D1014936

Laurie H

She's Got This

LAURIE HERNANDEZ

Pictures by Nina Mata

HARPER
An Imprint of HarperCollins*Publishers*

She's Got This

 For information address HarperCollins Children's Books, a division of HarperCollins Publishers, 195 Broadway, New York, NY 10007.
www.harpercollinschildrens.com

Library of Congress Control Number: 2018943090
ISBN 978-0-06-284058-5 (hardcover)
ISBN 978-0-06-284623-5 (signed edition)
ISBN 978-0-06-288922-5 (special edition)

The artist used Adobe Photoshop CC 2017 to create the digital illustrations for this book.
Typography by Alison Klapthor
18 19 20 21 22 PC 10 9 8 7 6 5 4 3 2 1

First Edition

To my parents, who have always supported my dreams

—L.H.

To my darling parents and Aaron, who never let me give up

—N.M.

Every day before school,
Zoe watched the birds perched in the tree
outside her bedroom window.

She loved the way they hopped and balanced on the branches. She loved the way they flew.

As she ate her morning cereal, something on TV caught Zoe's eye: A gymnast was dancing along a beam. Flipping and spinning and landing with her arms out.

Flying! For real!

Zoe wanted to do that, too!

Her dad took her shopping for a leotard.

Her mom drove her to her
first gymnastics class.

Zoe loved stretching, tumbling, and swinging on the bars.
But her favorite thing of all was the balance beam.

For a moment, Zoe flew.

Then she hit the mat with a thump.

Zoe's knee hurt. Her shoulder hurt. Her head hurt.

Inside, her heart hurt, too.

That night, Zoe told her parents she didn't want to go back to gymnastics class. "Because you fell?" her dad asked. "When you were learning to walk, you'd fall down and get right back up!"

But Zoe didn't remember learning to walk.
She *did* remember hitting the mat with a thump.

"One time I fell running a race," her older brother said. "Then I picked myself up. You can't let a fall make you quit!"

But Zoe's brother was big, and she was little.

"I fall all the time in karate," her older sister told Zoe. "That's part of what we do: learn to fall without getting hurt."

But falling *had* hurt. Zoe didn't want to fall again.

"Let's go out!" Zoe's mom said.

"Go out?" asked her dad. "Why?"

"To celebrate!" said her mom.

Celebration meant ice cream.
With hot fudge and sprinkles.

"What are we celebrating?"
asked Zoe's brother.

"Zoe's first fall!" said Zoe's mom.
"It's good news."

How is falling good news?

"Each fall makes you better," Zoe's mom told her. "Now you have to try again. Maybe you'll fall—but maybe not. You won't know unless you try."

A tiny bird soared
over Zoe's head.

The next week, Zoe went back to gymnastics.

She did somersaults and cartwheels. She turned flips. And she danced along the beam.

Sometimes she fell off.
But every time she did,
she got right back on.

After several weeks, Zoe's class put on a show for all the families.

When it was Zoe's turn, she hopped up onto the beam.
She paused and lifted her arms and her chin.

Her parents smiled, and her brother and sister cheered.
Her coach nodded.

Zoe breathed deeply. In a moment, she would jump into the air. She didn't know if she would fall or if she would land safely.

But she knew one thing. . . .

She was ready to fly.

As a gymnast, I've fallen more times than I can count. At first, every fall felt like a failure. I thought it meant that I wasn't good enough, that I wasn't meant to be a competitive athlete. Then I realized that falling is how you learn. What matters isn't how often you fall but how often you get back up.

Even as an Olympian, I still feel scared when I try something new, inside or outside the gym. But I never let fear hold me back. And neither should you. Because no matter what your dreams are, they're worth all the falls in the world—because eventually you'll fly.

You got this!

Love,

Laurie

D1014966

MAN MADE THE TOWN

MAN MADE THE TOWN

MICHAEL MIDDLETON

ST. MARTIN'S PRESS
NEW YORK

For information, address St. Martin's Press, 175 Fifth Avenue,
New York, N.Y. 10010.

Library of Congress Catalog Card Number: 87-42687

ISBN 0-312-01169-5

First published in Great Britain by The Bodley Head

First U.S. Edition

10 9 8 7 6 5 4 3 2 1

This book was sponsored by Shell U.K. Limited,
but this sponsorship does not necessarily
imply the support of any Shell company for
every assertion made by the Author.

● ● ●

CONTENTS

The changing face of San Francisco.

PREFACE

THE town, the city, notwithstanding its manifest shortcomings and failures, remains man's greatest collective achievement. This book is about some of its splendours and squalors, so often taken for granted by those who live and work within its walls. Others have analyzed particular aspects of the town in much greater detail—its history, its sociology, its economy, its transport, its administration, its architecture. What I have attempted here is an overall sketch of how towns and cities are actually shaped.

Opening chapters offer a generalized essay on the nature of the town — essentially the Western town—on why and how towns change, on what has gone wrong, and how we seek to control urban change. These chapters provide a context for the specific examples which follow of how a number of towns and cities have tackled particular problems—of conservation, of renewal, of housing, transport and land reclamation. Each of these case histories exemplifies something exceptional: exceptional imagination, exceptional tenacity, exceptional clarity of purpose, exceptional scholarship, exceptional acumen—and often in combination. My hope is that some readers at least will ask themselves why it is that such things remain exceptional; why similar efforts are not being made in their own community. Because, in no case, except perhaps in Williamsburg's ability to draw upon the resources of one very rich individual, were there special circumstances to make it easier in any of these places to turn ideas into action. Things got done because people—singly, in groups, collectively—saw an opportunity and determined to grasp it.

Mirror to the text are the illustrations. Words mean different things to different people. Pictures show the reality. This is how, for better or worse, things are—or were. For, of course, as tomorrow nudges today, and today dissolves into yesterday, the urban kaleidoscope shows ever-new configurations. The places pictured in this book, as too the statistics, laws, attitudes, do not belong to some perpetual now. They are already history. Kann's in Washington burnt down a day or two after I took the picture on page 44. Many other things will have changed. Skylines have changed, ownerships have changed, colour schemes have changed, signs and billboards have changed, greenery will have matured and trees been felled. It does not matter. All these things were thus, and are still thus somewhere. Hopes for some of the initiatives described here have faded, their promise seems unfulfilled. But who knows—another shake of the kaleidoscope and tomorrow may yet prove otherwise. These examples, these case histories, are not to be seen as recipes, as topical fashion plates, as blueprints for ultimate solutions. They are but pointers. In Bali the soft-stone temples are continuously being repaired, renewed, rebuilt, replaced, for if this process ceases they become no longer 'real', no longer a living home for the gods and the spirits. Thus too, endlessly, do we have to strive for quality in remaking our human settlements.

A whole literature has come into being to query the present usefulness of the traditional town. It has been suggested that the Western city is now no more than a museum-piece of bygone needs—of interest to historians and the tourist trade, but essentially a thing of the past, incapable of nourishing the needs and the new ways of life demanded by a changing world. Should cities in fact be left to die while new and more dispersed urban forms evolve? Today, with a terminal to hand and served by satellite, there is no longer need even to commute. Business can be done, information obtained, world-wide; conferences held, shopping ordered, entertainment enjoyed—all without moving from one's home, without losing the view of wooded fields, or peaceful lakeside, or mountain vista as the case may be. Conversely, the exploding cities of the developing world are out of control. Even were immeasurable resources available, could cities on such a scale be planned traditionally within a realistic time-scale? For these pullulating shanty-towns, without proper housing, proper drainage, proper transport systems, proper employment, the very concept of the traditional Western city has as much relevance, it will be said, as the gift of a bottle of French perfume to a condemned man. And yet . . . we are concerned here with the ultimate values of society. To study, say, the centre of Munich is to appreciate that the traditional city centre answers very deep-seated needs in mankind.

Renewal and conservation are not alternatives. They have to be seen, not as opposing philosophies, but as two facets of the same problem: the orderly and creative refashioning of our towns and cities. The urban problems of the Western world are now so great and so urgent that we can none of us afford to disregard the discoveries and accomplishments of others. That, of course, is why this is an international book. Some of our urban ills can only be dealt with by supra-national action; but in almost all spheres we have much to learn from one another.

Yeoman service has been afforded me, albeit unwittingly, by many people. Some of the authors upon whom I have leaned heavily figure in the short reading list in the bibliography. My understanding has been increased by a multitude of other reports and papers, too numerous to be listed. To all of these I am indebted. I owe particular and personal thanks to numerous organizations and individuals who have furnished me with documentation and information. Among these are, in Britain, Dr Neil Cossons, Leslie Forsyth of COMTECHSA, Maurice Howell, lately Director of Planning, and Dr Joan Rees, Swansea City Council; in the Netherlands, Jan Hengeveld and Paulein Hengeveld-Brand; in the United States, the city offices of Baltimore and Salem, Massachusetts including Commissioner Marion W. Pines of the former; the Tri-Met system in Portland, Oregon, for invaluable information; the San Antonio Conservation Society; Leopold Adler II of Savannah; Edmund C. Bacon; James R. Ellis of Seattle, for information about 'Forward Thrust' and Freeway Park; Richard Haag, also of Seattle, for information relating to Gasworks Park; Mary C. Means for information relating to the Main Street Center, and for having guided me towards so much of interest and value in America; and to Professor Robert Stipe for a sight of his comparative study of preservation legislation.

My special thanks are due to Swansea City Council for illustrations of the Lower Swansea Valley on pages 207 (the lower), 208, 209 (the sports complex grandstand), and 210; to the Ironbridge Gorge Museum Trust for the close-up of the Bridge's structure on page 129; to the Civic Trust/Ralph Erskine's Arkitektkontor for the illustrations on pages 161 and 162 (right); to the Civic Trust/Victor Rose for illustrations of the London pub on page 44, of Covent Garden on page 181 (the larger, right), and of Wirksworth on pages 194 and 197; also to Mary Means for the photograph of Chicago's Christmas lights on page 119. Tim Rock suggested the title, for which I am grateful. Andrew Hewson gave me moral support throughout a lengthy gestation period, during which David Machin and Guido Waldman of The Bodley Head have show exemplary patience. I must express warm appreciation to George Sharp for his handling of the book's design. Above all, I owe an immense debt of gratitude to Shell UK, who generously contributed to production costs, thus making possible, among other things, the large number of colour illustrations. It was, indeed, Shell's encouragement at the outset which emboldened me to set the wheels of the enterprise in motion; although it does not appear as such, this is in many ways the 'Shell Book of the Urban Environment'.

Telč, Czechoslovakia.

1 THE NATURE OF THE TOWN

THE heart of the town, to the transient visitor, approximates to theatre, the unknown actors performing their delicately complex rituals within a setting which itself bears heavily upon the plot. Café waiters set out their tables on the pavement. Cleaning ladies clump homewards from their offices. Schoolboys tumble about each other, satchels swinging. Shapeless little figures hurry back from the market with bulging baskets, mingling with the commuters as they fan out from railway station, metro or bus terminus. Newsmen cry the racing editions. Nets dry on the quays. There is the smell of new-baked bread, or crepes, or kebabs, or roasting chestnuts from street vendors. Prams and push-chairs are headed for the nearest park. Traffic police put parking tickets behind windscreen wipers. From out of sight comes the whine of a circular saw. Mailboxes are cleared, gutters and pavements swept, deliveries made. Proprietors of adjoining shops pass the time of day from their doorways. Tramps

Philadelphia, Pennsylvania.

and winos shuffle under the trees. Lovers pass. The light hardens as the universe turns and the sun moves to its zenith. Church clocks, as Virginia Woolf had it, debate the hour.

As a recollection of the European city the picture is pleasing but partial. Filtered out are vandalism, rampaging football crowds, street riots and the empty days of the unemployed. Out of sight are great areas of uneventful suburban streets, of grey apartment blocks and anonymous public housing; ethnic ghettos; sad stretches of waste land, with their scatter of old mattresses and rusting oil drums and abandoned cars; the ugliness and bleak monotony of industrial zones; the brutality of vast highway interchanges, crushing the life out of adjoining neighbourhoods; the squalid commercialism of the outer fringe. And what of the face of the city when the heat shimmer has given way to the darkening skies of winter? Empty now the streets at dusk, closed the parks, silent the school playgrounds. Beyond Europe stretch the endless mat-and-sacking shantytowns of the undeveloped world, the waterborne junk and bumboat communities of the Pacific, the dispersed sprawls that have no centre.

As images of the city these too are only facets of an infinitely greater whole. How then describe

The essential character of a town is shaped by the nature of its setting. Settlements came into being on coast and lakeshore, where a convenient anchorage offered; on high ground for defence or the sheltered pastures of the mountains; at river crossings, where trade routes met, or on alluvial plains where farming flourished—spreading outwards, in past centuries, from castle and church.

Cahors, France; Parga, Greece; Gruyères, Switzerland. Left: Biron, France. Right: Chicago, Illinois. Below: Norwich, England, and Salzburg, Austria.

Of greater significance to the character of a town than its individual buildings are its spaces. Road patterns, passages and pavements, arches, changes of level both slight and dramatic, now tease the eye by hinting at mysteries around the corner, now offer glimpses of more distant views.

Above: Fribourg, Switzerland; Sarlat, France; Gruyères, Switzerland. Left: the Duke of York's Steps, London; Telč, Czechoslovakia. Opposite: Corfu; Monpazier, France; Amsterdam; Montmartre, Paris.

the city? The city is ourselves, mirroring with precision our needs and our activities, our values and our aspirations, our confusions and our contradictions. Writers and artists have left us records and poetic insights; but it is not within human capacity fully to depict the city in its ever-changing complexity. For Disraeli London was 'a roost for every bird'. '*Lutetia non urbs est sed orbis*'* was Charles V's punning assessment of his capital. 'Paris', echoed Flaubert, is 'an ocean in which there will always be unexplored depths.' How could it be otherwise? If our homes reflect us as individuals, our towns and villages reflect no less the complex corporate nature of the societies which gave them birth, and which they subsequently and presently serve. World history, suggested Spengler, is city history.

The city is a kind of human coral reef, a palimpsest of values, charged with signs and signals made by distant generations, reflecting the motives which first caused people to come together, and then to stay together: the need for shelter and for safety from marauders; the opportunity to sell their skills, their labour and their produce; the possibility of education, and cultural and leisure opportunities; the chance to better themselves, perhaps even the hope of temporal or spiritual power.

Their settlements were sited for strategic and tactical reasons: on high ground, free from flooding, from which they could command the approaches (Luxembourg astride its gorges, Edinburgh on its rocky mount, Toledo, the hill towns of Italy); at river crossings, where trade routes meet, and agriculture could be easily irrigated (York, Paris, Prague, Samarkand); or on the coast, where safe anchorage offered itself for their fishing boats and for seamen from afar (Venice, Visby, Aigues-Mortes; or Cape Town which began as a market garden to counter scurvy among the Dutch sailors bound for the Indies). The character of cities is inextricably interwoven

* 'Paris is not a city but a world'

with the wider settings of which they are part: Rome, Bath, San Francisco on their hills; Stockholm on its islands; Telč in Moravia, conversely, garlanded by its lakes; Amsterdam, Bruges, Copenhagen, Hamburg, marked by the interpenetration of water and town. And that wider setting itself, in Europe, has been shaped and tilled and tended over millennia, having in consequence a very different feeling from that of the raw landscapes of Australia or the American mid-West.

Hundreds of today's European cities came into being as Roman garrison towns. Not only does the direct evidence remain in many places—the Maison Carrée in Nimes, the amphitheatre in Orange, the soaring Augustan aqueduct of 128 arches at Segovia, are but three of the more complete examples—but their very street patterns, as well as their names, embody evidence of the colonial settlement. The longevity of man's marks upon his environment—his communication lines, the configurations of his settlements no less than his enclosures of the countryside—is astonishing. The oval market place of Lucca follows the lines of the Roman forum; the Roman street plan remains almost untouched in Pavia; in Rome itself, the Piazza Navona was built on the walls of an ancient race track. Urban archaeology teems with such examples.

The nature of a town's layout reflects not only the period in which it was born but the urgency with which it was built. Colonizing Greeks and Romans parcelled out virgin sites in rectangles, as, millennia later, the nineteenth-century pioneers in North America and Australia parcelled out vast territories in great rectangular grids—of which the grid-pattern of the frontier post settlement was merely a smaller-scale elaboration. So too were Tang cities in China, like

Formal, informal, accidental, the spaces of a town are its outdoor rooms—open-air stages for the day-to-day encounters of community life.

Telč, Czechoslovakia.

Changan—by the tenth century the largest city in the world—divided by a grid layout into blocks, each of which, within the outer containing wall, was itself walled. In the more than three hundred *bastide* towns built in Aquitaine between 1220 and 1350, the English and the French placed their civic and religious buildings round a central square, from which a grid of residential streets spread outwards; as did the sixteenth century *conquistadores*, following the Royal ordinances—the 'laws of the Indies'—issued by Philip II in 1573. In the same way, from the seventeenth century onwards, the logic and convenience of the grid proved irresistible in the outward expansion of cities—Mannheim in 1689, Stuttgart, Vienna when development took place beyond the Ringstrasse in the third quarter of the nineteenth century. The British New Towns, built after the Second World War, in their informal layouts form an exception to the general rule that new towns follow the grid pattern (though they mostly failed to capture the authenticity of the organic development they sought to simulate).

Through the Middle Ages, and indeed for centuries thereafter, cities remained tiny by modern standards. In the East, by the second half of the thirteenth century, Hangzhou emerged as the biggest city in the world with a population of one million. In the West, Hangzhou was rivalled in size, wealth and sophistication only by Constantinople, the greatest trading centre between the Atlantic and the Urals. However, Constantinople's 800,000 or so inhabitants in the mid fifteenth century immensely outnumbered those of the other main trading ports—such as Genoa, Bruges, even Venice—and continued to outstrip even the capital cities of Europe for another two or three hundred years.

European towns began to expand from the twelfth century onwards, but slowly and by no means steadily. Many had their populations halved by the Black Death (London and Florence for example) and only recovered their earlier levels several centuries later. Those which had extended their outer wall systems were in many cases unable for generations to fill the empty space thus created.

After the collapse of the Carolingian empire, the castle was the source of power and protection; there were 99 in England in the eleventh century, of which half belonged to William the Conqueror. A small parasitic community huddled at the castle's foot. As armaments became more powerful, these growing communities had to be fortified by an enveloping wall, probably with corner bastions (for example Carcassonne), and perhaps a concentric ditch—with sometimes as in Breslau even a second, outer wall as additional protection. Outside the walls lay violence and pestilence. At night the gates were closed; the curfew was general; the watchman from his tower, ever on the lookout for fire, called the hours. Crowded within the walls, narrow streets, designed for pedestrians rather than traffic, offered protection from the summer sun and from the winds and sleet of winter. Castle and church formed the focal points, the liturgical orientation of the church influencing the spaces around it, as the need for room in which to accommodate the stalls of incoming merchants and in which to muster bodies of men for defence purposes, led to open squares immediately inside the gates. The feuding nobility came and went between their estates, but the citizens identified with the community within the walls, rather than with the province or nation without—think only of the frequency with which towns changed their allegiance during the private wars of the fourteenth century. This sense of independence lingered on for centuries, in one form in the princely centres of northwest Europe, in another in the merchant city states of northern Italy—though self-interest led sometimes to association based upon a common economic activity. The Hanseatic League, at its peak embracing some 80 towns (Berlin, Bremen, Breslau, Cologne, Cracow, Hamburg amongst them), controlled

Forming the town's spaces are its buildings, probably from many periods and infinitely various—well known and unknown, large and small, pompous and modest and kooky.

Above: Vienna; London; Bexhill, England.

the trade around the Baltic until, in the last quarter of the seventeenth century, the nation states assumed supremacy.

With the Renaissance came apprehensions of a perfect order, a perfect harmony, which would embrace all natural laws; a unity based upon mathematics, proportion and perspective. An ordered society needed an ordered urban framework. Alberti, in 1485, attacked the principles not just of individual buildings but of streets and city planning. 'A Citie is a perfect and absolute assembly or communion of many towns or streets in one' read the 1598 translation of Aristotle's *Politics*. The sixteenth and seventeenth centuries saw a flurry of plans for the Ideal City, first in Italy—Scamozzi's Palmanova for instance and Leonardo da Vinci's remodelling plan for Florence—later in France and Germany. They were essentially academic concepts, pattern-making which forced the forms and activities of the city into a predetermined mould.

Consequently few were built. Filarete's Sforzinda, laid out between 1457 and 1464, was perhaps the first Renaissance town; Palmanova, begun in 1593, remains within its nine-sided stellar rampart perhaps the most intricate of Ideal Town designs actually to have been completed, while labyrinthine Sabbionetta, dating from the 1550s, 'clean, white and silent', represents a more relaxed and realistic form. Out of such thinking was reborn the concept of urban design, the possibility of planning the city as a work of art. Baroque perspectives and symmetries and spaces, articulated by monuments and fountains and sculptures, were made magnificently manifest in the stage designs of the period; even, as in Michelangelo's unsurpassed Capitoline Hill in Rome, in reality. Great princes and absolute monarchs, from now on, sought to perpetuate their glory by imposing grand designs upon the ramshackle intricacy of the medieval town, cutting swathes through its fabric in orgies of destruction. In the 1560s the axial vista of Rome's Via Pia was something quite new, but thereafter, from Rome to St Petersburg, from Edinburgh to Brazilia, the geometry of the Beaux Arts vision continued to dominate the planned city.

To the shaping constraints and forces of terrain, of particular community activities, of constricting outer wall, of conscious improvement and aesthetics, or urgency of construction, a

The 'feel' of a town derives very directly from the materials used in its construction and the decorative idioms these engender. How marvellously the unknown craftsman used his timber to make this door in Bratislava, Czechoslovakia, such a pleasure to the eye.

Opposite: glazed brick (Brighton, England); cast iron (Savannah, Georgia); straw (Orvelte, Netherlands); tiles (St Stephen's Cathedral, Vienna); knapped flint (Norwich, England); seventeenth-century timber (Rademacher Forges, Sweden); stone (Ferrara, Italy); glass (Ipswich, England).

further factor in the development of a city's structure and character must now be noted—its transport systems. Amsterdam's canals were laid out before the houses and warehouses bordering them were built; the waterway system was thus the very armature of the city's form. Modes of transport have always governed the speed and degree of a community's expansion. The villages of Hampstead and Dulwich, for example, first became popular as dormitory areas for those working in central London because they were manageable by horse and carriage; just as, in the interwar period, the northwards extension of the London Underground led inexorably to the speculative development of 'metroland'. More recently still, the scale of American road construction has led to the massive outward dispersal of urban populations and has hastened the onset of inner city decay.

The interplay of all these factors has led to urban forms which are markedly different in detail. There are linear towns, seen in extreme form in the snaking terraces of South Wales mining villages, as they follow the contours of the valleys for miles on end. There are concentric-radial towns, of which Karlsruhe is a classic example. There are star-shaped settlements, the outwards thrusting fingers of which are interspersed with green fingers running in from the countryside to the central city. And there are cluster cities, composed of satellite communities grouped around a nucleus (though these tend to be modern concepts, such as La Défense on the edge of Paris, since, in the past, the nucleus has usually come to swallow the satellites). Nearly always the generative points of a settlement and the spread of their interlocking influence can be read clearly in its street pattern. Along main routes buildings cluster, like iron filings along lines of magnetic force.

Throughout history cities have suffered natural and man-made disasters—fire, flood, earthquake, pillage and war. The most moving and extraordinary item in the Pompeii exhibition of the nineteen seventies was the vertical scale which showed, hour by hour, the inexorably rising level of ash and lava. Most of Nuremburg was destroyed by fire in 1340. Two-thirds of Lisbon was destroyed in the great earthquake of 1775. Half the churches and three-quarters of the timber houses of Moscow were burnt in 1812. Four square miles of Chicago were laid low in the fire of 1871. Warsaw, Dresden, and Leningrad are but three of the great European cities to have suffered massive destruction in World War II. Occasionally—more usually for reasons other than disaster and assault—settlements have crumbled into oblivion. Old Sarum in England, for example, was left to rot when the bishopric moved its see to the new town of Salisbury less than ten miles away. In general, however, the city is tenacious of life. Rome's decline lasted for centuries—but Rome and Lisbon and Chicago and Leningrad are greater cities than ever. As, for Schiller, *'Das Alte stürzt es ändert sich die Zeit und neues Leben blüht aus den Ruinen'**, so too for Rudyard Kipling:

Cities and Thrones and Powers
 Stand in Time's eye,
Almost as long as flowers,
 Which daily die:
But, as new buds put forth
 To glad new men,
Out of the spent and unconsidered Earth
 The Cities rise again.

Symbolic of the time-scale of the city's will to live was the completion of Cologne Cathedral in the mid-nineteenth century, after work had been halted for more than four hundred years. Florence's Via Calzaioli was decreed in the fourteenth century, but mostly built in the nineteenth.

Sometimes, as we have seen, new cities are decreed: a Madrid (1561), a Washington (1790), a Brasilia (1956). Once in being, time works upon them as upon all other cities. The city expresses continuity, rising ever higher on the detritus of previous ages—so that, for example, carriageways end up above the level of the original doorsteps to old houses; the pavements of Bath are now twenty feet above the remains left by the Romans. So too, for the most part, cities have spread outwards, through the *faubourgs* which lay beyond the walls, until whole villages and communities were engulfed. Thus, for example, did London grow.

As urban populations increased, the balance of political and economic power gradually shifted, at different speeds, from court and church, through the guilds, the merchants and bankers, to the present variable mix of local government and capitalist enterprise. Streets and squares were widened, to ease congestion and provide space for civic events—parades and processions, festivals and fairs, tournaments, jousting, bullfights, horse-races. Formal, symmetrical squares were created from the end of the sixteenth century—the cathedral piazza in Livorno, the Place Royale (Place des Vosges) in Paris. At about the same time tree-planting began to be undertaken as an urban amenity—Antwerp's Groenplaats, along the ramparts of Lucca and the Amsterdam canals. From such as these the concept of the *cours*, the mall or promenade, widened to embrace parks and pleasure gardens—and eventually to resort towns. The increasing complexity of urban activity was reflected in new kinds of buildings: city halls, law courts, great covered markets and exchanges, hospitals, barracks, theatres—the Teatro Olimpico in Vicenza, for example, opened in 1585 with *Oedipus Tyrannus*—academies of this and that, docks and custom houses. Growing affluence was evident in the size and elaboration of these buildings, but—until the last hundred years or so—change was constrained by the limitations of traditional construction techniques and by a generally accepted syntax of architectural forms.

Architects and craftsmen moved freely across

* 'The old falls, time changes, and new life blossoms out of the ruins.'

Look down at the surfaces underfoot: brick, stone, marble, cobbles and granite setts. Before we inserted a network of underground services beneath our towns—services which themselves need constant servicing—paving could be a pleasure in itself.

Lisbon; near Delavan, Wisconsin.

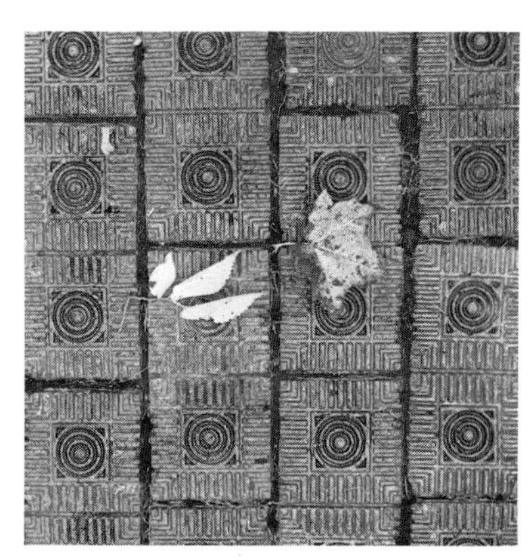

Europe, wherever work beckoned. French engineers designed the fortified castles of Wales for Edward I, and built the 88 towers of Avila's encircling walls; masons moved between the great cathedrals—Germans, for example, worked on Burgos; Italian stuccoists were in demand everywhere. Charles Cameron, a Scot, worked in Petrograd; Theophil von Hansen, a Dane, designed the Parliament building in Vienna. Backwards and forwards they went. Sir Thomas Gresham's Royal Exchange (1568–70) was designed by a master mason from Antwerp, Hendrike van Passe, on the lines of the Antwerp Bourse. Forty years later, Hendrick de Keyser was sent to London to study the Exchange in preparation for designing a similar one in Amsterdam. So, too, it may be said, has it been in more recent times: Lloyd Wright in Tokyo, Le Corbusier in Chandigarh, Jørn Utzon in Sydney, Richard Rogers in Paris. James Stirling, in England, designs museums for Stuttgart and Harvard. Robert Venturi in America designs the National Gallery extension in London. The grass across the valley, it seems, is always greener—but whereas in this century the eminent outsider is looked to for a distinctive and individual quality, in earlier days he was a master within an internationally accepted idiom.

Not that the idiom remained static. Styles evolved. Romanesque gave way to Gothic; Gothic was superseded by the rediscovery of the Classical; Baroque ripened into Rococo fantasy; Neo-Classicism sounded a call to order; intermittently, exotic by-ways, such as Chinoiserie, and pineapples on gateposts, beckoned seductively but proved dead ends. In the nineteenth century neo-Gothic all but swept the board, though at times it was a close-run thing.

Through all these modulations, and the passions and invective engendered by opposing camps, buildings, until the present century, continued to express their purpose to the community without ambiguity. The spire of a church rose high above the rooftops around, as befitted its spiritual purpose, but also signalling to the traveller the geographical heart of the community. The City Hall expressed stability and corporate pride—identifiable from the banking houses, no less anxious to communicate an unshakeable stability, by reason of its greater size. In the United States, the imposing, impressive court-house as often as not marks the pivot point of a community which was graduating from lawlessness to corporate order. The mill and the warehouse in town were as distinctive as farm and barn in the countryside. The marble fronts and slabs of the butcher or dairy, the polished wooden shelves and drawers of the grocer, the florid welcome of the pub, the brass plate and lettered window of the solicitor—these were the unmistakable signs of the trade or profession carried on within, even without the additional emphasis of hanging signs:

great pairs of spectacles framing well-lashed blue eyes, the barber's pole, the golden knee-high boot, and all the rest. Quarters became identified with particular callings, or particular ethnic groups—the Ponte Vecchio in Florence with jewellers; London's Inns of Court with the law; Wall Street with finance. Here lies Chinatown, or Germantown, or the Jewish Quarter—often separated from one another by no more than the width of a single street. Change took place within the human scale and within each generation's memory-span and understanding. The landmarks of the place where you were born were still there when you died.

The rhythm of a city's development—or lack of development—determined the face of its urban form as left by the receding years and centuries. The Baroque city expresses rationality, unity and the ultimate value of beauty. The authoritarian city offers a frame-work of awe-inspiring spaces calculated to impress and intimidate. The well-mannered façades on Dutch canals reflect the bourgeois values of the merchants for whom they were built. Present-day society is egalitarian, organized into very large and anonymous units, so our cities, and many of the buildings in them, are very large and anonymous too.

Layer upon layer, the city holds within itself the imprint of the values of successive generations, of great events and social movements, of the manifold activities of man which have lifted him above the animals. Jane Jacobs has traced, for example,[1] the development of Detroit from flour milling in the eighteen twenties and thirties, to the manufacture of mill machinery, to the development of shipyards (for the flour trade across the Lakes) and thereby to the first steamships, marine engines, smelting and refining, and, twenty years after the refineries closed down (because the ores ran out) to the automobile industry.

The city is man's greatest collective artefact, and sometimes his greatest collective work of art. Immense riches lie implicit in its fabric, for a

Decoration and embellishment flower at every level (opposite) on the skyline, on the street, sometimes sophisticated and sometimes charmingly less so. Trees and greenery soften the hard surfaces of the city, bringing colour and the changing seasons to its very heart.

Opposite: the Grand' Place, Brussels; Weymouth, England. Left: French formality in the castle moat at Angers, France; English informality at its height in a crop of churchyard daisies in Norwich, England, and the random placing of trees in a London street—with something of the same tradition to be seen on the canals in Amsterdam and in Boston Common and Public Garden.

The European city evolved over long centuries. The typical New World settlement lacks their complexity but can boast of other qualities. The little timber structures on the dirt road received new façades of greater pretension; the dirt road became Main Street; the grid stretched outwards, block by rectangular block; the buildings leaped heavenwards, and, within a century, America had given the world an awesome new urban image.

Far left: Philadelphia, Pennsylvania. Left: top, Illinois; below, both Eureka, California. Opposite: the Monadnock building (1891), Chicago; the generations leapfrog upwards in Boston, Massachusetts; the World Trade Towers in New York.

town can be 'read' like a book, yielding information, giving pleasure, at many different levels. Some of its statements require little background information to be understood; others demand detective work. Place names, street names, brim with references and meaning—often, but by no means always, self-evident. New Castle and (the Roman) Wall's End in England are straightforward. Self-evident, too, in Brussels, the rue du Bois Sauvage, running behind the cathedral, and in Paris, the little rue du Chat qui Pêche. Less so, perhaps, the delightful corruption, Pity Me (*petit mer*), in County Durham, or Charing Cross in London—site of one of the stone crosses marking the resting places, on the way to Westminster, of the *cortège* of Queen Eleanor, Edward I's *Chère Reine*. And surely baffling, unless you have the key, the passageway a few yards away, called Of Alley (now Formerly Of Alley). This was part of the Duke of Buckingham's estate; nearby streets are called Duke Street and Buckingham Street, and the inclusion somewhere of the particle was clearly irresistible. A church outside the city wall clearly betokens a degree of sectarian intolerance on the part of the community within; but who, from the street, is even to know of the existence of 'Our Lord in the Attic' the clandestine Catholic church built into the upper storeys of some seventeenth-century domestic premises in Amsterdam? For those with a developed sense of deduction, the iron rings set into the rock of Gibraltar are tell-tale signs of the ropes by which the army's canons were hauled to the upper galleries; but unless you know it is there, you are unlikely to spot, a yard from the pavement in central London, hard by the interwar German Embassy, the 1934 tombstone of 'Giro', the then Ambassador's dog.

An apprehension of the presence of the past constitutes one of the most affecting responses to the city. From this sense of the roots of our society we derive comfort: if on the one hand it points to the ephemeral nature of our own time, on the other it offers reassuring evidence of continuity.

Beyond the undertones and overtones of history, however, beyond the plaques recording that so-and-so once lived and worked in this house, that here stood Tyburn gallows, that from this quay the *Mayflower* sailed in 1620, there is the experience of the city itself, the city as work of art. Though none can fail to be moved by the knowledge that it was Michelangelo who placed Marcus Aurelius thus in his Capitoline Square, and relate this fact to the total view we have of an extraordinary man, the essential impact on us is the direct aesthetic experience of the reality itself: the slow approach up the long flight of steps to the level platform of the piazza, its subtle and unexpected shape, the controlled rhythms of the buildings, and the articulation of the central space by the great statue itself. In the exploration of towns there are moments, by no means confined to such obvious splendours, which cause the heart to leap.

A sentence, as any poet will demonstrate, can be a work of art—a world in itself. But great literature is built of sentences grouped into paragraphs, which form pages and then chapters. So is a building, however marvellous, but a sentence in the paragraph of the street, the chapter of the neighbourhood or quarter, the book that is the town. A book is not just an assemblage of sentences, it has its own internal structure, its own momentum and variations of pace, its forward and backward allusions and references. It exists in time, it unfolds as it moves from situation to situation, from insight to insight.

So, too, do the spatial inter-relationships of the city unfold to the circulating observer. Always there is more than can be perceived at any given moment, from any one vantage point. Under this arch, round this corner, up these steps, over the bridge, an ever-developing sequence of images, of juxtapositions and contrasts, unfolds. The kinetic experience of townscape is an aesthetic experience of a special kind—for those with eyes, one of the most rewarding pleasures in life.

It is akin to the experience of great architecture, but greatly extended spatially and demanding correspondingly greater time for its full assimilation. Gordon Cullen has analysed it sensitively and perceptively: the interplay of maundering alleys opening up into the release of a great square; the teasing secrecies of high walls, the mysteries of dark corners and the resonances of long perspectives; the games of visual hide-and-seek as towers come into view and disappear; hints and confirmation of the sea, or a great river, or mountains beyond, are glimpsed and lost again.

In this sense the city unfolds as music unfolds, with its contrasts of tempo, of key, of volume, of orchestral texture, the predictable balancing the unpredictable. Mumford, indeed, pointed the analogy nearly fifty years ago: '. . . through its complex orchestration of time and space,' he wrote, 'no less than through the social division of labour, life in the city takes on the character of a symphony.'

If we carry the analogy further, underpinning the variations on the main theme is the spatial framework defined by churches and public buildings, monuments and squares—and the vistas and the underlying relationships, often sensed rather than observed, which link them; echoes of noble concepts once held in minds long since returned to dust. More often than not it is the spaces of a town, rather than its individual buildings, which give it its essential character. Napoleon called St Mark's Square in Venice the finest open-air salon in Europe, and who would deny it? But think also of the great square at the centre of the little town of Kelso in Scotland, paved throughout with granite setts: the buildings do not rate as great architecture, but the space is an experience in its own right. It is in such settings that communities are made most keenly aware of their own identity.

Modulating the development of the main urban theme are the grace notes of differing materials, colour and decoration: the flowers, plants and trees of the region, stone porticos, iron balconies, oriel windows, fanlights over doors: the texture of timber and tile and brick and

Over and above the myriad other factors which combine to give each city its own special identity, there are the idiosyncratic quirks peculiar to it alone—images of the unexpected.

A ship berthed in a backyard in the heart of Baltimore, Maryland; a sheltering screen of ivy across a London window – protection, perhaps, from the harsh realities outside; a mountain of salt in Chicago awaiting the onset of winter; a wall of photographs of partisans killed in the war, facing the City Hall in Bologna; a car park wall in Cincinnati, Ohio.

VASILIA

colour-washed walls; the marvellous paving of a Lisbon or a Prague: monuments, statues, fountains: the umbrella pines of the Appian Way, poplars of France, Spanish moss drifting from the live oaks of Savannah, the silver birches of Scandinavia, mimosa and eucalyptus in Portugal or California. Compare the gravelly formality of a French park with the five great trees in the centre of the Circus in Bath, or with the great wedge of Fairmount park slicing into Philadelphia.

Some towns are very specialized. People go to Bayreuth for Wagner, to Assisi for its frescoes, to Baden-Baden for its waters, to Blackpool for a gregarious, jump-up holiday. But every city, every town, has its own special ingredients. Images in the mind's eye can seem to symbolize whole topographies: the circular nets of the fishermen in Stockholm, the tiled conical roofs of *trulli* houses in Apulia; the *Palio* in Siena; the high forest of television antennae over the roofs of Valletta (for the free capture of Italian transmissions); the tumble of starlings against the autumn sky above Trafalgar Square in London; the Olympia Brass Band parading through the streets of New Orleans, umbrellas twirling.

Over and above all these things—the historical, the sociological, the topographical, the architectural, the quirks and idiosyncracies—there is yet one more thing: the magic of the evanescent moment, touched by the weather and the seasons, as seen by one individual pair of eyes. The city is open to the skies, presenting its image in endless variations—touched by the first kiss of early light; shimmering in the softness of a summer heat haze or sharp in the relentless glare of the midday sun; glittering after rain, muffled by snow, glowing in an evening light. Who could forget the cold beauty of blacked-out, wartime London on a clear night under a bomber's moon? Or the towers of Manhattan seen from a helicopter in the after-glow of sunset, every window ablaze? or watching from the soft-lit rococo warmth of the Residenz in Munich, through the tall windows, the snow fall silently upon the marble statues of a darkening inner courtyard?

And what of the echoes within oneself? For Proust, 'The places we have known do not belong only to the world of space on which we map them for our own convenience. None of them was ever more than a thin slice held between the contiguous impressions that composed our life at that time: the memory of a particular image is but regret for a particular moment: and houses, roads, avenues are as fugitive, alas, as the years.'*

Returning to the places of one's childhood, fragments of once familiar scenes appear, like strains of a forgotten melody. Every city exists uniquely in the mind of each individual who knows it, its images shaped in part by his dreams, in part by his memories, in part by the circumstances of the passing moment. So was it to Wordsworth one September morning on Westminster Bridge:

> This City now doth, like a garment, wear
> The Beauty of the morning: silent, bare
> Ships, towers, domes, theatres and temples lie
> Open unto the fields, and to the sky:
> All bright and glittering in the smokeless air.

The rich diversity of the European urban heritage, with its monuments and works of art, represents the greatest cultural concentration in the world. But thousands, and tens of thousands, of other cities, towns and villages, throughout the five continents, each with its special character and qualities, each uniquely different, are no less part of man's heritage. Despite their squalors and imperfections, they constitute our greatest man-made asset, our greatest museum, our greatest collective achievement.

Perhaps we have taken them too much for granted, failed to appreciate their fragility and vulnerability. In our towns and cities, what has gone has gone for ever.

* The final words of *Swann's Way*, translated by C. K. Scott Moncrieff and Terence Kilmartin, Chatto & Windus, 1981.

There are moments of vision in a city which can never be shared—for the appearance of the city changes from moment to moment, modulated by the weather and the seasons and the time of day. A skyline at dawn, a misty silhouette, the hard hot sun of midday, a flicker of reflected light, the long romantic shadows of evening, the glitter of towers against a rolling thunder cloud—such evanescent moments remain personal to the individual observer.

Below: October starlings over the towers of Whitehall, London.
Right: hard midday dazzle and shadows in Corfu.
Bottom: reflected light in Boston, Massachusetts; sundown in San Francisco.

2 THE IMPACT OF CHANGE

THE design of towns is design in four dimensions. A town provides a framework for human activity and must needs change to meet the changing needs of those who live and work in it. Local resources are discovered, exploited, and worked out; industries rise and fall; populations ebb and flow; living standards change. Responsive to every nuance of demand, the city all the time adapts itself accordingly.

Jane Jacobs has suggested some of the mechanisms by which cities have grown—or stagnated.[1] Nearly every country has its ghost settlements from which life has fled: hill villages in Italy, the mining villages of County Durham in England, gold rush towns or dustbowl communities in North America. In historical terms, change can be very rapid. Between the two World Wars metropolitan London doubled in size; less than fifty years later, between 1971 and 1981, the population *dropped* by one tenth, falling, for the first time in the century, to below seven

The impact of change.

Previous page: Reconstruction in progress on the Coutts Bank building (John Nash), the Strand, London, August 1982. In the background, St Martin's-in-the-Fields.

This page: Fifty years separate the photographs on the left of the Hague. The church remains but canal, trees, buildings have been swept away. The views on the right were but a quarter of a mile apart. The previously unspoilt coastline of the Portuguese Algarve yields to the tower blocks of tourism. Eventually the visitor destroys the very thing he has come to enjoy.

million. Indeed, many of the great conurbations of Western civilization have begun, like trees, to rot at the core as their citizens have moved in great numbers from the centre to the periphery or beyond.

Within the city its neighbourhoods, too, are in a constant state of flux as, for modish, ethnic or other reasons, areas 'come up' or decline. In 1950 Brooklyn was ninety per cent white; a quarter of a century later the white population had dropped to sixty per cent. A single block may divide opulence from multiple deprivation. Here, a high class residential district is gradually colonized by big company offices, attracted by its snob value as an address. There, a hitherto featureless area becomes an immigrant stronghold. Elsewhere streets of conveniently sized working-class cottages are bought up and done over by the young marrieds of a now servantless middle-class; or, conversely, come to be regarded as a high-risk area and are 'redlined' so that mortgages and bank loans are withheld from them. Houses in single occupation change to multiple occupation; houses in multiple occupation revert to single family use. These processes may run their course in forty years, or forty months or less; but from them, in greater or lesser degree, no community is totally immune.

The concept of the 'Ideal City' has plagued men's minds for centuries, from Filarete to the *Ville Radieuse* of Corbusier. There can be no such thing. But even when a new town or city has been created from scratch, time works inexorably to erode its creator's conception. Accretions and adaptations are made to the buildings; materials weather, hideously or gracefully; landscaping matures, or withers; new growths, cankers, appear in the urban tissue; new roads are cut on lines at odds with the fabric through which they pass; areas of dereliction multiply.

So the design of cities is perforce design in time as well as space. Yet, given the complex patterns of urban administration and land ownership today, given the economic pressures—as like as not originating far from the settlement concerned—which push it into development or pull it into decline, can cities any longer be said truly to be *designed* at all? Mumford likened the city, in its multiple relationships, to a symphony. It has to be said, half a century later, that too many of the players in the urban symphony have been playing in different keys, in different tempos, and often just plain out of key.

The reasons are by now familiar: vast population increase; mass migration from the countryside to the city and from poorer to more prosperous regions; steadily rising standards of living; and, with new means of transport, almost total personal mobility. It should not be thought that violent change is special to our own age. The massive reconstruction of Paris in the 1850s and 1860s provoked the same sense of discontinuity engendered in so many cities a hundred years later. '"Old Paris" is dead,' wrote Baudelaire; 'unfortunately the pace of change is faster than that of the human heart.' Nonetheless the present century has seen agricultural economies transformed into manufacturing economies, the shift from production-based economies to service economies, and is now watching the transition from worker-based processes and activities to computer-based automation. It has seen the steady concentration of power into very large, centralized units of administration. All these things are mirrored faithfully in the changing city.

In retrospect, it is tempting to place the turning point in the nature of the city around the 1830s. To be sure John Evelyn, a couple of centuries and more before Ruskin, had wondered how it was that 'this glorious and ancient city [of London] should wrap her stately head in clouds of smoke and sulphur under which flowers die . . . and the very inhabitants are so affected by the fulginous and filthy vapour that catharrs, phthisicks, coughs and consumptions rage more in this one city than in the whole earth besides.' True, Jefferson considered cities 'pestilential to the morals, the health and the liberties of man'; and for Rousseau (of course) 'towns [were] the sink of the human race'.

Change begins almost imperceptibly. Buildings change hands, change uses. Services—for example plumbing and air-conditioning—are retro-fitted. Something is in the wind.

Kensington, London.

But it was with the coming of the railways that the awesome power of the industrial revolution reached its full gearing and the urbanization of rural populations began in earnest. By 1851, nearly two-thirds of the population in 62 towns in England and Wales had been born elsewhere. Cities expanded, exploded, as never before—not merely in Britain but subsequently in continental Europe, in North America—and now in the developing world.

To pick, almost at random, from the statistics . . . Middlesbrough, in the northeast of England, developed from a mere four houses in 1801 to a town of 60,000 in 1881 and 152,000 today. The population of Manchester rose from

72,275 in 1801 to over 203,000 fifty years later, and over 600,000 by the turn of the century. In North America Chicago, with a population of little more than 30 in 1830, grew nearly seven times in the single decade between 1845 and 1855, reaching almost 300,000 by 1870; 1,200,000 by 1890; and over 3,375,000 by 1930. Toronto grew by six times between 1881 and 1921. And so on. A hundred years ago there were five or six cities with a million or more inhabitants; today there are some 115, and it is estimated that by the year 2005 there will be over 90 with populations of more than five million. Tokyo has an average *annual* increase of 200,000; Bangkok of 300,000; Cairo of 350,000; São Paulo of 500,000; Mexico City 750,000. United Nations estimates suggest that, by the end of the century, Mexico City will have 31 million

In one scenario the area goes downhill. Upper floors fall empty first, then whole buildings, whole streets. 'Dangerous Structure' notices are served, the demolition men move in, and in next to no time what was a living community has become an urban desert where muggers and vandals roam.

Above: London; Bristol, England; and London. Right: central Chicago.

inhabitants, São Paulo nearly 26 million and Tokyo over 24 million—with New York and Shanghai not far behind.

The effects of such explosive growth have been twofold. First, cities push outwards to engulf the arable land upon which their swollen and swelling populations depend for food. Between 1957 and 1972, no less than 200,000 acres went to road building alone in the UK. In the 1970s it was estimated that in Britain agricultural land equivalent in extent to the county of Bedfordshire (125,350 ha, or 305,000 acres) was being lost to new construction every four years; with recession the figure has since dropped, but in the Green Belts and elsewhere development pressures remain intense. Urban America was estimated, during the same period, to be spreading at the rate of one million acres annually; and, in the developed world alone, 3,000 square kilometres of prime farmland were disappearing each year under new construction.[2] Some twelve per cent of the United Kingdom's land is now built up; no less than 26.6 per cent of Belgium's.

Second, the industrial revolution brought into being square mile upon square mile of appallingly inadequate housing, brutalizing in its squalor, to house the immigrant working populations. Densities could be staggering. Mark Girouard has pointed out that that of Calcutta in the 1960s was 101,000 people per square mile, whereas that of the tenth ward in New York in 1898 was 478,000. A Plymouth doctor in 1832 quoted cases of twelve to eighteen people sleeping in one room about twelve feet square. A Liverpool doctor in 1836 found a family of thirteen in a cellar, twelve of whom had typhus. Overcrowding, narrow streets, totally inadequate public hygiene, smoke, grime and every kind of air-borne and water-borne pollution, took their inevitable toll. In 1842 the average life expectancy of the labouring classes in Manchester was seventeen years (though for the gentry in more rural areas it could rise to fifty and more). As late as 1883 average expectancy for someone living in Swansea was 24 years.

Pigs roamed the streets of New York into the second half of the nineteenth century ('Take care of the pigs' wrote Dickens in 1842). It was reported in 1845 that 700 people in one part of Manchester were served by 33 lavatories. In Paris, sewage was still being removed in 1854 by private enterprise 'nightmen', whose charges deterred many from using their services. Private sewage disposal, and the failure to control burial areas, led to the gross contamination of water supplies everywhere. Until the mid-century, official intervention in housing and living conditions was minimal or non-existent. The railways crashed through the cities with powers of compulsory purchase—but without obligation to rehouse those displaced. Some 4,000 people were rendered homeless, for example, merely by the construction of Holborn Viaduct in London; in all, 100,000 are thought to have been uprooted by railway development in Britain. The effect was of course to exacerbate already existing overcrowding. Chadwick's 1845 Report to the Royal Commission on the Health of Towns found that, in Preston, in a block of 442 dwellings, 2,400 people slept in 853 beds. When, years later, the new London County Council cleared fifteen acres in the Boundary Street area of the East End, it still contained no fewer than 5,719 people living in 713 houses.

Arthur Morrison's *A Child of the Jago* paints these ghastly warrens and rookeries. Ruskin was rhetorical. In *The Crown of Wild Olives* he echoes John Evelyn: 'All that great foul city of London there,—rattling, growling, smoking, stinking,—a ghastly heap of fermenting brickwork, pouring out poison at every pore . . .' And again, in the preface to the *Notes on Educational Series*, '. . . of the myriads imprisoned by the English Minotaur of lust for wealth and condemned to live, if it is to be called life, in the labyrinth of black walls, and loathsome passages between them, which now fill the valley of the Thames and is called London, not one could hear, that day, any happy bird sing, or look upon any quiet

Central Chicago in the late 1970s.

space of the pure grass that is gone for seed.'

Foreigners came to Britain and wondered at what was happening. De Tocqueville wrote of Manchester, ten times swollen in only forty years: 'From this foul drain, the greatest stream of human industry flows out to fertilize the whole world. From this filthy river, pure gold flows. Here humanity attains its most complete development, and its most brutish; here civilization works its miracles, and civilized man is turned back almost into a savage.' It was upon this same city that Marx, with profound consequences for human history, largely based his analysis of capitalism.

This was the nature of the impact of change upon the city in the nineteenth century, change from which none can now escape. Today, for most in the Western world, clean water, sewage disposal, power, light and heat, are to be taken for granted. In general, families command enormously more space in their homes. Their living standards have risen out of all recognition. They have much greater leisure time in which to escape the daily grind, large numbers of them skipping off to the one-time playgrounds of the rich. But the nineteenth century led to a breakdown of urban form which we now almost take for granted; it changed the face of the city for good and many of the environmental ills it created are with us still.

The turmoil of change has continued unabated, gathering, with steady population increase, momentum all the time. Living conditions in the pullulating cities of the Third World are no better, for the majority, than those which existed in Europe in the nineteenth century. In the West the imbalance between housing need and availability grows no less. In Frankfurt, in 1975, 8,000 households were looking for somewhere to live; in 1980 the number was variously estimated as between 20,000 and 50,000. Amsterdam has some 20,000 *krakers*, or squatters, while in Berlin 160 blocks are occupied illegally.[3] Among the most acutely disadvantaged

123
itchie
TOW ZONE
NO
PARKING
LOADING ZONE
RESTAURANT
SUBS PIZZA
Instant Copies
BOSTON PHOTO SERVICE
PASSPORT PHOTOS

in terms of housing are migrant and immigrant workers and ethnic groups—present-day equivalents to the cheap labour of the last century. It is thought that there may be fifteen million migrant workers, with their dependants, in Europe. At the end of the 1970s some thirteen per cent of the population of Paris were of foreign nationality; one fifth of those in inner London had been born outside Britain. Such groups tend to gravitate to inadequate older areas where low rents make improvement impossible for the private landlord; if improvement *is* undertaken the rents rise beyond their tenants' means.

But to these perennial problems have been added, in our own day, additional factors, unknown in the past, which have heightened the impact of change. They include the *scale* upon which development now takes place; the *styles* of modern architecture; the desire to accommodate the unfettered use of the motor vehicle; and the changed pattern of land tenure and investment.

Until about a century ago the design of building was governed by traditional construction techniques, the use of familiar materials, and by the conventions of well-understood design languages, above all that of the classical Orders. With the slower pace of development, these constraints almost forced the designer to relate his work to traditional forms and the scale of the existing setting. Earlier prototypes might be adapted, modified, extended in this way or that, but the designer was in general building on the experience of the past, rather than attempting to create new forms *ab initio*.

The twentieth century changed all that. A new iconoclasm informed all the arts, and from this architecture was not exempt. The Modern Movement—with the possible exception of *art nouveau*, its immediate forerunner—was the first in architecture totally to reject the past. Architects and planners saw themselves, to a greater extent than ever before, as social engineers reshaping mankind; sickened by the moral and physical 'insalubrity' of the Victorian slum, they sought radically to change the existing environment rather than to modify and enhance it. Corbusier's 'We must kill the street. We shall truly enter into modern town planning only after we have accepted this preliminary determination' may be compared with Marinetti's 'Fire the museums . . .' etc. The break with the shackles of the past was to be absolute.

In the other scenario, change is fuelled by commercial pressures.
The Old State House, Boston, Massachusetts.

The means which made such thinking possible were threefold: Mr Otis' invention of the elevator in 1857, the 'skyscraper' construction techniques evolved in Chicago in the 1880s (in which a building's external cladding was borne by its internal metal framework) and the development of reinforced and pre-stressed concrete. Together these offered freedom from the tyranny of the load-bearing wall and gave the capability of building upwards to an extent never before dreamed of. Throughout history buildings have grown bigger, but these technical developments offered the possibility of a totally new urban form. It is this which, above all else, has changed the look of our towns and cities in the twentieth century.

New building no longer necessarily relates in scale and style to its surroundings. By 1913 the Woolworth Building had risen to 792 feet; by 1930–31 the Chrysler and Empire State Buildings had reached 1000 feet, plus or minus; by the 1970s the World Trade Towers in New York had risen to 1,350 feet and Sears in Chicago had topped 1,450 feet. By the 1980s New York alone had nearly 100 buildings of more than 40 storeys; a proposed development of 137 storeys for the Colosseum site was planned to reach 1,670 feet, and a World Trade Centre in Chicago no less than 2,500 feet. While these two cities edge competitively towards Frank Lloyd Wright's dream of a 528-storey, mile-high, cloud-topped tower which would house 130,000 inhabitants, towns and cities everywhere around the globe get on with their local pastiches of these New World wonders.

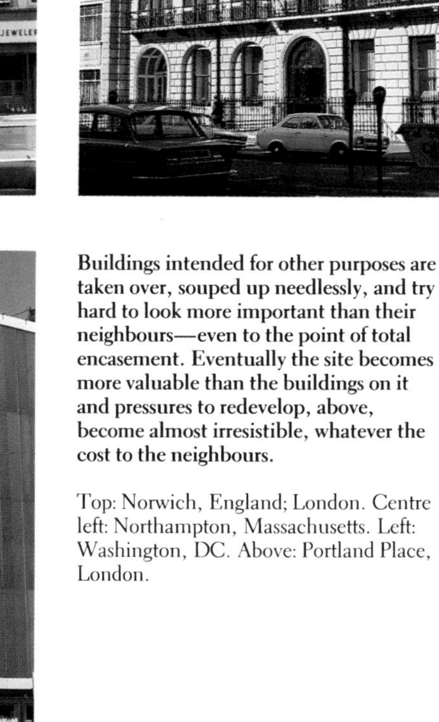

Buildings intended for other purposes are taken over, souped up needlessly, and try hard to look more important than their neighbours—even to the point of total encasement. Eventually the site becomes more valuable than the buildings on it and pressures to redevelop, above, become almost irresistible, whatever the cost to the neighbours.

Top: Norwich, England; London. Centre left: Northampton, Massachusetts. Left: Washington, DC. Above: Portland Place, London.

Corbusier's concentration of facilities within the big slab had the effect of 'liberating' it from its environmental context—from ancillary facilities and even, in a sense, from specific siting—it could be placed anywhere. The Modern Movement has thus tended to create buildings, on an increasingly monumental scale, rather than spaces. It has in consequence failed—ironically, in view of its determinist ambitions—as a generator of community life. 'We are concerned today,' wrote Mies van der Rohe in 1924, 'with questions of a general nature. The individual is losing significance, his destiny is no longer what interests us.' Every great city, and many a smaller one, has suffered over the past thirty years from the random—in townscape terms—implanting of towers and slabs into smaller-grain areas quite unfitted to receive them. All too often the result has been the creation of dark canyons, overshadowed for the greater part of the day; of violent wind vortices and little shelter; of covert spaces inviting violence; of alienation and the break-up of communities. Deck-access housing slabs in Manchester were reported in 1985, nearly a century and a half after de Tocqueville, as leaking, without heating, stinking from backflows of sewage, infested by cockroaches and damaged by vandals. Symbol of all the failure and the waste: Pruitt-Igoe in St Louis—2,800 flats in 43 blocks, built by the local authority in the 'fifties at a cost of $21 million, demolished less than twenty years later because there was no other way of dealing with the seething slum of violence it had become. Pruitt-Igoe was but the first of many. In England, Birkenhead, Hackney, Leeds and Liverpool are among the places that had to follow suit. In other places sheer size has dramatized failures of structural probity. A gas explosion brought down Ronan Point in London (its load-bearing wall joints stuffed with wadding, fag ends, newspapers and cans);[4] in Boston, over 10,000 windows had to be replaced in the ill-fated John Hancock building.

The concept of the building as a thing-in-itself a luxury object in isolation, is particularly evident in the American city. No other country has produced more ravishingly beautiful high-rise structures, albeit of a coldly anonymous beauty, than the United States—but nowhere else in the West is there a greater disregard for the relationships between such buildings, the spaces between them and the spaces around them. Chicago looks magical from the Lake—but it is chastening to look down upon the central city from the Hancock Tower and see what architectural self-sufficiency, the automobile and the clearance programmes of the 1960s did to urban coherence.

If *scale* marked one break with the past, *style* marked another. The pervasive influence of Alfred Loos, for whom ornament in any form was sinful, a measure of the degree of degeneracy of a society, permeated the Bauhaus ethic, De Stijl, and through them two generations of architects in the 'Modern Movement'. (Loos was not altogether consistent in his views, but this one on ornament lodged as some of his others failed to do.) Traditionally, buildings had been in large degree conceived from the outside in, the façade shaping the interior. The Modern Movement, conversely, postulated the primacy of a building's function as the starting point and regulator of its design. 'Form follows function'—exterior form should reflect, with complete honesty, the building's interior uses and relationships. Since exterior elevations were now regulated by the building's internal demands, it followed that every building could present to the world a face totally unrelated to those of its neighbours. In townscape terms, visual anarchy had been given a licence. The roof of the modern building was flat—a doctrinal requirement—and, except for high-rise construction, the visual emphasis of volumes and fenestration was horizontal. The face of the building was undecorated; it had, at least originally, to be all-white; concrete and glass were its chosen materials. From the outside its windows, serving different needs in different

rooms, could often appear wilfully random in their placing.

The break with the traditional languages of architecture meant that the interface between old and new was more intensely evident than ever in the past, the contrast much more abrupt. As, gradually, more buildings in the new manner made their appearance—usually in watered-down form—streets, quarters, and whole towns came to reflect a visual schizophrenia of a deeply unsettling nature. The confrontation of past and present is by no means necessarily to be regretted; in the right hands, as through the ages, it can enrich the quality of both, and thereby the character of the city as a whole. Unhappily, in recent times, it has too rarely done so.

At many levels, modern buildings have proved inadequate as an element of townscape. The right angle has supplanted the curve; buildings no longer wrap round corners but leave strangely shaped areas of fenced-off land to gather litter. In days gone by, buildings engaged the sky. Spires, turrets, statues, domes, rooflines, chimney stacks not only created the individuality of a particular sky line (think only of Wren's churches in London before they were submerged by new development) but contributed greatly, at street level, to the unfolding delight of the ever-changing street picture. The generic skyline of the modern movement, however, notwithstanding the great towers of the business districts, has been drawn with a ruler; there is little interplay between the city and the wheeling vault of heaven, as the sunlight shifts and falls and casts long shadows. With remarkable vision, a height restriction ordinance was passed in Washington DC, as early as 1901. As a result Washington is, exceptionally, a horizontal American city rather than a vertical one. But, in a thriving area, maximum building heights pretty soon turn into minimum building heights, and in Washington great lengths of street meet the sky uniformly, uninterrupted by the smallest visual event which might lend interest to the scene.

The cumulative effect of anonymity created by modern buildings *en masse* is destructive to any real sense of place. Ultimate anonymity is reached in the inward-looking, atrium building, cocooned within its windowless walls and reflective surfaces of bronze and mirrored glass. Clouds scud across the impeccable surfaces; perhaps rippling, fractured reflections of older, more comfortable buildings across the street create intriguing and unexpected patterns; but perhaps all that stares blankly from the high wall of glass is the abstract patterning reflected in an illusory vista from another such high wall of glass, no less reticent, introspective, anonymous. These are citadels, proud, self-sufficient, and ultimately destructive of urban community life, for the life within their glossy atria is selective, controlled, exclusive.

Of course a reaction was inevitable—crystallized in Britain in the Prince of Wales' 1984 reference to a proposed development as a 'carbuncle'. However, with only the minimalist functional ethos ('Less is more') as a basis on which to build, attempts to re-enrich the language of architecture have tended to spring either from the visual ingenuities of 'high-tech' constructional engineering, or from purely personal, and often wayward, forms of invention ungrounded in any commonly understood tradition. Of the first group, which are apt to exhibit to the public eye all those intimate details of

Height restrictions and controls on size do not of themselves produced good architecture or a lively skyline.

Far left: Devizes, England. Above: Washington, DC.

servicing which have hitherto been considered improper for public display, the Pompidou Centre was the first apotheosis. As a localized generator of community life, Pompidou has achieved its purpose triumphantly: but consider the effect upon our towns if whole quarters were to be redeveloped in similar manner. Rogers' building for Lloyds in the City of London, ten years later, bleached of Pompidou's stinging fairground colours and unified by the gleaming sheen of its steel, dropped on to a congested site so that it is never, at ground level, seen as a whole, is less destructive than its forerunner of the street scene, to which it brings an undoubted, if aggressive, drama. Across the roofs of neighbouring buildings, however, its bulk becomes apparent, and its top-heavy assemblage of seemingly autonomous pods and pipes and packages emerges overpoweringly. Despite the initial brilliance of their impact (which one hopes will survive the obvious problems of weathering and maintenance—a Lloyds man is quoted as saying 'Fortunately the pigeons haven't yet recognized it as a building, but when they do . . .')[5] neither building seems likely to offer lessons for the better redevelopment of our cities generally or for those ungeared to conspicuous expenditure.

To many in the second group the tag of 'post-modernist' has been applied—a loose-fit term which has been used to cover a whole range of oddball attempts to break with the puritanism of the Modern Movement. The deliberately anarchic include such things as Lucien Kroll's tumbled, half do-it-yourself accommodation for Louvain University; the odd, the litter strewn classical bits and pieces of Charles Moore's Piazza Roma in Los Angeles; the lighthearted, the surrealist fantasies of the BEST stores in the United States, in which walls crumble before your eyes, façades are displaced by several yards from the rest of the building, and so on; most publicized, buildings by Michael Graves and others, which are marked by the application of a simple, coloured geometry to their façades. The British reaction, particularly evident in housing, has tended towards the 'neo-vernacular'—would-be cosy compositions of low-rise, monopitch and hip-roofed buildings, faced in brick, with bays and set-backs to break up the line.

Clearly architects everywhere are feeling their way towards more decorative—and, where appropriate, more lighthearted—forms. As yet, however, real evidence of an emerging language which will provide a long-term basis for the transformation of our recent blunders in urban design is less clear.

If, in this century, scale and style have radically affected the appearance of the buildings in our

The *scale* of development has changed out of all recognition. The skyline of Chicago, opposite above, may stir memories of San Gimignano, but it is a trick of the eye: the city centre is miles distant. And when you reach them the citadels of the modern city are impassive, anonymous, impregnable.

Opposite below: New York.

towns, by far the most destructive impact upon their *spaces* has resulted from naïve and needlessly insensitive efforts to accommodate the motor vehicle. Western society has come to demand unlimited personal mobility—to the point where, in the United States, the automobile population is now around two-thirds the human; and the light vehicle fleet accounts for more than one-third of the nation's oil consumption—or about as much as *all* the oil used by Britain, France and West Germany combined. In Britain, in the single year 1983–84, traffic increased by ten billion vehicle-kilometres, or four per cent. Everywhere there has been massive investment in improved delivery systems—motorways, feeders and interchanges. But while these have been adequately, and in some cases magnificently, landscaped between cities, little real consideration has been given to how such systems can be integrated with the existing or redesigned fabric of the city itself; nor to what should be done with the proliferating vehicles once they have reached their destination. Multi-level interchanges and raised freeways have been brutally imposed on top of modest dormitory areas, slicing through historic quarters, severing communities and neighbourhoods. A single motorway interchange—for example, Birmingham's 'spaghetti junction'—can occupy 14 or more ha (38 acres); a really big one, as at 1-77 and 1-70 in Cambridge, Ohio, over 300 acres. Haussmann's restructuring of Paris was ruthless—but his 62 miles of avenues and great boulevards served to articulate the city itself; they were not an independent transportation system doomed to blight the areas through which they passed.

If big road systems have sterilized once lively neighbourhoods in the town, they have at the same time served to decant urban populations over wide areas of countryside. Initially, commuters worked in the city but lived outside it. Shopping followed, ribbon-built on either side of the highway, clustering, like the villages of old, where highways met. Factories, then offices,

BURGERS

came in their wake. In the United States suburban growth is spreading outwards sixty miles and more from the city centres. By the mid 1980s five times the new office space in Manhattan was being created in New York's suburbs. The dispersed city, the loosely built-up conurbation, is already a widespread reality. Think only of Tokyo or Los Angeles or Jakarta. Such places are no longer pedestrian oriented, they are not for exploration on foot. They are 55 m.p.h. settlements, linear, fragmented, often but one plot deep on the fringes of the eight-lane highway. Indeed, the commercial strip, brought to its finest flowering in America, has been extolled as holding new design lessons for the sensitive urban designer. Robert Venturi and his colleagues have written:[6] 'The parking lot is the *parterre* of the asphalt landscape. The patterns of parking lines give direction much as the paving patterns, curbs, borders and *tapis verts* give direction in Versailles; grids of lamp posts substitute for obelisks, rows of urns and statues as points of identity and continuity in the vast space.'

In close-knit Europe the problem is, so far, less extreme in this sense, but compounded by more urgent pressures in other ways. For example, in Britain 86 per cent of all goods—and 98 per cent of consumer goods—is carried by road;[7] Britain thus has many more heavy lorries (i.e. over ten tonnes carrying capacity) per motorway kilometre, compared with, say, France or West Germany (which subsidizes the transport of freight by rail). Unfortunately, sooner or later, perhaps repeatedly, road freight leaves the motorway and penetrates the town. If the country of Britain as a whole is compact, so too, are its towns, often preserving unaltered their mediaeval street patterns—roads intended for people on foot, hand carts, horses and waggons. The impact of the motor vehicle upon British towns has been dramatic. Streets have been destroyed to double the width of the carriageway; corner properties, pivot points in the town, have been torn down to improve turning circles; the enclosure of squares and market places has been blown open, so that the space leaks away meaninglessly along a ribbon of concrete and asphalt. The London Coal Exchange of 1846–49 was squandered because the line of a new highway encroached upon it by a few yards. Such piecemeal 'improvements', however, have often done no more than speed the motorist to the next bottleneck a quarter of a mile on. The economic justification for new road building in Britain turns upon aggregating the often tiny time-savings effected for large numbers of road-users. This has been likened to a form of fairy gold. What do they actually *do* with the fifteen seconds, or whatever, they have saved? Streets are still choked with traffic, juggernaut lorries still clog narrow streets and are trapped, their vibration contributing to sewer collapse,[8] bridges and historic buildings are damaged, fine squares and cathedral closes are turned into open-air parking lots. Across Europe, across America, everywhere the finest and most beautiful parts of our cities are submerged beneath the glittering metallic capsules that mean so much to us.

It is easier to describe the effects of urban change than its causes, for these are infinitely complex. People move, as did mediaeval craftsmen, to where there is work, or better paid work. Today, the 'rationalization' of manufacturing and administrative processes into very large units, to produce economies in overheads, is intensive and widespread. Factories and headquarter offices move towards the 'sun belt'; towards continental communications lines (freight movement increases steadily along the trade routes between Rotterdam and Hamburg to the Middle East, while the location of industry in Britain and northern France will be inescapably, if as yet unforeseeably, affected by the Channel tunnel); and/or towards areas which are already affluent, for these are likely to support a greater range of amenities and leisure opportunities—an obvious asset in attracting staff—than can less well-off areas. The disparity between towns of high economic pressure and those in economic decline becomes more marked.

On the one hand, sources of work, sources of revenue, dry up; unemployment rises; the more enterprising emigrate to places where there are better opportunities; spending power and the local tax base is reduced. Trade declines, essential maintenance is skipped, buildings fall empty and into decay, waste ground proliferates. Land is cheap because no-one wants it.

On the other hand, in more desirable areas, activity builds up, populations swell, there is pressure for more housing, more shops, more offices. Land values rise because land is in short supply. At the point where the site becomes more valuable than the buildings on it, there is almost irresistible pressure to tear them down and exploit the site more intensively so as to maximize its economic return. Market forces and architectural fashion thus combined to fuel the 1960s' and 1970s' drive to towers and super-towers and mega-structures. In this century, moreover, a major factor bearing upon the scale of urban development has been the changing nature of land tenure. The intricate warrens of the mediaeval town reflected its fragmented ownership patterns. A Baroque square, the controlled development of a great urban estate in London in the eighteenth century, the house building of the American pioneers on their democratically uniform plots of such-and-such a frontage and such-and-such a depth, reflected respectively the personal pride and aspirations of a prince, the landed aristocracy, the individual owner.

With the capacity to build high and build big, everything changed. A square metre of land could produce many more cubic metres of rentable space than ever before. The new commercial classes saw opportunities to amass great wealth, and grasped them. Individual entrepreneurs became millionaires almost overnight. And as the stakes grew ever higher, banks, insurance companies, pension funds lined up to fuel the development boom of the nineteen sixties and seventies with staggering amounts of capital. The values of these property companies, and of the commercial empires backing them, were not those of their predecessors. Lacking traditions of public service and a patrician sense of quality, lacking the personal pride (albeit sometimes misplaced) of the individual property owner, most of all lacking any roots in the area it chooses to develop, the twentieth-century board of directors has found its essential criterion of success in the balance sheet. Thus, for example, although twenty per cent of British pension funds are now invested in property, their investment capacity has but rarely been harnessed to the revitalization needs of the inner city. (In America Pittsburgh is said to be the one exception to this.)

Examples of the stakes involved could be taken from any country, but nowhere were they higher than in post World War II Britain. Oliver Marriott has cited figures from the boom years of the 1950s and 1960s (index them mentally for inflation). In London, the cost of land and development for D. E. and J. Levy's Euston Centre development was £16 million (1967 figures); the estimated profit, over and above this, was £22 million. In 1949 Harry J. Hyams, another English developer, acquired a moribund estate company for £50,000; by 1972 the company was worth £151 million and Mr Hyams' personal fortune was thought to be around £42 million. Two Hyams developments, the notorious Centre Point and Space House, both in the heart of central London, remained empty for decades while their capital value continued to rise. Centre Point was only fully occupied in 1981, some twenty years after its completion.[9] Since those halcyon post-war years the market has staged collapses and recoveries, and new types of developer have emerged. Things will never be quite like that again—but property prices have nonetheless contined to roar ahead of inflation and in the longer term have proved the fattest of investments.

By 1986 rental, service charges and rates in the

City of London had reached about £550 per square metre, the equivalent of £60 per annum for housing a wastepaper basket. (Costs in Tokyo were only marginally less; in New York your wastepaper basket would set you back a mere £45 per annum.)[10] As costs in the centre of the city soar, people begin to move out to the suburbs and the surrounding country—thus creating fresh strains on the commuter transportation systems. Business and industry, too, is attracted by the cheapness and unhampered ease of development on 'green field' sites. But the out-of-town shopping centre, for example, by sucking life from the downtown stores, exacerbates the process of decay at the centre. Thus, ironically, can both scenarios, for the boom town and the town in decay, lead eventually to a very similar picture, where only a massive injection of public funds is able to hold the community together.

In earlier centuries the people who paid for new buildings normally lived in the area. Today's entrepreneur roams the world, seeking sites where profits will come to rest. His movements are sometimes encouraged by the nature of national legislation. For example, United States banks have traditionally been locally based and, until very recently, have been prohibited from doing business across State lines; to put together a $50 million loan for a proposed development would normally mean putting together a consortium of banks. Canada on the other hand, has centralized banking and tends to lump construction and entrepreneurial activity together; this has helped Canadian development companies, to the frustration of their American counterparts, to become active south of the Forty-ninth Parallel. As property becomes investment, so on the one hand do funds flow into development activity from many

For the *styles*, too, of architecture have changed radically.

Opposite: the pilgrimage church of Die Wies (1745–54), West Germany, by the Zimmermann brothers. Above: I. M. Pei's extension to the National Gallery in Washington, DC (with a Calder mobile). Right: the Pompidou Centre in Paris by Piano and Rogers.

SAINT JOHN
SAINT PAUL

The confrontation between old and new is more marked than ever before. This can create visual drama and enrich the character of the town. No less can it thoughtlessly and insensitively play havoc with townscape values. Preserving the past by the mere retention of historic fragments has little to do with real urban conservation; it is like keeping the currants out of the cake and throwing the rest of the cake away.

Opposite: Trinity Church, Boston, reflected in I. M. Pei's Hancock Tower. Above: New Zealand House and Her Majesty's Theatre, London; Horseferry Road, London. Left: Vienna. Below: Brussels; London; Boston, Massachusetts. Right: fire plug painted for the American Bicentennial.

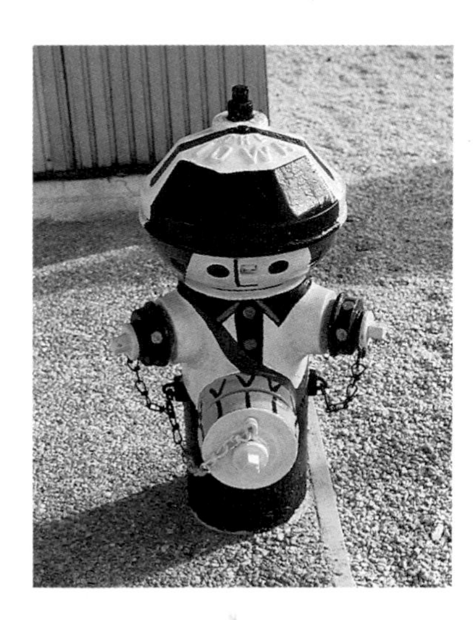

The sign on the filling station lavatories in South Carolina (left), reads: 'In order to preserve the architectural traditions of Charleston the brickwork and woodwork of the demolished Gabriel Manigault house 1800 AD were used in this station.' Increasingly, the boundaries between old and new, reality and make-believe, are being deliberately blurred—until, it may be, for some, the false becomes more acceptable than the real.

Below: a 'strip' restaurant in America; Disney World.

quarters of the globe—notable new sources, in the last quarter century, being the Middle East and Japan—while on the other, the actual development may be implanted into a city with little consideration for its secondary effects. The eleven million square feet of space suddenly made available by the twin World Trade Center towers in New York (seven times the floor space of the Empire State Building) put paid to the demand for office accommodation in lower Manhattan for about eight years and had, it has been said, 'as much economic justification as the pyramids of Egypt, and less social sense'.[11] Consider only the strains upon the street system of the Center's 30,000 workers and 80,000 daily visitors. Yet, by the mid-'Eighties, another eight million square feet of office space was going up on a 14½ acre site of reclaimed land immediately in front of these two towers.

The massive scale of today's redevelopment projects involves the methodical acquisition and assembly of sites, often over a long period. Peter Palumbo, a London developer, spent more than twenty years acquiring the many buildings and interests in an area adjoining the Mansion House, where he had hoped—as it turned out unsuccessfully—to put up a Mies van der Rohe office block. Such lead-times can result in many unforeseeable problems. Site owners can hold out and refuse to sell, immobilizing plans for the rest of the block; money markets can change and companies go into liquidation; governments and local authorities can make fundamental changes of policy or themselves change political colour. The results are apparent in every big city: festering waste land, weed-strewn temporary parking lots, empty and crumbling buildings—the unmistakable signs of planning 'blight'. Not infrequently the original project founders, and the community, is left with a running sore that may not heal for a generation or more, whereas the buildings which previously stood there could, improved and updated at a modest cost, have continued to justify their existence. The triangular site at the centre of London's museum area in South Kensington, originally intended for the National Theatre, remained unused for forty years; so, too, the site for the National Gallery extension in Trafalgar Square. In the 1970s the centre of Chicago was said to have seventeen square miles of wasteland—legacy of the demolition programmes of the 'Sixties; only now, two decades later, are the signs of redevelopment beginning to be apparent.

The speculative developer, then, has had as powerful an effect upon the face of the city in our day as did, in the past, the iron-master or mill-owner. Scarcely less, in places, has been the impact of mass tourism. Even Thomas Cook, who started it all when he organized excursions for three million people to the Great Exhibition in 1851, might be taken aback by the scale of the industry today. The number of tourists passing through Heathrow rose from 1¼ million in 1952 to 32 million at the end of the 'Seventies. In 1983 some 294 million international visits were made, and it is estimated that by 1990 tourist arrivals will be 250 million in Europe alone. Spain attracts around 25 million foreign visitors, Italy eighteen million, France seventeen million. Thirty-eight out of every hundred shoppers in London's Oxford Street are foreigners. In Greece the annual volume of tourists outnumbers the indigenous population. To these international flows has to be added travel within each country by its own residents, and short day-trips and excursions which must run into hundreds of millions in Europe: Italy alone receives 20–25 million excursionists each year from other countries.

Tourism then, growing annually in Europe (with temporary fluctuations) since 1950 at around fifteen per cent—a far higher rate of increase than any GNP—is a powerful economic force, which can be turned to good effect or ill. Towns and cities of character, lacking other means of support, can be saved from extinction by the revenues received from visitors—though the seasonal nature of the industry makes for instability of employment and creates problems in the provision of adequate infra-structure services which are not needed by the community itself. Unchecked and uncontrolled, however, mass tourism can destroy the very things the tourist has come to see—noble buildings, quiet backwaters, local character. The northern littoral of the Mediterranean, once so beautiful, has gone for ever; Benidorm and the Costa Brava have been colonized by packaged foreigners to the near extinction of indigenous values. Pisa, Mont Saint Michel, Stratford-on-Avon, New Orleans flaunt a squalid commercialism for the greater part of the year, their magic smothered, during peak tourist periods, by sheer weight of numbers. Tramping feet are now excluded from the Parthenon. In 'Third World' playgrounds, foreign values, buttressed by foreign spending power, and pandered to by quick-buck commercial interests, can quickly erode, crush and finally destroy, local traditions and cultures. Tourism has been called a form of prostitution. Yet how else are we to learn to live together?

Cities generate activity, and wealth, on an enormous scale. Great cities, though no longer expansionist sovereign states in the mediaeval-renaissance sense, nonetheless retain a large measure of political independence (and some of their tycoons, like Mayor Daley in Chicago, or the 'power broker' Robert Moses in New York), are perhaps not so very far removed, in their influence, from the renaissance princes. The budget of the Greater London Council (whose demise in 1986 may or may not result in significant financial savings) had a budget in the early 'Eighties which showed capital expenditure running at around £450 million and revenue at over £1,000 million. This represented only part of the

Traffic chokes the arteries of our towns, until almost the only escape seems to be that offered by the air. Of course new delivery systems for the motor vehicle have been devised (opposite) . . .

Top left: a jack-knifed lorry blocks Boston, Lincolnshire, England; New York. Above: Bradford-on-Avon, England; Sarlat, France. Opposite: Lake Shore Drive, Chicago.

public-sector spending in the metropolis. The boroughs between them spent another £4,700 million or so; the various utilities—water, gas, electricity, telecommunications, and the rest—accounted for millions more. Such figures overshadow the national budgets of the smaller nation states of Europe and many 'Third World' countries. The private-sector contribution, from the single owner-driver taxi to the big multinational corporation, is beyond computation.

Today the generators of change, as compared with those of past centuries, are powerful and infinitely numerous—and this simple fact lies at the heart of the urban design problem in the twentieth century. Even quite small towns are administered by scores of specialized agencies —the bus company, the police, the highway authority, the parks department, the telephone company, the education system, the planning or redevelopment authority, etc. All these, with the best of intentions, and the interest of the citizen at heart, are every day constructing, adapting, demolishing, inserting, repairing, signing, each

THE "HAWK" SHOPS
SUBMARINE
SANDWICHES
OPEN 7 A.M. to 1 A.M.
KAR
TOWNE
595-8974

. . . but what is their effect upon the fabric of the city (left)? And what are they like themselves? The American 'strip' represents the high point of motorway commercialism, but the highways of many other countries differ only in degree.

Left: Westway, London, in the 1970s. All else: anywhere in America (the 'Big Bird' is in fact in Medford, Oregon).

And what do we do with the vehicle when it has arrived? Buildings are demolished, canals filled in, to accommodate it. Famous squares and cathedral closes are turned into open-air parking lots. Multi-storey garages bully their neighbours—but the cars at ground level remain as numerous as ever.

Left: Mont St Michel, France. Right: the Plum Street Synagogue, Cincinnati, Ohio.

without reference to any of the others. Just on the carriageway Britain allows a score of different types of marking, regardless of their visual impact. How, within a democratic system, is the process of change to be controlled in the modern city?

In 1985 a sixty-metre length of the Great Wall of China was bulldozed by one Li Guobaio, to make space for an extension to the brick kiln he was operating. This was the result of ignorance. More serious by far, *owners* are beset by a passion for demolition. Some time after World War I the then Bishop of London proposed the demolition of nineteen City churches by Wren and Hawkesmoor. Nash's Regent Street went. The Adelphi went, and many of the Mayfair mansions. By 1934 there were proposals (halted, it is said, by the intervention of King George V) to rebuild Carlton House Terrace—and after World War II the Regent's Park Terraces. In 1984, one tenth of Bucharest was razed, laying low seventeen monasteries and churches, and over 9,000 late eighteenth-century houses.

Even as the main outlines of the city change and harsh new constructions replace the more comely façades and spaces of the past, a creeping proliferation of unco-ordinated trivia spreads across its face like a stain. Brutal festoons of wires drape the streets. Signs and posters cling to buildings until, in some cases, they totally encase them. Sky signs and their elaborate supports vulgarize once lovely skylines. Flyposting and graffiti disfigure historic monuments. Litter accumulates in the streets, flotsam and raw sewage in rivers and canals.

It was reported in 1982[12] that water authorities had identified about 2,000 different toxic impurites in the Rhine. In 1980 the river carried over the German–Dutch border—among much more—16 tons of mercury; 322 tons of arsenic; 80 tons of cadmium; 1,200 tons of lead; 890 tons of copper; 8,900 tons of oil; and 40 tons of phenols. So much for the mid-nineteenth century struggle for clean water. Between seventy and eighty per cent of the European Community's waste is disposed of in untreated form. The OECD has estimated that the cost of dealing with damage to the environment caused by the illegal dumping of waste—much of it toxic—amounts to between three and five per cent of the Community's GNP, or something between £30,000 and £87,000 million annually. A study for the USA's Environmental Protection Agency has estimated that 41 million tonnes of hazardous industrial waste is generated every year—or about 400 pounds per person. As industrial complexes grow in size and sophistication, so does the danger to urban communities; Chernobyl, Soweso, Bhopal are but three of the more recent warning signals; less publicized emergencies occur regularly in all countries.

The forms of pollution are manifold. Noise pollution, the OECD has stated, is 'escalating so rapidly as to become one of the major threats to the quality of human life'. The average daytime noise level from Mexico City's 130,000 factories and 2.5 million vehicles is reported to be a deafening 95 decibels, and is thought to be linked to the calls upon the organization known as Neurotics Anonymous. In relatively peaceful Britain, research has suggested that traffic noise may cause people in cities to take about three times as many tranquillizers and four times as many sleeping pills as do those in country areas.[13]

The devastating effects of sulphur and nitrogen oxides in the air, converted to sulphuric acid, and nitric acids, and falling as highly corrosive 'acid rain', have become a matter of major international concern. The sheer quantities of pollutants are daunting. It has been estimated in the United States that 22.3 million tonnes of nitrogen oxide and 29.7 million tonnes of sulphur dioxide are dumped in the atmosphere annually.[14] In central and northern Europe, sulphur levels doubled between the mid-'Fifties and mid-'Seventies. The resulting twenty-five years of air pollution have caused more damage to the Acropolis and to Ruskin's Stones of Venice than the previous twenty-five centuries of normal weathering. Eighty masons work year-round replacing the stonework of Cologne Cathedral. Elsewhere, to pick names almost at random, the mediaeval sculptures of Chartres, Bamberg, Lincoln and Wells are disintegrating or, to all intents and purposes, have gone for ever. It is said that the railway tracks in Upper Silesia are being eroded. No less disturbing are the effects upon human beings. In concentration, fumes from the motor car are thought to endanger public health, possibly producing brain damage in the young. For much of the time the dense yellow smog over Mexico City appears impenetrable; below it about 150,000 children a year die of respiratory diseases.[15]

Our cities have for too long been living beyond their environmental means, and failing to reinvest adequately in the maintenance of their fabric and their infrastructure. Road surfaces disintegrate; outworn services below ground are renewed piecemeal; trees die and are not replaced

(University of Liverpool studies have suggested that, after five years, half the trees planted every year in Britain to improve the environment have died—resulting in a waste of £10 million of public money per annum); buildings crumble because minimal repairs are not undertaken when the need for them first becomes apparent; waste land festers for a generation or more. In 1985 Manchester estimated that £600 million was needed to deal with the city's housing defects. A report by the Policy Studies Institute estimated that an extra £3,500 million a year was needed to stop further deterioration of the nation's roads, homes, water and sewerage systems, and infrastructure generally. Fecklessness on this scale is not peculiar to Britain. By the mid-1980s a new hazard had become apparent in litigious America. So crippling have the costs of potential legal liabilities become—and thereby the costs of insurance—that some cities are no longer able to cover themselves and have consequently been forced to close their public buildings and their parks, to mothball their automobiles, and cancel all but the most important council meetings.

Five pathological conditions have been diagnosed in the declining health of modern cities: declining standard of service provision; persistence of concentrated poverty; high levels of crime; movement outwards by the wealthier sectors of the community (in the United States, by the whites); and a resulting decline in the rate, or local tax, base. These conditions interlock in a spiral of decline which is inescapably reflected in the environmental quality of the city concerned. From them no city is wholly immune.

Change, from day to day, is almost imperceptible. Memories are short, the mind is preoccupied, the eye becomes anaesthetized to everything other than that which it is seeking. Were it possible to show the process of urban change in speeded-up form, like one of those films of cloud formations boiling and spilling over great mountain peaks, towns would be seen to be pulsating with change, development and

The need to do business so quickly gets out of hand. Traditional good manners get forgotten in ever more clamorous shouting matches as today's advertising looks for a surface, any surface, on which to come to rest. Left, the assault is actually in progress.

Opposite: Saumur, France; Lisbon; Chicago; London. Left: New York. Above: Chicago; Brussels.

Many cities are so enmeshed in their brutal wirescapes that it is hard to see much else. Man has walked the moon, but his terrestrial technology can be primitive in the extreme.

Opposite: San Francisco. Above: Poitiers, France. Below: Chicago.

decay. Return to the place of your childhood and the results of a generation of change are usually all-too evident.

Gone now the bell of the muffin man; the most characteristic sound of the great city today is the sliding wail of the sirens of police and emergency services. Gone now are the sailing barges of the Thames, the great Atlantic liners berthed only a block or two from Wall Street, the book stalls and print stalls along the right bank of the Seine—cleared to save a minute or two of driving time. Gone now so many reference points one took for granted, from the Euston Arch in London to the old Stock Exchange in Chicago.

The vestigial identity of once independent communities remains only in the invisible boundaries of city boroughs, parishes and voting districts. Once upon a time people in the city knew where they were: buildings spoke of their purpose. Now the natural logic has gone. We have to be provided with signs and directions: Town Centre, To the Station, To the Cathedral, Ring Road, No Entry and the rest.

Time was, as in country areas still, when strangers passing in the street greeted one another: Good day t'you. How do? In Germany, *Gruss' Gott!*—gossamer threads that helped to bind a community together. Today, alienation is far advanced. Encapsulated in their automobiles, many no longer experience such stray encounters; on foot they isolate themselves from their surroundings behind dark glasses and cassette-loaded earphones; front doors have fish-eye spyholes, and first-floor windows angled mirrors outside. There are areas where one does not go after dark; where the sweet smell of pot lies upon the air at street corners; where only the old, the poor, the weak, are left. To take but one example from many, there are said to be 350 gangs, of between 20 and 30 each, roaming the streets of Los Angeles.[16] At intervals frustration boils over and whole quarters become battlefields. Gone, irretrievably, are qualities and values which men had laboured to refine over centuries. Change seen

Pride of ownership can produce dangerous rushes of blood to the head. One must, after all, keep one's end up with the neighbours.

Left: Whitewater, Wisconsin. Below: Ann Arbor, Michigan; Wigan, England.

over the span of a generation appears overwhelming, and seldom for the better.

The picture, it will be objected, is an extreme one. It is true that not *all* cities suffer from *all* these ills—or to such an extent. But no city is totally free of some of these things. Every fire, however big, however destructive, starts as a little fire. Change in the city is never so small as to be unimportant. Somehow we have to bring the processes of urban change under more effective and more creative control. We may find that to do so we are having to recast our own values and attitudes.

We take care of the rooms inside our own homes, but whose job is it to look after the outdoor rooms of our towns? Maintenance is skimped, repairs are left undone. Rubbish accumulates. We defile our surroundings—and ourselves—with paintbrush and aerosol. We pollute our rivers and canals, and the very air we breathe.

Cockermouth and London, England; Bologna, Italy; Aberystwyth, Wales; Port Angelos, Washington State.

Cheltenham, England.

3 CONTROL OF CHANGE

ONCE the control of towns had passed from the top of the feudal pyramid to more democratic forms of administration, the extent of official intervention over the nature of urban change became subject to publicly held concerns and attitudes. Today there is broad agreement that, in the interests of society as a whole, the processes of change have, in some measure, to be guided, directed and controlled. This realization, however, developed slowly and fitfully.

'Let every house be pitched in the middle of its plot,' wrote William Penn in 1681 to his agents in the New World, 'so that there may be ground on each side for gardens or orchards or fields, that it may be a green country that will never be burnt and always be wholesome.' Philadelphia was perhaps the first city to be planned in advance of its first buildings—an example subsequently followed by Moravian settlers in the New World, who sent their plans to Europe for approval before breaking the ground. New settlements, or reconstruction after war or natural disaster, have made unified design possible, for how, without a regulatory concept, is one to begin? An existing settlement, however, is another matter. To bring the continuing, day-to-day, process of urban change under effective control has proved altogether more intractable. It is one thing to postulate criteria, but change is generated by individual aspirations and initiatives. How, except by compulsory acquisition and the use of public funds, are those criteria to be *enforced*? In other than totalitarian societies, towns stand on land which is, for the most part, privately owned. Officially to regulate the use or development of that land constitutes a restriction upon the rights and liberties of the owner, quite apart from whether or not he can afford to meet the demands made upon him. Planning, in the Western world, is therefore directly bound up with the nature and ethic of democracy. The pace at which planning concepts have evolved, and the form which they have taken, have thus varied enormously from one nation to another, coloured by each country's legislative and administrative structure and cultural traditions, as well as by the pressures, or otherwise, of its economy. On the whole, older countries more readily accept the concept of intervention than do younger, where the pioneering spirit remains strong. Massive urbanization tends to speed the process; non-industrialized societies come later to its acceptance. Even today a good many 'developed' countries have planning systems which are so minimal and unevolved that, except on paper, they barely exist; while for the most part the under-developed world, obsessed by the objective of intensive development, allows a free-for-all which it is bound, eventually, to regret.

Town planning is not a new concept. As we have seen, the colonial cities of the ancient world were constructed on planned grids. More recent excavations in London have indicated the rebuilding of Roman roads, after their total obliteration by the debris of great fires, to precisely the same line as previously—suggesting the existence of a planning office where plans and records were stored. As cities developed, civic authorities sought increasingly to limit their outward spread, deal with congestion in the streets, and provide sewerage and water. These are still major considerations today. Attempts were made in the fourth century BC to limit the growth of Rome; Julius Caesar prohibited vehicular movement between sunrise and an hour before sunset (which led Juvenal to complain, a century and a half later, that 'it is absolutely impossible to sleep anywhere in the city. The perpetual traffic of waggons in the narrow winding streets . . . is enough to wake the dead.') From the fourteenth century onwards, as cities' big families and merchants' guilds pushed for the right to make laws and impose taxes, mediaeval boroughs came increasingly to exercise a measure of corporate responsibility over water supplies, building, and the provision of simple community services. Areas were paved—in Paris by the twelfth century, in Florence and Lübeck by the thirteenth and fourteenth centuries. Drainage and street cleaning systems of a kind were initiated, though for the most part citizens were still required to carry their refuse to the fields beyond the town. In 1524 Paris decreed that citizens put candles in their windows to light the streets (the effect of which can perhaps be gauged by those who have passed through Campden Hill Square in London on Christmas Eve). Attempts were made to enforce a measure of infilling on unbuilt-up plots. Bologna passed an ordinance in the fifteenth century (which is still in force) requiring all property owners to provide pedestrian arcades on the street side of their buildings—as a result of which the city's 35 km (22 miles) of arcading today constitutes its main distinction.

The citizen's right to a planning appeal process became recognized. The 1419 Liber Albus of the City of London (compiled by John Carpenter, Town Clerk, while Richard Whittington was Mayor) included such provisions as this:

> Be it known, that if a person builds near the tenement of his neighbour, and it appears unto such neighbour that such building is unjust and to the injury of his own tenement, it shall be fully lawful for him to impede the erection of such building, pledge and surety being given unto the Sheriff of the City that he will prosecute; and thereupon shall such building cease, until by the twelve men aforesaid, or the greater part of them, it shall have been discussed whether such building is unjust or not.

A century and a half later, in London and in Paris, primarily for health reasons, the long struggle to contain the cities' growth was already joined—though in neither case to great effect. In 1580 Queen Elizabeth issued a proclamation banning all new building, except on existing foundations, within a three-mile belt (later extended to five miles) beyond the City gates. Acts, ordinances and proclamations to the same end followed over the next century or so (James issued a 'peremptory commandment' in 1615 that *all* private building must cease) but proved well-nigh unenforceable in practice (though Cromwell imposed a retrospective fine, in 1656, of one year's rent on any building illegally erected after 1620). The last such attempt foundered in 1709 with the withdrawal of yet another Parliamentary Bill, until resuscitated in the present century as the still-operative Green Belt policy: by 1983, in Britain, over 4.5 million acres of Green Belt had been designated in fifteen areas, with over 1.2 million surrounding London.

Other matters continued to be the subject of regulation—building materials, the thickness of walls, the size of rooms, the amount of land round new buildings. As we have seen, water supply systems of a kind were installed, streets improved, public gardens and open spaces created. It took disaster to focus public thinking on more integrated objectives. In London, for example, the Great Fire led to a ferment of planning ideas which was scarcely to be rivalled until the end of the nineteenth century. One proposal, by a Colonel Birch, was that the Crown should acquire the whole of the City of London, which would then, after replanning and redesign, be sold back to the original landowners. This got to the nub of the matter. However, rather as with the rebuilding of bombed cities after World War II, speed was seen as essential (the Rebuilding of London Act of 1667 allowed any building site left empty for more than three years to be acquired compulsorily by the City authorities); to a great extent expediency triumphed over long-term planning. The Rebuilding Acts also contained a form of 'betterment levy', whereby a sum settled by jury was payable to the City in respect of values increased by public improvement, thus tackling an intractable problem with which modern Britain has tangled repeatedly but unsuccessfully.

However, though advances were made, new building lines imposed, Commissioners for paving and drainage created, substantial progress was less through these Acts than through the subsequent Street Improvement Acts and the Towns Commissioners laws of the eighteenth and early nineteenth centuries. The 1774 Building Act, by grading classes of houses and imposing detailed requirements as to the measurements and materials of each, tightly controlled the development of London for a hundred years and brought into being the Georgian terraces and squares which are still part of its character today. In developing their great London estates, the aristocracy put out the actual construction work to speculative builders, but, by adding their own constraints and guidelines to those of the 1774 Building Act, exercised the most rigid control not only over basic layout, the width of streets, the provision of garden squares, and so on, but over the most detailed aspects of elevational design and unity. Typical leases suppressed gin shops, gaming houses, brothels and schools (presumably because of the shrill clamour of the young), and contained long lists of forbidden trades and activities. Original aspirations faded as leases fell in, and much of what the great estates left us has been grievously eroded in our own day. By the 1980s, for example, the Grosvenor Estate had been forced to sell some twenty per cent of the houses it owned in Mayfair and Belgravia, under the Leasehold Reform Act of 1967 (upheld by the European Court of Justice), which allows occupants of leasehold properties the right to acquire them freehold. Even now, though, considerable areas of Bloomsbury and Belgravia testify to what unity of ownership can achieve.

Though London was exceptional in this form of land ownership, her efforts to achieve orderly development were not unique. Paris exerted increasingly tight controls over her street façades from the seventeenth century onwards. Edinburgh appointed a city architect in 1728. The City of Stockholm had already, in 1640, drawn up plans for outer suburbs; and after suffering eight great fires over the following century, then appointed a chief planner (or 'conductor') to what must surely be one of the oldest municipal planning departments in the world. Big-scale developments and improvements were put in hand in many great cities. Craig's plan for Edinburgh New Town was published in 1776; Nash's proposals for the reshaping of central London were adopted in 1811; Haussmann's for Paris were commissioned after the 1848 revolution; the Ringstrasse in Vienna dates from the same period.

With the coming of the Victorian era, however, cities faced problems of an altogether new order. Mechanisms which had sufficed for a time of more orderly development proved totally inadequate for a period of explosive expansion. In England the very success of the great private estates as enlightened developers had tended to slow the pace of official intervention, while the energies unleashed by the industrial revolution were fuelled by self-interest rather than social or aesthetic values. It was in the living and working conditions of the nineteenth-century proletariat that town planning, as we understand it today, really found its roots.

The contradictions of the century—the brutality of its attitudes to the labouring classes, coupled increasingly with individual examples of paternalistic reformism aimed at ameliorating their lot—are well illustrated by two examples taken from the very same year of 1816. On the one hand, here is Richard Arkwright giving evidence before the Select Committee to Enquire into the State of the Children employed in the Manufactories of the United Kingdom:

> At what age do you admit children into your mills?—Not until they are ten years of age.
>
> What are the hours of work per day in your mills?—Thirteen hours, including meal times.
>
> What other ages have you heard of their being taken into factories at?—I have heard of their being taken in at six.

On the other hand, here, in the same year, is Robert Owen, first of the century's doggedly deterministic reformers:

> I know that society may be formed so as to exist without crime, without poverty, with health greatly improved, with little, if any, misery, and with intelligence and happiness increased an hundredfold; and no obstacle whatever intervenes at this moment, except ignorance, to prevent such a state of society becoming universal.

The cholera outbreaks of the eighteen thirties triggered a period of intense self-examination which continued to the end of the century. In 1842 the Poor Law Commissioners reported on public health. This resulted in the appointment of a Royal Commission on the Condition of the Towns, whose report in turn led to the Public Health Act of 1848. Thereafter Government commissions and voluntary committees reported endlessly—and painstakingly—on overcrowding; on sanitation and water supplies; on factory conditions; on child labour; on the education and improvement of the masses; on drunkenness; on crime. Improvements were put in hand, most successfully in the first instance to the supply of water, to sanitation and to the control of burial—at a stroke dramatically improving the life expectancy of the city dweller, and incidentally establishing the link between health and housing, so that, seventy years later, it was the Ministry of Health which was made responsible for housing and town planning. Legislation was passed in 1847 enforcing the disposal of household sewage by public sewers. (Since, however, these mostly discharged into the rivers, the effect was to make the Thames, for example, so grossly polluted for 150 years that nothing would live in it.) However, most of the reports gathered dust on the shelves. Public action requires appropriate machinery and as yet this did not exist. The Municipal Corporations Act of 1835 had unified the local government system throughout the country, and regulated the functions of town councils. Over the following half century some fifty amending Acts were passed, gradually extending the powers of local councils, but property rights constitute the corner-stone of capitalism, and interventionist policies were only accepted by the landed and new mercantile classes, if at all, with grudging reluctance. Innovation was left to social reformers and a few paternalistic industrialists.

There was no shortage of theories on how best to end the depravity of the slums. Minter Morgan proposed Christian communities of 300 families; Dr Benjamin Richardson's *Hygeia* offered healthy conditions for 300,000. There were more practical propositions too. In 1841, the Rector of Spitalfields founded the Metropolitan Association for Improving Conditions of the Industrious Classes. Philanthropic housing societies and trusts became increasingly active. The Shaftesbury Society (1844), the Peabody Trust (1862) and the Improved Industrial Dwellings Company (1863) were notable, and many of their buildings are with us still. George Peabody, an American merchant settled in London, wrote in 1866 to the trustees of his Fund: 'A century in the history of London is but a brief period comparatively with the life of man . . . it is my ardent hope and trust that within that period . . . there may not be a poor working man of good character in London who could not obtain comfortable and healthful lodgings for himself and his family at a cost within his means . . .' Peabody was one of the 'Five Per Cent Philanthropists' for whom total charity would have seemed destructive of moral fibre in the recipient, but, even more to the point, incapable of being self-supporting and therefore sustainable over a long period. In the conditions of the day they achieved a good deal. Between the 1840s and the 1880s nearly 60,000 were rehoused; by 1905 the number, for nine major trusts, stood at 123,000—but by then a great structure of municipal services was coming into being. The 1885 Housing of the Working Classes Act, in particular, led, over the following century, to a massive intervention by local authorities, on a scale which is more or less unique to Britain. By the 1980s local councils in Britain housed around eighteen million people, and were rehousing some 300,000 families a year (though under pressure from central government to encourage home ownership by sale of their housing to their tenants).

But improved living conditions in the city did not of themselves exorcise the horrors of working-class existence. To the Victorian reformers new working communities seemed to offer another solution. Estate villages had been built by the British nobility during the eighteenth century—Blanchland, Inveraray, Lowther and Milton Abbas for example. W. A. Madocks, a late eighteenth/early nineteenth-century Member of Parliament, dreamed of forming an ideal community on land reclaimed by damming the Glaslyn estuary in North Wales. First, however, of the industrial communities was New Lanark (see p. 97) created by David Dale in 1784 at the Falls of Clyde in Lanarkshire, and developed from the turn of the century by Robert Owen, his son-in-law—the nature of whose beliefs have already been noted. Within twelve years, four mills were in operation, employing a work force of 1340, and the practical evidence of Owen's reforming zeal soon brought New Lanark up to 2,000 visitors a year.

From the middle of the century new industrial communities, on paper and in reality, proliferated. Some were simply streets of houses like those built for their workers by the railway companies in Swindon, Derby and Crewe. Some were conceived as true communities. In 1849 Titus Salt, Congregationalist, mill-owner and ex-mayor of Bradford, decided to rationalize his mills at a new site—Saltaire—four miles out from the city. There seems little doubt that he was influenced by Disraeli's notions of a model factory and village in *Sybil, or, The Two Nations*. 'I will do all I can', wrote Salt, 'to avoid evils so great as those resulting from polluted air and water, and hope to draw around me a well-fed, contented and happy body of operatives.' The housing he would build was to be 'a pattern to the country'.

And not only in Britain. Promotion of ideal communities became quite the thing. Fourier, a French Robert Owen, saw his big communal buildings for workers realized by J. B. André at Guise. In the 1874 Meunier village of Noisel near Paris, tenants' rents were progressively reduced until they finally retired to free accommodation in the village almshouses. George Pullman, of railway carriage fame, is thought to have been inspired by Saltaire (which he probably visited in 1873) when he began his new town to the south of Chicago in 1880—a town on 300 acres of a 4,000-acre site which eventually housed nearly 12,000 people. (Pullman's less than philanthropic wage cuts, however, finally brought about a walk-out which turned into a national strike in 1894, from which he, and the venture, never really recovered.) Back in England, George and Richard Cadbury began to lay out Bournville in 1879; in 1887 W. H. Lever and his son started the construction of Port Sunlight. Indeed, by 1883, there was even a Society for Promoting Industrial Villages.

These communities varied considerably in size. Saltaire still houses about 2,500 people in its 800 houses on 22 streets, though in 1986 it was announced that the great central mill building itself was to be vacated, posing a threat to the whole nature of Saltaire. Bournville (which was never intended to be a 'company' village but open to all) today has around 13,000 living in 4,000 houses and flats. What they all had in common was that they were provided with laundries, shops, doctors, churches and community meeting places, and all coloured by a high-minded concern for hygiene and moral rectitude—for these determinist reformers saw themselves as social *and moral* engineers. (Owen not only created an Institute for the Formation of Character, and instituted fines for drunkenness and impropriety, but conducted weekly inspections of each household for cleanliness and order.) In their layout, these little towns included green spaces and avenues of trees (Bournville deliberately picturesque, with its housing grouped around cul-de-sacs and closes; Port Sunlight rather more in the Beaux Arts tradition). These paternalistic communities for the working class were, in some measure, prototypes for the Garden City Movement—the voluntary, middle-class equivalent, the ethos of which was enshrined in Ebenezer Howard's *Tomorrow—The Peaceful Path to Real Reform*, of 1898. The Garden City concept stretches from the creation of Bedford Park in London, laid out in 1871, through Letchworth, begun in 1903, and Hampstead Garden Suburb, begun in 1907, to the 32 New Towns built after World War II. It was to prove one of the most tenacious elements in the orthodox wisdom of twentieth-century planning. If Le Corbusier's *Ville Radieuse* was a diagram for the future inner city, Ebenezer Howard's Garden City proved one not only for new towns but, watered down and bereft of charm, for endless miles of sprawling local authority housing in Britain during the second and third quarters of the twentieth century. The main twist to the diagram came from America, with the Radburn concept of separating traffic and pedestrians by turning the houses back-to-front and linking them by foot-paths.

If these various efforts to free the labouring classes from the nightmare squalors of the industrial city formed the central thread of a developing concept which we now call planning, they were soon to be joined by others. Escape into the countryside gave a new significance to its protection. Revulsion against the brutalizing effects of industrialization induced nostalgia for a lost way of life, for the dignity of labour, the loving work of the artist-craftsman, and the ancient buildings that reflected his handiwork. In the princely German states and in centralist France, the thrust towards protection of the countryside and historic buildings came from Court and Government. In the English-speaking world it was by and large individual reformers and private associations who made the running.

Attitudes to change have probably always been ambivalent. In the eighteenth century the new landscape of enclosure in Britain was reviled as unnatural and disgusting by countrymen and connoisseurs. 'The beautiful wild scenery—all swept away,' lamented Bewick. But this is the landscape, made lovable by familiarity, the passing of which to accommodate mechanization the present generation of non-farmers in its turn laments. (The loss of hedgerows was running, by the 1980s, at 4,000 miles a year).

Past centuries, however, were seldom beset by self-doubts in the remodelling of buildings and towns. Change was synonymous with 'improvement' and it seems never to have occurred to anyone much before the nineteenth century that the new could in any way be inferior to what went before. Romanesque was reclad in the pointed armour of Gothic. Gothic buildings were remodelled in the classic manner during the Renaissance; Tudor buildings in England were given Georgian fronts; great churches were reshaped without a qualm by the confident Victorians.

During the eighteenth century, however, change began to be seen against a wider historical background. 'Whatever is good in its kind', wrote Hawkesmoor in 1715, 'ought to be preserved in respect to antiquity as well as our present advantage, for destruction can be profitable to none but such as live by it.' Increasingly, painting, architecture and landscape mirrored the values, real or imagined, of a newly discovered golden age, the actual monuments of which formed the main objectives of the Grand Tour. (According to Horace Walpole, 40,000 English passed through Calais in 1763–64.) Palladian villas began to appear in England. The Poussins and Claudes upon the walls were the inspiration of the Arcadian parkland through the windows. By 1728 Betty Langley was calling for theatre-scenery ruins to lend a sense of history to the design of gardens ('It is not every man that can build a house who can execute a ruin . . .'). 'Virtuosi' began to collect assorted fragments and curiosities from the past. The Society of Antiquaries was incorporated in London in 1751, and the earliest plea, in Britain, for the systematic preservation of old buildings (for the purpose of historic study) was made by a Director of the Society, Richard Gough, in 1788. With the French revolution, neo-classicism became the approved, and it was hoped ennobling, manner in France. History painting flourished and scholarship began to flesh out understanding of previous ages. The nineteenth century has been described as 'obsessed with history'.

In Britain especially, a parallel development was a fresh perception of nature in her many moods, but particularly the awesome, the picturesque and the 'sublime'. The Rev. William Gilpin helped a whole generation to look afresh at landscape. The cognoscenti prized above all what we would now call 'wilderness' for its power to move the spirit by reminders of man's insignificance as measured against the elements. The essential pleasures of the countryside were growing more popular; by mid-seventeenth century people of taste were setting off for a ramble and a picnic. Dr Russell's *Dissertation Concerning the Uses of Sea Water in Diseases of the Glands* appeared in English in 1753 and twenty years later Smollet remarked the bathing machines along the beach at Scarborough. By the end of the century Constable and Turner were transmuting the transient effects of the weather and the seasons into painting of incomparable freshness and power, and thereby ushering in a great period of *plein air* artists throughout Europe. Nash's nine *cottages ornées*, informally laid out in 1811 as Blaise Hamlet, near Bristol, embodied current principles of irregularity and the picturesque. Would an earlier engineer have written, as did Telford while engaged on the Menai Bridge, 'whenever I am commissioned to build a bridge I have a fear of my design not blending, not fitting in with the surrounding countryside.' The sense was developing, as Wordsworth wrote of the Lake District, of landscape as 'a sort of national property, in which every man has a right and an interest who has an eye to perceive and a heart to enjoy'.

These new perceptions of the built and natural environment were eventually to spread through society. They began, however, as aristocratic concerns of the Church and in monarchist and absolutist states. A Constitution of the Council held at St Paul's, London, in 1236 (presided over by the Papal Legate, with the Archbishops of Canterbury and York among those present) reads: 'We strictly forbid . . . Rectors of Churches to pull down ancient consecrated churches without the consent and license of the Bishop of the Diocese, under the pretext of raising a more ample or fair fabric . . .' In Rome, Pius II issued a Bull aimed at protecting the ruins—but permitted the demolition of the Portico of Octavia; Sixtus IV tried to clamp down on the export of antiquities—but allowed the demolition of the Temple of Hercules. Leo X was persuaded by Raphael to stop quarrying for St Peters—but it went on after his death until Benedict IV's ban in the mid-eighteenth century.

Some sporadic listing of monuments began in the sixteenth and seventeenth centuries—in Bavaria, in Württemberg, and in Sweden (the 1666 Proclamation on Historic Monuments and Antiquities). Sweden, indeed, had a Curator of National Antiquities as early as 1630. James I commissioned Inigo Jones to undertake a (not very sophisticated) survey of Stonehenge in 1620. By the eighteenth century a number of German princes were ordering inventories to be made (for example in 1780, Margrave Alexander of Ansbach-Bayreuth), followed by the first protective *statutes* (Württenberg in 1790, Bavaria in 1835). Ludwig I's decree of 1826 remains topical. 'We have learnt that in a number of places in Our Kingdom public monuments of ancient art and specially precious buildings have been robbed of their essential character through unsuitable renewal, supposed embellishment or disfigurement through painting. Since We wish to preserve these same objects with all care in their original state, so We promulgate the command that no alteration will be permitted to any public work of art, in particular churches and other buildings, without permission from the district government.'

Then in 1832 Victor Hugo published his *Guerre aux Démolisseurs*, calling for legislation to save monuments threatened with demolition or excessive 'restoration'. After the 1830 revolution the French government did indeed set in motion ambitious moves to document and protect all France's historic buildings and ruins, which Prosper Mérimée, succeeding Ludovic Vitet, cut down to size (reckoning that the original plan would take 200 years and 900 volumes). He himself traversed the country to make the first list of 59 buildings, all of them mediaeval or earlier (it was not, for example, until 1889 that the classical Place Royale, now the Place des Vosges, was listed). But, no less significantly, Mérimée secured a small government budget of 105,000 francs towards the preservation of listed monuments. France thus became the first country in modern times to make government funds available for this purpose (Mérimée's first restoration job, La Madeleine at Vézelay, went to Violet-le-Duc); the first, too, in 1841, to legislate to permit the State compulsorily to purchase monuments—though (how familiar it sounds) implementation was inhibited by inadequate funds.

In Britain, the only action was that initiated by informed opinion. In York a group of citizens, calling themselves the Association for the Preservation of Ancient Footpaths, in 1826 issued an appeal for funds with which to restore the thirteenth-century city walls, damaged during the Civil War and threatened with demolition by the city council. About £3,500 was collected—an enormous sum in those days—enabling the restoration work to be carried out. By 1847 the first, still-surviving local conservation society in Britain was founded at Sidmouth, on the south coast—its first task being to raise the funds for a new footbridge. In January 1850, Lord Cockburn up in Scotland recorded, 'I went yesterday to see the house believed to have been John Knox's, under restoration. An attempt has been carrying on, for nearly a year, to get it removed as dangerous, which before the Dean of Guild was always successful. A public subscription to keep it up has saved it, without any material change in its air or its composition. I could scarcely keep my pen off the subject . . .'

So, throughout the second half of the century, public opinion gathered weight and momentum. Lord Cockburn in Edinburgh, and Ruskin in London, called on citizens to form protectionist associations; a quarter of a century later, the still flourishing Cockburn Association and, through William Morris, the Society for the Protection of Ancient Buildings came into existence. Darwin, Gladstone and Hardy were only three of the early supporters of the SPAB; Royal Academicians abounded among the early members. Foreshadowing the efforts of UNESCO and Venice in Peril a century later, the Society sent Holman Hunt and George Street to report on repairs to the Dome of the Rock in Jerusalem and St Mark's in Venice. While such as these were throwing their weight into the battle against Victorian church 'restoration', the protagonists of the countryside were no less active—in the first instance against the 'enclosure', or annexation by private interests, of common land. Here is Lord Eversley's 1894 account—taken from a contemporary newspaper report—of one of the best known counter-attacks:

> On March 6th 1866 a special train left Euston shortly after midnight with a force of 120 workmen aboard armed with implements and crowbars. The train reached Tring in Hertfordshire at 1.30 a.m. A procession was formed at the station and a march of three miles in the moonlight brought them to Berkhamsted Common. In detachments of a dozen strong, the workmen loosened the joints of the five foot high railings surrounding the Common with hammers, chisels and crowbars. Before six a.m. the whole of the fences, two miles in length, were levelled to the ground, and the railings were laid in a heap, with as little damage as possible. It was seven o'clock before the alarm was given, and when Lord Brownlow's agent appeared on the scene, he found that Berkhamsted Common was no longer enclosed. Meanwhile the news spread and the inhabitants of the district flocked to the scene. Gentlemen came in their carriages and dogcarts; shopkeepers from Berkhamsted and farmers in their gigs; labourers on foot tested the reality of what they saw by wandering over the Common, and cutting morsels of the flowering gorse, to prove, as they said, that the land was theirs again. Thus were 430 acres restored to the Common.

And thus was the oldest national society of its kind in Britain, the Commons, Open Spaces and Footpaths Preservation Society, brought into being. Among its founder members were Octavia Hill, Robert Hunter, T. A. Huxley and John Stuart Mill.

From such beginnings grew Britain's dense network of over 1,000 unofficial associations, which has largely set the aims of planning in Britain. Societies for the preservation of Dartmoor, the Lake District and Hampstead Heath in London came into being in 1883, 1885 and 1896. By the end of the century, there were the Metropolitan and Public Gardens Association (1882), the National Trust (1891), the National Society for Checking Abuse of Public Advertising (1893), and the Garden Cities Association (1899) (later to become the Town and Country Planning Association). Many more were to follow. Nor of course were such initiatives confined to Britain: The Mount Vernon Ladies Association had acquired George Washington's old home in 1858; the Association for the Protection of Old Bamberg, in Bavaria, came into existence in 1875—and so on. With the new century came a wave of national preservation societies in Germany, in Switzerland, in the Netherlands, Denmark, Poland and elsewhere.

Through the decades spanning the turn of the century traditional concepts were in the melting pot. Barriers were being breached in all directions—in the arts, in political thought, in the exploration of matter and the exploration of the human mind. Wireless, the motor car and the aeroplane gave promise of a world rendered unbelievably accessible. The future had arrived and all things seemed possible. The environmental concerns of the Victorian era began to come together and planning, as a system of control, at last emerged: timidly, tentatively, its practice to start with permissive rather than mandatory. John Barns' Housing, Town Planning Act of 1909 laid the first, rather insubstantial foundations in Britain. Just what the process of planning meant in practice was still not very clear, though the second part of the Act set out—and this is its main interest today—the main elements to be taken into account. They embraced streets and highways, including their stopping up or diversion; buildings and structures of all kinds; the preservation of objects of historical interest or of natural beauty; drainage and sewage disposal; lighting; water supply; ancillary works; and provision for compensation and betterment (values increased by public works), though these proved more or less unworkable in practice.

A planning profession came into being. The (now Royal) Town Planning Institute was born at the beginning of 1914 (with 115 members—most of them architects, followed by surveyors and engineers). Patrick Geddes, a key figure, battled to bring the aims of planning into sharper focus. His message, in brief: survey, plan, implementation. Geddes, more than others at that time, appreciated the complexity of town planning. It had to be 'a veritable orchestration of all the arts, needing all the Social Sciences'.

However, the administrative framework was still lacking and little real progress was made between the wars. The main concern lay with zoning, density and the development of greenfield sites. The most potent theoretical framework put forward between the wars was that embodied in the 'Athens Charter' of 1933. This stemmed from the influential CIAM (*Congrès Internationaux d'Architecture Moderne*) which, between 1929 and 1963, was *the* forum for the Modern Movement. In the Charter's codification (generally acknowledged to be largely a personal manifesto by Corbusier) the functions of the city—housing, work, recreation and transport—provided its armature; the Charter called for high-rise development, industrial zones, parks and sports grounds, and an hierarchical street system for traffic at different speeds. These things, for better or worse, entered the architectural/planning vocabulary world-wide and carried all before them in the decades immediately after World War II.

It was indeed the Second World War, and the urge to create a better world when it had ended, which gave planning—at least in Europe—an inevitability it had previously lacked. Massive reconstruction had to be planned in countless war-devasted cities—Rotterdam, Cologne, Warsaw, Coventry and many others. It was, however, Britain's Town and Country Planning Act of 1947 which sought, finally, to bring the day-to-day process of change, right across the board, under continuous control. The experience of war-time government regulation of so many aspects of life paved the way—almost without demur—for what was the biggest single transfer of power from the individual to the State ever made in Britain outside times of national emergency. Planning had finally arrived, or so it seemed.

The central aim of planning is to regulate change—to maximize its potential for the public good, to minimize the possible harm. At the core of any planning system must lie the capability of controlling the *use* to which land is put, and any proposed *changes* of use. It may, for example, be thought desirable to designate 'zones' for particular purposes or of particular kinds—industrial, residential, of historic interest, etc. By this means the householder may be spared the noise, pollution and heavy traffic generated by industrial uses; inappropriate commercial activities can be excluded from historic areas; the outward sprawl of cities into the countryside can be contained, and so on.

No less important is the capability of controlling the *density* to which a site is developed—the number of people to be housed on a hectare of land, or the number of square metres of office space permissible on a given site. This is the planner's weapon against the overcrowding of the Victorian slum and the gross over-exploitation of a site for private gain. It gives him, at the same time, the ability to control the height and bulk of buildings.

Around these central powers may be grouped a multitude of others, enabling him to deal with such things as traffic management and exclusion, the protection of historic properties, clean air and smokeless zones, the protection and planting of trees, abuses of outdoor advertising, and so on.

Most of these powers, it will be apparent, are 'negative'—they will be used to *prevent* something happening. This is not to be sneezed at—the British countryside, for example, is virtually free of the vast billboards which disfigure the motorways of other nations. Can planning do more? It has been said that planning only exists because of the tendency of real estate to develop; in the absence of pressures to develop, there is nothing to plan. This is only half true. New towns can be created, industry induced to move to areas of low economic pressure by grants and fiscal reliefs, tourism encouraged by improved access and facilities. Nevertheless, it is what planning prevents which developers and the general public are most likely to be conscious of, and the British system, it has to be admitted, has in general failed to balance control with equally purposeful creativity.

In outline, solutions look obvious. Here is an historic square, one side of which was demolished between the wars for road widening. The replacement buildings—a public lavatory and some ugly little shops—are separated by waste ground; the whole site is an eyesore. A quarter of a mile away, a national company acquires a site for a thirty-storey headquarters block which can only be totally out of keeping with the Regency streets around. Why can this tower block not be moved a quarter of a mile away and laid on its side to complete the square once more—not necessarily in a pastiche way, but in scale and in suitable materials? Site acquisition costs would be greater, but construction costs considerably less. The company would have a prestige building; the character of the town would be enhanced.

The trouble is, of course, that, lacking ownership of the land, the planning authority can only suggest, wheedle, perhaps offer some financial incentive (if it can afford to and if such a move be legal), possibly hold up its approval in respect of the one site in the hope that some deal may emerge on the other (in the square). But it will not dare to play this game for too long lest the company decide to move elsewhere and the promise of 900 new jobs is lost.

At what level and at what stage should official intervention begin? If one householder replaces a Georgian sash window with a metal-framed 'picture' window, or falls for the blandishments of a door-to-door salesman and clads his house with what looks like vertical crazy paving, it can scarcely be regarded, unless the area is of the greatest historical importance, as a matter of life and death. But suppose that ten, fifty, three quarters of the householders in the area do likewise? The essential character of the area will have been totally destroyed and everyone may regret what they have done.

Pitfalls abound. If a site is compulsorily acquired, should compensation be paid to the owner at its existing use value, or its potential use value? If the latter, why should personal gain accrue from increased values created solely by publicly financed works? (In Singapore, for example, land is acquired by the government at existing use value, and sold to developers at its enhanced value, thus ensuring that the 'betterment' element passes to the public purse.) To what extent should development by official agencies, governmental and local authority, be exempt from planning control? If they are not to be exempt, how can government and local planning authorities be judge and applicant at the same time? To what extent is 'open government' fully possible in planning matters? Public knowledge of eventual possible redevelopment, with all the uncertainty created thereby, has blighted vast areas of our towns and cities, sometimes for a generation or more—and sometimes, as it has proved in the long run, needlessly.

The manner in which these things are handled is very much a matter of the political and cultural traditions of the country concerned. For example, it is illuminating, if ironic, to compare the power of control which can be achieved by private enterprise in the United States with that of a communist administration in Western Europe. Disney World offers a fascinating glimpse of control by ownership. The transport systems complement one another. The monorail is totally integrated with buildings. Power, heat and water are recycled. Litter and rubbish are whisked away at 60 m.p.h. through underground ducting. Disney World is a kind of free-enterprise utopia, cocooned from the real world by its 43 sq. miles (110 sq. km)—of which only one tenth is as yet developed—and by its monopolistic powers over every aspect of development and use (as an 'improvement district' under Florida law, it is a sovereign authority in all but policing and matters affecting the individual).

Ideologically, this is how things should have been in Bologna, in Italy, but the realities were different. Bologna began to establish long-term conservationist principles in the early 1960s. These were based on a very detailed survey of the city's structures and open spaces. The city's 1969 plan had as its objective the rehabilitation of the entire historic core—but without displacement of the lower-income groups living there. To this end, the city proposed, as had been suggested in the City of London after the Great Fire, to acquire the whole central area compulsorily at 'existing use' levels (i.e. far below the potential market value), and to lease back the properties after restoration. However, in Italy, local councils receive no revenue from local taxes, and what Bologna received back from central government was totally inadequate for the purpose. The grand plan, in its original form, had to be jettisoned. In fact, a more modest approach has been devised, based on subsidies to owners for rehabilitation work, coupled with a means test, no displacement and controlled rents. But that, as they say, is another story. There are no absolute rules, then. What works in very centralized systems—for example the French—could not work in a federal framework such as Germany, Switzerland or the United States, or in countries where executive power is largely delegated to local level—as in the Netherlands and Britain. (Interestingly, in the middle 1980s France appears to be moving towards greater decentralization, while in Britain central government is taking to itself increased responsibilities.) Britain's machinery, however, provides a conveniently integrated pattern against which others may be compared.

The 1947 Planning Act brought into being a single statutory system for the whole of England and Wales (the Scottish equivalent differs marginally). The Act has been much amended since then, and Britain's local authority structure has twice been radically redrawn. Further changes undoubtedly lie ahead but, in greatly simplified outline, the British system as it evolved during the first thirty years is as follows. The Department of the Environment is centrally responsible for all land-use planning, housing and environmental protection. Two tiers of local authorities exercise compulsory responsibilities—counties (or in Scotland, regions) at a strategic level; districts (and London boroughs) for local and day-to-day control. The former are responsible for the preparation of 'structure plans', which are broad policy statements (at present subject to government confirmation); the latter for 'local' plans, which form the basis for continuing control of proposed development (and have to conform with the structure plan).

All applications (save proposals by Government and statutory undertakers) to develop a site, or change its use, or alter a building listed for its architectural or historic interest, must be submitted to the district or borough for planning permission. Any scheme affecting more than a few people must be publicized and local authorities are obliged to seek the views of the public in the preliminary stages of planning their own proposed developments. The public may make representations for or against applications; in the event of planning permission being withheld, or coupled with unacceptable conditions, applicants have the right of appeal to the Secretary of State. The

Minister can himself 'call in' an application for decision at government level if he considers it desirable. Any application of substance is likely to become the subject of a Public Inquiry—rather on the lines of a court of law but more informal—under an Inspector appointed by the Department of the Environment. Third parties—i.e. other than the applicant and the planning authority—can make representations at such Inquiries, in writing or in person. Smaller cases may now be decided by the Inspector alone; where the decision is taken by the Secretary of State, he will normally—but not necessarily—accept his Inspector's finding; where he does not, he must state his reasons for differing.

The British system was initially regarded with wonder, and sometimes envy, by other countries. However, the pattern which looks so neat on paper is by no means uniform in practice. It is not open to a local council in Britain to draft its own land-use ordinances and regulations, as happens for example in Austria (Salzburg, Graz) or in the United States (where on the other hand, the absence of any *requirement* to plan means that many smaller communities are subject to no planning control at all). However, while the powers and obligations of local authorities in Britain are established statutorily, the manner in which those powers are exercised is largely discretionary. Official *advice* is offered by central government in the form of Departmental Circulars (and a measure of clumsy, broad-brush stroke constraint is exercised by government financial policy), but, in normal circumstances, there is no question of detailed government *direction* on specific jobs. In its legislation the government often retains reserve powers to act directly in the event of default by a local authority, but such powers are rarely exercised. Performance standards therefore differ widely at the local level and the problem poses itself of how, within this kind of framework, can democracy *ensure* minimum performance levels. So far in Britain the democratic ideal has taken precedence over consistency of effort.

In North America, in Australia, property rights are regarded as sacred and any intervention an unwarranted intrusion upon the liberty of the individual. The American Constitution entrusts the federal government with certain powers and obligations; all else is a matter for state regulation. Federal planning legislation is minimal (though by dispensing very large sums at the local level, federal agencies such as the Department of Housing and Urban Development, or the Federal Urban Mass Transportation Administration, can offer or withhold powerful support for local initiatives. In the high-spending nineteen seventies there were said to be some 400 channels of federal grant aid.

State legislation is variable, to say the least (Oregon and Vermont have good frameworks for nature conservation, pollution control, and energy saving, and Massachusetts has been active in other aspects of planning, but few others come up to their level). Urban planning is an almost totally local responsibility, with the strengths and weaknesses attaching to this. Fundamentally, the exercise of development control in the United States turns upon the provision of the Fifth Amendment, which forbids the taking of property (or property rights) without just compensation—though powers of 'eminent domain' (or compulsory purchase) are widespread in many States, and the constitutionality of public control over private lands was upheld by the Supreme Court in a landmark case.

To a large extent planning, in America, has been left to private enterprise—not only in the construction of new towns like Reston, in Virginia, and Columbia, in Maryland, but in the very initiation of city plans; Baltimore offers one example (see p. 187). Houston, spurning even zoning regulations, offers the most extreme example of American *laissez faire*, though the results are not markedly different from those in the central business districts of other big American cities. Lacking the statutory obligation to plan, a municipality's usual procedure, if it wishes or is pushed to move positively, is to set up a semi-autonomous agency for the purpose —as like as not called a local Redevelopment Authority—which has more in common with one of Britain's New Town Corporations, or with the special Development Corporations created for London's and Liverpool's Docklands, than with a British local authority planning department. Often such agencies are given a set term of existence—which concentrates the mind wonderfully; the rules they make are clear-cut—so that developers and public know exactly where they stand; and regulations, once made, are enforced more rigorously than is often the case in Britain.

Local finance is raised by taxes and, after public approval has been voted for it, the issue of bonds. In the absence of national or State legislation, constitutionality, as has been stated, is the touchstone in relation to any specific proposals; the courts become the battleground of opposing interests and the arbiters of the degree of regulation considered admissible under the Constitution. During the nineteen seventies the Environmental Impact Statement emerged as a new planning tool. This required federal agencies to furnish detailed evidence, in advance, of the effects of any proposed action significantly affecting the quality of the human environment. An element of overkill attached to the EIS for a time, as initiating agencies sought to blanket possible opposition by the sheer volume of material tabled. However, the practice seems to have settled down—Urban Impact Analysis now is required of all federal agencies—and has since been welcomed by the European Community which has made it the subject of a Directive for incorporation into the laws of member states. In Britain it seems likely to be used for very big Public Inquiries for which the normal planning process is not really suitable.

To compare the planning systems of the Western world in any detail would be baffling in its complexity. Differences abound in all directions. In the United States National Parks are totally owned by the nation; settlement in them is discouraged and public use of them limited. In Britain, pressure on space demands that National Parks remain in multiple use and multiple ownership. In America, property owners are encouraged into the ways of righteousness by fiscal reliefs (see p. 95); in Britain, by direct government grants. In federal Switzerland, decisions are taken by local referenda on matters which, in France, may well end up on the Presidential desk (for example the motorway proposed some years ago for the Left Bank of the Seine; the redevelopment of Les Halles; the courtyard pyramid of the 'Grand Louvre'). A change of incumbent can thus produce dramatic reversals of policy.

Consider merely the protection of the architectural heritage. In some countries—for example Bulgaria—the listing process is regarded as complete; in others—like Spain and Luxembourg—work has only been initiated fairly recently. Many younger countries have no inventory at all, while many inventories are incomplete or open-ended if only because the frontiers of 'historical interest' are all the time expanding, and any official list must take account of this.

Standards, criteria and mechanisms diverge no less. France's 1913 Act, which is still in force, established two grades of value—Monuments Classés (about 12,000) and those listed on the Supplementary Inventory (about 18,000). Germany prefers to work to a single category; Bulgaria has four. Against France's 30,000 listed monuments, Germany has around 400,000 (of which a quarter are in Bavaria). In some countries —for example the USA—the owner's agreement has to be obtained before a property goes on to the National Register of Historic Places; in France you are informed of the decision to list and can appeal against the decision in the case of a *Monument Classé* (though the Government can override the appeal): in Britain at one time you were not even formally told that your house had been listed—until you sought to alter or demolish it. National psychologies can be detected with particular clarity in relation to the architectural heritage. Italy, oppressed perhaps by a greater weight of monuments of international importance than exists in any other country, has tended to take her incomparable riches for granted. They have always been there; what if a few crumble away?

For exactly the converse reason the younger nations—until very recently—have paid scant attention to *their* older buildings; these have not seemed unusual in any way, except, perhaps, for associational reasons. Thus the American emphasis on the historic building, or site, as shrine. Buildings were preserved, if at all, in an *ad hoc* manner as mementos of great men (most frequently the founding fathers of the Union)—as museums which, by their associations, would move the visitor and uplift him with reminders of the patriotic virtues. If redevelopment proved compellingly attractive, the obstructing building might be moved to some quieter spot; or broken up, but with a room or two (or a door, or a fireplace) carefully installed in a museum. For a period the big museums vied with one another in plundering historic properties.

From this tradition stems the talismanic magic with which Americans have imbued tangible fragments of the past: Col. McCormick's bits of stone from around the world which he embedded in the outer walls of his *Chicago Tribune* building; the free-standing façade of the old Pennsylvania Fire Insurance Company which fronts the Penn Mutual tower looking up Independence Mall in Philadelphia. History has tended to be the American touch-stone in such matters. It persists in the glamour now attaching to interwar 'diners', drive-in cinemas, Coney Island hot dog stands, and the Sankey milk bottle which was given a civic welcome in the harbour when it was moved to Boston in the mid 'Seventies. In this sense the American people forcefully continue the collecting habits of the eighteenth-century cognoscenti in Europe.

A different ethic obtains in France—the France which has for centuries found *la gloire* in artistic pre-eminence and her self-appointed position as guardian of the world's cultural standards. Buildings, and later towns, have been protected and preserved primarily as great works of art in their own right. The Napoleonic Code Civil made it logical that their care and maintenance should fall to the Government and the Ministry of Fine Arts. The Revolution divested the Church of ownership of cathedrals and churches (the former falling to the Government, the latter to local authorities). As we have seen, France was the first nation to make official funds available for the protection of historic buildings. And it is significant that France has designated some sixty *secteurs sauvegardés*—her show-piece towns and quarters—as opposed to the nearly 6,000 conservation areas designated in Britain (though it has to be added that in the middle 'Seventies the French Government listed the entire central areas of 100 of the 350 towns of over 20,000 population). This view of historic buildings as art works has tended until recently to divorce their problems from those of land-use planning generally—though, with Gallic logic, since 1913 the French have insisted on a 'buffer zone', or protected area, around the monument itself so as to ensure it an appropriate setting. This has given France very complete control over large parts of towns; only in 1974 did Britain make *all* demolition in conservation areas subject to control.

In Germany and northern Europe the emphasis has been different again, coloured by an almost mystical sense of national identity. Old buildings are linked with folk art, folk music and dance, crafts and folk lore, as containing the cultural roots of the people. The *Neu Romantik* philosophy of the last century, centred upon a rejection of foreign influences, in some degree represented, like the backward-looking dreams of the Pre-Raphaelites and the Arts and Crafts Movement, an attempted escape from the harsh realities of the present day. *Heimat*, as a word, overlaps 'home' and 'fatherland'. It was the association of this nationalistic element underlying the *Bund Heimatschutz*, founded in 1904, with the tenets of the Third Reich, which led to the renaming of the organization after the Second World War as the *Deutsche Heimatbund*.

It is tempting to suggest that official action has always come in the wake of private initiative; but in France the reverse is true. In America it was the professionals within the National Park Service who were largely responsible for the creation of the National Trust for Historic Preservation. It is tempting to assume that Europe has always led the way—but the Trustees of Reservations in Massachusetts predate the English National Trust by four years (and the latter is based upon the former's constitution). Charleston's zoning provisions of 1931, recognizing the city's historic quarter, predated Malraux's *secteurs sauvegardés* by thirty-one years and Britain's conservation areas by thirty-six.

Breakthroughs have stemmed from chance encounters and from totally unforeseeable circumstances. Had Ann Cunningham caught the return river boat from Mount Vernon to Washington, and not been forced to return for the night, finally to convince her host in the morning of her sincerity, would Washington's mansion ever have passed into the Mount Vernon Ladies' Association's hands? Had Dr Goodwin not found himself seated next to John D. Rockefeller at dinner, would Colonial Williamsburg ever have come into being? Had it not been for the Depression of the 1930s and Roosevelt's political response in the shape of the Works Progress Administration programme, would the National Park Service have been able to swing preservation in America into becoming a professionally-based activity? Without the Second World War, could Britain's planning system have been introduced in 1947?

From different starting points, then, and moving at different speeds, subject to chance inputs and influences, the nations are grappling with the problems posed by intensive environmental change. It is a measure of the distance planning has come that the great international agencies —UN, UNESCO, OECD and the rest—as the collective conscience of their peoples, are now struggling to establish standards, codes, and controls. The Council of Europe has initiated, with considerable success, a series of campaigns aimed at alerting the European peoples to the environmental imperatives of our time. The European Community has worked steadily, since 1973, toward an environmental policy through a series of Environmental Action Programmes. The EEC's Directives, dealing as they do with specifics, have a direct bearing upon national legislation (and therefore policies). And indeed, by these various means, progress *is* being made on trans-frontier problems—the pollution of the Rhine, pollution in the Mediterranean, acid rain, noise and emission standards for the motor vehicle, and so on. For example, UK figures for 1984 show a 49 per cent drop in the average urban concentration of sulphur dioxide since 1973, and more than 70 per cent since 1963. Airborne lead pollution was down by 13 per cent as compared with ten years earlier.[17] At the same time it has to be said that Britain has aroused deep resentment in Scandinavia over her reluctance to take additional measures to curb acid rain. It is a complicated issue, but even the measures promised by the British government in 1986 were hailed as half-hearted. Nevertheless, how utopian it would all have seemed a century ago.

Never before has man invested so much effort, at so many levels, in the attempt to control and improve his surroundings. By the mid 1980s, for instance, the original 115 members of the Royal Town Planning Institute in Britain had increased to nearly 13,500. And yet . . . Planning has not saved us from enough. Unwittingly and with the best of intentions, it has even created horrors of its own. Too many planning studies and reports and recommendations have gathered dust upon the shelves. It has perhaps always been so. A French regulation of 1893 required the demolition of any city block in which more than ten people had died of tuberculosis in one year. A 1918 survey of the 11ᵉ *arrondissement* revealed seventeen such blocks, inhabited by 200,000 people. More than forty years later, one had been demolished; no others were scheduled.

Too often planning decisions have been based on erroneous assumptions, overtaken by events, or overturned by political decision. Peter Hall has put a number of 'great planning disasters' under the microscope, in his book of that title.[18] The convoluted history of the Third London Airport is one such. In the early 1960s an interdepartmental government committee recommended a site at Stansted, to the north of London, for a new airport which would complement Heathrow and Gatwick. The proposals were rejected at a public inquiry. In the middle 'Sixties they were resurrected and confirmed by the Government. Local opposition was such that an independent commission was set up and, after the most prolonged and sophisticated enquiry undertaken up to that time, recommended a different site, at Cublington. The Government rejected these findings and in 1971 announced that the airport would in fact be built at a third site, Maplin; a decision which was itself abandoned three years later. Some ten years after the first commission had sat, and another committee had reverted to the Stansted suggestion, a second Public Inquiry, which ran for two years, was instituted to review the arguments yet again—as a result of which in 1985 the Government decided to expand . . . Stansted. On a smaller scale, such long-running sagas of indecision in British planning are commonplace.

Too much planning has been too negative. Planning cannot of itself *create* quality or diversity—though it can create the opportunities for both. In practice legislation has too often been backed by insufficient funds (so that, for example, grant aid which is available in theory has been totally committed within the first few months of a new financial year). Too many loopholes exist (for instance enabling government departments and agencies to sidestep normal planning procedures—in Britain because of the long-standing doctrine that statute does not bind the Crown). Too often decisions can be fudged, particularly at the local level, by the clout of a well-placed citizen and/or corruption within the City Hall or Capitol. Too often mistakes are made through inadequate public consultation, so that decisions simply do not accord with the wishes of those most closely concerned. The belief in ideal, finite solutions, stemming from utopian models, dies hard and tends to make planners wary of intensive public participation lest the solution they see as preferable to all others be diluted or rejected.

In Britain, over the past twenty years, the concept of the 'pure' planner has emerged; for many other countries—West Germany, Italy, the United States—planning is a multidisciplinary activity in which people become planners by practising planning. Can planning ever be based on more than pragmatic aspirations, a general belief in man's ability to better his condition? Can it truly achieve the kind of systematic and conceptually rigorous body of theory, free of value judgments and political pressures, which underpins the traditional professions?

All planning is a matter of trade-offs. There are many routes to many solutions, but there is never any perfect solution. Mechanisms do not of themselves create policies and strategies. In the last analysis, the machinery of planning is turned by attitudes, vision and political will. If our environmental programmes are too often tentative, short-term and lacking in consistency, it is because society itself remains uncertain as to its real objectives, and its leaders too often fail to foresee the secondary effects of their decisions. Some of the problems to be met with in trying to marry attitudes with strategies will be examined in the next chapter.

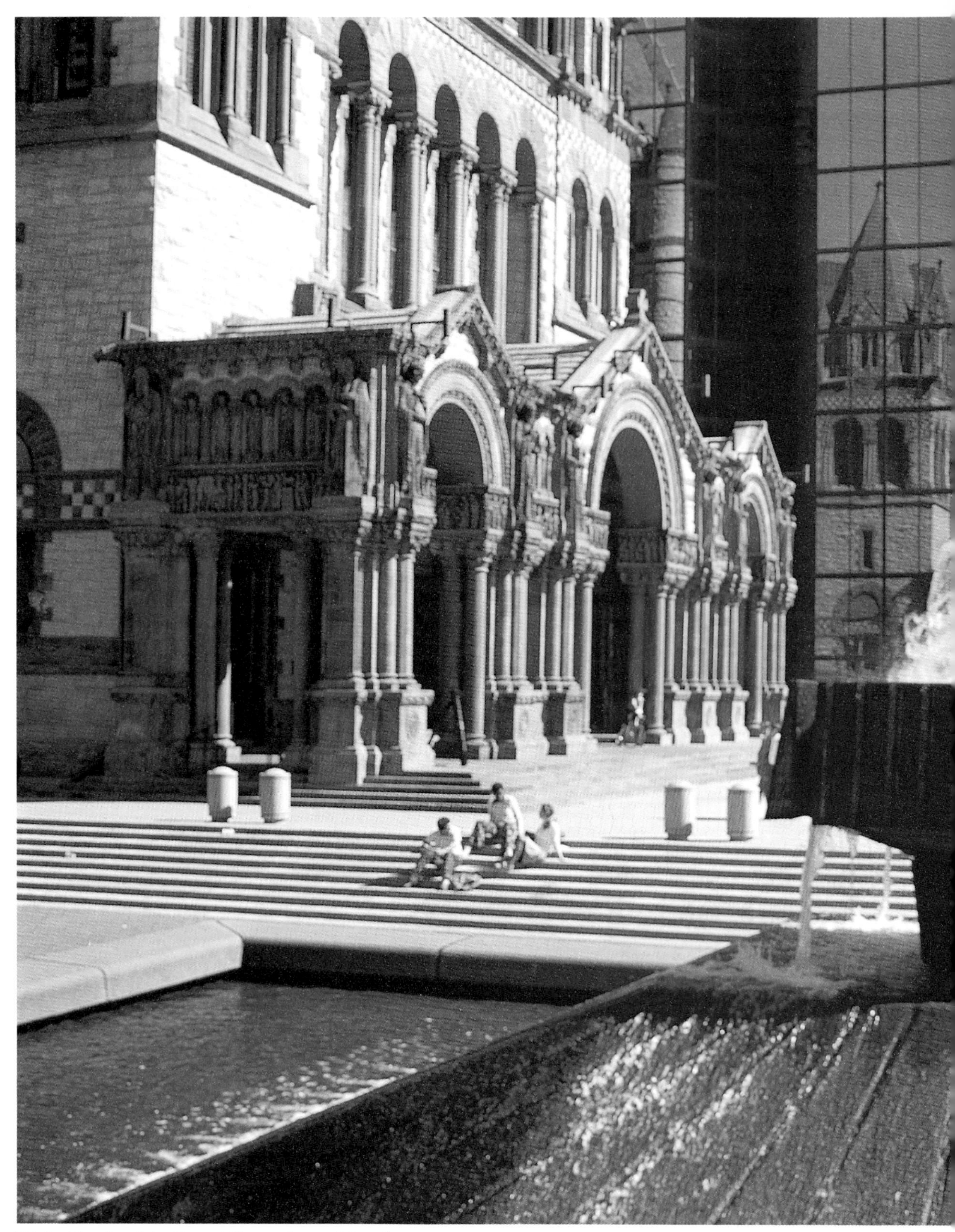

Trinity Church and the Hancock Tower, Boston, Massachusetts.

4
THE ART OF THE POSSIBLE

CITIES are very delicate organisms, the balance of their relationships is fragile. Blundering, broad-brush gestures are more likely to damage their well-being than strengthen it. Optimum solutions are unlikely to be found at policy extremes. Corbusier told us to abolish the street; thirty years later Jane Jacobs told us to put it back. We need to beware the pendulum swing of fashion, and get back to that more organic form of change which shaped our settlements before the industrial revolution.

The *outlines* are simple enough. We must keep what is best from the past, replace what is less than good with something better. We must get inessential traffic out of central areas and hand them back to the pedestrian. We must provide good public transport, social facilities, lots of trees and greenery. We must ensure that maintenance is constant. And so on. These things are easily said; tiresomely, the reality is more complicated. Strategic planning can have two essential thrusts; on the one hand to control change, to slow it down, to protect and conserve; on the other to promote and encourage change —to restore derelict land, to replace outworn housing, to introduce new industries, new uses, new jobs, new transportation systems, new shopping and leisure facilities. There are still those who see these two broad functions as incompatible alternatives—'progress or preservation'. In fact they are but opposite sides of the same coin. When Liverpool's magnificent Albert Dock is brought to life once more for new activities and new uses, is this to be regarded as conservation, or renewal? They are the same thing, and it is planning's task to reconcile them creatively.

Let us start with what we have. What should we keep and what replace? Why should we preserve *anything*? Twenty-five years ago the Civic Trust in Britain put forward five criteria for retaining buildings, and I see no reason to change them.

First, the building is a work of art in itself; its very existence enriches the environment.

Second, it is a notable example of a particular style or period. (The fact that public taste may not currently endorse the value of that style does not invalidate the building's claim to survival.)

Third, the building holds an historic place in the community. (Few would deny the right of a parish church to be preserved, even though its value may lie only in the accretions of time.)

Fourth, the building has particular historic associations with great men or great events.

Fifth, it lends to its surroundings a sense of the continuity of time. (A town without old buildings has been likened to a man without a memory.)

To these judgements of architectural or historical value can be added the townscape significance of buildings—their interest as a group, the skyline they create, the way this building terminates a vista, or that one provides a pivot point for converging streets. Indeed there are towns—for example the *bastides* of Aquitaine—where the road pattern is of no less historical interest than the buildings themselves. All these things are beyond price; they simply cannot be assessed in

monetary terms—which creates confusion, to say the least, in administrative and real-estate minds.

The essential preliminary to any rational conservation programme is an accurate inventory of what society considers to be of value; without that, informed decisions are impossible. But what criteria should be used to draw up the list? How extensive should it be? France lists about 30,000 historic buildings; Britain, after a re-listing process due to be completed in about 1987, is expected to have nearly half a million. Clearly, different values are at work. How close to the present day should the list be brought? Is there to be an arbitrary cut-off point, as though history ceased at midnight when a particular monarch died, or when one century ended and another started? Can we yet judge the true significance of the inter-war filling stations and 'diners' which now exercise the attention of historians and 'commercial archaeologists' in America?

What is it that we are really trying to achieve? 'Preservation' and 'conservation' are compendium words. They mean quite different things to different people. Preservation can seek, among other things

(a) To retain, as far as possible intact and without replacement, the original fabric of a monument. (The Pyramids; Jerash; Harlech

Cleaning is essential in the big cities to preserve brickwork and stonework; the simplest buildings can 'sing' when paint is applied with imagination.

Opposite: London. Above: Fribourg, Switzerland. Right: an Oriental rug shop, London.

Castle in Wales.) The structure will eventually decay and crumble, for nothing lasts for ever, but even as a ruin it will remain a valid historical document of the materials and methods of its day.

(b) To replace individual elements of a structure as they become defective. (The great cathedrals and palaces of Europe.) If done regularly and faithfully, this will keep intact the form of the original, even though eventually none of its original component parts remain.

(c) To restore parts of a building which have disappeared through decay or accident; in extreme form, to re-erect a monument which long ago collapsed, maybe from the original stones and materials which litter the site. (The palaces of Leningrad; parts of Colonial Williamsburg; Giles Gilbert Scott's reconstruction of the lantern of Ely Cathedral.) Unless precise records of its original form and construction exist, a degree of conjecture is inevitable in such reconstruction and the result may be no more than one generation's guess as to how the work of another *may* have looked.

The past *need* not be thrown on to the scrapheap. Character and craftsmanship, wherever they remain, must surely be retained?

Regency caryatid in Montpellier Walk, Cheltenham, England; tiles outside a Welsh pub; Louis Sullivan's luxuriant ornamentation on the Carson, Pirie, Scott store in Chicago; and a restored shop window in Nottingham, England.

Eighty colours are said to have been used on this house in the Haight Ashbury district of San Francisco (Far left) – the prototype for California's now numerous 'painted ladies'.

(d) To remove buildings at risk and re-site them for safe keeping elsewhere, either as an open-air museum, or, more rarely, as the framework for a new community. (Skansen in Stockholm; Zaanse Schans in the Netherlands, Hoyt Street, Portland, Oregon—see p. 123 and 97.)[19]

To what extent can this kind of thinking be applied to the broader canvas of a whole district? It is not possible—even if it were desirable—to halt the process of change in the entire fabric of a town. Were we tempted to try, what philosophical questions would arise! Should this gap site be left in perpetuity, because it was empty at the time of designation? If not, what style should the new building have? Should this burnt-out building be restored to its original Gothic form, as it was in Renaissance times, or as it looked last year? By what process of reasoning can such arbitrary decisions be justified; and who is to take them?

Conservation, then, seeks to slow down change and to bring it under more purposeful and creative control. This may mean preserving outstanding buildings, and small areas, totally. More frequently it means adapting old buildings to new uses, as far as possible in the spirit of the original design—even sometimes keeping the exterior as an outer skin to new construction behind. It may involve the replacement of structures which have lived out their time, or the filling of gap sites, with buildings of modern design which respect the height, scale, materials and architectural rhythms of their neighbours. Above all it means keeping the character and quality of a town's street pattern, its squares and open spaces; and beyond the town its wider landscape setting.

The *motives* underlying conservation are no less various. They spring from a range of functional and emotive sources: from the cultural, through the need for energy and resource conservation, to a simple dislike and fear of change. It is important to be clear about our objectives. The adaptation of an old building can destroy its validity as an historical document. The retention of an ancient street plan need not necessarily entail the retention of the buildings. And for whom, anyway, is this area being rehabilitated? 'Conservation' aimed at attracting tourists may well be at the expense of the resident community during the high season, and turn the place into a morgue for the rest of the year.

To what extent should—or can—the prohibition of demolition or alteration of an old building be absolute? Should the quality of what is proposed in its place affect the decision—and can we be sure that future generations will concur with our judgement? How, anyway, can we enforce the retention of a building for which no appropriate use can be found—for example, a 1930 cinema, built to seat 3,000, which cannot be subdivided into a number of 'mini-cinemas' because the ripe fantasy of its interior is the very *raison d'être* for its preservation, (though the astonishing Fox cinema in Atlanta, Georgia, happily saved by a local group from demolition, shows that all things are possible). If an owner cannot afford to maintain a listed building adequately, is it right to expropriate it forcibly from him at the public expense? And if this be done in exceptional cases, will it not lead to a plethora of owners pleading poverty and thereby crippling the finances of the acquiring authority? And if a zone of protection has been established round a monument or an ensemble (as in France), how far, in a democracy, can the rights of individual owners be denied, in respect of buildings which may be, in themselves, unexceptionable?

How far, indeed, can those in authority be expected to *know* about the condition of private property? In our older city centres, many of their shopping streets have unocuppied floors. Surveys have shown that seventy per cent of Chester's upper floors are unused or under-used; in Worcester and Shrewsbury the figures are fifty-three and fifty-four per cent—space that could provide flats for 500–600 people. A British trader has been quoted as saying that if it rained for half an hour, he had no need to bother because the water did not reach the ground floor; but that if it went on all day, he had to put the buckets out.[20] How is a planning authority to *know*, until it is too late, that the upper part of such a building is rotting away? How is it to *enforce* an alternative use if there is no possibility of providing separate access, adequate means of escape in case of fire, and so on? The Netherlands introduced legislation in 1981 aimed at ensuring that premises do not stand empty for socially unacceptable long periods (and thereby aimed to some extent at squatting). This makes the reporting of empty premises to the municipality compulsory; after five months the municipality has to decide whether or not to requisition them. The City of Bath has acquired groups of shops, converted their upper floors laterally, and leased back the ground floor shops to tenant traders. Ipswich, in Suffolk, has voted £150,000 a year to provide 'top-up' grants to help the conversion of upper floors into flats; within eighteen months six schemes had been tackled.

These are only some of the factors affecting urban conservation. They are compounded by social and economic pressures, and all the other elements of land-use planning—housing, transportation, the siting of industry, shopping and leisure provision. Policies may conflict. In Britain it is not uncommon, for example, to find the Environmental Health Department of a local authority condemning older housing as fit only for demolition, while the same authority's Planning Department may feel strongly that the property is suitable for rehabilitation. In such clashes the relative costs of demolition/new construction as compared with rehabilitation are likely to swing the issue—and the intrinsic desirability of the one or other course may well be blurred by fiscal structures. For long periods after World War II many countries made it more economic to demolish and redevelop than to restore and adapt (in the 1970s Britain imposed Value Added Tax on restoration work while 'zero-rating' new construction). Conversely US legislation creates real incentives to adapt older buildings to new uses. The American Tax Reform Act of 1976, which allowed the cost of rehabilitating buildings to be written off at an accelerated rate of depreciation, corrected a previous bias in favour of demolition and redevelopment. Successful beyond expectations (2,500 projects over four years or so, involving a total investment of more than $1.2 billion), it was followed by the Economic Recovery Tax Act of 1981. This offered a 25 per cent investment tax credit for certified rehabilitation of historic buildings; and an accelerated cost recovery system allowing investment to be recovered in fifteen years. (It left intact the earlier Internal Revenue code which forbids the demolition costs of historic buildings to be offset against federal tax—i.e. costs set as 'business losses' to reduce an individual's or a company's adjusted gross income.) The provisions, within a framework of three different options, are complex, depending upon the option chosen, the age and quality of the building, whether the building is sold within five years, and the tax bracket of the applicant. In a typical case it might amount to about one quarter of the total cost of building, including restoration costs. The effect of these new provisions has been even more marked. Together, these two Acts, by late 1983, had stimulated over 7,500 projects, involving $4.8 billion in private investment. Housing accounted for 48 per cent (more than 38,000 units); 27 per cent was for office, commercial and hotel use; 22 per cent for mixed uses. A National Park Service survey showed that 64 per cent of owners would not have undertaken certified rehabilitation—i.e. to federal standards—without these incentives. By 1985, ironically, the very success of the legislation was leading to concern in the US Treasury at the amount of tax 'lost'.

Whatever the incentives or penalties, the city must renew itself. Not all old buildings can be adapted for today's uses. Specialized functions—research laboratories, telephone exchanges,

multi-storey car parks, sheltered housing for the elderly or the handicapped, for example—require purpose-built structures. But the problem goes much wider than that of the individual building. As the flight from the city continues, whole quarters fall into festering decay. Fearful dereliction marks vast areas which were at one time the pulsating centres of the first Industrial Revolution and today have desperately to seek new ways of earning their living. Planning, it is now recognized, has to balance the control functions appropriate to an expanding economy with the more positive, promotional, entrepreneurial activities called for in the rejuvenation of areas of economic decline. For planners in Britain, this is a new ballgame—and in a democratic society, not an easy one.

There is widespread acknowledgement that the British planning system—in the 1950s a model, it seemed, for much of the world—has become in the 1980s cumbersome, bureaucratic, time-consuming and too often unresponsive to the needs of the private sector. A would-be developer may have to consult an Approved Town Map, a Submitted Structure Plan, a Draft Interim Local Plan, and a whole range of government Circulars—and that is before he becomes embroiled in the cycle of application for, and possibly refusal of, planning permission, appeal, public inquiry, amended application and the rest. 'In the sense of preventing desirable things from happening,' wrote the Director-General of the British Property Federation in 1985, 'it could be said that planning control is too effective . . .' In recent years there have been moves, of a rather *ad hoc* kind, to speed up the process and make it more flexible. To coax private investment into areas of decline, however, more positive inducements are required.

In all countries financial bribery, or barter, probably remains the biggest single argument to both public and private sectors. It is rumoured that, in 1985, the State of Minnesota offered (as it turned out unsuccessfully) no less than \$3

To save an old building of merit is always worthwhile. To bring back into use a whole complex of buildings is a much more demanding challenge. In New Lanark, Scotland (left), architectural character is coupled with a remarkable social history (see page 75). Over the past decade or so a specially created trust has been steadily bringing New Lanark back to life.

Sometimes buildings can be saved only by moving them physically. Here in Portland, Oregon, individual owners, calling themselves the 'Hoyt Street Group' have moved timber-framed houses from nearby blocks to fill the gaps in their own. Additionally, they have pooled their back gardens and landscaped them for common use.

billion to General Motors, in the form of tax credits and other incentives, to attract the 'Saturn' project—a new, 6,000-jobs car plant—to the State. The reverse process has been no less common, whereby the planning authority requires a developer to donate to the community some land or facility, not always connected with the proposed development itself, as a condition of granting him permission to go ahead. Between 1961 and 1972—and the process did not stop then—New York clawed back some twenty acres of land for public use, in return for allowing developers an extra ten square feet of commercial floor space for every square foot they surrendered at ground level. Many an English town has, by not dissimilar means, acquired a multi-purpose sports hall, or small park, or new library. Aspects of 'planning gain', as it is termed in Britain (or 'incentive zoning' in America), are coming to be regarded as an unacceptable form of blackmail—if not, indeed, illegal—but there is no doubt that it has assisted the renewal process.

Continued life for old buildings will often turn upon finding new uses for them. Here between two parallel canals in Amsterdam, seventeen old warehouses and merchants' houses have been converted into a modern hotel. Rear accretions were removed and a series of gardens created around the new link between the two sides. The coffee shop, lower right, was restored by Stadsherstel (see pages 149–151).

This church in Krems, Austria, right, has been turned into a museum; and that, far right, in Leeds into a shop.

At national level more systematic approaches are called for. One such mechanism is America's Urban Development Action Grant (UDAG) and its British equivalent (UDG); under both schemes central government grants are used as incentives to the private sector to invest in renewal projects which might not otherwise be carried out. UDAG, in its first six years, made grants totalling $2,700 million towards 1,700 projects; by 1984 UDG, which started only in late 1982, had put £55 million towards 122 projects. To what extent does such public investment take the place of money which would have been spent by the private sector anyway? A Federal review in the United States found that in 64 per cent of the cases no substitution had taken place; in 21 per cent there was an element of substitution; and in 15 per cent the evidence was inconclusive. Do the benefits of such schemes outweigh their shortcomings? Every UDAG dollar is thought to have levered $5.5 from the private sector (so far the British experience is not dissimilar); a degree of substitution may be felt to be the price that has to be paid for the overall impetus created by such means.

A second mechanism on the test bed is that of the 'Enterprise Zone'—initiated in Britain in 1981, in the wake of a proposal by Professor Peter Hall for the creation of 'freeport' areas—and subsequently taken on board, in principle, by America. (Federal legislation is introduced annually, but year by year fails to convince Congress; at the same time a mixed bag of around 1,250 'zones', in assorted shapes and colours, have been designated locally.) In the first three years of Britain's scheme, 25 Enterprise Zones were designated, their incentives including freedom from rates, or local taxes, for ten years; freedom from Development Land Tax; and minimal planning restrictions. Officially, they are a success story. By early 1986 the Government stated that over 2,000 businesses, employing 48,000 were located in the zones (as compared with 28,000 on designation). In the special case of London Docklands—special because it comes under one of two special, unelected Corporations (akin to one of the British New Town Corporations) created to redevelop the decaying dockland areas of London and Merseyside—160 companies had been relocated within the Enterprise Zone; 1.8 million

square feet of new floor space had been completed with another 1.9 million under construction; 2,500 houses had been built, with 4,600 more under construction. Investment of over £800 million by the private sector had been leveraged by £141 million of public money—with infinitely bigger proposals in the pipeline. These include a vast development at Canary Wharf, embracing the three tallest buildings in Europe. And this is only part of the story. The whole Docks area covers some 8½ square miles and the overall figures mushroom while you watch. £300 million spent by the Corporation has led to something like £1.4 billion private expenditure; land values have risen over five years from £75,000 per acre to around £2 million. Seven and a half miles of light railway and a short-take-off-and-landing airport are in hand. The whole centre of gravity of central London has moved eastwards.

Nonetheless, elsewhere doubts persist. The ten-year time span for the initial incentives seems to have deterred major financial institutions from investing in the smaller zones. In some cases firms have simply relocated across the zone boundary, in order to qualify for the inducements, and neighbouring land values have dropped by ten per cent. Interestingly, consultants employed to monitor results found that freedom from planning controls had a negligible effect upon decisions to go into the zones. The Government, notwithstanding, in 1985 announced proposals for further 'Special Planning Zones' in which a greater-than-normal freedom from controls would be allowed, and in 1986 for a number of new Urban Development Corporations to undertake the regeneration of inner city areas of the big conurbations. How

In Boston, Massachusetts, the granite warehouses of the Waterfront, dating mostly from the first half of the nineteenth century and in galloping decay by the middle of the twentieth, have now been restored and converted into apartments, with shops, chandlers, restaurants and professional offices at ground level. Hard by is the new Waterfront Park and, a quarter of a mile away, the happy-go-lucky bustle of Faneuil Hall Market.

these and similar mechanisms work long-term remains to be seen.

What other factors bear upon the revitalization of dying areas? Transport and communications networks, obviously. Although there is no hard evidence that new roads lead to the creation of new industry, easy access to motorways, ports and airports is, nonetheless, of major importance. The existence of local data networks is likely in the future increasingly to affect decisions to locate here as opposed to there. Above all, the scales are likely to be tipped by the quality of life and quality of the environment offered by alternative sites. Outworn industrial areas will have to make a major effort drastically to improve their image before they can expect new investment to come their way; city centres, no less, must become places where people actually want to be.

By what means can planning and urban design teams put quality back into urban life? For a start . . . not *all* the high-rise housing estates of the 1950s and 1960s, so powerfully castigated by Jane Jacobs and Oscar Newman and Alice Coleman, *have* to be blown up in the wake of Pruitt-Igoe. A growing number, in Britain, are being totally redesigned to make them safer, less impersonal, friendlier. Upper walkways and bridges, so handy for the escaping mugger, are being abolished; blocks are sub-divided vertically, with each group of apartments given its own main entrance; two-dimensional elevations are remodelled to give a greater sense of individuality and 'place'; windy areas of concrete and tarmac are being 'greened'; walled or fenced gardens and spaces created for each group of homes, and traffic slowed down or excluded. Some of these rescues are being

To fit a new building into an existing setting is one of the most demanding of architectural tasks. Sometimes full-blooded pastiche seems right, as with the arch in Bath (top left), which thus completes the square. More often it is a matter of scale and rhythm. Stratford-on-Avon and Ipswich, England, offer contrasting examples; sometimes paint alone can do the trick—as in Munich, above.

How slim a face this airy addition to a bank in Columbus, Indiana, (left; see page 226) presents to the street. Sometimes it may be appropriate to develop behind existing façades—below, a shopping centre which has been slotted in behind the famous 'Rows' in Chester. But how far should the process be allowed to go? Coutts' Bank, in London, a new steel and concrete building with a Nash exterior, bottom, and pages 34–35, represents a growing trend towards 'façadism'.

effected by the local authorities concerned; in some cases the tenants have been rehoused elsewhere and the properties sold for similar treatment by the private sector. A more modest technique used for older terraced housing in rundown areas in Britain is 'enveloping', whereby the local authority repairs and renovates the exterior of the houses without charge, leaving the interiors to the owners or tenants. The tonic effect upon decayed districts has been remarkable.

New building may be governed by a multitude of requirements relating to zoning and use; to height, bulk and density (i.e. intensity of use): to the street or building line, and provision of access. To a greater extent than a generation ago, development proposals in Britain are now considered in the context of their surroundings and not in a vacuum—but by no means sufficiently. These things can prevent the worst environmental disasters; they cannot stop the mediocre; and they cannot ensure a building of quality—only a skilful architect, armed with the right brief from his or her client, can do that. Excellence calls for imagination and understanding between architect and client. All that planning can do is ensure an orderly city, and provide a framework within which excellence can be achieved.

The degree to which elevational control should be exercised—that is to say the withholding or granting of planning permission on stylistic and aesthetic grounds—is a matter of controversy, though long taken for granted in central Paris, and to some extent since World War II, in Britain. Architects tend to resent criticism of their designs by planners and 'lay' planning committees (overlooking the fact that many planners are themselves architects, or will have architects in their departments). Planners in Britain point out that the great majority of planning applications are not architect-designed anyway. One County Council, Essex, has pioneered a more positive, 'design guide' approach, offering guideline advice to speculative developers as to what may or may not be regarded as in keeping with the traditional character of the county. This has provoked ridicule in some architectural quarters, as inhibiting the architect's freedom and leading to a kind of 'Noddyland' or Disney World tweeness. There is an element of truth in the charge, but it is hard to believe that quality and innovation have thereby been suppressed directly—that is to say by the planning authority. What *does* seem to have happened in too many cases in Britain in recent years is that developers, fearful of the public opposition that has been aroused in the past by the sheer awfulness of their paltry 'modern' buildings, and conscious of the cost of delays occasioned by long consultations and public inquiries, have opted for 'safe', pastiche designs which they can be reasonably sure will pass painlessly through the local planning committee and be producing revenue more quickly than might a more controversial design.

Genius will look after itself. What the public has the right to expect in all new building is a minimum level of architectural good manners. Very large schemes—a Beaubourg in Paris, a Byker in Newcastle—create their own ambience, but for the day-to-day darning of the urban fabric, the knitting together of old and new in High Street and Square, an altogether different and more subtle skill is needed. A degree of humility too. Not every new building *needs* to be, *should* be, a masterpiece. Hamburg, extensively rebuilt after the war, offers an instructive example of the difference between great architecture and good urban design; little is remarkable as architecture, but it has been assembled to make an agreeable city to move about in.

In the traditional European city, the spaces between buildings create its character to a greater extent than do the buildings themselves—yet for fifty years the visual analysis of urban space was practically forgotten. Both in new construction and in rehabilitation, there are endless opportunities to create new focal points, new spatial relationships, new walkways, new squares and

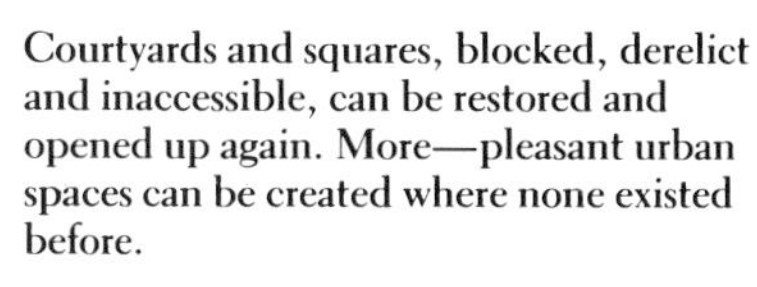

Courtyards and squares, blocked, derelict and inaccessible, can be restored and opened up again. More—pleasant urban spaces can be created where none existed before.

Above: Hobhouse Court in central London, and the way it used to be. Left: Society Hill, Philadelphia, Pennsylvania. Right: Krems, Austria. Below: a mini-park in Singapore.

courts, new kinetic experiences—in a word, new urban assets. Some of New York's mini-parks, such as Greenacre Park, tiny in relation to the scale of the city, offer pleasures out of all proportion to their size. London and Glasgow and Liverpool have, since World War II, been creating splendid new riverside walkways which did not exist before. Baltimore has opened up its Inner Harbour (see p. 187). Seattle has created a public park in the airspace over a motorway (see p. 173). But how rarely are such opportunities seized. Britain completed, at the end of 1982, a nationwide register of unused and under-used

Public spaces can be created in the most unlikely places. Slicing through Madrid is the multi-lane highway of Paseo de la Castellana/Paseo de Ricoletos. How amazing to find there, embedded between carriageways, a peaceful linear park, where prams are pushed, lovers look at their reflections in pools, and sleepers slump between the trees.

land in public ownership, detailing over 11,000 sites amounting to more than 40,470 ha; and much of it urban land. A real drive to put such sites to more positive uses—even temporary use—must be an essential part of revitalizing the inner city.

Any consideration of urban spaces is inextricably bound up with the problem of what to do with the motor car. The invention of the internal combustion engine has had more far-reaching effects upon the nature of urban communities than has any other in this century. The car's attraction lies in its ability to transport people and goods from door to door. Any restrictions upon the owner's rights to utilize that ability to the full produce howls of anguish. At the same time, Western towns and cities—and increasingly the larger settlements of the developing world—are now so clogged with vehicles, moving and stationary, that the need to free urban arteries has become an urgent priority. The means of doing so are clearly understood in principle; their implementation is another matter. (The New York businessman setting out for lunch and asking his partner, 'Shall we walk, or is there time to take a cab?' has become a touch too apt.)

Public transport is a key factor. Inadequate public transport leads inevitably to greater use of private cars; greater use of private cars diminishes the number of travellers using the public transport system, and therefore its income. So the system is thrown into decline. Bus passenger traffic in Britain fell from 42 per cent in 1953 to a mere 8 per cent in 1983. To reverse this requires bold moves—generally massive capital expenditure and subsidized running costs. Most big cities have recognized this. A number of American cities—Portland, Oregon (as described in later pages); Denver, Colorado; San Antonio, Texas—now offer totally free bus travel in their central areas. So, for the elderly, do London and other cities. 'Park-and-ride' schemes, aimed at divorcing the commuter from his vehicle on the outskirts of the town, are widespread in many countries. In the 1970s, metro systems became the new urban prestige symbols, much as national airlines have for newly emerging Third-World countries. Prague, Amsterdam, Vienna, Washington DC, were only some of the places which suddenly saw the underground railway as the solution to their traffic problems. Others—San Francisco; Glasgow and Newcastle in Britain—installed or reconstituted other rapid-transit systems. And of course, from time to time, thoughts of novel 'people-moving' systems come to the boil—monorails, travelators, electric runabouts. There is no doubt that, in the short term, a cheap and efficient public transport system, publicly subsidized, can dramatically increase 'ridership' and reduce the number of private cars on the road (London Transport's fare reductions in 1983, coupled with the introduction of travel cards and wheel clamps for illegal parkers, resulted in a 21 per cent reduction in car arrivals in central London). However, as costs continue to escalate—in Britain bus subsidies nationally rose from £10 million in the mid-'Seventies to £522 million in the mid-'Eighties—consideration is increasingly being given to fundamentally different ways of assisting the disadvantaged and those without other means of transport. A flexible form of personal 'entitlement', for example, in the form of vouchers which could be used to meet the cost of bus travel, rail travel, taxis, petrol (for shared trips), or indeed any form of transport available, up to a given limit, would be likely to lead to a more rational and flexible use of vehicles (including more flexible routing), less waste (fewer empty buses on scheduled services), and greater choice for the public.

Nothing however, unless it be an insupportable rise in future fuel costs, seems likely to stem the inexorable rise of car ownership. All big cities—London being a rare exception—have constructed massive urban motorways as means of relieving congestion. Colin Buchanan, in 1963, published his study of *Traffic in Towns*,[21] the essential message of which was that every urban area has a traffic saturation point; the greater the volume of traffic, the more radical the reconstruction of the area has to be if its environmental quality is to be maintained. There were those who read his book as a plea for rebuilding for the sake of traffic; more accurately, Buchanan was saying that the trade-offs had to be faced: if you are determined on such and such a course, you must realize that the implications are this and that.

The trouble with the urban motorway is twofold. Its great overhead roads and interchanges crush the traditional urban fabric; communities and ground-level activities are severed, noise blasts through the windows of homes, large tracts of land are sterilized and dead areas created—which readily become spawning grounds for violence. Once built, it sucks up and creates additional traffic flows which, disgorged into the feeder roads of the inadequate system it tried to replace, result in congestion no less clogged than before.

The European city suffers especially from the movement of heavy freight by road. Its mediaeval street patterns were designed for ox and cart, not the 'juggernaut' lorries on which the road haulage industry now depends. And in Europe, Britain has perhaps suffered most. Compact in size, Britain carries far more of its freight by road than the other major EEC countries. The annual roll-on/roll-off figures for cross-Channel lorries passing through the port of Dover rose from 21,000 in 1967 to 510,000 in 1981—a twenty-three fold increase. But of 700 towns or villages astride the Government's proposed heavy lorry network, the Civic Trust in 1981 found that only twenty-five per cent had been by-passed;[22] and the quieter lorry, promised since the late 1960s remains a promise.

At what point does the environmental impact of this means of distribution become unacceptable, socially and politically? What would be the cost of by-passing all the towns needing to be by-passed (where local factors allow, for in some cases it may be physically impossible)? How do true rail costs compare with true road costs, once the hidden elements are brought into the open? What would be the true cost of road transport if the cost of road construction and maintenance were included; if transhipment from 'juggernauts' into smaller runabout lorries for deliveries to central areas were insisted on; if adequate sound-proofing of property were undertaken; if the damage to buildings, to pavements, to underground services, were charged to the operators responsible?

The physical impact of the car and of the heavy lorry can be mitigated. Through traffic routes can be diverted underground as in Dürnstein in Austria, in Colonial Williamsburg and in Chicago. Heavy lorries can be banned from particular routes and areas—in Britain the 'Windsor Cordon' has been operative for some years, and the Greater London Council, before its demise in 1986, introduced widespread bans in the capital—while the Netherlands has built depots outside towns, where large consignments of goods can be broken down for central-area delivery by smaller vans. What long years it has taken to realize that traffic can be excluded from particular streets or quarters. One of the first closures was in Essen in 1926 but it was forty years more before the first in Britain, in London Street, Norwich. Another twenty years on, notwithstanding the reluctance of traders to accept the evidence that business almost invariably increases after the removal of traffic, the number of pedestrian areas in Europe can be counted in four figures—West Germany alone is estimated as having 800 such areas, many with networks of 5,000 metres or more. In many places—Durham, Munich, Rouen—the ban is to all intents and purposes total; in others—Minneapolis, Portland (Oregon), Zurich—it is selective, allowing, for example, trams and buses but not private cars. Such measures help to keep the area alive after dark when purely pedestrian zones can tend to slide into eerie, echoing spaces. Sophisticated design techniques of layout and landscaping, by means of which traffic is allowed, but tamed and domesticated and reduced to a walking pace, have been evolved since 1976 in the Dutch *Woonerven* (literally, if inelegantly, 'living yards'). Four years later, in 1980, West German legislation introduced the *Verkehrsberuhigung* concept, based upon the Dutch regulations. Applied first in residential streets (where accident figures dropped as a result) the approach is likely in both countries to be extended to shopping and other types of area. Even where traffic flows unrestrictedly, the pedestrian can be protected and isolated from it all by arcades or screening. In Nürnberg half the dual carriageway of Fürther Strasse has been turned into a foot street; in Waldstrasse, Berlin-Moabit, one carriageway into an urban park. Madrid has created an astonishing oasis of green—a linear park—between the many lanes of its broadest thoroughfare, Paseo de la Castellana.

At the end of their journey, cars do not have to come to rest in multi-storey parking structures (though these *can* be sympathetically designed—see Salem, on page 204). Underground parking is common, even if its necessary corollary—the prohibition of parking in the street—is not always rigorously applied. And even open parking lots, normally so disruptive to townscape and character, *can* be decently landscaped and screened—

Cumulatively, the small things assume enormous visual importance. Skylines *need* not be forested with television aerials and hung with overhead wires. Underfoot, decent paving is still possible, and elegance given to things like ramps for the disabled. Street furniture *can* be simple and well designed.

Left: Lacock, England. Below: Chester, England, and San Francisco. Bottom: Boston, Massachusetts and San Francisco again.

Traffic can be routed around towns—or underneath them, as in Dürnstein, Austria, on the banks of the Danube (above and left)—thus freeing central areas for pedestrians (Bolton, England, facing page centre left). Vehicles can be parked out of sight, below ground, as in Chartres, opposite, top left and centre—and how discreet the entrance until you are on top of it—and in Strasbourg, also in France, top right. Above-ground parking need not offend the eye: how great the difference made by a screen of trees and shrubs (Columbus, Indiana, centre right); by a single wall of ivy in an otherwise commonplace space in Portland, Maine, and by grass to a car park in Scotland.

COIFF

BENO
THRIFT

Lettering, signs and decorative features do not have to be old to be beautiful. Left: a street number in Washington, DC, and store lettering in France. Below: a shop sign in Sweden, a baker's window in London, and an elegant peacock in Prague. Opposite: a well-known kettle in Boston, Massachusetts.

in Columbus, Indiana, for example, they are a pleasure to the eye.

All this is part of making places where people *want to be*. The Roman city had its forum: a gathering point in time of crisis, where great events unfolded—but also the stage for the small exchanges of daily life, bumping into friends, strolling with one's family, watching other people, catching up with the news. The Puerto del Sol in Madrid in the evening, or the Place Beaubourg in Paris on *le quartorze Juillet*, or Quincy Market in Boston at almost any time—these are proof enough that the forum still meets one of man's deepest needs. For several generations the art of creating such places fell into abeyance. Pompous, windy and characterless open spaces were the best that we could do. Only within the last decade or two have

we begun to grope our way back towards an understanding of what we really require of our towns.

William Whyte, in his book *The Social Life of Small Public Spaces* (see p. 233), has pinpointed many of the basic requirements. Since 1961, as already noted, New York has squeezed out of developers some twenty acres of open space at street level for public use—a tremendous plus for a city starved of space—in which visitors and residents alike can take the weight off their feet and enjoy the sun. But wait. Why, asked Mr Whyte, were some of these spaces so crowded, when others, just as small were all but deserted? Over a period of years he traced, by means of time-lapse film, the comings and goings, the ritual dances, of the New York public as they congregated and split up, ate their lunches, moved from the sun to the shadow or from the shadow to the sun, slept, stretched their legs, drank, watched girls and generally did what people do. He tried to find out why people sat on ledges not designed to be sat on, and refused to sit on seats expressly designed to be sat on. 'The findings', writes Mr Whyte, 'should have been staggeringly obvious to us had we thought of them in the first place. But we didn't. Opposite propositions were often what seemed obvious.'

Whatever they *say*, people *like* the presence of other people. They like movement. Somewhere to sit is vital (about seventeen inches from the ground and thirty to thirty-six inches across for sitting on both sides). It should be flexible in what it offers (the Metropolitan Museum of Art leaves about 200 moveable chairs by its front steps; there is little vandalism). Shelter is important; trees, water, sculpture, food and happenings help. And how the plaza or square links up with the street is very important: the transition between the two should be as imperceptible as possible. (The lessons provided by Whyte's survey provided the basis for a whole regiment of amendments to New York's Open Space Zoning Provisions in 1975.)

All the elements that add up to a good open space in a town need to be studied separately in greater depth. Take trees . . . Engineers and maintenance men hate trees. Town trees shed leaves, cause cars to skid and people to slip, and impose a fearful burden every autumn on the street cleaners. But the rest of us rather like them. Trees bring sunlight and the passing seasons into the canyons of the city, they can filter out noise and fumes—yet, oddly, few attempts have been made to establish standards. Could there be such a thing? City squares in London and Edinburgh have 27 and 35 trees to the acre; inner suburban areas can vary between 25 and 50 to the acre. Perhaps more important than their number is the siting of urban trees, and the greening of hard surfaces by ground cover and massed shrubs. Tokyo and Singapore are two cities which plant as though they really mean it, and the City of London has achieved wonders in establishing green reference points in the most unlikely situations.

Water—its flash and sparkle endlessly fascinating and refreshing to the human spirit. The Japanese are masters of the flat sheet of water, *just* spilling over at its edge. The West, with its *penchant* for 'wedding cake' fountains, is at last moving—especially in America—towards more imaginative displays. Great waterfalls and catar-

Exterior murals can hide eyesores, lend colour to drab surroundings, bring wit— and propriety—to the street. Above: Fay Jones' birds in Seattle, and a flank wall in Hamburg, Germany (how boring if it had been left blank). Left and right: two *jeux d'esprit* by Richard Haas in Boston and the SoHo area of New York. In the latter, two real windows in the side wall of a cast-iron fronted building have been jokily incorporated in the design.

acts, by the very crash of their fall, isolate the passer-by from the sounds of the city and offer the illusion of escape.

In many countries national or local legislation now requires a proportion of the cost of new building to be spent on sculpture, murals or other decoration. Sweden was perhaps the first; France, West Germany and the Netherlands are among those which have followed suit. Calder's big red 'Flamingo', so marvellously right in scale for its setting, is an example from Chicago where a local ordinance requires 'one per cent for art'. And Seattle's manhole covers, depicting a relief map of the city, are another. The American bicentenary produced a rash of paint-up whimsy (especially on fire-plugs) but also numerous exterior murals

Public sculpture is so often so hopelessly wrong in scale for its setting. A splendid example to the contrary is Calder's 'Flamingo' in Chicago. Left and right: Henry Moore in London and a sculptural relief on Cologne's rebuilt City Hall.

which are witty, beautiful and exhilarating.

Fountains, sculpture, greenery, street furniture, lighting, signs, outdoor advertising, overhead wires, the paving underfoot—how, in the ever-changing city, are all the conflicting elements of the street scene to be fashioned into, and kept as, a harmonious whole? Highway engineers will construct multi-lane motorways through the heart of the city; food will be brought to market, merchandise to the stores; water will flow through the pipes, power through the switch; shelter will be provided; social workers will apply themselves to the misfits . . . but whose job is it to see that the city as a whole is a fine and seemly place, unless it be the planner and the urban designer?

It is not merely how high the seating should be in the plaza, nor what sort of trees should be planted, nor even what the street lighting should be, which have to be brought into common resolution; it is also providing the right housing, making public transport work, siting industry properly—things not resolved by feeding data into a computer. Detailed programmes will stem from policies, policies drawn up on social and political premises. How much public housing is needed compared with private development? Can this eighteenth-century mansion be used as an art gallery? Should waste land be cleaned up as public open space or be used as a site for offices, which might create jobs? Is tourism destroying the towns which the tourists come to visit? Or can one more hotel be squeezed in? There can never be an absolute answer. Different people, different ideologies, will see things in a totally different light—and our successors, we may be sure, differently again. There are no facts about the future.

At what point, in the quicksands of differing values and tastes, does the false drown the real? Where does conscious become self-conscious? Revival slide into the routine ingredients of beautification? Behind so many 'period' shop fronts are to be found identical candle-and-craft stores, scented soap and tea-towel nookeries, indoor plant shops, butchers-block and wheelbarrow restaurants. Every piece of 'façadism', however scholarly, diminishes the genuine. Every newly installed Gold Rush shop-front in Main Street blurs the difference between the real and the make-believe. It is but a step to preferring the make-believe. The Chateau Louise Resort in Illinois describes its attractions as '. . . a complete ancient village, transported out of time—21 minutes from O'Hare Airport . . . Wandering passages lead to every great resort delight. Nell Gwyn's Snug, a multi-level bar where Nell's Belles sing and dance on the tables . . . steak by the ounce . . . spacious armoires gracefully conceal colour televisions. Hung on the walls, genuine oils . . .'

Differing tastes, differing values. Whenever an area is given a new lease of life, there is likely to be talk of elitist values being imposed upon a hard-used public. Moves to bring about greater participation in the decision-making process will be derided by some as so much window dressing—as advocacy of an already chosen course or at best the offer of choice from pre-determined alternatives. In this view, planning is the instrument of an elitist-professional *cadre*, encapsulating the values and standards of middle-class pressure groups. Only when people can decide for themselves what they want, and where, and how, will their surroundings fit their needs. Many attempts have been made since the late 'Sixties to find workable methodologies by which a creative public input into planning and development can be achieved—some more successful than others, all laborious and infinitely time-consuming. In the 1980s the self-build form known as 'community architecture' came to the fore.

This is an area in which issues become muddled. The most, as Dryden put it, can err as grossly as the few. Excellence has nothing to do with class, or numbers, as such; it is simply the best of which mankind is capable. Standards, though they can never be absolute, nevertheless embody a corpus of opinion built up over many generations—sieved and confirmed through the years much as is the corpus of British case law. The works of art which survive the judgement of centuries are those rich enough in content to offer something fresh to meet the needs of each succeeding generation. In today's egalitarian society, there are great pressures to establish the supremacy of 'popular' values—but values are values. There is nothing sinful about quality. Mozart is demonstrably richer in content than those who come and go at the Top of the Pops; Michelangelo than the graffiti 'artists' of the New York subway; Venice than Las Vegas. This has nothing to do with political and social justice, or with equality of opportunity. And if it is only a minority which responds to such standards, that must be accounted a failure of our educational systems. Let us not seek to make a virtue of that failure by sliding trendily into the supposition that because, for example, large numbers identify with pop groups, such sub-cultures must therefore be more important than the real thing. This is akin to saying church attendances are dropping, so let us relax the doctrinal message to make it more acceptable; or: too few children are passing their 'O' and 'A' level examinations, so clearly the pass levels are too high and must be lowered. That way lies social, as well as cultural, suicide.

Social justice is another matter. There are powerful cultural arguments for offering special protection to areas of high environmental quality; but there are no less powerful social arguments for concentrating public funds on the underprivileged areas. The displacement of those who have long lived and worked in a district is all too commonly the result of the increased rents and rates which inevitably follow its revitalization. The problem has dogged many of the great rescue operations of recent years: the Marais, in Paris; Covent Garden in London; housing in central Amsterdam. In the Jordaan, in Amsterdam, and in the Victorian District in Savannah, Georgia, official fiscal mechanisms have been used with some success to bridge the gap between workers' incomes and fair market rentals for restored properties. In the Byker district of Newcastle, England, special efforts—though only partially successful—were made to keep together the community which had previously existed there. Both these latter schemes are detailed in later pages.

The problems of displacement, whether of poorer families from newly desirable areas, or small shopkeepers pushed out by new supermarkets, or small craft workshops by office development, simply point the need to consider each and every kind of urban change in the overall planning context of the city as a whole. There will be times when social change has to be. The mechanization of farming has led to the depopulation of many English villages; the sociologist and the historian may deplore the acquisition of empty cottages as holiday and weekend homes, and the consequent disappearance of the traditional village life—but were it otherwise the village would cease to exist. Conversely, improvements may be necessary to keep existing uses in a particular district, as with Rochdale's Industrial Improvement Area in England (an exemplar subsequently copied by a number of other towns). The principle of keeping displacement to a minimum is almost universally accepted. The *Declaration of Amsterdam*, the culminating statement of European Architectural Heritage Year in 1975, stated: 'The rehabilitation of old areas should be conceived and carried out in such a way as to ensure that, wherever possible, this does not necessitate a major change in the social composition of the residents. All sections of society should share in the benefits of restoration financed by public funds.' What cannot be spelled out universally are the means by which these objectives are to be achieved in differing circumstances.

Town and country are interdependent. Social and economic factors are interdependent. Housing, transport, leisure and shopping facilities are interdependent. Until fairly recently, planning meant the formulation of finite proposals for an area—so called 'master plans'—in much the same way that past centuries drew up plans for a processional way, or a new suburb. It is now appreciated that planning is an open-ended *process*. Circumstances change. Needs change. Accordingly objectives, too, must change. Long-term plans have to be flexible enough not to crack under pressures unforeseen, and perhaps unforeseeable, at the time of their drafting.

The design of cities is the most complex of all design problems for this very reason that it has to take account of the passage of time. Its business

Water, flags and lighting, in a thousand forms, lend flash and sparkle to the city. Above: a man-made waterfall in Portland, Oregon—nearly twenty feet high and half a block wide. Below: Victoria, British Columbia. Opposite: Christmas lights in Chicago.

is never done. The most, perhaps, that we can hope to do is to endow our cities with ideas, and qualities, and physical reference points, which will continue to reverberate down the years, and open up for future generations opportunities which would not otherwise exist, further to enhance their surroundings. Edmund N. Bacon, for long the force behind Philadelphia's post-war planning, has written of Rome that it 'is a city in which the quality of living, the joy of being there and indeed the function of getting around, are far more deeply influenced today by the vision and conviction of Pope Sixtus V than they were in his lifetime.'[23] To shape a city in this way requires vision, confidence and a corporate and imaginative tenacity of purpose over very long periods—but these things are not impossible.

In the following pages many of the matters we have been considering are brought together, no longer as separate items on a check-list but interlocked one with another. The individual 'case histories' deal with the dialogue between past and present which must take place in any living, changing community; with new building, new housing, which does not look like Levittown or the outskirts of Rome, Berlin or Madrid. There are demonstrations of how transport can be made to heal the city and of how real meeting places can be newly created in city centres. Programmes of integrated urban design are examined, one of renewal on the big-city scale; others in which renewal and conservation are so inextricably mixed that a new word needs to be coined for what has been done there. Finally, there are three examples of how, with vision, the most daunting of liabilities can be turned into positive assets.

Nearly every one of the areas described was a problem area a generation or so ago. Now they attract visitors and tourists in considerable numbers. The Marais, Lowell, Ironbridge Gorge, the Béguinage in Louvain, Byker, Covent Garden, Baltimore's Inner Harbour, Salem in Massachusetts, Wirksworth in Derbyshire, the Lower Swansea Valley—all these were in decay, largely written off, their potential unrecognized. Today they represent an affirmation of what vision and steadfastness of purpose can achieve; they offer irrefutable reminders that nothing is impossible if we will it so. Each, in its different way, offers pointers to the never-to-be achieved Ideal City.

PARK

Lowell, Massachusetts: the great mill wheel symbolizing the city's past.

5 POINTERS

I

THE TOWN AS MUSEUM

THE museum concept has changed fundamentally during the present century. At first museums, like the *cognoscenti* of the eighteenth century, were content merely to accumulate artifacts and exotica; these were sufficient wonder in themselves. Even today, large collections like the Field Museum of Natural History in Chicago are endearingly apt, on occasion, to label a plate 'plate'. Increasingly, however, the need is seen to place exhibits within their context—to relate them to their period, their region, and to the form of society which gave them birth. For their greater understanding by the general public, the story each has to tell must be 'interpreted'. Some see this as vulgarization, at odds with scholarship and academic rectitude. Certainly, displays can be over-designed and essential information compressed into statements of gross over-simplification. Nonetheless, attitudes towards collections have changed for ever. Something of the same shift is evident in attitudes towards historic buildings and towns. We have moved from a concern for the retention of individual buildings to an appreciation of whole areas. Where now does the idea of town-as-museum merge with what should be everyday conservation?

Progenitor of all open-air museums of buildings is Skansen, in Stockholm, initiated in 1891 by Arthur Hazalius as part of the Nordiska Museet which he had founded eighteen years earlier. Almost instantly, open-air museums sprang up in ever-increasing numbers, at first all over the Scandinavian countries, then in central and eastern Europe. Romania today has some 1,400 buildings in ten such museums.

Hazalius saw Skansen essentially as a folk centre, where buildings from different parts of Sweden would be linked with other traditional arts, customs and festivals. Crafts like glass-blowing were introduced. The eighteenth-century church is used for weddings. Geese clack around farmyards. 'Here', says a guidebook, 'on summer evenings thousands of citizens sometimes gather to sing hearty Swedish folk-songs under the leadership of an official song-master, while attendants in charming peasant costumes of the various provinces carry round refreshments.'

From Skansen at one end of the spectrum, to the historic city struggling to earn its living in today's world at the other, a progression can be marked in fairly clear-cut stages. Zaanse Schans, ten miles or so north of Amsterdam, is an open-air museum—but at the same time something more: a little village, because the imported timber buildings have been grouped as though a community had grown up there over a long period. The windmills turn, the houses are occupied, there are rowing boats tied up at the ends of the gardens. Zaanse Schans *is* a tiny community—of a kind. But it is a community which did not exist until the second half of this century. It has been wholly contrived.

Colonial Williamsburg, too, has been contrived—the word seems inadequate for such single-minded drive—but in a totally different way. Here the town has existed for three centuries, and many of the buildings in it. What has taken place is the idealization of the settlement as it was in 1780 when the State legislature moved to Richmond. This has involved the demolition and removal of some hundreds of later buildings, and the reconstruction of those which preceded them. The historic area is lived in, and worked in; it is part of the larger town to which it pays the usual taxes; but it remains an artificial community, pulled now towards the Disney World parade of daily battles and cannon salutes, now towards the precious isolation of academic research.

Research and historicism lie at the heart of the transformation taking place in and around the Ironbridge Gorge, in England. Yet scattered communities remain there, rooted in the realities of the twentieth century. Indeed, Ironbridge and Coalbrookdale fell within the boundary of the New Town of Telford; the evidence they offer of Britain's industrial heritage remains *in situ*—other material is grouped in museums elsewhere.

Ironbridge perhaps represents the dividing line between the full-blooded urban museum and the conservation of a working community. A city like Lowell in Massachusetts, or the Marais in Paris, or Bath, or Venice are all living communities seeking to renew themselves in the light of their own history.

In all such places, the pressures to clean up, to prettify, are great and insidious. The sanitized museum town anyway lacks the smells, the filth, the vermin, the overcrowding, the building decay, from which it once suffered. How far can the process be allowed to go without totally destroying the very attributes which call for the area's protection and retention? It is against this question that the validity of the town-as-museum has to be judged.

ZAANSE SCHANS—*Netherlands*

The picture is familiar from countless paintings. The flat Netherlands landscape; the wheeling sails of windmills; villages strung out along the banks of river and canal, the ditches and paths of the *polders*. In the second half of the nineteenth century the picture was already fading; by the mid-twentieth century little was left. Alone along the banks of the River Zaan was the 'Gortershoek' in Zaandijk, some sixteen kilometres north of Amsterdam.

The Zaan River, now dammed, once led to the Zuyder Zee, and at this point had one of the most important shipyards in Holland. It was here, in 1697, that Peter the Great came, incognito, himself to work in the yards and learn the trade. And it was here, on the east bank opposite Gortershoek, that the newly formed Zaanse Schans Foundation in the late 1950s identified a site of about twenty acres on which to recreate a traditional Zaans village by bringing together buildings from the area which were otherwise doomed to perish on the developer's bonfire.

First approaches for assistance were made to the industries which had grown up along the river. However, it was eventually the eight municipalities of the province, pushed a little by central government, which made the necessary initial funding available; the municipality of Zaandam acquired the site, and twenty-odd years later, a new village of some forty buildings had come into existence there.

The buildings were brought bodily by water and by road. With the exception of some deep piling, reconstruction was entirely traditional in manner. Merchants' houses mingle with simple vernacular homes, shops and workshops, the oldest dating from about 1620. Most are entirely of timber, painted Zaans green, on brick foundations, in a few cases with brick façades. Few buildings are of more than one storey. In the vicinity are fourteen working windmills—five of them on the river's edge (and eleven owned by the Zaans Windmill Society). The oldest of these was built in 1610 as a pumping mill, converted in 1672 to grind peanuts for salad oil. Others include a snuff mill, built in 1790, which now grinds mustard, and a cocoa mill, the last of its kind in the world. Zaanse Schans includes several museums, a bakery, an antique shop, and a clog-maker with 6,000 pairs of different kinds in

stock. An excellent restaurant, in what was once the old orphanage of Westzaan, has been joined by a second, seating up to 150 inside and an equal number outside. Parking is provided for several hundred cars and coaches.

The Foundation is managed by representatives of the eight municipalities, which also contribute to the running costs on a *per capita* basis. Central government pays thirty-five per cent of the cost; industrial and private donations—plus income from letting and entrance fees—make up the difference. Technical and construction problems are dealt with by a Building Committee, composed of architectural advisers, an architect from the government's Monumentumcare, and members of the Board.

Zaanse Schans has been joined by a rather similar project—the outdoor Zuider Zee Museum at Enkhuizen. Both are safety nets. Both offer a coherent glimpse of a vanished way of life. The excellence of Zaanse Schans' layout, paving, planting and maintenance present a standard of quality which some, at least, of its visitors must surely take away with them. What is inevitably lacking, as compared with a Williamsburg or an Ironbridge, are the undertones and overtones, the resonances, sounding down the years from real people and real events of long ago.

Across the River Zaan from Zaanse Schans (previous page), the green timber houses of Gortershoek. In Zaanse Schans itself the windmills turn, the gardens dazzle, the paintwork gleams, the paving underfoot is immaculate. A generation ago Zaanse Schans did not exist.

COLONIAL WILLIAMSBURG—*Virginia*

In 1699—about seventy years after a small stockaded outpost had been established there—Sir Francis Nicholson, Lieutenant-Governor of Virginia, drew up a plan for the small town on the same site, which was later to be called Williamsburg. When the Statehouse at Jamestown, a few miles away, burnt down yet again, Virginia's General Assembly moved to Williamsburg. George Washington, Thomas Jefferson and Patrick Henry are only three of the names associated with the town and its Capitol. Here, in May 1776, Virginia's legislators voted for full freedom from England; acting on these instructions Richard Henry Lee introduced the Motion in the Continental Congress in Philadelphia which led directly to the Declaration of Independence.

Nicholson's grid plan was bisected by a great central avenue, the ninety-nine-foot wide Duke of Gloucester Street, running nearly a mile from the Capitol at the eastern end to the College of William and Mary at the western end, with the Governor's Palace at the northern limit of the main cross-route. After 1780, the seat of government reverted to Richmond and Williamsburg relapsed into the gentle rhythms of a quiet college town. In 1920 the population was no more than 2,000.

Today, the telegraph poles have gone from the centre of Duke of Gloucester Street. Buildings and gardens are immaculate; the only vehicle to be seen is an occasional horse-drawn buggy. Colonial Williamsburg is world-famous, and thirty million visitors have come there to capture what life was like in a small town in the Virginia Tideway in a stirring decade two centuries ago.

How it happened is scarcely less well known: how the Rev W. A. R. Goodwin restored the Bruton Parish Church there, of which he was rector, in 1907; left and returned to Williamsburg in 1923; found himself by chance seated next to John D. Rockefeller Jnr at a dinner in New York in 1924, and lodged in Rockefeller's mind the possibility of restoring some of the main buildings in the town. Rockefeller allowed himself to be convinced only step by step. So methodical was he that, in retrospect, the progress made over the following decade—the heroic first phase—is astonishing. By 1927 Rockefeller had accepted Goodwin's romantic notion of restoring not merely a couple of areas but the whole historic core. A three-cornered administration came into being, linking Goodwin and his staff in Williamsburg, Rockefeller's office in New York and the architects Perry, Shaw and Hepburn in Boston. A team of up to twenty draughtsmen was built up in Williamsburg; archaeologists, historians and researchers followed. In 1929 the Rector's cousin, Mary Goodwin, discovered in Oxford some copperplate engravings of the original Capitol, the Palace and the second College, which provided the essential evidence for their restoration. By spring 1931 (accompanied by much ethical and philosophical agonizing) no fewer than 321 'modern' buildings had been demolished and thirty-four old ones restored. In 1934 the project was officially 'dedicated' when Rockefeller addressed the Virginia legislature in the rebuilt Capitol.

From the mid-1930s a new phase developed, marked by the fifteen-year leadership of Kenneth Chorley, and by the policy of filling in the gaps left by the demolition programme. In 1939 Edwin Kendrew presented a massive and authoritative *Report of Proposed Ultimate Restoration Work*. The interpretation and education element, in the hands of Goodwin's journalist son, Rutherfoord, built up. Twenty years after the start of the project half a million people a year were visiting Williamsburg.

The 173-acre Historic Area which they come to see today is not the little Virginia Tideway town of two centuries ago. How could it be? It nonetheless remains an extraordinary achievement. Of its buildings, eighty-eight—more than half the major structures—are original. Some, such as the church and the President's House in the College grounds, have maintained their original function uninterrupted. The remainder have been reconstructed on their original foundations with the aid of archaeologists, historians and voluminous documentary evidence—'wills, deeds, journals, eye-witness accounts, early drawings and even photographs'. Of these the best known are the Capitol and the Governor's Palace. One hundred acres of gardens and greens have been meticulously recreated, mostly from English examples, since none of the originals had survived; into them 500 species in use in the eighteenth century have been re-introduced; over 100,000 new bulbs are planted every year. Inside the buildings are important collections of painting and furniture. About 100 master craftsmen and apprentices work in their shops and smithies, perpetuating and demonstrating the skills of their calling.

Previous page: This is Williamsburg, Virginia; the date, the second half of the 1770s.

The Capitol, above, rebuilt in the 1930s to the original plans, stands at one end of Duke of Gloucester Street, the spine road of Colonial Williamsburg (opposite). At the other end, almost a mile distant, the College of William and Mary, chartered in 1693 and the oldest academic building in the US to have remained in continuous use.

Williamsburg is a peaceful and beautiful place

to wander about in. Contrived it may be, but a certain innocence nonetheless permeates the atmosphere. Everything has been fashioned with the sturdy tools of Colonial days. The guides to the public buildings are moved daily so that they never speak by rote, but from their general knowledge and understanding of the town's whole historical background. The objective, from very early days, has been not merely to restore the architecture but to inspire the visitor with the simple virtues of the founding fathers. The truth is that Colonial Williamsburg is the product of enormous integrity and the most meticulous research, at every level. The musician playing at the tavern where you take your meal is likely to have worked at the British Museum on the manuscripts from which his tunes are taken. In the 1930s and '40s the project was the proving ground for a whole generation of specialists, without whom later American conservation policies could not have been sustained. Garden history has been immeasurably enriched by Williamsburg research. The Foundation keeps alive a multitude of craft skills and traditions which would otherwise have died out. It has forged new approaches to 'interpretation'—Goodwin himself coined the term in 1930.

As a museum, then, Williamsburg is unique. Has it lessons for the workaday town in the real world? Like Dürnstein, Williamsburg has tunnelled its through-traffic beneath the town; a bus service loops the Historic Area and makes traffic exclusion possible. Like Disney World, it is litter-free and maintenance is immaculate. Such things are made possible by unified ownership and control. No public authority could have demolished a harmless mid-nineteenth century Greek Revival building like the Maupin House simply because it did not exist in 1780. The houses in Williamsburg are lived in and worked in, some still occupied by their inter-war owners or their descendants (purchase was often linked to a life tenancy for existing owners), but more by employees of the Foundation. The town can certainly be said, therefore, to be a living community—smoke rises from the chimneys, washing hangs upon the line—but a community of a very special kind, free of the social pressures and discords of less protected places.

The Historic Area is only a part of the whole town of Williamsburg, which has a population of 10,000 and is administered in the usual way by mayor, council and city manager. To the council, the Foundation pays its rates, or local taxes, as any other property owner, but there is no mistaking the two Williamsburgs. Cross the boundary of the Historic Area and billboards, wires, neon signs and the vulgarities of the 'strip' are quickly rampant. Even with the example on their very doorstep, it is not easy, it seems, for the wider community to understand what brings the visitors flocking to Colonial Williamsburg.

IRONBRIDGE GORGE—*England*

'Ironbridge in the 1940s', begins one of the Museum Trust's publications, 'was a remote and mysterious place . . .' And so it was—its wooded fastnesses on either side of the River Severn overgrown, its buildings largely abandoned and derelict, its bridge closed to traffic. Yet, it was here, in 1709, in a furnace dating back even earlier, to the 1630s, that Abraham Darby I evolved the technique for smelting iron ore by the use of coke in place of the traditional charcoal. Coal, waterpower, iron—it was the proximity of these things which gradually released the full thrust of the Industrial Revolution.

New activities sprang into being in the Gorge—smelting, casting, brickmaking, potteries. Everything was made of iron—from steam engines to farm utensils, buildings to cooking pots. Three generations of Darbys played their part in this, together with other ironmasters like William Reynolds (1758–1803), who was responsible for the Shropshire Canal and the creation of Coalport 'new town' in the 1790s. By the mid-eighteenth century there were more than 200 barges on the river, carrying, amongst other things, coal, iron, lead, bricks and tiles; and an inclined plane had been constructed (by Reynolds) which could raise a six-ton boat 207 feet from the river to the canal in three minutes. Spanning the river itself was the world's first iron bridge, cast at Coalbrookdale in 1779 (and put together in the manner of a carpenter, with dovetail joints and mortice and tenon joints). It gave the little town on the northern bank—largely laid out as a result of the building of the bridge—its name.

By the end of the nineteenth century, many of the area's natural resources were exhausted and the Gorge was in decline. One by one the collieries and the works closed. In 1926, china production at Coalport was transferred to Stoke; in the 1950s the last brick and tile works—of national importance at the beginning of the present century (the Maws Works was once the largest in the world and claimed to turn out thirty square miles of tiles a year)—shut its doors; in 1960, the railway line was abandoned. Ironbridge Gorge was included within the boundary of the new town of Telford—conceived in the mid-'Sixties with the object of revitalizing the East Shropshire coalfield area—in the hope that it could be rescued from dereliction.

Interest in industrial archaeology was already gathering pace. Michael Rix, who had coined the term in 1955, was by 1964 suggesting the creation of national parks of industrial archaeology—with Ironbridge as a priority candidate. The concept was embodied in a report to the New Town Corporation by their planning consultants, the John Madin Design Group, who proposed that the various sites of interest in the Gorge should be placed under the integrated management of a specially created trust. In 1967 the Ironbridge Gorge Museum Trust was set up as a non-profit-making, limited company, registered as a charity, under the chairmanship of E. Bruce Ball and with two honorary curators.

A 'Friends' organization was created and volunteers, between 1969 and 1972, cleared much undergrowth; in particular they excavated and repaired the upper level of the Shropshire Canal (which is linked to Coalport by the inclined plane). An initial appeal brought in £73,000, which permitted the first staff to be appointed. In 1970 Allied Ironfounders, the owners, handed over to the Trust the Old Furnace site and museum at Coalbrookdale on a ninety-nine-year lease. In 1971 Neil Cossons, who for twelve years did so much to bring the Museum to its present position, was appointed Director.

Today, the multifarious activities of the Trust are reflected in its structure. Flanking the central body are, on one side, the Ironbridge Gorge Museum Development Trust, the sole purpose of which is to raise funds for the Museum Trust

itself; on the other, the Ironbridge Trading Company, which handles publishing and sales activities (which would otherwise attract Corporation Tax). A third arm is a more recent addition—the Upper Severn Navigation Trust, which is restoring the last surviving Severn sailing barge or 'trow', the *Spry*, and aims to preserve certain features of the river navigation.

The museum area covers a flattened U-shape, some three square miles, the base of which is formed by the River Severn. Here the Iron Bridge itself, symbolic centre of the area, links Broseley on the south bank with the little town of Ironbridge on the north. Repair work on the bridge began in 1972: a reinforced concrete invert arch has been constructed between the two abutments and the approaches have been restored and strengthened. In the town itself, the little market

Above: the world's first iron bridge, cast in 1779, which gave its name to the little town on the north bank. In Ironbridge Gorge a whole complex of industrial activities developed—right, the remaining bottle kiln of the Coalport China Works, and the inclined plane which could lift a six-ton boat 207 feet from the river to the Shropshire Canal above in three minutes.

Ironbridge itself, spruced up and improved; above, the central motif on the bridge's handrail.

place has been refurbished (one of the larger buildings facing on to it by the Landmark Trust). Westward, up a small side valley of the main Gorge, lies the Coalbrookdale Furnace (Abraham Darby I's) and the Museum of Iron—the latter a magnificent display of the flowering proliferation in the uses of iron in its heyday, housed in the 1838 Great Warehouse. The Coalbrookdale Company still makes castings a stone's throw away. Between here and Ironbridge, on the river, is the quirky Severn Warehouse, a Victorian Gothic building of the 1840s now used (having done service at different times as a lemonade bottling factory, a bicycle factory, a bicycle frame assembly shop, and a garage) as the main interpretive centre, together with its adjoining wharf.

In the opposite direction lie the Coalport China Works Museum, with its remaining bottle oven, and Coalport Bridge. To the north of this lie the forty-two acres of the Blists Hill Open Air Museum, embracing three early nineteenth-century blast furnaces and blowing engine houses, two beam-engines, *David* and *Sampson*, a colliery mineshaft and steam-driven winding engine, and reconstructed buildings of various kinds. A small Shropshire town is here being recreated as it might have been at the end of the nineteenth century, its gas-lit streets comprising shops and houses, offices and works. Most important of these is the Iron Foundry, operating in the traditional way, which opened in 1985 and is now producing a wide range of castings—from tables and benches to pulley wheels, from weather vanes to bootscrapers. Linking Blists Hill with Coalport is the Shropshire Canal and the Hay Inclined Plane.

Other recent projects include the restoration of the Bedlam blast furnaces of 1757, the only ones of their type and date in Shropshire of which anything substantial remains; and putting back into productive use on the south side of the river the Victorian Craven Dunhill tile works at Jackfield—12,000 original moulds of which remain intact—with forty young people in a training workshop. Scattered about the Gorge are buildings and groups of buildings of historical interest, which the Museum has taken into its care—the houses the Darbys and other Quakers built for themselves; the Shelton tollhouse, one of a range built by Thomas Telford for the Holyhead road; a row of black-and-white cottages already there when Darby arrived in 1709. Throughout the area, walls have been rebuilt, paving and ground surfaces restored, planting undertaken—all done with sturdy reticence.

From the outset the Museum aimed to create a serious research centre. Its library of over 30,000 volumes has been extended by the Elton Collection, the main reference point in Britain for study of the visual aspects of industrial and technological development. In 1978 the Institute of Industrial Archaeology was launched; links were established with the University of Birmingham; and a post-graduate Diploma in Industrial Archaeology is now offered.

The general educational use of the Gorge has been steadily developed. Of the quarter million or so visitors each year (the figure rises steadily), half are children. Residential accommodation (administered jointly with the Youth Hostels Association) is now available for sixty-seven students, together with classroom facilities, based on the Coalbrookdale Literary and Scientific Institute.

The Museum today has a staff of around 100, and employs an average 200 or so young unemployed each year under the government's Manpower Services Commission schemes. Its own financial turnover is well in excess of £1 million. It is estimated that the Museum is worth £6 million to the locality, about half in wages and half through shops and hotels (a big new hotel opened in 1986). In 1978 it received the European Museum of the Year Award.

Ironbridge has come very far, then, in its first twenty years. It cannot, however, avoid some fairly fundamental changes during the years ahead. The Trust is not only exceptional in being the only agency of its kind in Britain designed to plan and conserve an area of this size; it has been a unique mix of the charitable, non-statutory, organization *plus* the statutory powers of Telford Development Corporation—from which it has derived considerable clout.

However, the British New Town Corporations are wound up when their job—the planning and construction of the new settlement—is done. The town then slots into the normal elective local authority framework. Telford's support for the Museum must inevitably decline steadily through the 1980s, in anticipation of its own demise at the end of the decade. What then will follow?

The potential problems are two-fold: those of finance and of ultimate control. Could the Museum ever be self-supporting? Certainly not until its capital development programme is substantially complete. Beyond that? Colonial Williamsburg was making substantial losses half a century after work began there, and long after the Historic Area became a national attraction. To a degree, Ironbridge could be expected to build upon its own reputation. The Development Trust's initial target of £1 million, set in the early 'Seventies, was reached in six years; by the late 'Seventies it was able to gain half its second £1 million in less than one year. Nonetheless, the drying up of a main source of funding (which has already begun) poses difficulties.

The other problem concerns the exercise of planning power and control. The Trust will surely wish in the coming years to seek some guarantee of the inalienability of the sites in its care—not all of which it owns. Should the answer lie in Michael Rix's 1964 call for the establishment of national parks of industrial archaeology? Certainly there can be no doubt now of the national significance of Ironbridge, and the creation of a national museum there—albeit of a new kind for Britain—would be one answer. The demands of the museum town are new to our generation; it seems clear that new patterns of administration have to be established to meet them—as Lowell, Massachusetts, has discovered.

LOWELL—*Massachusetts*

As the Industrial Revolution slips further into history, uncertainty envelops the tough grandeur of its once confident cities. In the Pennine mill towns of England, the great stark buildings, of hard red brick in Lancashire and millstone grit in Yorkshire, are but empty husks now; the forests of chimneys which once punctuated the skyline —an industrial equivalent of Wren's church spires in London—are smokeless and fast disappearing; the only movement on the canals which thread their way through the blackened canyons of the mills is that of an occasional pleasure boat pushing towards the open country.

Industrial areas, shaped by their functions and their period, have much in common. Images of Bradford and Halifax and Oldham in England, for example, easily overlay those of Lawrence and Lowell and Manchester in New England. From all such textile cities, for common reasons, work and prosperity eventually ebbed away. By the second half of the present century their need to find new purposes had become paramount. Some, like Manchester, New Hampshire, and Oldham, in England, put their faith in renewal; a 1977 Borough report in the latter stated that 'efforts should be made to largely clear Oldham of [up to 150] mills by the end of the century'. Others, like Halifax in England, with its splendidly restored 1774–79 Piece Hall, and Lowell, in Massachusetts, have opted for all-out coordinated conservation programmes as the basis for their economic revitalization. The former embarked on a ten-year 'Inheritance Decade' in 1985; the latter was heading in the same direction ten years earlier—and therefore, as yet, has more to show on the ground.

Lowell was founded in a bend of the Merrimack River, to the west of its junction with the Concord River. Here, in 1821, reconnoitering, came five industrialists from Boston, the 'Boston Associates'. There was a powdering of snow on the ground and there were fewer than a dozen houses. The place was called East Chelmsford. Ten years before, Francis Cabott Lowell had visited Britain, had memorized the details of the automated looms he saw there—an early example of industrial espionage—and, on his return, had developed with Paul Moody his own power looms based on the British designs. In 1815, with the 'Boston Associates', two years before his own death, he had formed a company with its works in Waltham—today a westerly suburb of Boston. The Associates now sought an alternative site where a greater source of power offered itself—and they found it at East Chelmsford where the Merrimack drops over thirty feet at the wide Pawtucket Falls.

Many others were to follow them, but the Associates' company was to dominate the whole development of the area. Kirk Boott, their agent, not only masterminded the company's expanding affairs but those of the community also. The company acquired 400 acres; and then, a year or two later, took over the 'Proprietors of Locks and Canals' who owned such part of the system as then existed. From 1837 James B. Francis, their Chief Engineer for forty years, steadily developed the waterway system which put the city in the forefront of hydraulic engineering. Eventually more than 5½ miles of canal, with associated locks and dams, had been constructed to distribute water power to scores of mills. In the 1820s the community was renamed after Lowell; by 1836 it became the third city incorporated in Massachusetts, with a population of 17,000; by the mid century it had become the largest producer of cotton textiles in the world.

Paternalistic employers at first sought to provide decent conditions and amenities for the mill girls, who attended lectures and even ran a literary magazine, 'The Lowell Offering'. It is of interest to recall that it was in 1826, the year the city took its name, that Robert Dale Owen left New Lanark to join his father at New Harmony, Indiana.

Lowell's power source—the wide Pawtucket Falls on the Merrimack River—and the Gatehouse controlling the entry to the Northern canal. Channelled through the canal system (far right: Francis Gate), it drove great works like the Massachusetts Mills on the other side of the city.

Lowell became, like New Lanark, of wide interest; visitors came from afar to study the 'Lowell Experiment' (to an observer from England it seemed 'a commercial utopia'). But the paternalism failed to outlast the early years. The first strike took place in 1843; by mid century, notwithstanding increased output, the mill girls' pay was less than it had been at the outset.

Irish, French Canadians, Greeks and Portuguese were only some of the immigrant groups who flocked to Lowell. By the early twentieth century, however, the industry was moving south. Increasingly mills and associated housing fell empty and into disrepair; by the mid 'Seventies only two mills remained open; the population had dropped by one third; and unemployment at fifteen per cent was the highest in the State. Some mills were demolished and consideration was given—as in Dutch and Belgian towns, and Bologna, and England's declining docklands—to filling in the canals to provide sites for new industry.

It was possibly the loss of so much of Manchester's industrial heritage during the 1950s and 1960s—ironically enough, fuelled by federal renewal money—which prompted efforts to save Lowell from a similar fate. In 1966 two Boston architects, Michael and Susan Southworth, in association with the federal 'Model Cities' programme, put forward the concept of the 'Lowell Discovery Network'—an exercise aimed at developing public awareness of the city's past and saving the most essential elements of its industrial and social fabric. Over the coming years the idea was to receive powerful backing from one time city councilman, now Senator, Paul Tsongas.

In 1972 Lowell City Council adopted a resolution basing future development on the historic park concept. By 1974 the State of Massachusetts had earmarked nearly $10 million for land acquisition for the Network, and its development as a Heritage Park. The New England Regional Commission was putting up around $700,000 towards the creation of pedestrian walks. The National Park Service was examining the idea of creating, in Lowell, a National Cultural Park which would be the first of its kind.

Nor was it all planning. By 1974 a number of small improvements had already been accomplished—the creation of nine small canalside parks and an information centre; tours were being organized. Over the next few years it all came together. Three agencies have assumed interlocking responsibilities for shaping the city's response to its past. The National Park Service exercises certain functions, notably interpretation, in respect of the area designated in 1978 as a *National Historic Park*—a chunk of the central area across, but mainly east of, the Merrimack Canal; the big Wannalancit Mill complex (part of which now houses a museum display, 'Spindle City'); and the canal system. Surrounding these is the *Historic Preservation District* of more than 200 ha or about 500 acres, embracing some 800 buildings, which is administered by the fifteen-member *Historic Park Commission*, representing local, state and federal interest. Interlocked with these is the *Heritage State Park*, focused particularly on the canal system and its associated locks and structures, which is managed, essentially for recreational purposes, by the Massachusetts Department of Environmental Management. Underpinning all this, of course, there remains the City administration with all its normal duties and functions to perform.

It sounds needlessly complicated—it has not proved easy to explain the difference between these overlapping agencies to the public—but there were, after all, no clear precedents to follow. The National Park Service is used to managing its own—largely wilderness—territory. The proprieties of revitalizing private property in an urban area were not to be taken for granted and the administrative partnerships necessary to run a living city as a national park had to be devised from scratch (a similar problem arising concurrently in respect of the Charleston Navy Yard in Boston, thirty miles to the south). The mechanisms chosen were, in fact, largely extensions of practices developed for natural areas.

Key to the whole programme is the Commission, the first agency of its kind in the United States. It meets monthly (its first director Fred Faust, one time assistant to Tsongas); it has a small professional staff; and it has been established for ten years only, after which it expects to be dissolved. The task it set itself in its 1980–81 Plan are:

(a) to compile a register, or index, of historic and cultural properties, in both the Park and the Preservation District;

(b) to devise standards for rehabilitation and for new building; and, with the City, to convert these into local ordinances—a new approach in

It was from buildings like these that the strength of Lowell sprang. Left: the big Lowell Manufacturing Company group (1881). Above: part of the even vaster Boott Mill complex (1835) and right: the Old Market House (1837) under repair.

the United States, hardly possible through normal zoning provisions (though Massachusetts State law provides a better framework than most);

(c) to assist with the conservation of ten specific buildings;

(d) to assist with trolley (tram) and barge transport systems for Park visitors.

The Index consists of four categories: buildings considered to be of national importance (about one third of those in the Park and Historic District); buildings of local importance only; buildings which neither contribute to, nor detract from, the scene; and buildings which are 'inconsistent' and undesirable in their context. (The Commission aims, for example, to acquire and demolish the undistinguished buildings on either side of Central Street where it passes over the Pawtucket Canal, so as to open up views of the —now invisible—waterway on either side.)

The Commission's budget for its decade of life was set at $20 million. Its funds have been concentrated—to the extent of ninety per cent of the total—in four areas: the city centre, Lower Locks, Acre and Chapel Hill. As far as possible the emphasis is put on incentives to the private sector; the gearing anticipated is $20 private expenditure for every dollar of grant. In these four priority areas, in which about eighty properties are considered eligible, owners are invited to submit proposals and applications for assistance. Grants (made only for exterior rehabilitation) are administered by the Commission; loans jointly by the Commission and the Lowell Development and Financial Corporation—the latter being in effect a non-profitmaking revolving fund, to which the Commission will loan in all $750,000 for a 35-year period. Maximum grants are $75,000; interest on loans is pegged at forty per cent of the base rate.

Five particularly important buildings, or complexes, have been earmarked by the Commission as essential for conservation. These include the giant brick and granite Boott Mill, of over 700,000 square feet (some 78,000 square metres), and the two sizeable blocks remaining of the Lowell Manufacturing Company, covering 270,000 square feet (buildings can be even more massive in America than in Britain because pro-

Far left: one of the informative 'interpretation' drums which set your surroundings in their social and historical context. Left: a detail from a cleaned building in Palmer Street. Right: the 1840 Welles Block (and National Historical Park offices) and St Anne's Church (1825), both in Merrimack Street.

cesses were more concentrated there). A grant of $500,000 towards the exterior repair and restoration of the Boott Mill complex clinched Wang Laboratories' purchase of the 1871 Capehart Building (which had had over 450 windows missing and the weather coming through the roof). Other parts of the building will be acquired for other uses; feasibility studies and options are under examination. The Lowell Manufacturing Company buildings, grouped round a central courtyard space, the roof and top floor of the later building destroyed by fire, have already been converted, in a $12 million scheme in conjunction with a private developer, into apartments on the upper floors, with a Park Service Visitors' Centre ('the Gateway') and commercial uses at ground level.

The Commission offers architectural advice and assistance to individual owners within the District; it brings architects and designers together weekly from all the official agencies involved to enable them to co-ordinate their work; it sets performance and design standards for paving, street furniture, planting and landscape; and, with the City, has established machinery for the control of development and granting of permits where appropriate.

Lowell today is still a city in transition, but seemingly very clear as to its direction. Through the early 'Eighties scaffolding abounded in the central area. Larger blocks, as in Market Street, were being brought back to life; handsome smaller buildings, as in Palmer Street, had already been restored and cleaned. Small gardens and sitting areas are appearing in odd corners which were previously untended. At vantage points circular drums carry excellently designed interpretative material. Park Service rangers conduct three-hour tours for schoolchildren and visitors. From the Park Service's headquarters, outside which stands, as sculpture, an enormous driving wheel from one of the mills, an old tram, 'The Whistler', will take you northwards and westwards to the Lowell Museum, where perhaps you may join a boat to the 1848 Gatehouse across the entry to the Northern Canal—there to admire the counterbalancing of the big sluice gates. Not far away, on the Pawtucket Canal, the Francis Gate, a 1850 flood prevention measure, has been repaired. The new Visitor Centre is in operation.

Lowell hopes, in the second half of the 1980s, to be receiving three quarters of a million visitors a year. It does not seem unreasonable. Great problems remain, for the sheer size of buildings like Boott Mill and those of the Suffolk Manufacturing Company are daunting. Nonetheless, Wang alone now employ 15,000; there is a new Hilton hotel; and in all directions an unmistakable air of purpose and optimism about the place. The mechanisms adopted there offer interesting comparisons with those of France's *secteurs sauvegardés*.

II

THE PROTECTED AREA

IF the town-as-museum be likened to a lecture, the historic area of a living town represents a continuing dialogue—a dialogue between past and present, in which neither must be allowed to shout down the other. In the protected area contrivance and artificiality have no place. Monuments may provide its glories, famous streets and squares its atmosphere, but ordinary life has to go on. Uses must be found for its buildings; housing must meet modern standards; people and goods must be transported; there must be jobs, shops and opportunity for leisure pursuits. Yet at the same time the Conservation Area or the *secteur sauvegardé* or the National Historic Landmark must meet the demands of today with such discretion that its essential character remains unharmed, is perhaps even enhanced. Museum towns, by definition, are nurtured by one single-minded agency or consortium; the historic area in a living town remains a multi-purpose area in multiple ownership, a cockpit of warring forces. How are such areas to survive?

Here is a handful of examples, ranging from the grand, centralized approach of the French *secteur sauvegardé*, through the recycling of an area by a private proprietor—a university—to the work of private associations seeking to save little vernacular towns in Scotland and the black-occupied Victorian District of Savannah, Georgia.

There are many ways of darning the urban fabric: France concentrates maximum resources upon very limited areas, working to very high standards; Britain has evolved the much looser 'Town Scheme'. Under Britain's system, government and local authority (often both County and District councils combine) put up equal sums annually, normally for a minimum period of five years; this money is available as grant-aid to the owner towards the restoration and essential maintenance of key buildings within a conservation area (up to fifty per cent of the total cost). This has given good value for money—the steady application of relatively small sums serving to keep nearly 200 towns in England and Wales in a reasonably good state of repair.

A third technique—like the Town Scheme, a means of what might be termed 'dispersed restoration'—is that of the 'revolving fund'. The revolving fund is generally employed by private trusts and foundations to purchase, restore and, usually but by no means always, sell historic buildings so that the proceeds can be ploughed back into more acquisition and more restoration. In this way, with minimum capital, a rolling programme can be built up which, through the years, can underpin and revitalize whole areas and even whole towns.

The revolving fund is not a magic formula. Where demand exists, normal market forces ensure a property's survival. Where there is no foreseeable use for a building, no revolving fund can save it. Between these extremes, however, a vast number of old buildings, for one reason or another, remain unattractive to the real estate world—either because they look like being difficult to restore or (the other side of the same coin) they promise too low a return on investment or may not sell readily and quickly. These are just the sort of buildings so casually demolished on a vast scale in the 1960s, the passing of which is now so widely regretted. These are the buildings which, through sheer commitment and dedication, can often be saved by private groups with low overheads. If a particular building is judged important enough, they may even decide to *lose* money on it.

Loss-making charities, profit-making companies—revolving funds come in all shapes. Some trusts sell the buildings they have completed; some retain them. Some restore completely; some partially, leaving the rest to the purchaser, who knows his own needs. Some do not even buy the building, but undertake restoration on the purchaser's behalf. These different approaches can be noted in the work of four organizations in three different countries: the National Trust for Scotland; Maatschappij Tot Stadsherstel in Amsterdam; and two in Savannah, Georgia.

The Marais district of Paris was one of France's first secteurs sauvegardés. Here, the Place des Vosges, the oldest square in Paris, before and after restoration.

SECTEURS SAUVEGARDES—*France*

As the pressures of the post-war development boom began to make themselves felt, André Malraux, the then Minister of Cultural Affairs, saw the need to establish for France's principal historic towns some means—within the planning process—not only of protecting them, but of fitting them for continued existence in the future. The grand sweep of France's single-minded approach could not fail to arouse the envy of less practised and more pragmatic countries. As the first results began to emerge—the magnificent *hôtels* of the Marais, freed of the unlovely accretions of generations; the almost too-painstaking restorations of Sarlat—Malraux's grand design came under increasing scrutiny by conservationists everywhere. Was this the pattern for which we were searching? In the event, the task has proved infinitely more expensive and more complex than was then foreseen. Under the Malraux law of 1962 it was hoped to schedule 200 *secteurs sauvegardés* in ten years; in fact, twenty-five years later, from an initial list of 400

The great 'hôtels', or town houses, of the Marais were most of them crumbling and down-at-heel; after restoration their quality is evident. The Hôtel Béthune-Sully, overleaf, was one of the first to be tackled. Page 140: the street entrance to the front courtyard as it had become, and today. Page 141: the courtyard itself and the recreated garden at the rear; details from the dazzling stonework and from the main door.

towns and quarters of towns, sixty-odd have been designated—with work going on in only a tiny proportion of the areas they cover.

Designation is effected by the Ministry of Cultural Affairs—in the last resort, it could be, even against local wishes—after consultation with the mayors, councils and Prefect concerned, and with relevant government departments. Responsibility for subsequent action falls to the Ministries of Cultural Affairs and of Equipment, co-ordinated by the more recent Ministry of the Environment and Quality of Life, and the *Commission Nationale des Secteurs Sauvegardés*.

Until later amendments to the process, designation was followed by a two-year moratorium on change of any kind, during which an architect was appointed to draw up a *Plan Permanent de Sauvegarde et de Mise en Valeur* (note that 'permanent'). This replaced all other plans and laid down which buildings were to be restored or demolished, which sites should be earmarked for new building, the activities to be allowed, road proposals, and how gardens and open spaces should be treated. With the publication of the plan, the exterior appearance of buildings became subject to control and all changes subject to the requirements of the plan.

Initially plans were for the most part undertaken by *Sociétés d'Economie Mixte*, created specially for each *secteur sauvegardé* or for defined areas within it. The SEM, a company financed jointly by the public and private sectors (medium- and long-term loans of up to eighty per cent of its expenditure are available from the government) would draw up detailed plans for the *îlot* or *secteur operationnel* for which it was responsible, within the terms of the permanent plan. The *Société* may undertake work by agreement with the owner, or by compulsory purchase and re-sale on a non-profit basis; in which case the original owner has first refusal, provided he refunds the *Société* his share of the expenditure incurred—otherwise the *Société* has the power to evict the owner and sell to somebody else.

To follow the system through in any detail means taking a look at specific examples. Clearly it is impossible to generalize. Not only do designated *secteurs sauvegardés* vary enormously in size—that at Chalon/Saône covers a mere three acres or so, while that at Loche, south-east of Tours, covers 370 ha of which 84 ha are built upon—but their problems and their approaches differ widely.

Some have been subject to little more than minimal maintenance, some to radical reshaping (it is not easy fully to square the extent of redevelopment in Avignon with the conservation ethic). Rouen has freed almost 2 km of its medieval streets from traffic and a good many others have managed to exclude traffic to some extent; the Marais has merely realigned some kerbs and elim-

inated some on-street parking. Sarlat, bisected brutally by the inter-war rue de la République—'la Traverse'—has yet effectively to get on top of its traffic management problems, let alone create underground parking space as Chartres has done.

Nonetheless, fundamental problems of execution, finance and the displacement of existing inhabitants have been common to most of the *secteurs sauvegardés*. They may be conveniently studied in one of the first to get off the ground: the Marais.

The Marais district of Paris lies athwart the great east-west route which runs from the Arc de Triomphe to the Bastille. Once marshland, it became popular with the Court and aristocracy in the fifteenth and sixteenth centuries. Some of its streets date back to the thirteenth century; the Place Royale, now the Place des Vosges, was begun in 1604 and is the oldest square in Paris; the area as a whole embraces some 1,900 buildings of high architectural quality from the sixteenth to the eighteenth centuries,* and three quarters of all its buildings are more than one hundred years old.

By the mid eighteenth century the aristocracy were moving westwards. Houses were divided and

* The formal inventory lists 56 as of the highest quality (Hôtels de Sully, de Beauvais, Lamoignon etc); 121 *monuments historiques*; 526 unclassified but which would merit listing; and around 1,000 more of architectural interest, plus others having details of quality.

sub-divided as they were occupied by more and more families. Artisan businesses and workshops —weaving, working and dealing in precious metals, and so on—which had come to the area to serve the Court, began to occupy and fill in courtyards and back land. By the first decades of the present century, the Marais had perhaps reached its lowest ebb, but at mid-century it remained one of the most densely populated districts in the whole of France. Part of the St Paul area had been scheduled for demolition in 1923 as *insalubre*; when designated as a *secteur sauvegardé* in 1965, the Marais had some of the worst living conditions in the city. Open space amounted to no more than 1.7 per cent of the land surface. Of 536 dwellings in the Carnavalet district, 416 were sub-standard. In some blocks thirty-six per cent of the dwellings had no water supply, seventy-four per cent no private lavatory; there were parts where nine people lived in two rooms.

The *Plan Permanent* covered 126 ha. It envisaged moving some 20,000 residents out of the district, and the regrouping of wholesale trades and workshops into areas where access would be easier and the buildings of little architectural importance; the amount of industry and warehousing would be reduced from eighty-four per cent to thirty-two per cent (in 1965 there were around 7,000 small businesses in the Marais, employing some 40,000). In all, the built-up area was to be reduced from seventy-seven per cent to forty-four per cent; 24,700 buildings were to be demolished; commercial activity reduced; and parking provision increased.

In 1967 a first *secteur operationnel* of 3.5 ha (later reduced to 3 ha for financial reasons)— the Region Carnavalet already referred to—was selected by the newly formed *Société d'Economie Mixte pour la Restauration du Marais* (SO.RE.MA). Of the latter's capital fifty-one per cent was held by the City of Paris, eighteen per cent by SARPI, twenty-seven per cent by banks and four per cent by insurance companies.

The *Société*'s programme for the *secteur* called for the removal of 186 dwellings and sixty-seven commercial premises, totalling forty-two per cent of the total floor area. These were acquired by agreement or compulsory purchase; of them eighty-five per cent were demolished at a cost of over thirty-five million francs. The restoration work required was set out and owners had to decide whether to do it themselves or hand it over to the *Société*. In the event, three-quarters of the work on the *hôtels particuliers* was undertaken by the owners, ninety per cent of all other work by the *Société* (at a 1976 cost of twenty-five million francs). It had been hoped that new flats and offices would be built by private developers. However, the property market took fright at the constraints imposed, with the result that the *Société* has had to shoulder this part of the programme as well. By 1976 a total expenditure of 166 million francs had been incurred, 150 million francs of which it was hoped to recoup from sales (though sales have been slower than anticipated).

However, by the end of 1975—ironically, the year of the Council of Europe's Heritage Year campaign—the 1967 Plan for the Marais was scrapped, and over the next few months totally revised. Costs were escalating; demolitions, outside the SEM areas, were more or less non-existent; speculative improvements at the upper end of the market were increasing. The new plan —from the title of which, significantly, the word 'permanent' was dropped—was intended to be a good deal less rigid in its approach. Renewal was greatly reduced; demolition restricted to totally unfit living accommodation and structures at odds with major monuments; small departures from the plan were to be permissible in appropriate circumstances. Much greater weight would be given to co-ordinated initiatives by property owners themselves (the formation of consortia of owners had all along been seen as an alternative to the SEM approach).

Owners' consortia, called *Associations Foncières Urbaines*, originally proposed in a 1967 law for rural areas, can be set up by a majority of owners within a defined area of a *secteur sauvegardé*, and attract exactly the same official grants and loans available to an SEM—with which, indeed, they are in competition. By definition, work by such associations does not produce the massive displacement which followed the first SEM initiatives. It is said to have worked well elsewhere—for example at Le Puy.

How, then, does the balance sheet stand in the Marais a quarter of a century after André Malraux's 'grand design' was promulgated in 1962? The great mansions are still being brought magnificently back to life—most recently, for example, in 1985, the Hôtel Aubert de Fontenay (the 'Hôtel Sale') as the Picasso Museum. However, it would be a mistake to identify the whole programme with the work of the quasi-governmental agencies. Indeed, it was only because of various earlier initiatives that the official programme was able to get under way so quickly. The City of Paris has been active in the St Paul area—now, after clearance and reconstruction, the 'Village Saint-Paul'. Elsewhere façades and shop fronts have been stripped, scraped and sand-blasted by the *Agence des Bâtiments de France du Marais*. In 1961 the *Association pour la Sauvegarde et Mise en Valeur de Paris Historique* was founded. In 1962 the first Marais Festival, now comprising an annual four-weeks' programme, was held in association with them. At all stages a number of individual owners have been prepared to do further work to their own properties.

Nevertheless the official agencies have continued to provide the main leverage. As the changes of 1975–76 make clear, however, it is simply not possible today, even within an administration as centralized as has been that of France, for government and local authorities alone to enforce pre-determined physical change upon urban areas of any size. It was originally hoped to deal with fifteen hectares of the Marais each year; in fact, a mere half hectare has been achieved and it is admitted that the full programme will take a century or more to complete. Over France as a whole, of the 3,400 or so hectares making up the total area of all the *secteurs sauvegardés* so far designated, a mere forty hectares are covered by *secteurs operationnels*. How many of the buildings already at risk today, one wonders, will still be standing when the programme finally catches up with them? It has been estimated that it could take 300 years to deal with merely the *secteurs sauvegardés* already designated.

Conservation on this scale must always turn on the availability of massive finance. Thereafter the overwhelming problem in the revitalization of decaying areas—whether in the Marais, or Bologna, or Amsterdam, or other *secteurs sauvegardés* like Colmar—is that of the social displacement it involves: 'gentrification'. Restoration and modernization cost money. Short of substantial subsidies from one source or another, there is no way that improved properties can be sold or let at the same level that they commanded as slums.

In the Marais fifty-six per cent of those displaced have been rehoused in the *arrondissement*; the rest have been dispersed all over Paris. Of 432 new dwellings foreseen in the original plan, only 101 will be for low-income tenants. It is perhaps not surprising that the eviction of sitting tenants in the St Paul area led to violence in 1977.

If *enforced* emigration of large numbers from an area they regard as their own, as a result of official action, is to be avoided, flexibility is called for at many different levels. France's *secteurs sauvegardés* can point to impressive achievements. In all parts of the country, work continues steadily and strikingly. Their weakness has been to let the best be the enemy of the good, in that their rigidly perfectionist approach has led to cumbersome procedures allied to a certain ruthlessness of outlook. In less grand areas, as we shall see, other methods may be more appropriate.

GRAND BEGUINAGE—*Louvain, Belgium*

The cultural schisms which divide Belgium have turned Louvain, in Brabant, into Leuven. Before the rise of Brussels, the city was the capital of the province. In 1426 Duke John IV of Brabant founded there a university which has ever since remained pre-eminent—in the sixteenth century there were no fewer than 6,000 students attached to it. But, with the granting of 'cultural autonomy' in 1971, the University and its institutions were split, the Flemish-speaking elements remaining, the French-speaking moving to the new university town of Louvain-la-Neuve, created to the south-east of Brussels.

In 1963, before the split, the University purchased the whole of the Grand Béguinage from the local authority, to provide accommodation for dons and students. The Béguinage was not so

Self-contained and traffic-free, the Grand Béguinage in Louvain, for long in galloping decay, has been brought to life again as accommodation for 800 university students and staff. The occasional new building (above) has been slotted in with becoming discretion.

much a nunnery in the conventional sense as an area of housing for nuns. Founded in the thirteenth century, it covers five hectares (or nearly twelve and a half acres) on either side of an arm of the River Dyle: a fortified enclave within the city. It embraces a fourteenth-century church, some hundred houses from the sixteenth and seventeenth centuries, and a small park. With the confiscation of church property at the end of the eighteenth century, the Béguinage was turned over to ordinary housing, gradually degenerating into an overcrowded and ruinous slum. Most local authority members—or their officers—seeing it at the end of World War II, would have called without hesitation for its demolition and redevelopment.

By the 1970s it was unrecognizable. Restoration and adaptation, under the direction of Professor Raymond Lemaire of the University's own architecture department, were spread over about ten years. The residential buildings now provide accommodation for some 800 students and staff; a hospital has been turned into a faculty club; there are reading rooms and a library, recreation rooms and a cafeteria restaurant.

The Grand Béguinage is today a peaceful enclave, free of traffic and largely insulated from the city around it. Its spaces lead intriguingly from one to another. Brickwork has been meticulously cleaned and restored. New additions—and they are not numerous—have been slotted in with a becoming humility (though never as pastiche). Interiors are simple, with wholly modern fittings and furniture. Between 1978 and 1985 the church—Gothic in structure, Baroque in its fittings—was itself restored as splendidly as befits the parish church of the University.

Other universities—for example Durham, in England—have made signal contributions to the conservation of their parent cities. What distinguishes the Grand Béguinage of Louvain—or if preferred the Begijnhof of Leuven—is the exemplary manner in which the whole project was carried out; but, no less, the fact that its restoration and adaptation cost less than equivalent new accommodation would have done.

Overall costs in fact amounted to £55 (early 1970s) per square metre. Total expenditure was equivalent to seventeen million French francs, broken down as follows:

> Purchase of land and buildings—2 million fr. Services infrastructure, river control etc—2.5 million fr. Interior restoration and fittings—180 fr per cubic metre, or twenty-five per cent less than the figure for new student accommodation built by the university elsewhere; however, because rooms in the Béguinage are larger and more comfortable, the price per room, at 17,000 fr, was approximinately the same. Purpose-made furniture cost 3,000 fr per room. Restoration of the church and conversion of the social centre cost 5 million fr.

It would be rash to extrapolate costs generally from any particular example—the variables are too numerous—but in this case at least, conservation, to a high standard, proved the more economic answer.

LITTLE HOUSES SCHEME—*Scotland*

The National Trust for Scotland was founded in 1931. Like its parent body—together they now form the largest landowner in Britain after the Crown and government—the Trust exists to save historic buildings and areas of outstanding landscape, through acquisition and ownership, in perpetuity. However, in Scotland, the Trust has often been interventionist and entrepreneurial in the wider field. One example of such initiatives is its 'Little Houses Improvement Scheme'.

From its earliest years, the Scottish Trust has shown a concern for more than castles and great homes. It began restoration work on some of the little houses in the historic and royal Burgh of Culross, in Fife, in 1932; with similar work twenty years later in Dunkeld in Perthshire. However, income from these buildings was so small —Scotland's rents have traditionally been much lower than in England—that, if such rescue work was to be continued, a new approach had to be found. A survey by the Trust as far back as 1936 had identified over 1,100 vernacular buildings of interest in one hundred towns. The Trust decided to experiment with a revolving fund.

The 'Little Houses Improvement Scheme' was launched in 1960, the fund itself the following year—initially with £10,000 from the Pilgrim Trust and a similar sum from the Trust's own General Fund. Since then, 'refreshed', as the

A far cry from the show-pieces of the Marais, little vernacular houses like these are no less part of the European heritage—and, collectively, no less deserving of preservation. Above and right: part of Dysart before restoration—and after. Facing page, below: St Monans, another of the coastal towns of Fife, given fresh life by the National Trust for Scotland.

Trust has it, by donations, grants from local authorities, interest-free loans, legacies and the profits from sales, the figure grew (inevitably the total fluctuated upwards and downwards) and today stands at well over £200,000—though inflation has greatly reduced the spending power represented by such a sum.

The scheme's most concentrated effort has centred on the County of Fife. Fife has been called 'a beggar's mantle fringed with gold'—the fringe being a marvellous coastline to the Firth of Forth, stretching eastwards from Aberdour to St Andrews and embracing a string of picturesque little towns of great character: Culross, Dysart, St Monans, Pittenweem, Anstruther and Crail amongst them. By the 1950s these places were in decline, their buildings, many of them, empty and crumbling. If now they present a more confident and colourful face to the world, it is primarily because of the Trust's Little Houses Scheme. Between the early 1960s and the mid 1970s, the Trust acquired, restored and sold some 150 vernacular buildings—mostly houses but also shops, two museums and a handful of other types (by the mid 'Eighties the number had risen to about 170). In all, some £2 million of restoration work was thus sparked off. The scheme formed one of the Council of Europe's fifty demonstration projects in European Architectural Heritage Year, 1975.

Criteria for selecting a property include its architectural or historic merit; vacant possession; costs of purchase and restoration; and eventual saleability. The identification of suitable buildings springs initially from the Trust's network of supporters; detailed investigations are carried out by staff surveyors. Restoration is undertaken by one of three means:

(a) the building may be purchased from the Trust and restored by the new owner using his own architect;

(b) the purchaser may ask the Trust to undertake the work on his behalf and, within reason, to his specifications;

(c) the Trust may restore the building itself after purchase and then seek a buyer or tenant.

In the two latter cases rehabilitation is organized by one of the Trust's area surveyors. Direct costs are recovered, including that of the surveyor's time, but general administrative and overhead costs are not charged. In all cases purchasers are required to enter into a Conservation Agreement—ie a restrictive covenant—designed to ensure the integrity of the building in perpetuity. Over recent years, with increasing calls upon its resources and the value of the Fund eroded by inflation, the Trust has sought more and more to work through the 'restoring purchaser' who will himself, directly or through the Trust, undertake necessary restoration—thereby relieving financial pressures upon the Trust. Even by 1970, nearly half the work in hand was being financed by this means; today it has become common practice. Nonetheless, more recently still, the Trust has sought to renew the original impact of the Fund, and has begun to move once more towards selective 'in-house' restoration.

Two further points may be made—one specific, the other more general. Although the Trust has sought, up to a point successfully, to apply the revolving fund principle to other, hardly less delightful towns, the same momentum has not been achieved. One reason lies in the completion of the Firth of Forth road bridge in 1964, which brought the Neuk of Fife, the coastal strip, for the first time within commuting distance of Edinburgh. Suddenly cottages in these small communities became desirable as weekend or retirement retreats. The Trust's initiative came at exactly the right moment. Might the normal market forces eventually have achieved the same results anyway? Who can now tell? The fact is that the process of decline in these towns was halted—and restrictive covenants now safeguard the appearance of many of their buildings indefinitely, which no other means could have ensured.

The second and more important point lies in the influence the Trust's work has had on others. Not only have the local authorities primarily concerned—originally for example the County Councils of East Lothian and Fife, and now, since local government re-organization, a number of regional authorities—become active partners in the scheme, but a number of local trusts have come into being to work alongside the Trust and reinforce its efforts. The Elgin Fund and the Crail Preservation Society date in fact from 1945 and 1959 respectively; but others include the East Neuk of Fife Preservation Society (1961), the Central and North Fife Preservation Society (1962) and the Banff Preservation Society (1965). To groups such as these—for example in Anstruther, Banff, Ceres and Tayport—the Trust has made interest-free loans to enable them to purchase and restore buildings. Thus a rolling programme to deal with thirty estate cottages on the shores of Loch Lomond includes, as partners with the Trust, the Regional Council, the District Council, a housing association and the Scottish Civic Trust. In this kind of flexibility lies some of the potential of the revolving fund technique.

It was primarily the example of the Little Houses Scheme which led to the creation in Britain, following a study by the Civic Trust, of the Architectural Heritage Fund—a £2.6 million fund which makes low-interest loans to local trusts to ease their cash-flow problems during restoration (see page 222). This has in turn led to a significant increase in the number of such trusts.

STADSHERSTEL—*Amsterdam*

Amsterdam, of all the major cities in Western Europe, has most obviously retained its traditional character. The layout of the city is still determined by the triple crescent of tree-lined canals—Prinsengracht, Keizergracht and Herrengracht—constructed in the seventeenth century. From that century, and even more from the eighteenth, date the greater number of red brick, ornate-gabled, bourgeois houses which give to central Amsterdam its particular, civilized, architectural character.

Of the 7,000 or so listed buildings in the central area—roughly one third of the national total—most remain in private hands. The Dutch take their heritage very seriously and government grants for conservation are generous. Over the past quarter of a century, some 2,300 buildings have received official assistance towards their restoration and repair. The municipality has long maintained an advisory service for owners and their architects on restoration problems, quite apart from its own major initiatives in areas like the Jordaan. But over and above such official machinery, Amsterdam has benefited from a range of private initiatives and programmes by foundations created specially to acquire and restore historic buildings.

There are over forty such trusts and non-profit-making companies in the country as a whole, with a handful operating in Amsterdam. Some have been in existence for a very considerable time—for example, the association Hendrick de Keyser (named after that same seventeenth-century architect who was sent to London to study Gresham's Royal Exchange) was founded in 1918. Of them all, the limited company Amsterdamse Maatschappij Tot Stadsherstel NV—the Amsterdam Company for Town Restoration—has expanded the most rapidly.

Stadsherstel was formed in 1956, by a director of an Amsterdam brewery. As a businessman, he took the view that substantial investment would be required to make any significant impact on the conservation of the city, and that this would only be possible if properties were acquired and a return made on the capital involved. Conservation must be made to pay—if only modestly.

On this basis Mr Six van Hillegom approached nine Dutch insurance companies, two shipping companies and two banks. Together they were persuaded to put up a combined share capital of more than one million guilders, or about £¼ million; shares were to offer only five per cent—but that was to be accumulative. This formed the basis of the operation. The company does not differ administratively from any other limited liability company. Policy is laid down by a Board of Directors; day-to-day control is exercised by the Managing Director—a post held from 1966 by Dr J. M. Hengeveld. Additionally, however, Stadsherstel is registered as a Housing Association, which in the Netherlands brings with it certain tax advantages.

In the initial period up to 1966, yields—and profit margins—were small. Income from rentals of restored properties was swallowed up in loan charges, capital costs and the expenditure involved in getting the whole programme moving. During this period no dividends were paid. By the early 1960s, more capital was needed. It was obtained through mortgages on the buildings already restored, provided by the same founder supporters of Stadsherstel, but at normal interest rates. This injection of fresh capital enabled momentum to be maintained and increased, so that from 1966—ten years after the company's formation—it became possible for the first time to pay a dividend of three per cent.

In 1976 shareholders received all the dividends which had not been paid to them since 1956—in other words, five per cent on the capital employed has now been paid for every year the company has been in operation. All further surpluses have been ploughed back into restoration work. By 1966, Stadsherstel owned ninety houses, of which twenty had been restored. Ten years later, the company had 213 properties in its possession, of which 123 had been restored. By the end of 1982, the totals had risen to around 280 and over 180 respectively. The company now aims to purchase between ten and twenty houses each year, and to restore about fifteen of them annually. This steady expansion of its programme has meant an equally steady expansion of its capital. In 1968 Stadsherstel successfully launched a share issue to the total value of nearly 4 million guilders, or about £1 million. At the same time Amsterdam City Council acquired a stake in the share capital to the tune of 600,000 guilders, or £150,000. Via further issues of shares in 1972, 1976 and 1980, Stadsherstel's capital assets stood at about 75 million guilders in the early 'Eighties, with an issued share capital of 28.5 million guilders. Rental income amounts to 4.5 million guilders a year.

This astonishing success story makes clear what adequate funding and professional management can do for conservation. At the same time it is necessary to recall the aims which lie behind the financial success. The company's essential objectives are to save and bring into use older buildings which would otherwise be lost, thereby revitalizing areas of the city and providing housing accommodation at reasonable rentals. These objectives have obviously guided the choice of properties acquired. Thus Stadsherstel prefers to acquire *groups* of buildings wherever possible, and shows particular interest in corner sites. Concentration of effort upon several adjoining buildings will make a bigger impact upon a street than the same amount of work split among random individual buildings; it is more likely to 'bring up' nearby properties not in possession of the company. Preserving the *corners* of blocks stabilizes the whole block, for once the corners have gone, there is little hope of saving the rest.

Most of the older buildings in Amsterdam were originally houses and lend themselves fairly readily to conversion to modern apartments. This has formed by far the greater, but by no means exclusive, part of Stadsherstel's work. In one case the company acquired part of a small shopping street (ten properties), improved and re-let the shops at street level, and provided accommodation above for nurses from a nearby hospital. In another case a corner property was let to form part of an hotel fashioned from a block of seventeen merchants' houses and old warehouses backing onto each other (see p. 98). Elsewhere parts of premises have been let as professional offices, flats and restaurants.

Two reservations have been raised in connection with Stadsherstel's operations. One relates to the nature of the work carried out, in that some of the properties acquired have been so dilapidated that rebuilding, rather than restoration, has been necessary. The second, which will have a familiar ring in most other countries, is that Stadsherstel's operations are 'elitist'; that existing tenants are driven away by the increased rent chargeable after restoration. To such questions there are no easy answers. Counsels of perfection cannot always be followed in real life. The right housing mix for a city can only be achieved through municipal action—and the municipality in this case is itself a Stadsherstel shareholder. It has to be said that in certain areas, for example the Jordaan district, the Amsterdam City Council has made strenuous efforts to avoid 'gentrification'.

What is undeniable is that, over a quarter of a century, Stadsherstel and its colleague organizations have made a major contribution to the protection of the character of the Dutch capital. Their achievement provides further justification for the small, self-motivated private agency, for it is hard to believe that a similar volume of work could have been done by any official organization with a staff of sixteen (twelve professional and four clerical) and overheads of twelve per cent of the annual turnover.

Left: tell-tale signs—the well-known boards of Stadsherstel on the scaffolding of another Amsterdam house under repair. Above: a corner building restored by the company, and the neat plaque recording its ownership.

SAVANNAH—*Georgia*

Savannah, Georgia's port and first capital, was founded by James Oglethorpe and nineteen of the original settlers, who arrived there in February 1733. The city was laid out on a steep bluff on the south side of the Savannah River, fifteen miles above its mouth. Oglethorpe's grid plan was based on a sequence of wide streets broken by large, open squares. As the city rebuilt itself after the war of 1776 and two catastrophic fires in 1796 and 1820, and spread across the flat land stretching back from the river, Oglethorpe's original conception was maintained. To his original six squares, eighteen more were added—of the total twenty-one remain today, three having been lost in the 1950s to a highway—giving Savannah with its tree-lined streets a particularly park-like character. It is also a city of considerable architectural distinction, having fine Regency and Greek Revival buildings; much splendid ironwork in balconies, porches, stairways, gates and railings; and the charms of Factors' Row, built against the bluff so that goods could enter the warehouses at the foot directly from the river, while the cotton factors', or brokers', counting houses and offices on top linked straight to the city across bridges spanning lower access roads.

Today, Savannah has a population of around 142,000. The air is soft, and fragrant with flowering shrubs. Spanish moss hangs from big shady trees. Brick and stucco glow in the sun; clapboarding gleams with new paint. Children play in the streets. Motorists are unaggressive. Front doors are often left unlocked. All in all, Savannah is one of the most congenial of American cities, the pride of its citizens and increasingly beloved by tourists (revenue from tourism rose over twenty years from $500,000 to $130 million). It was not always so. Thirty years ago, much of the city was down at heel; trade was being lost to out-of-town shopping centres; decaying Georgian houses, occupied by several families, were declining steadily into slums; the more affluent had moved, or were

Savannah, Georgia. It will be snapped up quickly—but things were not always so.

moving, to the suburbs. The downtown area had been virtually abandoned. One organization, above all others, was responsible for setting the city on a new course: the Historic Savannah Foundation.

It was the destruction in 1954 of the old city market for a multi-storey car park—an eyesore to this day—which led to the creation of the Foundation by seven ladies, led by Mrs Anna Hunter. Originally fairly informal in character, and tagged by some the 'Hysteric Savannah Foundation', the group has come to wield considerable political power; its impact on the city over twenty-five years has been remarkable. An original outlay of only $38,000 'seed' (pump priming) money used as a revolving fund, has triggered off some $60 million worth of restoration. Of 1,100 historic buildings in the two and a half square miles (6.5 sq km) central district, the greater number have now been restored. As a separate operation, the Gardens Club has restored and replanted many of the city's squares. Factors' Row, threatened in the 1950s, has been brought back to life and embraces a ships' museum, ships' chandlers, restaurants, taverns and shops. An $8 million renewal of the river front has been completed. The Chamber of Commerce now occupies, and has superbly renovated, the redundant railway station. A new organization, the Savannah Landmark Rehabilitation Project, has been formed to tackle the seventy-eight-block 'gingerbread' Victorian District—predominantly black—with the aim of avoiding the displacement of present owners and tenants.

How did it all come about? The start was much like beginnings everywhere. Concurrently with the loss of the City Market in 1954, the distinguished Isaiah Davenport House (1815–1820), having degenerated into a decayed tenement housing eight families, came up for demolition. It was the new Foundation's first purchase. Five years later, the Foundation failed to acquire four fine, 1855 terrace houses of grey Savannah brick—Marshall Row. However, a young investment banker, Leopold Adler II, stepped in, bought the land on which they stood for $45,000, then negotiated with the demolition company—which had already knocked down the mews building at the rear—offering them $9,000 in place of the $6,000 they had already paid for the much-sought-after grey bricks. The purchase was completed in the names of Adler and three other business men, one the then President of the Foundation. This action sparked off the entire restoration programme.

A new steering committee met twice weekly. To get a proper foothold in the property market, members of the Foundation raised substantial funds amongst themselves on a short-term basis;

Facing the river is Factors' Row—now in use by ships' chandlers, as offices, restaurants, a ships museum . . . On the landward side the upper floors bridge across to the higher ground on which stands the city itself.

badgered, cajoled and wheedled smaller amounts from reluctant bankers. Responding to emergencies as they arose, the Foundation, with the help of outside consultants and a team of students from the University of Virginia, began a systematic and authoritative survey of the historic central area. Completed in 1962, it cost them $50,000. Armed with this detailed inventory, the Foundation was able to convince the Chamber of Commerce of Savannah's tourist potential. A $75,000 annual budget was approved to implement a joint conservation/tourist report by the two bodies. The inventory also enabled the Foundation to enlist for the first time the business community's support for a proper revolving fund. $200,000 was subscribed—$75,000 from the Foundation and $125,000 from private and commercial sources.

Things now began to move rapidly. Over the following eighteen months—that is to say, between 1963 and 1965—the Foundation quietly, through agents, acquired no fewer than fifty-four key properties in the Pulaski Square/West Jones Street area. The project was then announced, publicized and promoted—through estate agents, guided tours, publications and the press. The first really sizeable programme thus got off the ground. More acquisitions followed steadily, commercial area improvements were put in hand and, most encouraging of all, private individuals began to move in and independently reclaim more buildings. No fewer than fifty were restored by one group of three people; fifteen more by another married couple. By 1967, thirteen years after the Foundation came into being, nearly 500 buildings had been saved. In that year the Foundation launched a capital drive to raise a further $500,000—$350,000 for the revolving fund, $100,000 for the development of major landmark buildings and $50,000 for general administrative and operational expenses.

In 1966, the central 2½ square mile area was designated as an Historic Landmark by the Federal Department of the Interior. In 1968, the Foundation published the definitive inventory for the area and this became the basis for the City Authority's historic zoning ordinance enacted in 1972, though battles with the City Council still took place—notably a bitter controversy over a high-rise development on the waterfront. Savannah now has an official Historic Review Board which has set down sixteen criteria for restoration and commands near-absolute powers of veto over exterior changes in the centre.

Left: the Owen Thomas House, a typical Savannah terrace, and the Davenport House. Right: one of the score of garden squares which give the city so much of its character. Right and below: restoration in the Victorian District, and one of the first houses completed in the district by Savannah Landmark.

Throughout its existence, the primary aim of the Historic Savannah Foundation has been to *save buildings*. It has not normally sought to retain ownership (though its restrictive covenants are firm, and it retains the right to repurchase if the owner wishes to sell); it has not normally itself become involved in the actual process of restoration (although it will advise owners and

tenants on the historical and technical aspects of restoration). Its method has been to acquire threatened properties for resale to organizations or individuals, who will themselves restore them within a specified period. Sometimes it has been a matter of years before resale has become possible; sometimes the Foundation has sustained deliberate losses.

A fairly typical building operation was the 'Cluskey Complex', a handsome double balconied residence, due to make way for a fourteen-storey, steel, glass and concrete annexe to the Courthouse behind it. The owner's asking price was $175,000. To get it, he allowed the Foundation to name its own terms. The Foundation's formula involved $1,000 down as a six-month deposit, with $14,000 at the end of that period; thereafter interest only was to be paid for eighteen months and from then on, $1,000 a month for eight years, with the remainder knocked off in one fell swoop at the end of eight years. In other words, the Foundation's outlay for the first year would be somewhere around $20,000–$22,000, and maybe $14,000 p.a. thereafter, the general assumption being that if the Foundation couldn't get rid of the building over several years there was something wrong with the Foundation. In fact a purchaser took it off their hands at $25,000 below their own commitment—but the Foundation considered the low return to be an appropriate contribution to the quality and vitality of the city.

Today, the Foundation's headquarters are in Davenport House—its first purchase—open to the public six days a week. The Foundation has 800 members, who subscribe $25 a year each; a professional staff of six; and a Board of Trustees numbering thirty, with an Executive Committee which meets monthly. Success breeds success. Savannah bankers are now prepared to make restoration loans of up to ninety per cent of the cost of a project. The Foundation still sees its function as saving buildings. Though it has been responsible over the years for some $60 million of work going to the local building industry, and some $18 million of fees going to local estate agents, there is still, it feels, work to be done.

Much of that work, however, needs to be in other parts of the city. Lee Adler left the Foundation in 1967 to take up the more difficult challenge of the Victorian District lying to the south of Oglethorpe's original settlement. This is a forty-five-block area, covering some 160 acres originally built as a middle class suburb in the late nineteenth and early twentieth centuries. The streets are tree-lined; the houses—detached, semi-detached or in short terraces—are largely timber, gingerbread and 'Carpenter Gothic' (ie trimmed with detail chosen from a builders' catalogue). With the continuing drift outwards from the centre after World War II, the area was left in the hands of absentee landlords and in recent times has mostly been occupied by low-income, elderly blacks. Decay is widespread, living conditions are often deplorable. However, the kind of approaches to rehabilitation which were appropriate for the older part of the city, much of it unoccupied thirty years ago, could not be expected to work in the Victorian District (although in earlier days Mills B. Lane, a retired Atlanta banker, has restored twenty-seven old properties in the central area for use by poorer families, but this was an act of personal philanthropy). If large numbers of blacks were not to be displaced different means had to be found.

Adler set up the Savannah Landmark Rehabilitation Project in 1970, as a private, non-profit-making corporation. Its first plans were invalidated by changes in government policy; it now plans to buy and restore nearly half the 1,200 homes in the District, at a rate of sixty a year. First building work began in 1977; by February of the following year, Savannah Landmark owned forty properties (buildings have been, or will be, purchased in each of the forty-five blocks of the District). Three years after the project began, forty homes had been restored, twenty-four others were under way, and it was planned to acquire

100 more. There were 700 families on the waiting list.

Savannah Landmark has attracted some substantial backing, from national as well as local sources. Above all, however, the programme involves a perpetual juggling act with all the subsidies—local and Federal—the work can possibly attract: for housing rehabilitation, for training craftsmen, and by the way of rent subsidy. The key to the operation—the Netherlands has a rather similar provision—is the Federal 'Section 8' rental subsidy programme. This provides for low-income tenants to pay up to a quarter of their income towards rent, the difference between that and the proper market rental being made up by government grant (through HUD, the Department of Housing and Urban Development).

Savannah Landmark's twenty-three-member Board has on it both blacks and whites. Loan capital to the legal limit has been provided by the Carver State Bank, Savannah's only minority-owned bank (the white-owned banks only came in, reluctantly, later). All the first building work was undertaken by William Mobley, a black contractor, using largely unskilled black workers under the Comprehensive Employment Training Act (CETA) comparable with the Manpower Services Commission programmes in Britain. Savannah Landmark looks forward to mixed neighbourhoods, partly rented, partly owner-occupied, where blacks and whites will live alongside one another in comparable housing. All the first houses rehabilitated, however, have been let to black families.

The dividing line between preserving buildings for a social purpose, and using older buildings to meet a social need (as is often done by housing associations) is tenuous to the point of non-existence. The terminology is unimportant. What is stimulating about initiatives like those in Savannah is their confidence, and professionalism. Savannah Landmark works to a critical-path analysis and monthly cash-flow projections for three years ahead.

III

MAKING NEW PLACES

THE ideal cities of Ebenezer Howard and Le Corbusier were little more than conceptual diagrams; watered down, they produced between them half a century of housing of exceptional monotony—monotony not merely of detail and style (after all the Georgians created uniformity and we love it) but of gross insensitivity to the *genius loci*—the essential difference between one site and another, one region and another. There has been an awful sameness about British local authority housing estates, from Land's End to John O'Groats, as there has been about the cheerless high-rise slabs ringing every big city in the world from Stockholm to Singapore.

Here are two new-built communities which are otherwise. One is a holiday village for the rich on the Côte d'Azur; the other a public housing estate in the north of England. They could not be more different, architecturally or socially. Their differences as places serve only to emphasize that character is not just a question of architectural style. It is the way that buildings are laid out—and respect the lie of the land—that creates spaces and views which make *this* place immediately distinguishable from *that*. In neither of the examples that follow do you ever pause to wonder where you are.

PORT LA GALERE—*France*

Mass tourism has caused the once-beautiful Meditteranean littoral to be lined with an almost endless cliff of white hotels and apartment blocks, spreading up the foothills of the Alps, and leap-frogging skywards to steal views over those in front. In the 1960s, France, while steadfastly allowing ever more monolithic blocks of this kind to be built (la Grande Motte, in the Languedoc, is an intimidating example), also saw the appearance of new holiday villages between the Spanish and Italian borders. Of a very different sort, these villages were conceived as 'places'. Among the first were Port Grimaud, a marina development in the form of a Venetian fishing village, built on piles around ten km of quays, and Port la Galère.

Both have been derided as rich men's playgrounds. Port Grimaud, rather unfairly, has been called 'a deplorable fake' (to the unprejudiced eye it seems merely to have settled down into being itself). Port la Galère is too idiosyncratic to be faking anything. From a distance, it resembles a familiar kind of Mediterranean village, tumbling vertiginously down a rocky cliffside to a small harbour below. At close quarters, however, the architecture turns out to be unlike any other—unless perhaps Gaudí and Rudolf Steiner had collaborated to create a holiday village in the sun. The concept was that of the Provençale artist-architect, Jacques Couëlle, and it is interesting to note that the designer-developer of Port Grimaud, François Spoerry, at one time studied under him (he is said also to have been influenced by Clough Williams-Ellis' Portmeirion in north Wales). It was reported in 1986 that Spoerry and Couëlle have been invited to collaborate in the creation of a new water-bound community in New Jersey, looking across the bay to Manhattan.

Port la Galère clings to a rocky point between Théoule and Miramar, about eleven km west of Cannes. Here in 1960, Charles-John Tiffen, the Parisian promoter of the scheme, purchased a big nineteenth-century house in twenty-three ha (sixty acres) of secluded grounds. Clothing the volcanic red-brown Estorel rock were eucalyptus, palms, umbrella pines, blue cedars, mimosa and cactus in profusion. Into this setting, over two decades, has been woven a compact and intricate development of over 400 houses and apartments —seemingly grown out of one another over generations.

The aim has been to offer each balcony, each terrace, each main window, at once privacy and a 180° view. Apartments range from two rooms to six, from about seventy sq metres (650 sq ft) to around 260 sq metres (2,300 sq ft). They may be

Port la Galère, tumbling down the rocky cliffside to the Mediterranean, its buildings as intricately interlocked as if they had grown out of one another over long years. The port itself has shops, bistro and moorings for 190 boats.

A single aerial serves the whole community.

on one floor, or two, or three. The interiors, like the exteriors, avoid the right angles of the drawing board like the plague—Port la Galère, says a promotional brochure, 'has beaten that terrible scourge of the modern age, uniformity.' Lines, curves, levels, screens, whether exterior or interior, have been carefully shaped to direct the eye, or the light, in certain ways; interior spaces and divisions are by no means evident from the exteriors. The evolution and execution of this most complex development inevitably called for exceptional teamwork between different disciplines. To the engineering problems posed by the nature of the site were added the intractable problems of setting down on paper forms which move in every dimension. It is not surprising that Couëlle's intentions were communicated largely by maquettes and wire models (the latter indicating interior and exterior surfaces simultaneously). Detailed design control in the final drawings and execution of the project was by a group of architects headed by Abro Kandjian and Leopold Vitorge.

Winding paths and walkways weave in and out of the cascading roofs and balconies. There are steps leading to miniature coves for bathing. At an upper level there is car parking for 200 cars and access to a multi-level underground garage; at a lower level, round the point to the east, a newly created port with space for 190 boats, and a quayside of shops, bistro, banks, ship's chandlers, and so on. The main club buildings are centred on the original house, radically adapted and extended; there are swimming pools, a tennis court, and another restaurant. The Club (*Société Civile du Club de Port la Galère*) is in fact the agency responsible for the management, operation and maintenance of the whole enclave. Club membership is compulsory; this, together with the fact that purchasers become shareholders in the parent company and co-owners of the estate, gives them overall control and direct say in the day-to-day running of its affairs.

Port la Galère demonstrates yet again what can be achieved by unified land ownership; by designing the inter-relationship of individual buildings and, in turn, their relationship to their sites; and by total attention to detail—from the intensive landscaping (by R. Joffet and J. M. Leclef), to the elimination of television aerials by a single, slim mast; from the careful composition of roofs and the view to be had from every single window, to the design of its harbour wall (the result of an architectural competition). The significance of Port la Galère stems not from architecture in the narrow sense, but from the vision which sustained it from start to finish. Something of the same tenacity underlays the very different Byker redevelopment in the north of England.

BYKER—*Newcastle, England*

Newcastle-upon-Tyne is the regional capital of north-eastern England—a city of some 300,000 people set within a substantially larger urban area, and reached across the river by five large bridges. It was founded as a minor fort on Hadrian's Wall and was for centuries subjected to, and a base for, marauding raids across the Scottish border. In the nineteenth century, coal, and then shipbuilding and heavy engineering, brought a period of great expansion. Changes of level answering Newcastle's dramatic topography give their own character to the city, and the streets planned in its commercial centre by Richard Grainger and John Dobson between 1835–40 are among the most handsome of their kind in England.

Over the last fifty years Newcastle has had to face industrial decline. Spirited efforts at renewal were made in the 1960s, with some success—but also not without blunders. Most striking of the city's post-war initiatives, in housing anyway, is Byker. Byker lies about one mile east of the city centre. At the start of the 1960s, it was a community of 17,000 people, typical of hundreds of similar working-class communities all over the north of England. Its long, steeply sloping terraces of Victorian housing, orginally built for skilled workers from the heavy industries downstream, ran down towards the river; the houses consisted of 'Tyneside flats', one on the upper floor and one below. Parts had been condemned. By 1963 the city council saw no alternative to total clearance and redevelopment.

The site covers some 200 acres (over eighty hectares). The English architect Ralph Erskine, who has spent his working life in Sweden, was invited, first to reappraise the city's own proposals for the area; subsequently to undertake the actual scheme. Building began in 1970 and continued for some thirteen years.

Erskine's objective was to build an integrated community for and with those already living in

Throughout Byker, there are glimpses of the unexpected: an ever-changing skyline, colour, courtyards and private gardens.

the area. His brief set a density of 247 persons per hectare; for the most part in low, two-storey buildings; it required the maximum number of private gardens, and extensive soft landscaping, generous parking space, and corner shops for each of the fifteen projected phases of the programme. To shut out a projected urban motorway immediately north of the site, Erskine planned a continuous perimeter wall, quickly to become known as the 'Byker Wall', which would shelter the rest of the development from the noise and disruption of the motorway (as well as from winter winds from the north). By building *along* the contours rather than *across* them, he would open up the view over the river and the city for as many people as possible, as well as minimizing the gradients for residents who had previously had to labour up slopes of one in seven.

Construction began with the 'Wall', because the site had been cleared for the motorway, and those living there already rehoused elsewhere. Thereafter, the City's original ambition to clear

up to 1,500 houses at a time was reduced to 250 or so, to enable a rolling programme to be planned—build/rehouse/clear/build/rehouse and so on. One other small parcel of cleared land was available, and it was decided to use this as a pilot for developing housing suitable for use elsewhere in Byker, and as a test-bed for tenant participation—above all with the forty-six families to be rehoused in this first area.

The architects had, at the outset, in September 1969, taken over corner premises on Brinkburn Street (of all things an undertaker's parlour) as a headquarters and information centre for the community. Two of the staff moved into the flat upstairs and more or less held 'open house'. People were encouraged to come to discuss the way the scheme was developing, their likes and dislikes, their requirements, their concerns and their problems (not always crucial: a missing hamster or 'can I use your phone?'). During the early years, many—especially the forty-six 'pilot' households—visited the office. The corner of Brinkburn Street, a colourful striped balloon painted on its flank wall, represented an exceptional attempt—in public housing—to bridge the gap between designers and users. Its success was not unqualified. *Before* moving in, residents were mostly concerned with the date of their move; *after* moving, problems and grievances emerged—which led in 1972 to the formation of a Tenants' Association to deal directly with the City Hall. One positive result, at Erskine's insistence, was that a system of 'forward allocation' was eventually instituted, by which people were told which house they would be offered, three to six months before its completion.

The new Byker which emerged reflects a long period of generalized soundings rather than individual participation in its creation. How could it be otherwise in so large a scheme? The main *raison d'être* of the Wall was removed by the later decision not to proceed with the proposed motorway (now the line of the city's new metro system)—or would Erskine have retained something of the kind anyway for the sense of enclosure it gives the rest of the scheme? His work in Sweden has made him very conscious of the need for shelter from the elements. The Wall itself is an undulating cliff, varying between two and twelve storeys high, which curves sinuously, on plan, for the best part of a mile from end to end. Its northern face, broken by minimal windows, is relieved by bold patterns of brickwork in deep reds and ochres. Roofs are bright blue, and its inner, southern face supports staggered timber 'clip-on' balconies—also in bright red and blue—which look out towards the city. The lower housing is grouped around private gardens and courtyards, linked by walkways and steps, thickly planted throughout. Not only has each phase of the scheme its own identity, but there is a great variety of housing, the characteristics of which—as in Port la Galère—ensure an absence of uniformity and give each tenant a sense of having his or her own particular home. Considering the size of the development as a whole, it is astoundingly non-monumental. Throughout, bright toytown colours—both paint and wood stain—have been used liberally to reinforce the sense of identity. The old Byker had neither colour, nor trees, nor gardens; the effect now, in a generally blackened industrial area, is enormously cheerful and exhilarating. Proof that people love living there is to be seen in the burgeoning gardens (the architects were always ready to advise on planting and even ran a plant shop for tenants) and in the low level of vandalism and graffiti. There is an effective and rapid re-planting policy to take care of what damage there is to the greenery.

Is this then the old Byker community come into its own? Only to a limited extent. Since 1970 the total population of the area has fallen by nearly sixty-five per cent. By 1980 the population was about 4,500, of whom it has been estimated that not much more than half are original Byker residents. Clearly the reasons for this are many, but perhaps most important are the intrinsic complications of trying to dovetail a rehouse/clear/build programme of this size. Between 1971 and 1973 around 500 dwellings were built, but about 2,300 were due for demolition. There were substantial buildings delays—stemming partly from increasing inflation. Uncertainty as to when their new homes would be ready led many families to opt for accommodation elsewhere. In the formative stages of the scheme so much emphasis was placed upon keeping the existing community intact that the exercise is now seen by some as a failure, notwithstanding its good intentions.

Perhaps there is no way in which an entire community of this size *can* be rehoused without losing some of the original inhabitants; Byker has retained many more than most such schemes even attempt to do. And it has attracted back the second generation of many of those who moved out from the old Byker in the 1950s and 1960s. It is very evident that at Byker—as at Port la Galère—a place has been created where people like to be.

The big 'Byker Wall' shelters the lower buildings of the development, where the lavish and sprightly planting is matched by immense efforts put into their own gardens by those who live there.

IV

INTEGRATING TRANSPORT

THE effect of urban transport systems upon the environment can be profound—not merely in the negative sense of rendering neighbourhoods untenable by reason of inadequate access, poor or costly service, noise, vibration, air pollution and so on, but, conversely, because they can make possible environmental improvements which would otherwise be impossible.

In the following pages are three examples of very positive approaches to the integration of transport and urban planning. The first is in Munich, where the finest traffic-free zone in Europe—perhaps in the world—provides a constant source of pleasure to all who use it. Many factors bear upon the success of this scheme: the inner ring road, the provision of generous parking space outside the ring, the street pattern and the traffic management measures within. The single most important factor, however, is the rapid transit metro system, which provides access to the heart of the pedestrian area; without this it is doubtful whether a scheme of such sophistication would have been possible.

Not all cities have rapid transit systems—but all cities have bus systems. Portland, Oregon, used the death of its main private enterprise bus company in 1969 as the occasion to create a municipally sponsored three-county network; and then used the need to restructure and improve the system itself as the occasion to reconstruct and improve a twenty-two block stretch of the centre of the city. Portland now has not only arguably the best bus system in the world, but also an exceptionally agreeable downtown area in which to stroll and shop.

Every city offers particular challenges and has particular potentialities. Seattle, in the State of Washington, brutally severed by an interstate highway, fought back by decking it over and creating a new park of particular lushness and verve above it. Only in the airspace above land already purchased and amortized, would such a park have been possible, for the cost of land acquisition in the city centre would have been prohibitive. Here, then, is a different example of how imaginative exploitation of a transport system can offer an environmental gain. If the will be strong enough, nothing is impossible.

Munich's traffic-free central area stretches for nearly one kilometre east to west, and not much less from north to south.

MUNICH—*West Germany*

Munich, the capital of Bavaria, is the third largest city in West Germany, with a population of around 1.5 million and growing by about 40,000 a year. It is an industrial centre, claims the biggest university in the country and attracts more than 3.5 million visitors every year.

The foundation of the city dates from the early fourteenth century, when it was fortified for the second time by Emperor Ludwig of Bavaria. Three gates remain from that time. In the twelfth century, the Duchy of Bavaria passed to the Wittelsbachs, whose association with the city continued until the close of the First World War. From them, Munich gained a continuing taste for the arts, as well as an extraordinary wealth of artistic treasures—not only its remarkable churches, its royal palaces and its splendid civic buildings, but the great collections and works of art which they house, of which the Alte Pinakothek is but the most famous. Musical life has ever been strong; there are some forty theatres; shopping (the city sees itself as the fashion centre of Germany) and food are excellent. Small wonder that Munich plays host to 1,200 or more conferences annually.

The city suffered sixty-six air raids during World War II. Damage was extensive, particularly to the historic inner city—the traditional cultural and shopping centre—which accounts for perhaps one and a half square kilometres of the fifty covered by the city as a whole. Redevelopment plans were aimed, first, at restructuring the Old Town so as to restore to it its original functions—threatened by new hypermarkets and other shopping facilities springing up on the city's outer fringes; secondly, at developing public transport systems integrating the city with its region and the Land as a whole.

The means were unexceptional. In a city with a forty per cent car ownership, they included a drastic reduction in the use of cars in the central area, coupled with a large measure of pedestrianization; an inner ring road at a radius of about three-quarters of a kilometre from the centre, with parking spaces outside the ring and firm traffic control within it; and a very high level of public transport—specifically a new U-Bahn or metro system and a sub-surface railway link between the main Federal Railway station and the East station, which would increase the forty-five-minute catchment area of the city from 500 sq km to 1,500 sq km. The city centre became accessible at a stroke to many more people. Similar proposals have been made for many great cities in the last twenty-five years. What was exceptional about Munich's plans was that they were implemented scrupulously and have succeeded triumphantly.

Studies were made through the 1960s, but doubtless it was the city's hosting of the 1972 Olympic Games which concentrated minds; detailed plans were approved in 1969. The arm-

ature of the proposals lay in the cross formed by the north/south-west axis running between Odeonplatz-Marienplatz-Torplatz and the east/west axis running between Karlstor-Marienplatz to the Old City Hall. This effectively quarters the historic centre, enclosed by the inner ring road. Both axes are approximately one kilometre in length. Until the 1960s the area was choked with motor vehicles and trams.

The viability of the pedestrian area depended on access provided by new transport. The subsurface railway link between the two mainline stations was therefore begun in 1967, more or less concurrently with the first sixteen km of the metro (the full network, serving the whole city, was scheduled for completion in 1985). Work on the mall itself was undertaken between the completion of the latter in autumn 1970 and the opening of the Olympics in the summer of 1972. Its design was the subject of a competition. The two winners, the architects Bernhard Winkler and Siegfried Meschederu, were selected to work on the final scheme.

The area is extensive, but filled throughout with visual incident. Neuhauserstrasse/Kaufingerstrasse are for most of their length around twenty to twenty-two metres in width, and contrast intriguingly with the narrower spurs off on either side. Historic buildings—the 1710 Bürgersall with its orange walls and white pilasters; the Old Academy and St Michael's Church, both of 1597; the Old Town Hall of 1474; and a few yards away the Frauenkirche Cathedral, the eleventh-century Church of St Peter, and the Baroque Theaterkirche of 1677—lend a strong sense of continuity to the area.

Post-war building—mostly commercial—is either straightforward reconstruction or in the blandly non-committal modern style which Germany has used rather effectively in rebuilding its historic towns. The big, chunky Kaufhof store which looks across Marienplatz to the new Town Hall is totally of today. All in all a lively mix, avoiding preciosity, eschewing vulgarity.

There are pools and fountains, the largest at the Karlstor Bastion, with 200 jets, and in the Frauenplatz, where the lines in the pavement lead into an amphitheatre-like depression filled with water. There is a constantly changing display of shrubs and flowers, massed in 300 hexagonal

Visually the area is richly various, with old buildings and new in juxtaposition; lively but dignified paving, planting and lighting; and cafés and restaurants adding sparkle and life. Left: the Richard Strauss fountain by Hans Wimmer; the Burgersaal of 1710. Far right: the City Hall and Marienplatz, from which, below, the northern spur runs towards the Theaterkirche.

stacking concrete troughs containing plant boxes. There are show cases; lighting is by decorative clusters of plexiglass globes; and, apart from the cinemas, theatre and museum, some twenty eating places provide open-air seating for 1,200 (Munich probably lives out of doors more than any other city north of the Alps.) At night many of the buildings are floodlit.

The paving patterns are strong yet restrained, in grey and red granite, sometimes separated by mosaic strips. Great care has been taken to integrate stop-cocks and valve box covers into the design, and to lay underground services under a relatively brittle crust of mineral concrete so that repairs cause minimal disruption.

Vans and lorries deliver to the shops and restaurants between 10.30 p.m. and 9.45 a.m. (or midday in the area round the Frauenkirche)—though seventy per cent of the stores have rear access anyway. The maximum permitted axle-load is three and a half tonnes; vehicles are kept at walking pace speed and are not allowed to turn. Small electric run-abouts clean the streets, and a shuttle service of electric buses is proposed for the elderly and infirm.

There were doubts at the outset whether such extensive outdoor spaces would come to life. The fears were groundless. A survey undertaken in 1966 showed 72,000 people passing through Kaufinger-Neuhauserstrasse during a twelve-hour period; in 1972 there were 120,000. The figures for the same area as a whole are in excess of 300,000 daily, and trading profits have risen by a spectacular forty per cent. Throughout the year there are seasonal events, and during the Christmas Market, even under a blanket of snow, the Marienplatz remains alive with movement and activity.

A few further points to complete the picture. A proposal to enlarge the inner ring to three-lane motorway standards involved so much destruction that public opinion vetoed it. A more modest road was built and this appears to work perfectly adequately. Parking within the ring has been reduced from 16,000 places to fewer than 5,000 in multi-storey and underground garages, with strict curbs on on-street parking; there is generous provision outside the ring, with park-and-ride facilities.

Bavaria was one of the first German states to concern itself—in the early nineteenth century—with the protection of its architectural heritage. Munich today retains the same strong sense of tradition and local pride. For instance, in 1968, the City Council launched a campaign to cheer up and enrich its streets; so successful was this that in the following year the Council offered ten prizes of 1,000 DM for the best renovated façades—and from 1973 the number was increased to twenty. As a result, between 300 and 400 such renovations are now registered annually, at an estimated cost to their owners of DM 10 million. Again, at a time when the municipality was not keen to do so, the reconstruction was mooted of the tower-gate of the Old City Hall, at the eastern end of the Mall; the citizens responded by subscribing around DM 1 million, half the cost, for its rebuilding. Finally, the entire capital cost of the pedestrian zone—DM 1.6 million—was met by the City itself, without subventions from elsewhere. Societies get the surroundings they deserve; Munich, one feels, deserves its historic centre.

Marienplatz, against its backdrop of the City Hall, buzzes with activity throughout the year. In December, it is the site of the city's Christmas Market.

PORTLAND MALL—*Oregon*

Portland, Oregon, America's tenth largest port, is a city of 363,000 people, within a wider metropolitan area of well over one million. At the foot of the Cascades range, astride the River Willamette, its western setting is of afforested hills. It has some magnificent parks, and two historic districts on the fringe of the downtown area. It can claim more cast-iron fronted buildings—even though only twenty remain from the original 180 or more—than any American city, save New York. It likes to be called 'a city of fountains'. The concrete freeway system has been blanketed with shrubs, creepers, heathers and trees. And since the late 1970s, Portland has boasted the most civilized bus system in the world.

Ten years earlier, Portland was suffering ills common to many big cities. The port's container traffic was moving downstream. The downtown shopping and office area was in decline. There was serious air pollution. Public transport was caught in the familiar descending spiral of falling passenger figures, rising fares and increasing cuts in services. By 1969 the position of the two main private bus companies—Rose City Transit and the Blue Lines Bus System—had become impossible (annual passenger figures on Rose City had declined from 60 million in 1960 to 15 million in 1969).

Oregon State Legislature having voted the enabling legislation, Portland City Council, set up a three-county transport district and operating organization. Tri-Met came into being, taking over Rose City's elderly and faltering system at the end of 1969, Blue Line's nine months later.

Concurrently, in 1970, the city's business and property community, alarmed at the continued decline of the downtown area, formed a Downtown Committee to press for more positive action. As a result of their efforts, the City sponsored a planning study—jointly financed by the public and private sectors. A Citizens' Advisory Committee was appointed by the Mayor to assist in its formulation.

In the best Oregon tradition, the plan, when it appeared in 1972, integrated proposals for transportation, renewal, environmental improvement and the reduction of air pollution. A better bus network, it was suggested, could wean the public from their cars: the vehicle load on the road system would be reduced, air pollution diminished, fuel consumption cut. At the same time, the transport modernization programme could improve the centre of the city and put new heart into the ailing downtown area. The concept of Portland Mall, approved in principle by the City the previous year, was finally established.

The Tri-Met network, now divided into seven service areas, covers more than 1,000 square miles and over 1,750 route miles, the whole system funnelling through Portland. It was proposed that the complicated trans-city routing should be consolidated into two parallel streets—Fifth and Sixth Avenues—from which other traffic should be virtually excluded. For Tri-Met this, in conjunction with scheduling changes, could cut the time taken to cross the city by as much as half, thus tripling the system's potential carrying capacity. The proposed package included eliminating over 1,750 on-street parking spaces by 1975 (and limiting any newly constructed off-street spaces to no more than that number), together with park-and-ride facilities.

Skidmore, Owings and Merrill were appointed as consultants to design the scheme in detail, with Lawrence Halprin Associates (now CHNMB Associates) responsible for much of the landscaping. Their proposals were accepted in principle by the City in 1963, published in 1964, and were made the subject of a formal City ordinance, following approval by the Federal Urban Mass Transportation Administration (UMTA), who were to be responsible for much of the funding, in the same year.

The Mall involved the redesign of Fifth and Sixth Avenues over a length of eleven blocks—more than half a mile each—making it the largest of its kind in America. The fifteen-foot pavements were increased by half as much again; two twenty-four-foot bus lanes run throughout, one-way in each street, and a third lane for access vehicles runs past eight of the eleven blocks—the three restricted stretches serving as barriers to through traffic. Cross movement, at right angles to the Mall, is permitted.

The whole twenty-two-block length of the Mall has been completely repaved in brick and granite, and 290 new trees—sycamores, limes and plane trees—have been planted. All street furniture is new, save the refurbished cast-iron street lamps and the drinking fountains donated to the city during the Prohibition era to help save Portland citizens from the demon drink. The Mall is further enlivened by five fountains and waterfalls ('city of fountains') and at least eleven big sculptures, which were specially purchased or commissioned. Portland Mall makes a good place to

Buses and pedestrians only in the two parallel avenues which make up Portland Mall. Throughout there is new paving, planting and street furniture—except for the occasional refurbished drinking fountain left over from the Prohibition era. Route maps (left) explain the bus system; bus shelters (above) include a free phone for information and a closed-circuit screen announcing the arrival of the next bus.

shop and saunter, even if you are not using the bus system.

If you *are* so minded, but a stranger to the town, you would start with one of the eight trip-planning kiosks. The 'Rider Information System' co-ordinates maps, television screens, charts and coloured symbols. Maps of the system display the network; detailed route maps identify the points served by a particular line; the seven service areas are each coded by a separate symbol and a different colour, which will direct you to your proper shelter or stop. Buses, shelters, timetables—everything will be signposted by this symbol and this colour. Is something unclear? Lift the free phone for a direct line to transit HQ, and when they have solved your problem, punch a computer terminal for a timetable and the arrival time of the bus you want at this particular shelter. Tri-Met was the first—and perhaps remains the only—bus system in the United States to use closed-circuit television in conjunction with such a computerized route and scheduling system.

The shelters themselves, of bronze and plexiglass, suggest an up-dated and slightly festive memory of Art Nouveau; they are weatherproof, very unclaustrophobic, friendly, clean, with plenty of room to sit. There are thirty-five of them altogether in the Mall, and they cost (1979 figures) $37,000 apiece.

The Mall lies within Tri-Met's 'Fareless Square', covering over 300 city blocks, within which any bus, any time, is free. Outside the Square there are now three regular fares, depending on distance, (the system is divided into five zones). A whole range of reduced fares is available on different buses: there are 24-hour tickets; there are Monthly Passes—which for evenings and weekends become Family Passes, allowing up to three children to travel free; there are Youth Passes for students; an 'Honored Citizen' card, or Medicare card, allows free travel outside working hours and reduced fares at other times. Fifteen mini-buses are specially equipped for the physically handicapped. More than seventy park-and-ride points provide 3,600 parking spaces, and from them a Bus Pool scheme serves sponsoring centres of employment on request. Tri-Met further administers a Car Pool scheme (outside the Mall, bus and three-person car pool lanes are provided), seeing all forms of transport in the area as part of a single, integrated system.

Until 1980, the system handled over 40 million

passengers a year, on sixty-six routes. Whereas, over the region as a whole, four per cent of all journeys are by bus and ninety-six per cent by car or other means, in central Portland, it could be claimed, thirty-six per cent of all trips were now made by bus. The service, including the direct phone information service, operated well-nigh round the clock, seven days a week.

Tri-Met's income is derived from fares, plus an employment pay-roll tax of 0.6 per cent on payrolls of employees in the three-county area, plus (at the end of the 1970s) an operating subsidy of approximately $5 million p.a. from the federal government through UMTA. Support was also available from UMTA for eighty per cent of the nearly $16 million capital cost of redesigning Portland Mall. But in cities nothing stands still. That is the challenge. By the start of the 1980s the Western world was slipping into recession. Tri-Met, tied tightly by its payroll tax revenue to the state of the Oregon economy, found itself faced by a decline in its bread-and-butter passenger traffic and in its payroll tax income. Concurrently the Reagan administration announced it would be phasing out federal (UMTA) operating subsidies by 1985. There was nothing for it but to trim back—by staff cuts, service reductions (5,000 hours over 1984/5), and restructuring fares and zones. Over three 'tight' budget cycles something like $11 million has been lopped off the expenditure column.

A painful period. But it was not all gloom. Nearly fifty miles of bus lanes and exclusive bus roads are to be established. In 1981 the first new advanced-design buses were ordered. And the big news was the development of the Banfield Light Rail line—today's equivalent to the tram, or streetcar, of yesteryear. The fifteen-mile line, due to be opened in 1986, aims to carry people from Portland to Gresham in 45 minutes, to take tens of thousands of commuters off the road system, and, it is claimed, to save $4 million annually as compared with the bus service (each unit will carry 300 passengers). At an outlay of $211.7 million, it has been Oregon's biggest public works programme. Almost willy-nilly it has involved further environmental improvements—widened pavements, repaving, tree planting. Around half a million cobbles or setts, retrieved from under the asphalt and stored by the city since 1975, will have been used.

It seems all of a piece with city programmes generally—the Urban Conservation Fund of $550,000 which provides loans to private owners, and the waterfront redevelopment which is turning a decaying wasteland into housing, a marina and a park. There are familiar complaints that business in Portland Mall is not what was hoped for. Could it have been? Would anyone wish to turn the clock back? Portland has given itself a civilized central area; its innovative transport system gathers award after award, year after year. It is impossible to separate the two.

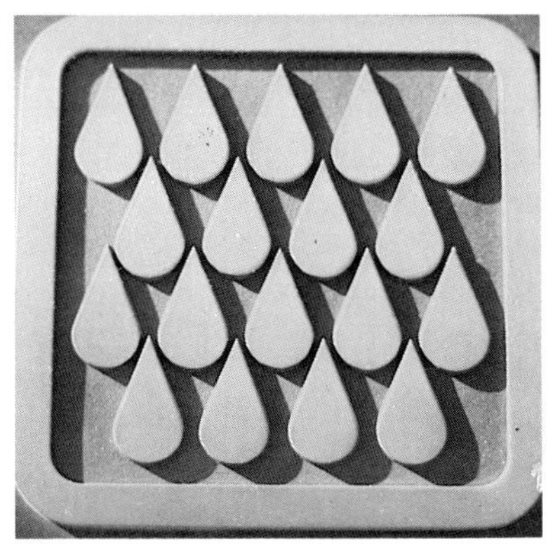

Each route, each bus, shelter and stop, is identified by its own symbol.

SEATTLE—*Washington State*

From Portland, Interstate 5 runs northwards to Seattle, on its way from the Mexican border to Canada. In 1966 the final link through Seattle was completed, cutting a canyon through the heart of the city and severing pedestrian access between First Hill, with its hospitals and residential blocks, and the main downtown office and commercial area to the west. Along the ten lanes of this concrete ribbon surge around 133,300 vehicles every weekday, rising at peak periods to 13,000 an hour.

Even as the Freeway was being completed, there was talk of putting a 'lid' on this downtown section, but the idea remained unrealistic for some years. However, factors gradually came together to make the suggestion worthy of serious consideration.

First, as part of the wide-ranging Forward Thrust campaign (see page 228) the voters of King County, which embraces the City of Seattle and Metropolitan Seattle, approved bond resolutions to the tune of $334 million for social and environmental programmes. Of this, a sizeable chunk was ear-marked for parks and park facilities in Seattle. Second, the city was seeking a site for a large municipal multi-storey car park near the Freeway to reduce central area congestion. Third, a developer—Richard C. Hedreen—was seeking a site for a new twenty-one-storey tower block. Fourth, Federal and State highway funding was secured to deck over the freeway between Seneca Street and University Street (further funds were subsequently made available for the construction of a second deck to the south of Seneca Street). From these and other sources—not least the determination of certain leading citizens, led by James R. Ellis, Chairman of the Forward Thrust campaign—sprang Freeway Park, a unique example of city planning which was opened to the public at a dedication ceremony in April 1976.

Freeway Park covers 5.4 acres. It spans more than 400 ft of Interstate 5, and has parking space for 630 cars. On the south side it builds up from the bottom of the freeway canyon in a series of transitional boxes and terraces, growing more extensive until they coalesce into the upper decks of the main park, the whole supported by precast concrete girders up to 133 ft in length. As the planting matures, the hanging boxes leading up to the park will be totally hidden by their greenery.

The park itself was designed by Lawrence Halprin Associates (now CHNMB Associates)—who were responsible for landscaping the Portland Mall. It ranges from a simple 'meadow' over the garage to sumptuously rich planting in the Central Plaza to the north. Spaces flow easily and intriguingly into one another. Water—as in

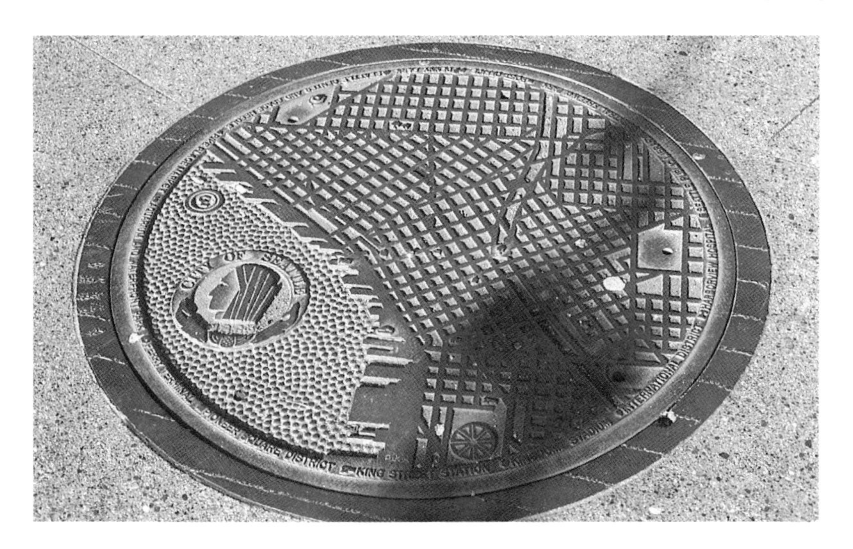

Pride of place is strong in Seattle. Even the manhole covers are special—a simplified map of the city.

so many other American cities—has been used with panache. The Naramore Fountain was relocated in the southern section; in the Central Plaza there is a cascade and a 'canyon' in which 27,000 gallons of water are recirculated every minute—the crash of its thirty-three-foot fall totally drowning the sounds of the city.

Planting was designed to cope with intense summer sun, harsh winds resulting from the park's exposed position and higher-than-average air pollution. Soil is inevitably shallow—a mix of ⅔ fine sand and ⅓ peat moss for light weight and drainage—and the automatic irrigation system maintains a constant level of nutrients in the soil by means of a system of fertilizer injection. Species include Bradford pear, deodar, Douglas fir, small leaved lime, magnolia, maple, English oak, red oak and sweet gum. In all, 279 deciduous trees were planted and 195 evergreens. The 'Friends of Freeway Park', an association of five business firms, have made themselves responsible for the constant display of flowers, at a cost of $30,000 per annum.

The total bill amounted to over $13.75 million (1976 figures). This was broken down as follows:

Decks bridging over the freeway	$5,525,000
Parking garage	$4,200,000
Park	$5,067,000

The decks were paid for out of Federal and State Highway funds; the garage by local authority bonds. A whole range of sources, official and unofficial, met the cost of the park itself, including $17,000 from the American Legion, who presented the children's pool. $2,800,000 was provided through the Park Bonds of Forward Thrust.

The garage is expected to pay for its construction, bringing the total public investment figures down to $9,594,000, or $45 per sq ft. What this means is that, as a result of co-operation between city, county, state and federal authorities, together with private enterprise, Freeway Park cost the ratepayers less than the land alone in this part of the city would have cost to purchase and clear (assuming it could have been purchased at all), and without counting the cost of works on the park itself at all. Further, construction of the Park Place building (developer Hedreen's new block) has meant an increase in rateable value (property tax revenue) from which the city benefits. Thus downtown Seattle has, at a cost which will seem increasingly derisory as the years go by, acquired an exceptional place in which to saunter and relax.

Ten lanes of interstate highway slice through downtown Seattle; part is now decked over to form Freeway Park. Opposite: the build-up to the platform.

This page: the sparkle of the Naramore Fountain and the flash of flowers; below, a glimpse of the meadow—all man-made in the airspace over the motorway.

V
MARKET PLACE

SHOPPING has long provided the force which has held together the different elements of the urban fabric. Now, in the space of a generation, shopping has changed its whole nature, raising profound issues of urban design. By rationalizing distribution into large units, costs have been cut; and the concentration of a wide range of goods under one roof has proved convenient and time-saving for the customer. As a result, in most cities, the number of neighbourhood stores and small family shops has shrunk dramatically; bankruptcies have escalated.

In the process, shopping has become an impersonal activity. It will probably become more so with the impact of the micro-chip upon ordering and delivery patterns. The friendly greeting, the neighbourly contact, the gossip at the corner shop —little encounters which help to give stability to a community—for many people, these are already no more than a romantic memory. In reaction to the bleakness of the supermarket a quite different form of shopping is beginning to develop—in malls, in markets, in arcades: shopping as a leisure pursuit in its own right.

It began with the hypermarkets and out-of-town shopping centres. Their controlled and traffic-free environment, enlivened by fountains, banners, sculptures, murals, mobiles, trees and flowers, sought to bring back an element of glamour to shopping. The atrium building offered not only security, particularly comforting to the American public, but new design possibilities—dramatically exploited, in another context, by John Portman in his hotels. As shopping centres proliferated, their promoters decked them out with ever more exotic trimmings. The first result, as we have seen, was that life was sucked from traditional trading areas in the city. Increasingly, older shopping streets have given the impression of hanging on against the tide, of being tired, worn-out, and rather inconvenient. Premises tend to look uncared-for or else frenetically jazzed-up in a sad simulation of prosperity. Small shop-keepers go out of business first; then the larger stores.

And yet—was not something lacking in the big hypermarkets too? William H. Whyte has described the effect of the megastructure building. 'There is no sense of place. One feels disembodied. Is it night? Or day? Spring? Or Winter? And where are you? You cannot see out. You cannot tell what city you are in, or whether it is in the East or the West or even a foreign country. Piped music gives no clue. You are in a universally controlled environment. And it is a deadly bore.'[24]

People began to have second thoughts. The rising cost of petrol began to make the suburban and out-of-town centre less attractive as a regular trip. High Street traders looked again at their traditional assets—personal service, speciality goods, shop fronts and counters not made of plastic, the nostalgia for a vanished past. In Britain, at the end of the 1950s, the Civic Trust demonstrated how quite ordinary streets could be brought back to life—at a modest cost—by a collective, co-operative effort. The superficialities of the operation were picked up by North America under the tag of 'beautification', and for the Bicentennial hundreds of Main Streets began to deck themselves out in instant 'history'—'gas' lamps, phoney colony signs and fascias, beetling 'mansard' brows, and Wild West taverns. On the whole Disney did it better.

Latterly the American National Trust has been nudging Main Streets into a more sophisticated type of rescue operation (see page 221). At the same time new US tax reliefs have made the conversion of old warehouses, cinemas and courthouses attractive to commercial developers. Many such buildings have been turned into shopping centres offering more genuine, or at least friendlier, settings than their suburban counterparts. This recycling caught the mood of the moment; shopping began to be fun.

Creating communal spaces for shopping, eating and meeting is hardly new. Resorts and spas were built around the idea. Milan's Galeria, opened in 1867 was a resounding success from the outset (though sadly it has lost much of its one-time elegance since World War II). Towns all over Europe sought to emulate Milan (Balzac has described something of the life of the Parisan arcades) and the idea caught on in America too (Cleveland, Ohio's 1890 arcade, the largest, has in recent years been restored to something of its former grandeur).

The traffic-free shopping street which has emerged in the past thirty years, seen at its most splendid in Munich, differs only in extent and the absence of an overhead canopy from the arcade. In malls, markets or arcades, people rediscovered the pull of the Roman forum—the pleasures of a place in which to congregate, to sit in the sun, to watch the passing show and to debate eternal truths.

Ghiradelli Square, in San Francisco, was the daddy of one kind of these new market places. Looking east across the Bay, and marked by a handsome clock tower, it was originally a chocolate factory; in 1962 the whole complex was threatened with demolition. However, William Roth, a San Franciscan, and his mother acquired it to demonstrate that such buildings could still have a useful life. Over the following six years they gradually transformed Ghiradelli Square into a speciality shopping centre which rapidly became one of *the* places any visitor to San Francisco had to see. In the Californian climate, who needs a canopy?

Ghiradelli Square begat a host of offspring in North America: Trolley Square in Salt Lake City (an ex-tramway terminus), Underground City in Atlanta, Gaslight Square in St Louis, Market Square in Victoria, Vancouver Island—as well as countless individual buildings like Georgetown Market House in Washington DC, and the white cream-cake Century Theatre in Chicago. Not all sustained their initial success. The major breakthrough came with the Rouse Company's commercial triumph in Quincy Market, in Boston—until the 1960s the city's main fruit and vegetable market.

It is interesting to compare the different approaches of three great cities—Paris, London and Boston—to the same problem. In each case the decision to move their central market was taken, for the same reasons, in the early 1960s; in each case first thoughts turned to grandiose redevelopment.

Paris moved forward—tragically—to the demolition of the magnificent nineteenth-century structures of Les Halles in 1971, despite widespread protest. The project quickly became a political shuttlecock (ending up as the personal responsibility of Mayor Chirac—who pulled down a building designed by Boffil which was under construction on the northern side), and no one had any clear idea of what to do with the site (even by the beginning of the 1980s half the area had yet to be redeveloped). From 1968, however, one reference point remained firm, which was to create a new shopping centre on part of the site, and this was in fact opened in 1980. The Forum des Halles is a vast, sunken, four-level shopping complex around a central piazza with glazed arcades at the upper levels. It contains about 200 shops, led by such internationally known names as Pierre Cardin and Yves St Laurent, as well as

Three twentieth-century marketplaces. Fun-shopping, in its present form, began in Ghiradelli Square, overlooking the Bay in San Francisco (left) and below. Paris took a different direction and replaced Les Halles with a modern hypermarket/entertainment centre (foot of page).

restaurants, cinemas and various cultural facilities (financed by an annual levy on the traders of initially seventy francs per square metre of trading space). Shops stay open until eight p.m. five nights a week, and most of the Forum (the restaurants forming an initial exception) is crowded and animated. The promoters claim an average annual turnover of F. Fr. 47,000 (over £4,500) per square metre.

Boston, after various twists and turns, backtracked from comprehensive redevelopment and opted for the re-use of Quincy Market and its two parallel warehouse buildings as a speciality shopping centre of the new type. Faneuil Hall Market, as it is known, broke new ground: because it is in a downtown area; because its 150 outlets were not underpinned, as is usual in hypermarkets, by any major retailers; and because the exploitation of its space, masterminded by the Rouse Company, was intensive. In the first year of trading, even push-cart stalls cleared sales of $500 per square foot; a mere couple of years after the market's re-opening in 1976, total sales had reached nearly $40 million per annum; eight years later they were running at more than $88 million. Eighteen million people are now said to pass through the market in a year, and a major problem is how to dispose of the trash (needless to say, maintenance is in fact excellent).

From the outset, proposals for London's Covent Garden area envisaged retaining the market building itself, re-building practically everything else. How redevelopment was transformed into conservation is touched on below. Covent

When Boston, Massachusetts, banished its fruit and vegetable market, it took a lead from Ghiradelli Square and recycled Quincy Market—to be followed in turn by Covent Garden in London (overleaf).

Garden is infinitely smaller than Les Halles; smaller than, but more comparable with, Quincy Market. Nonetheless, in its quieter way, Covent Garden is squarely in the growing tradition of shopping for fun.

Central area hypermarkets are not unknown. Gruen Associates can maybe claim the earliest with their Mid-town Plaza in Rochester, N.Y.; Eldon Square in Newcastle, is an English example; Toronto's Eaton Centre another impressive example. However, the Boston experience fired the Rouse Company—ironically, until then a firm concerned with just those out-of-town sites which have had such a dire effect upon central area shopping—to look at a host of downtown sites which might work in the same way: Market Street in Philadelphia; South Street Seaport in Manhattan; the railway station in St Louis; the old Navy Pier in Chicago. If there were no old buildings but the site seemed right, they set out to create the same atmosphere in new buildings (for example, Santa Monica Place, South California, and Harborplace in Baltimore (see page 187).

These are not hypermarkets in the accepted sense. Like the Galleria in Milan all those years ago, with its 100 shops, restaurants, cafés and bars, they offer a blend of shopping, eating and meeting. Traders and caterers chosen with immense care, are guided towards a particular sector of the market, and their services are monitored in great detail (the food, for example, is sampled by Rouse's marketing people, and its style and content amended on their advice). Frontages and signs are controlled by a Manual of Tenant Criteria, which, in effect, forms an extension of the lease. 'We like flags and banners and perpendicular signs because we think they add to the festive quality of the public area.' Showmanship and the fiesta spirit, a sort of controlled informality, have been brought into the market place; the objective, as in the resorts and spas of a century and a half ago, is to offer release from the workaday world—to create places where people like to be. 'We'd like to have the kind of environment in our malls', says one Rouse quote, 'where somebody could bring a bag lunch and sit down by a water fountain or a mini-park and feel very comfortable, even if he doesn't buy anything (though it goes on: 'we believe that he will buy something, and researches have told us this is true').

As with any form of transition, control is not easy. The Faneuil Hall area now seethes with people like a successful 'theme park'—and indeed the border between some of these brasher developments and the theme park is not always clear cut. Allan Temko, of the University of California, has laid into Pier 39 in San Francisco—a 'reconstruction' of the city at the turn of the century—as 'Corn. Kitsch. Schlock. Honky-Tonk. Dreck. Schmalz. Pseudo-Victorian Junk creating an ersatz San Francisco that never was'. The sophisticated have dismissed even a more straightforward formula of boutiques and ethnic fast-food eateries as trendy nonsense, their settings as cliché-ridden pastiche. But then fantasy has always been part of escape—think only of Prinny's Brighton Pavilion. Success *need* not push objectives over the top. What is important about such schemes lies surely in the pointers they offer as to why people enjoy being in one kind of setting more than another. And that has implications everywhere.

There is the further point that, almost by definition, such developments take place in decayed areas which are in need of renewal. To what extent can they themselves spearhead renewal? Leo A. Molinari, President of American City Corporation, a subsidiary of the Rouse Company, has said: 'Retail follows. It does not lead. It comes when there are people there to use it.' Nonetheless, successful centres of this kind can clearly create powerful economic generators and, at the least, strongly reinforce wider planning objectives with that same magnetic force that shopping always has. This was certainly the strategic aim behind the decision to restore and adapt the Fowler building in Covent Garden.

COVENT GARDEN—*England*

With the removal from Covent Garden of the traditional fruit, vegetable and flower market in 1974, there passed from central London one of the capital's most colourful spectacles—a great jostle of barrows and baskets and movement, of smells and colour and language no less colourful; a place where the pubs opened long before dawn—and the place where Eliza Doolittle continues to be rediscovered under the portico of St Paul's Church each time the curtain rises on *Pygmalion* or *My Fair Lady*.

To Londoners generally, and to planners in particular, 'Covent Garden' is also used to describe a much bigger area of 100 acres (40 ha) lying between Shaftesbury Avenue and High Holborn to the north and the Strand to the south, Charing Cross Road to the west and Kingsway to the east. It is an area in which only about 3,000 people lived but 37,000 work; an area long in decay, partly because of uncertainty about its future. With the removal of the market, the whole area seemed ripe, in the atmosphere of the 1960s, for comprehensive redevelopment and renewal.

It was just such a plan that the Greater London Council produced in 1968: a drastically hygienic plan of big blocks and 'big thinking'. A storm of public abuse resulted.

Covent Garden: today, looking out from the restored building towards the portico of Inigo Jones' St Paul's Church.

Revised proposals were published in 1971 and went to public inquiry. Odhams Press, a major newspaper publisher in the area, closed. The Covent Garden Community Association was founded to fight the GLC's proposals. In 1973, the Secretary of State for the Environment, Mr Geoffrey Rippon, rejected his Inspector's report arising from the public inquiry and, almost overnight, created a new set of constraints by officially listing 250 buildings in the area as of architectural or historical interest. He instructed the GLC to draw up a new plan with full public participation.

A long period of confused lobbying, confrontation, special pleading, changes of course and community initiatives of one kind and another followed; to some extent this continues. Essentially, however, the concept of incremental—rather than blanket—renewal has been accepted and is being steadily pursued, the starting point being the revitalization of the old vegetable market.

The Market has been centred upon Inigo Jones' 1630s' piazza—an arcaded square, conceived in the manner of the Place Royale in the Marais but which never quite materialized. In the middle of this square sits the main market building, the 'Dedicated Building' as it was first called, designed by Charles Fowler, and built between 1828 and 1830. A little like Quincy Market in Boston, it consists of three parallel buildings—but fronted at the east end by a stone colonnade. Over this runs a terrace, partly covered by two conservatories. In 1875 and in 1888 the two courtyards between the buildings were glazed over by cast-iron roofs.

From the moment it was known that the Market would be leaving, it had been decided to retain the Fowler building, but a variety of uses for it had been mooted—including use as a helicopter pad.

In the event however—almost inevitably it now seems—the decision was taken to use it, much as Quincy Market, as a speciality shopping centre, and as such it was opened to the public in the summer of 1980. The approach is lower key than in Boston, the activity less frenetic. This is partly a matter of size: the Fowler building is only one third the size of Quincy Market and the numbers passing through, about four million people in the first year as opposed to around twelve million, reflect this. Partly perhaps it is because the building itself was regarded as all-important, and its scrupulous restoration by the Historic Buildings Division of the GLC took precedence over commercial trading values.

Marketing of the building was undertaken by the GLC's Covent Garden Planning Team, from its office on the corner of the piazza, in conjunction with a well-established firm of chartered surveyors, Donaldsons. Certain principles were

Restored and opened up, the Market consists of three parallel ranges of buildings, the spaces between which were covered over in the nineteenth century. Shops, cafés and restaurants are at two main levels. In the background there is likely to be a traditional jazz band or a string quartet. Right: a temporary witticism fills a space nearby until long-term development.

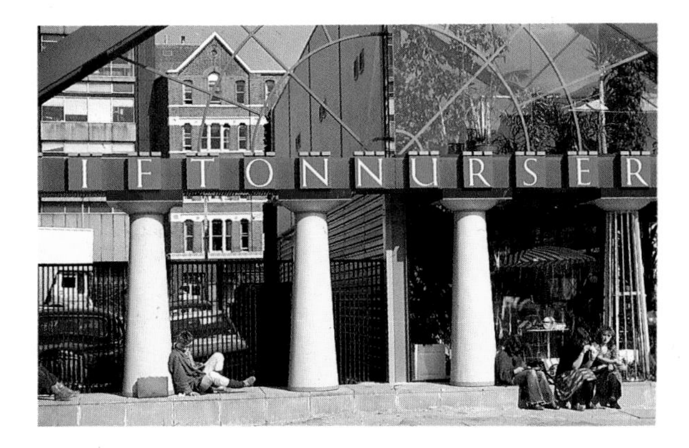

established at the outset. The Market was to be an integrated unit, a combined magnet, the elements of which should complement and not compete with one another. It should avoid the more routine concerns of the workaday shopping street (some prohibitions were quite specific—no souvenir shops, no denim clothing). These criteria meant that the mix must not be dictated simply by the highest bids (and in fact there is no set rental level—some trades pay more than others). Food and drink was seen as a magnet—but not so overwhelmingly as in Boston. Shops must remain open until 8 p.m.

A first trawl produced over 1,000 applicants. From these, 250 'potentials' were selected for further interview, from whom seventy-seven retailers and twenty-five caterers were finally identified for detailed negotiations. Leases of twenty-five years or more, with five-year reviews, were offered to caterers; of fifteen years, with three-year reviews, to traders. The final mix of forty-five to fifty included, at random, shops dealing in game and poultry, children's books, plants and flowers, original and rare newspapers, dolls' houses, kitchenware, confectionery, Pollock's Toy Theatres; there is an art gallery, a show of holograms, a crêperie, a health food bar—in addition to wine bars, restaurants and a pub. In the Northern Hall is the 'Apple Market', where forty brightly painted old iron flower stands and some coster barrows salvaged from days gone by are used free by 250 craftsmen a week, on a daily licence basis, to sell their work. (Provision for longer-term licences, valid for one or two days a week, has since been made.)

The units are none of them large, varying from 80 sq ft (9 sq metres) to 1,800 sq ft (200 sq metres) for shops, 1,500 sq ft (165 sq metres) to 4,000 sq ft (440 sq metres) for caterers. Although the building offers 52,000 sq ft (4,800 sq metres) of lettable space, no less than 30,000 sq ft (2,800 sq metres) of this is at basement level—and the warren of small vaulted spaces forming the basement areas was one of the real problems faced by the design team. Another was that, in its previous existence, the building was exempt from certain fire and safety regulations; it had to be brought up to standard, and this affected the handling of the 700 spaces in the buildings and in particular the opening up of the basement.

The treatment of the different premises is nicely varied. The GLC team restored all shop fronts as part of the contract, but interiors were at the discretion of tenants, within guidelines set out in a tenants' handbook; tenant expenditure varied from a few thousand pounds to several hundreds of thousands. The openness of the building, pierced by its cross-routes, engages its interior spaces with those of the piazza and the streets around, and lends an air of informality to its more austere elements. There are loading bays at either end but direct servicing to the shops is not permitted (double handling is apparently accepted by the traders as being in their own interest); as a result, all shops are double fronted and there is none of the unsightly back door clutter to be seen, for example, on the northern and southern 'outside' walls of the warehouse blocks of Quincy Market. Street shows, licensed by the GLC, include not only the now ubiquitous

From the Market the ripples spread outwards. Above: a Christmas fairground. Right: the surrounding streets take on new life, and new housing brings in new residents.

fire-eaters and escapologists, but Punch & Judy, mimes, string quartets and bowler-hatted jazzmen. A Christmas fair at one end has included merry-go-round, Big Wheel and Helterskelter among the sideshows. Total cost to the GLC was about £3 million; the initial annual rent roll was about £500,000.

From the new market the ripples have spread outwards. In one corner of the piazza the London Transport tram museum has opened in the old Flower Market. Hard by, the Jubilee Hall, notwithstanding pressures to retain the original (and not very distinguished) building, is being rebuilt. In another corner the first, long-awaited extension to the Royal Opera House is complete; plans are in hand for a big, further, arcaded extension which will complete the northeast corner of the piazza. St Paul's churchyard, that wonderful oasis, is cleared of the cars that once parked there. In the network of small streets around the market, scaffolding and cleaning and restoration have given way to restaurants and speciality shops of every kind. It is a far cry now from only the middle 'Seventies when a 'Trade Promotion Group' was set up to hawk empty buildings around at £1 a sq ft. One recent development has achieved, it is

said, £23 a sq ft, and rentals generally have soared to the point where original plans for a big open space in the middle of the area have long since been abandoned—the land has become far too valuable.

The 1978 plan provided for a local population increase from 2,800 to 6,000; and the number of dwellings from 1,600 to 2,400. Seven years later 600 dwellings had in fact been completed, with more in the pipeline. On the one-time site of Odhams Press there is now an international award-winning, casbah-like, housing complex of some character, with many miniature hanging gardens. The number of children attending St Clement Dane's School has more than doubled, and there is a waiting list.

The complaints continue: that there are still only 5,000 living in the area; that the businesses moving in are trendy design groups and P.R. firms; that the shops are too up-market and that the Garden has become a tourist rip-off. Covent Garden is, indeed, now the second most popular tourist attraction in London after the Tower.

Tourists however do not make up the majority of those who now throng the area. A 1982 survey by the Greater London Council showed that nearly sixty per cent of visitors were Londoners. Covent Garden needed a new economic generator, and it has got one. New life is spreading throughout the quarter. But, in the last analysis, what is important is that Covent Garden has brought back to the capital an experience taken for granted in most big cities but long lost to Londoners themselves: the simple pleasures of eating, drinking, shopping, meeting friends, listening to music, watching the world go by, in an open-air setting designed for the purpose. It is clear from their faces that they love it.

The abolition of the Greater London Council in 1986 posed crucial questions about the market's future. Might it be sold off, in line with current government thinking? Would not any relaxation of the GLC's controls be bound to result in a concessionnaires' free-for-all? At the time of writing it appears likely that the market may pass to a specially formed trust, on which the two main Borough Councils will be represented, ensuring that reasonably unified management and control will thereby be maintained. It would seem a happy solution.

VI
RENEWAL

TWENTY-FIVE years ago the word 're-newal' radiated faith in a perfectable future. Fifteen years later it had become synonymous with stained concrete, broken communities and urban violence. Yet towns and cities need to renew themselves. Inner city decay now is widespread. It has been subjected to intensive survey and study. The problem—lost jobs, population exodus, falling local revenue, leading to multiple deprivation for those remaining—is well enough understood. Solutions, however, have proved more intractable—usually because the 'action' demanded is politically or economically unacceptable. To reverse the forces which drive an area into decay requires exceptional and sustained effort.

Most of the work shown in the immediately preceding and following pages represents renewal in some sense—Munich, Byker, Covent Garden and the rest. Most embrace more than one planning ingredient. What is intended by the word here is something even more radically comprehensive, bringing together housing, shopping, offices, leisure, transport or pedestrian improvements, landscaping . . . Two examples happen to be American—though that does not mean that America has the sole rights in such things. Baltimore, however, represents one of the most sustained and successful programmes anywhere to revitalize and upgrade a big city. Wirksworth, in England, is by comparison minuscule. Salem, in Massachusetts, between the two in size, is a remarkable example in design terms of how to integrate renewal with conservation. Between them these places, so very different, have lessons for towns in many other countries.

For, while renewal is, in greater or lesser degree, social engineering, the glib polarities of 'progress' *or* 'stagnation' must be discarded. The reshaping of outworn urban tissue needs to be an organic process, creating growth by fitting new assets into the framework of existing assets.

Looking north across Baltimore's Inner Harbor from Federal Hill towards the city; the big buildings of Charles Center pile up in the distance. Bottom: the reverse view, towards Federal Hill, Rash Field and the marina.

BALTIMORE—*Maryland*

At the outbreak of the American Revolution, Baltimore's population was 5,000. Over the following twenty-five years the figure more than quadrupled. The river was dredged, marshes were filled, and the city's docks extended until they rivalled New York's. Strategically, the site was exceptional. Southward-bound shipping enjoys one hundred miles of the sheltered waters of Chesapeake Bay before reaching the open sea; at the same time, itself well inland, the city offers competitive land access. By 1810 Baltimore had become the third city in the United States. When the completion of the Erie Canal threatened her northern trade, Baltimore responded with America's first passenger railway (the Baltimore and Ohio). Its impact was great. The population doubled again; with steadily increasing affluence, modern services and amenities began to be introduced.

It was not to last. The Civil War cut the city's inland communications; markets were lost; the port slipped from second to eighth place in national importance. By the mid-twentieth century, Baltimore was economically stagnant. No major office building had gone up for nearly thirty years. Twenty per cent of its housing was decaying. The better-off had emigrated to the suburbs. Its non-white population was increasing steadily (it is now approaching sixty per cent of the total of around 800,000). Many of the ethnic neighbourhoods were slums. Firms were moving out, shops closing, social services deteriorating, crime increasing. The city developed a massive inferiority complex.

The problems are common to many places. Baltimore's response, however, was exceptional, and has led to a revival in her fortunes which is quite remarkable. Two factors bear upon this. The first is the city's form of management: Baltimore was removed from county administration in 1851, becoming what used to be known in Britain as an 'all-purpose' authority. This is unusual in America, and made more so by the city's 'strong mayor' structure which allows the mayor a powerful voice in policy formulation and execution—giving him, for example, three out of five votes on the Board of Estimate which controls the budget. His office is thus more comparable with that of a French mayor, or a Dutch Burgomeister, than with the 'figurehead' mayor of British local politics.

The second factor was—and is—the sense of civic responsibility of Baltimore's business community. A good many American cities, in their relatively short histories, have suffered appalling disasters which have called forth a powerful community response. So perhaps in Baltimore were community links forged in the aftermath of the 1904 fire, which destroyed more than 1,500 buildings over 140 acres. Be that as it may, it was in fact the business community which took the first positive steps, in the early and middle 'Fifties, to combat the apparently inexorable erosion of their city's well-being.

In 1954 the Retail Merchants Association set up a Committee for Downtown, which then joined forces with the Greater Baltimore Committee (of influential businessmen—among them James Rouse, to become, as already noted, one of America's most influential property developers) to produce a plan for the city. For the purpose they created their own non-profit planning team—the Planning Council—in 1956 (something of a key year, which threw up a whole clutch of ideas and initiatives) and then contracted with it to produce proposals for 1,000 acres of the centre city. Realism supervened, and it was a plan to carve out 33 acres of the business district for redevelopment which was in fact presented to the mayor in 1958 and turned over to the city's Urban Renewal and Housing Agency (now the Department of Housing and Community Development) for more detailed study. By 1959 it had been officially adopted and the

'Charles Center Management Office' created to supervise its implementation.

From the outset it seems to have been agreed that quality should be a primary objective. The Charles Center plans aimed to retain the most significant existing buildings, as well as to create new economic generators; additional open space was to be provided; the separation of pedestrians and traffic was to be helped by means of linked decks and walkways (a concept assisted by the nature of the site, which falls steadily to the waterfront of the Inner Harbor—then a ramshackle and largely derelict wasteland of rotting piers and shacks). Land was acquired from over 200 owners. An Architectural Review Board was set up to assess the quality of each development and to ensure its consistency with the overall objectives. The Board's initial task, in fact, was to supervise an architectural competition for the first new building, One Charles Center, which, in the event, was won by Mies van der Rohe (from Marcel Breuer amongst others).

For some time now the Charles Center programme has been to all intents and purposes complete. It embraces fifteen or more major new buildings offering 1¾ million square feet (nearly 200,000 sq metres) of office space; 600 apartments; 335,000 square feet (37,000 sq metres) of retail and commercial activity; a hotel, the Mechanic Theatre, and 4,000 underground parking spaces. Interspersed among these are a number of public squares and gardens. Public investment (relating to the Federal office building, but otherwise to these gardens, walkways, fountains and sculpture) was around $35 million; private sector investment has been around $175 million.

Overall, Charles Center has proved enormously successful. It has created jobs. It has increased revenue to the city from rates and property taxes from little more than $750,000 to something like $6 million a year. However, Charles Center was only the first, confidence-boosting element, which helped to trigger a much wider city programme. Long before Charles Center had got into its full stride, other initiatives were already being taken. In 1956—that year again—the Maryland Port Authority was created to rejuvenate the city's port facilities, as a result of which Baltimore now once more stands second among United States ports. And in 1963 the decision was taken to redevelop the crumbling Inner Harbor area, primarily for cultural and recreational purposes (as, too, had first been mooted in 1956).

The administrative structure established for Charles Center provided the pattern. For the initial planning the City put up $35,000, the Greater Baltimore Committee $25,000, and the Committee for Downtown $25,000. The task was again entrusted to the Planning Council. The Charles Center Management office was expanded to become Charles Center—Inner Harbor Management, Inc.—a kind of local authority 'quango' (quasi autonomous non-governmental organization). This is financed on a contractual basis by the city administration, but is free to operate entrepreneurially without the constraints natural to local government itself. The machinery has been endorsed by successive mayors; the cost to the public purse no more than two per cent of the public funds involved.

The outline proposals for the Inner Harbor envisaged the renewal, in three phases, of an area of some 240 acres. The first phase, covering the ground immediately adjoining the Harbor itself, is today more or less complete; at the time of writing phase two, embracing a more extensive area to the West, towards the big Camden Street railway station (where one, or even two, stadia are proposed) and the spirited Florentine folly of the Bromo-Selzer tower (now housing the Mayor's Advisory Committee on Art and Culture), is in hand and partially complete; phase three, to the East, is still being planned.

Not only is the total area to be dealt with vastly greater than that of Charles Center; the range of uses is much more varied. Flanking the Inner Harbor are I.M.Pei's 28-storey World Trade

Center—the largest pentagonal building in the world; on Pier 3 a dazzling $21 million aquarium by Peter Chermayeff of Cambridge Seven Associates, visited by well over one million people each year, and soon to be expanded to Pier 4 to embrace a big whale and dolphin exhibit; 'Harborplace'—two pavilions offering 150,000 square feet of specialized shops and eating places, by Benjamin Thompson for the Rouse Company (he had been responsible, too, for Faneuil Hall market in Boston); a large, half-buried and therefore marvellously low-set Convention Center for 7,500 people, which has a welcome sense of open-ness by reason of its 30,000 sq feet of interior-exterior glass walls—said to be Pilkington's largest system of suspended glass so far in use; a 500-room Hyatt Regency hotel in mirror glass; the McCormick and Company building—retained from the past—wafting its exotic odours of processed spices across the water is now, it seems, sadly, to go; but the museum/planetarium/exhibition of the Maryland Science Center, from the office of Edward Durrell Stone—permanent home of the Maryland Academy of Sciences has recently been expanded and joined by an IMAX theatre. Interspersed among and around all these are the playing fields, and stands for 4,000 of Rash Field; a marina; the USF *Constellation*, the nation's first commissioned warship, built in Baltimore in 1797; and on Pier 6 a multi-tented concert pavilion—the biggest canvas structure in the country—which can seat over 3,000 people three times a week. All this, enlivened by fountains and sculpture, is linked through to the decks of Charles Center by raised walkways at the northwest corner. A baseball-throw to the west are the 'homestead' streets and new housing of the Otterbein neighbourhood.

One result of all this is that Baltimore, apparently sliding out of existence thirty years earlier, has become a considerable tourist attraction. Visitors flock to the Inner Harbor. In its first year Harborplace drew more visitors (eighteen million) than Disney World. The annual City Fair draws between one and two million people a day. Overall, the city now attracts more than twenty million visits a year by some six million people, seventy per cent of them from out-of-town and out of Maryland. The city is now mounting major tourist promotions in Europe, offering itself as the ideal gateway to the Virginia-New England coastal zone. But all this is a spin-off, hardly to be foreseen in the middle 'Fifties, least of all as an economically valuable

Baltimore's regeneration began with the Charles Center area. A system of walkways and spaces link right through to the Inner Harbor, past the mirror-glass Regency Hyatt hotel (overleaf).

one—direct tax receipts from tourism now amount to $10 million a year. The true success of Baltimore has to be sought in the lives of its own citizens. However Charles Center and the Inner Harbor are merely the present show-pieces of a city-wide drive which continues at many levels.

It was Baltimore which first saw through an effective 'homesteading' programme, in which old properties (often slated for demolition) were sold off at a dollar a time to those who undertook to renovate them within six months and live in them for at least eighteen (Barre Circle, Otterbein, Stirling Street and Washington Hill were the first areas where this was done). By mid 1978 there were over 500 homesteaders. It was Baltimore which, in 1977, extended the principle to 'shopsteading' with, eventually, 60 stores going at $100 each. To these and other property owners the city offers up to one hundred per cent low cost loans to cover the cost of renovation (seven per cent over twenty years.) Elsewhere over 250 middle-class terraced houses designed by Moshe Safdie, 'Coldspring New Town', have been created on a joint public-private basis, again with generous mortgages. For its more than twenty historic districts, the City has set up the 'Salvage Depot', where doors, mantels, windows, materials retrieved from older buildings which have been demolished, may be bought. The 'Loading Dock' stocks cheap reject components for use by non-profit and community groups. A 'Neighbourhood Incentive Programme' matches dollar for dollar, private funds and 'sweat equity' put into local environmental improvements.

As a big port Baltimore has always been a settling place for ethnic groups from elsewhere, and the city's neighbourhoods play a particularly important role in its affairs. The Citizens' Housing and Planning Association was founded in 1941. Mayor William Donald Schaefer, who came to office in 1971 after nineteen years as a city Councilman—the most forceful and dedicated to date of a succession of admirable leaders—made special efforts to put new heart into the neighbourhoods. Amongst his other steps he set up eleven 'mayor's stations', or district offices, to act as local 'consulates' for the City Hall and its departments. In how many other cities could not such area offices be set up with advantage?

It was Mayor Schaefer, too, who initiated a running programme of free public events—concerts of every kind, theatrical performances, ballet, fireworks, ethnic festivals—first in Charles Center, subsequently in the Inner Harbor where they culminate each year in the Baltimore City Fair. The essential purpose was to encourage blacks and whites to come together and give them a sense of common identity; to draw people into once decayed areas which were previously considered unsafe; and to give confidence to potential developers. The 1968 civil rights disturbances affected Baltimore, as so many other cities. Safety and security became new imperatives for the ordinary citizen, and for years the central business district was deserted at night. These daily and nightly events, largely open air, have proved spectacularly successful in creating places where people like to congregate, and which did not exist before.

Has it, then, all gone smoothly from the outset? Inevitably not. There was a head-on collision between public opinion and officialdom throughout the 1960s, over proposals to drive a section of Interstate 95 directly through the Harbor area. Public opinion won, and one must be relieved that it did. Once public access to the Inner Harbor had been gained by clearance of the decaying structures which had lined it for so long, public opinion was at first strongly against any redevelopment of this new-won space (10,000 signatures were gathered in a petition to halt all further construction). However, the issue was put to public referendum, and won. Harborplace is there, and humming—and there must be few now to regret the fact.

Facing page: the Regency Hyatt; the northern quayside passes beneath the tall World Trade Center, as it curves round to Pier Three and the glittering aquarium. Above: a corner of the aquarium itself.

Problems remain—how could they not? The city worries about the state of the social services (for demographic and other reasons demands upon the social services are above average and create problems of adequate financing); about the continuing decay of the older shopping areas; about the likely future of the Inner Harbor area—will its use decline if the present flow of community events should be tapered off, or, conversely, will it attract more and more tourists, to the point where the citizens no longer feel it to be their own? about the massive cut-backs in Federal funding. However, the thrust of its policies seems unabated. Steps have been taken, for example, to improve and renovate a number of shopping areas: the traffic-free Old Town Mall, Broadway Market in Fells Point, Lexington Market, the city's big food market. Plans are afoot for important downtown schemes—the big Market Center development, co-ordinated by another 'quango' corporation, which calls for investment of the order of $250 million. The new metro, the first section of which was opened in 1983, will, it is hoped, help to restore some of the ailing shopping streets to better health and splice them into the growing liveliness of city life elsewhere.

Two indicators must give profound encouragement to those who have led Baltimore through the past thirty years. The drift from the city has been halted and the population level has been stabilized; crime rates, which were rising sharply a quarter of a century ago, have decreased from their peak levels.

In the last analysis, Baltimore's renaissance has been due to two things: to a succession of exceptionally able public figures, headed by the city's mayors—above all, Mayor William Donald Schaefer, in the mid 'Eighties re-elected for an unprecedented fourth term—and such men as Robert C. Embry Jr, the first Commissioner of the Department of Housing and Community Affairs; and to the relationship between public and private sectors, and the exceptional community spirit of the latter. It is a measure of the pressure generated by the city's manifold programmes that, over the years before the Reagan administration, it was the second biggest recipient in the nation of Federal Urban Development Action Grant aid (UDAG) at nearly $300 million. However, God, and governments, help those who help themselves. The Greater Baltimore Committee is still at it after thirty years. The 'Blue Chip-In' campaign, backed by five business leaders, has created 18,000 summer jobs, privately funded, over five years. Another group of businessmen is seeking to persuade a couple of dozen firms to contribute up to five per cent of their taxable income for civic causes. It was the business community which financed the city's programme of public events and performances. As Harborplace got off the ground, the Rouse Corporation and City Hall made exceptional efforts to bring about an above-average minorities participation in its affairs. The manager was black; forty per cent of the work force is non-white; and as a result of very positive recruitment, involving a good deal of work on banks and sponsors from other Rouse developments to produce the necessary financial backing, around sixteen per cent of the trader-tenants are non-white. These are higher figures than usual by far, and they symbolize much of the *type* of effort which has underlain Baltimore's thirty years of renewal.

That renewal has been based upon long-term *ideas*, the needs of people, and the understanding that these will inevitably change. Mayor Schaefer has written: 'This city will continue to be recycled. One of these days Inner Harbor will have to be completely redone, and there will always be houses that have to be rehabilitated. It never ends. You redevelop Inner Harbor and in 25 years maybe there will be an entirely different concept for it. People ask me when the Inner Harbor project will be completed. I say "Never". They look at me as if to say "What do you mean, it will never be completed?" But that's true. No neighbourhood will ever be complete. Neighbourhoods get older, they become stable, and then they might start to decline as older folks leave and the houses become too big. Then, in comes a group of young people and they change the neighbourhood entirely. Some people worry that if they hurry and finish a job, they'll be out of work. But I say "Do the job now, and when you're finished there will be other jobs to do"'.

Already, after twenty-five years, the Charles Center plaza is being refurbished. And for Shaefer himself another job: in the autumn of 1986, on a landslide 82 per cent vote, he was elected Governor of Maryland.

Left: the tented bridge leading to the Maritime Museum and the big music pavilion for open-air concerts. Above: masts of the 1797 USF *Constellation* reflected in Harborplace. Below: a Harborplace pavilion glimpsed past the ship herself.

WIRKSWORTH—*Derbyshire*

Wirksworth is a small town of just under 6,000 inhabitants. It is tucked into a bowl of hills at the head of the Ecclesbourne Valley in central Derbyshire, a mile or two to the south of the Peak District National Park—an area of rolling uplands and dry stone walls which was the first of the British National Parks to be designated. The town has a long history—it was once one of the most important in the county—going back to Roman days and earning its living successively through lead-mining, textiles, especially tape-weaving (not least, huge quantities of the famous bureaucratic red tape), and limestone quarrying. Quarrying, indeed, by reason of a big, worked-out hole at the back of the town, has made its own contribution to the often spectacular views to be had into, and across, Wirksworth.

This was the town used by George Eliot as the main background for *Adam Bede*. For so small a place its layout has considerable urbanity. Like a miniaturized cathedral city, its parish church stands at the centre, surrounded by a 'close', beyond the perimeter buildings of which lie the irregular Market Place and the rest of the town. Facing the Market Place stands the 1871 Town Hall. Scattered through the centre of the town are handsome, even quite grand, buildings from more prosperous days. Indeed, by 1978 65 of them were officially listed by the government as of architectural or historic importance. Threading through these and the more modest stone cottages which make up the bulk of the place are walled pedestrian ways, given drama by abrupt changes of level. More modern housing has been built at the edges, but in general the town remains compact.

A place of visual character, then, but one which, by the 1970s, had long been showing all the usual symptoms of rural decline. Unemployment was rising; buildings were empty and decaying; shops were generally poor in quality. With local government reorganization in 1974, control of the town's services—housing, planning, roads, public health and refuse collection—passed to the new District Council situated some distance away. Morale was low. The town itself was down-at-heel and pretty unprepossessing.

It was at this point that the Civic Trust, an independent charitable organization, appeared on the scene. The Trust was founded in 1957 to raise environmental standards. Its concerns have ranged from the reclamation of industrial dereliction to the environmental impact of heavy lorries; from urban conservation (it drafted the legislation which brought the conservation-area concept into the British planning system) to the design of new development. It supports a network of 1,000 local groups. It makes awards. Its films have reached all parts of the world. Amongst these and other activities, it has regularly initiated practical programmes of improvement as exemplars from which other places can learn. The Wirksworth Project was one of these.

With funding from another charitable foundation, the Monument Trust, the Civic Trust proposed and, at a Town Meeting of the local people, gained acceptance for, a programme aimed at rejuvenating the whole community. The programme had five main aims:

— to increase people's sense of pride in Wirksworth;

— to encourage more people to live in, and take more care of, the older properties in the centre of the town;

— to create more job opportunities;

— to encourage greater investment in the town's shopping and businesses;

— to develop the town's tourist potential.

Wirksworth, tucked into the head of its valley in Derbyshire, has found the confidence to reshape its future.

These aims were not set out in any order of priority; they were seen as totally interlinked.

Support was promised by the local authorities concerned—the County Council, the District Council, the Town (or Parish) Council—and by the Civic Society. (There were useful links between these: Councillor Bernard Truman, Mayor in 1978, was concurrently chairman of the Society, and Barry Joyce, a planner with the County Council lived in Wirksworth and was a member of the Society.) The Civic Trust set up a Project Office in the town. Here the Project Team, representing these organizations, could meet weekly with the Trust—in particular Gordon Michell, the architect Project Leader, who had privately purchased a cottage in the town. On Tuesdays—Market Day—the office was open to all members of the public to bring their problems and discuss aspects of the Project which affected them. Continuing talks were held with all local organizations likely to have some part to play in the scheme—amongst them the Chamber of Trade and Commerce, Rotary, the Wirksworth Ladies Group and the sixth form of the Anthony Gell School. Throughout, the message was the same: the Civic Trust was not there to impose solutions; if Wirksworth was to be revitalized it could only be by local people themselves, working together.

Nonetheless, a lot of initial spadework had to be done before any real action on the ground could commence. Possibilities had to be explored, options set out, thoughts clarified. An attitudes survey was commissioned, to establish what local people themselves saw as their main problems. A landscape survey was commissioned, to clarify the area's assets and liabilities, and to indicate exactly what needed to be done to improve the town's spaces and character. A list was drawn up of sixteen 'Buildings at Risk'. A study was put in hand, bearing in mind the need to attract tourists, to establish the basis for an interpretive strategy for the town. The Conservation Area was enlarged and a 'Town Scheme' set up to provide grant aid towards the restoration and maintenance of listed buildings. (See page 000). In this case it was £3,000 each from the two main local authorities, doubled by the DoE to make £12,000 available as fifty per cent grant to owners—rising in subsequent years to £29,000 and more than £34,000. A 'General Improvement Area' was created, to bring in official funding for housing improvements. A Wirksworth Heritage Education Group was set up to involve the schools; through this school children of all age groups began to undertake surveys and projects which culminated in a sizeable exhibition in the parish church—'Our Town, Our Schools'. Arrangements were made with a big Building Society to make mortgages available anywhere within the Conservation and General Improvement Areas.

And then, suddenly, everything began to happen. Scaffolding appeared on buildings in all parts of the town. Walls were repaired and rebuilt. Advance factory/workshop units, built by the Council for Small Industries in Rural Areas (COSIRA), were opened. An unsightly public lavatory was removed from a corner of the Town Hall, allowing a much needed extension to be created for the public library within. The Derbyshire Historic Buildings Trust acquired and restored several houses as the start of a rolling programme in the town. New shops appeared—a bookshop, toyshop, delicatessen, a pet shop, an art gallery and, a little later, a showroom for hand-made furniture. Between 1979 and 1982 some £134,000 of official grant aid led to building work costing nearly £360,000—but over and above this other owners, spurred by what was happening, got on with their own improvements without official funding.

The tonic effect of this visible activity, starting in the summer of 1980, built up steadily. When the time came for the Civic Trust to pull out in 1982, after three and a half years, there was no doubt that the show was on the road. A second Town Meeting, called by the Trust in July 1981,

31–33 The Dale—one of the first buildings to be restored. Scores of premises have since been brought to life again—as homes, as shops, as workshops.

had considered possible options for continuing the Project; by the end of the year the Town Council had formally assumed responsibility for its future implementation. A Special Steering Committee of elected members was created, with respresentation from the County and District Councils; a Working Group was set up composed of officers from the three Councils and representatives of the DHBT, the Conservation Area Advisory Committee, the Civic Society, the Chamber of Trade, Rotary and the schools. Gordon Michell, the Civic Trust's project leader, was retained on a one-day a month basis. Barry Joyce was seconded to the Project half-time by the County Council (in fact, since he lived in the town, his commitment was considerably more).

Such was the momentum already built up that, on this basis, the programme continued triumphantly. Since then the Market Place has been repaved. Amongst other buildings, the important and central ruin of 1,2,3 Greenhill has been brought back to life by DHBT. More new shops have opened. The Civic Trust's commissioned interpretive study has led to the restoration of another derelict building for use as a Heritage Centre, run by the Civic Society and opened in mid 1986. Proposals for a National Stone Centre at a nearby worked-out quarry have found favour, and preparatory work on this is going ahead. In 1984 the Project received the Royal Town Planning Institute's Jubilee Award for achievement in planning; it has received an international Award from Europa Nostra; the Prince of Wales has referred to it as 'brilliantly imaginative' and the town attracts regular study tours of professional and other groups. As the second stage of the operation gave way in 1986 to its third, and one may hope permanently self-supporting, phase, the auguries could scarcely have looked better. Problems remained. There was more to be done. But Wirksworth, so sorry for itself ten years earlier, had not only been transformed physically; the town was filled with a new confidence—in itself and in its future.

How was it done? The Civic Trust brought a fresh eye to the town's problems. It was able to suggest courses of action; bring together agencies and people who could help such a programme forward; advise on putting together financial packages and use its contacts to help in this; bring in additional specialist consultants where necessary; assist individual members of the public with technical and professional expertise, and help them through the tangles of bureaucracy. All these things, it may be objected, could surely be done by one or other of the authorities and agencies which already existed locally. The fact is that they were not. The Civic Trust—through its project leader Gordon Michell in particular—was seen by all to have no axe to grind, but to have commitment, enthusiasm and professional know-how. It became the catalyst which released the local potential which lay dormant in the area. It is hard to believe that such potential was, and is, peculiar to Wirksworth. In how many other communities are similar possibilities not awaiting similar realization?

SALEM—*Massachusetts*

The story of Heritage Plaza in Salem, Massachusetts, is in many ways archetypal. It is the story of the change in taste that took place in so many countries over the 1960s and 1970s.

Salem was founded in 1626 and became an important seaport in the India trade from the last quarter of the century. Apart from that mysterious bout of witchcraft and hysteria, the city's claims to fame include the first provincial assembly of Massachusetts in 1774 and the first armed resistance of the Revolution in the following year. Nathaniel Hawthorne was one of its sons, and Hawthorne's 'House of the Seven Gables' is one of the attractions which brings a summer influx of 700,000 tourists.

A pleasant place then, well rooted in the past, with a wealth of seventeenth-, eighteenth- and nineteenth-century buildings. Stable as a community too—its largely 'blue collar' population today of 40,000 is only a couple of thousand less than it was at the end of World War I, despite the gravitational pull of Boston thirty miles or so to the south.

That stability was shaken, however, by events in the 1960s. It began with the construction of Route 128 as a ring road to the Boston metropolitan area. This by-passed Salem to the north and the magnetism of the new highway led to the relocation of some major industries and the creation of two multi-million dollar shopping malls at the interchanges. Salem had previously been the main shopping centre for the communities north of Boston, and these developments accelerated the city's economic decline. The municipality was led to drastic action.

At the prompting of the local Chamber of Commerce, the Salem Redevelopment Authority was set up in 1962 to inject new life into the city centre. By 1965 the Authority had produced a twelve-block, forty acre renewal plan based upon large-scale clearance, the construction of a sixty-foot inner ring road and high rise commercial development described as 'futuristic'. Traffic and construction were its blind priorities and demolition its hallmark, wrote Ada Louise Huxtable in the *New York Times*; the plan, she suggested, was the product of a 'bulldozer mentality'.

In 1968 massive demolition commenced and the northern third of the area, consisting of decayed but fundamentally sound eighteenth-century housing, was levelled. However, the Authority ran into a snag. One house, dating from 1811, belonged to an elderly lady, by name Bessie Monroe, who refused to budge. Through

Downtown Salem, Massachusetts. Let us take a stroll through Heritage Plaza East. The western entrance is there, across the road. See that white building . . . ?

kindness, or perhaps fear of adverse publicity, the Authority took no steps to evict her and there she stayed until her death in 1971. Around her house the cleared land remained empty; no developer came forward; local protests mounted. By the early 1970s the number of shops and stores had halved—from around eighty to forty. By 1971, however, attitudes had changed. Opposition to the Authority's proposals from local conservation groups had become increasingly bitter. (Abbott Cummings, Director of the 1910 Society for the Protection of New England Antiquities, felt impelled to resign from the Design Review Board in 1970 because its work appeared to him irrelevant in the face of the demolition then in progress.) The city's mayor retired after twenty years' service and his forceful successor, Samuel Zoll, began to reconstitute the membership of the Council's various boards and commissions. In 1971 Timothy J. Noonan became Chairman of the Redevelopment Authority; William Tinti, member of Historic Salem—the leading conservation group—became its Vice-Chairman, and two years later its Chairman. The Authority was charged with producing new proposals within six months.

Zoll, Noonan and Tinti threw out the 1960s road proposals and insisted on retaining the existing street pattern of the central area. The rigid approach of the master-plan was abandoned: the Authority aimed to spend all its money as soon as possible, so that it should not decline into a self-perpetuating bureaucracy. It decided to concentrate initially on the area centred on Essex Street, now known as Heritage Plaza East. In part because of the Mayor's brisk timetable, in part because of the Authority's new philosophy, the plan developed as they went along. There was no formal report. Broad proposals were put to a town meeting of 300, and well received. Work on site began ninety days after proposals were put forward.

Spelled out in detail was the sort of renewal envisaged—permitted uses, plot ratios, permitted heights, interior rehabilitation standards, responsibilities for off-street parking (to re-establish the confidence of the business community, the Authority undertook to provide 1,000 parking spaces within the Project area), and provisions for compulsory acquisition and purchase of easements (or restrictive covenants). No building would be demolished unless real efforts to save it had been made and failed, and until a new building for the site had been approved and its construction scheduled.

The same year, 1972, saw three further formative events. A development team initiated by the Boston architect Nelson Aldrich was selected

1 A few yards in, opposite it, we turn to the left

2 towards the big office block of One Salem Green.

from twenty-two others as the 'designated developer', under the name of 'The Salem Corporation'; the Corporation was associated with, and eventually became wholly owned by, the Canadian development company Mondev International (Aldrich having relinquished any financial interest in the organization). Second, a start was made on the ground with the construction of a new market place around the 1816 Old Town Hall for use by produce stalls, craftsmen and outdoor gatherings. Third, the proposals for Heritage Plaza gained the recognition of the federal government's Department of Housing and Urban Development, which granted them a Bicentennial Project Design Honor Award. This, and the arrival on the scene of a big development company in the form of Mondev, provided a much needed psychological boost. The Project began to gather momentum.

Ten years later it was to all intents and purposes complete. It contained over forty shops and restaurants; new office space; around 225 housing units and sixty apartment units, with some housing for the elderly. Traffic had been rerouted.

Through the area runs the east-west spine of Essex Street, now paved and traffic-free—save for an occasional goods vehicle servicing one of the shops. Pedestrian spurs lead off on either side. Here, adjoining One Salem Green—a five-storey office block offering 50,000 square feet of space and completed in 1974—a new mini-park forms a green oasis, replacing the backland jumble at the rear of City Hall. Here, fronting the restored Old Town Hall, are the trees and benches of Derby Square, leading to the New Market Place on the other side and, further on across Charter Street, to the simple open structures of the Lower Market (an area which, like Quincy Market in Boston, once formed the waterfront to the harbour). Returning to Essex Street by another route, one reaches an arcaded approach to East India Square, the focal point of this end of the scheme. Faced on one side by the venerable Peabody Museum of maritime history (1825) and its modern extension, the Essex Institute, the Square is formed on two of its other sides by the second big Mondev redevelopment—the multi-storey car park which the traders had requested—and at ground level, the shops and restaurants of East India Mall. The Square itself, thickly planted round the perimeter, has at its centre a fountain and water feature in the form of a coastline map of the area. Some few yards further along Essex Street, one reaches the eastern boundary of this part of the renewal area.

Heritage Plaza is thus an intelligent mix of conservation and renewal. The older buildings, well restored and cleaned up, anchor the scheme

3 Through the entrance lobby we can see a sunny oasis created by clearing the backland mess of generations.

by their continuity. The new buildings are appropriate, without being precious. The extension to the Salem Five Cents Savings Bank quite deftly echoes the arch of the original main door. The fairly massive block of One Salem Green nonetheless bridges the walkway to the north, offers a glimpse through a glazed lobby to the dappled greenery of City Hall Plaza, and provides a not-inappropriate foil to the Lyceum Building (scene of General Tom Thumb's wedding and now a restaurant). At the other end of Essex Street, the parking garage of East India Square must be one of the most self-effacing of its kind in North America.

All this is admirable. What is exceptional about Heritage Plaza East, however, is the way the whole area has been pulled together by its faultless landscaping. Everything is simple, sturdy, nicely detailed and very well executed (the contractors sometimes even exceeded the specifications they were given). The siting of trees and bollards and other items at ground level is informal—as dictated by the underground services—and this relaxed approach has a good deal to do with the sense of organic unity which permeates the whole area—a quality so lacking in post-war development throughout the Western world. This disciplined yet sensitive control stemmed from the landscape consultant John Collins and his colleagues, introduced into the scheme by Edmund Bacon, by then of Mondev, with whom he had worked in Philadelphia.

Costs are not easy to pin down, partly because of inflation, partly because the renewal programme continues to roll and figures become outdated. However, in 1980, when to all intents and purposes Heritage Plaza East had been completed, the overall cost was estimated at around $90 million. Of this some $70 million stemmed from the private sector; city and State had put up around $4,350,000; and possibly $15 million had been injected by the Federal Government (for example, the Department of Housing and Urban Development put some millions of dollars into the paving and landscaping of Essex Street and its offshoots, and into the structures of the Lower Market).

Over $3 million went into the rehabilitation of older buildings, and a technique adopted by the Redevelopment Authority is worth noticing. From 1972 onwards the Authority began to purchase 'façade easements' (or the covenanted right to control the exterior elevations in perpetuity) of historic buildings which it did not own—initially twelve which were eligible for listing on the National Register. By way of payment the owners received up to $90,000 for exterior renovation (executed under the guidance of the Authority's

4 Turn back now to rejoin Essex Street by the Bank;

5 almost opposite, we sight the fine Old Town Hall.

Review Board and architects). The total charge to the Authority was $600,000. 'This', said William Tinti, 'was the best $600,000 we ever spent.' Of the forty-eight historic buildings requiring restoration, easements were finally purchased by the Authority for thirty-three.

Overall, this must be one of the most environmentally successful operations of its scale and period anywhere—the more so considering the radical change of direction required to rescue it from its original objectives. How sad, then, to have to record its failure, as yet, to achieve the economic hopes pinned to it.

At various stages along the line reservations had been expressed. One or two good buildings were lost. It took a dozen years or more after the clearance of the northern area to start the replacement housing. Local opinion was not unanimous about Mondev's role. There can be no doubt that, in the early 1970s, the intervention of a major international company (its backers include the Montreal Trust Company, the Royal Bank of Canada and the Fidelity Mutual Life Insurance Company of Philadelphia) had a powerful tonic effect upon the unconvinced Salem business community. Futhermore, as we have seen, Mondev directly or indirectly brought along some impressive design talent. Some claim, however, that the real improvement to the area stems more from small owners putting their own money into their own properties; they point to the contribution made by Historic Salem with its manual 'The Salem Handbook: A Renovation Guide for Homeowners', and to the fact that for a considerable period new trees and planting had to be maintained voluntarily by members of the public. They complain that, the City having leased a sizeable chunk of One Salem Green for its own use and having thereby relieved Mondev of much of the cost, Mondev's East India Mall remained uncompleted for a number of years; and that, even on eventual completion, with rentals which are considered high for the area, and leases of a length and complexity to fox any small town trader, the development failed to let well from the outset.

Here is the nub of the matter. Within the city, the sophistication of Heritage Plaza East has not grabbed the blue-collar community. In relation to the surrounding area, Salem's revitalization, it seems, has failed as yet to achieve the 'critical mass' necessary to compete with neighbouring centres. What was to have been Heritage Plaza West has yet to materialize. The 'picturesque' private development of 'Pickering Wharf' on the site of a redundant tank farm, is aimed primarily at the tourist trade—and the partial link between Plaza and Wharf, via Nathaniel Bowditch Park,

6 At its rear, New Market Square. As we head back,

7 notice this neat parking space, nicely screened.

8 In Essex Street, paving and detailing are worth a second look. Another new building, arcaded, brings us into East India Square; facing the 1825 Peabody Museum, the new shopping mall.

9 **In the Square, a watery map of the New England coastline.**

remains tenuous. Yet, in spite of local complaints, and a city centre which is still deserted at night, tax returns from the Plaza area had increased fourfold by 1980. Perhaps what Salem needs is not less of Heritage Plaza East but more. Tastes, after all, are not immutable. A convenient and ironic footnote can point the pendulum swing of fashion. Bessie Monroe's house, which she refused to vacate for the demolition men in the 1960s, is now designated an historic landmark. It is hard to believe that Salem's Plaza will not attract equal regard in years to come.

10 **Beyond, shops, a restaurant and—so screened that you would hardly know it—multi-storey parking.**

VII

SOW'S EARS

FINALLY—the eyesores, the wasteland, the neglected canal or railway track: all the flotsam and jetsam of the years, so often allowed to fester for decades while they spread their creeping blight throughout the surrounding areas. To bring derelict buildings back into use is often difficult enough; to find appropriate uses for unwanted and disfigured land is likely to call for very special qualities of tenacity and imagination. The three examples which follow, however, demonstrate convincingly that there is almost no land so difficult that it cannot be turned to creative purpose. Liabilities *can* be turned into assets.

They are very different in extent and complexity. The Lower Swansea Valley Project, in Wales, covers some 1,200 acres (500 ha); Gasworks Park in Seattle a mere 20 acres. Pressures on land in a country the size of Britain make it imperative that none be wasted, but the effect of quite small areas can be profound upon the centre city anywhere. San Antonio's riverside walk and Seattle's Gasworks Park represent problems and possibilities which are replicated in hundreds, if not thousands, of towns and cities everywhere. First: the Paseo del Rio in San Antonio, Texas.

THE PASEO DEL RIO—*San Antonio*

Texas remained Spanish until 1821. Then, when Mexico threw off the Spanish yoke, Texas, far from Mexico City, became a sort of vacuum into which America was—not altogether unwillingly—sucked. The Spanish Missions in and around San Antonio are among the oldest buildings in the United States, and it was one of these, the 1718 Mission San Antonio de Valero, become the Alamo fortress, which saw some of the bloodiest and most famous fighting before Texas was finally annexed by America in 1845.

San Antonio takes its name from the river which winds through it, itself named after St Anthony of Padua. The village which was founded in the first half of the eighteenth century has become a city of 650,000, upon which the heat presses down relentlessly in the summer months. The visitor is likely to find himself taken, within hours of his arrival, to the Paseo del Rio for a meal or a drink. This tree-lined riverside walk is the city's biggest environmental asset. That it is there to be enjoyed results from a struggle that took place more than half a century ago.

The river makes a big horse-shoe loop through the central area, about twenty feet below street level. Subject to flash floods of some severity, the city determined, after a disastrous one in 1921, to seal off this loop, roof it over to form an underground storm sewer, and to build on top. At that time the river was indeed for long periods not much more than a glorified ditch. Nonetheless, fifteen ladies of San Antonio banded together to fight the city's proposals and then, in 1924, to form the San Antonio Conservation Society. The Society is the oldest citizens' group of its kind in the United States (and no less remarkable for its choice, at that time, of the word 'conservation'). It has as its motto: Shall I say 'Yes, I remember it' or 'Here it is, I helped to save it'? The story goes that Emily Edwards, a high school art teacher and the Society's first President, deflected the city fathers from their designs upon the San Antonio River by means of a persuasive boat trip, followed by what was clearly a no less persuasive puppet show, suitably titled 'The Goose that Laid the Golden Eggs', at the City Hall. It has to be recorded that, in its earliest years, the Society was held to be run by rather eccentric white-gloved ladies.

At all events, by one means or another, the Society's lobbying resulted in the river being kept open and the construction of a new by-pass channel to link the two ends of the horseshoe, creating a continuous loop of river in the centre of the city, with flood-control barriers at these two points. Over the following years a great deal happened. The Paseo del Rio today is green and shaded by magnificent trees. There are open-air cafés and restaurants. A hotel comes down to water level. There is an open-air theatre, with a stage on one side of the water and a grassy amphitheatre the other. Backing on to the river are the Herzberg Circus Museum, the city's main library and an interesting botanical garden. You can cruise in a flat-bottomed boat, from which you will catch, over the bridges and through the trees, glimpses of the city above, from which the Paseo del Rio is so isolated and yet with which it is so closely integrated.

The proposal to create a continuous riverside walk was put forward in 1926 by a young architect, Robert Hugman. Much work was done in the late 1930s under the WPA (Works Progress Administration) programme, Roosevelt's forceful drive to counter unemployment in the Depression years. The river channel was cleared, the banks landscaped, and La Villita, for long a slum area, turned into a humming centre for craft workshops. And when San Antonio staged its 'Hemisfair' in 1968, the Paseo was extended by a new spur running into the Fair grounds.

Today it is all taken for granted. It is a place to meet your friends, to stop over at on your way

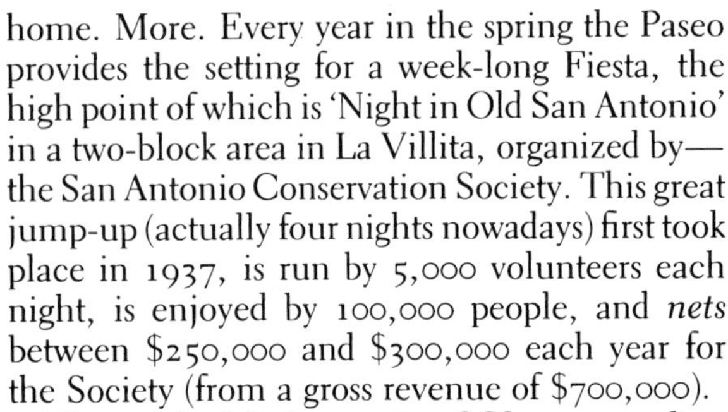

home. More. Every year in the spring the Paseo provides the setting for a week-long Fiesta, the high point of which is 'Night in Old San Antonio' in a two-block area in La Villita, organized by—the San Antonio Conservation Society. This great jump-up (actually four nights nowadays) first took place in 1937, is run by 5,000 volunteers each night, is enjoyed by 100,000 people, and *nets* between $250,000 and $300,000 each year for the Society (from a gross revenue of $700,000).

The original little coterie of fifteen crusading ladies has become an organization of over 3,000, still run almost entirely by women, (although one hundred or so men members are now tolerated), with an annual budget of around $400,000. Of this about half is expended on the historic properties which have been acquired through the years (a number have been given away, or sold, deliberately, at a loss—the remainder were valued in the 1970s at $2 million). But the Society is much more than a property-owning body; it has moved into planning, tax legislation, transport, central area revitalization and everything to do with environmental quality. It runs a scholarship programme for architectural students; makes awards for good restoration; and has built up a useful library and photographic archive. Its then President was also the first President of 'Preservation Action', the very effective lobbying organization on Capitol Hill in Washington. With a full-time staff of half a dozen, it has made itself a major force in the city of its birth, having infiltrated many of the agencies of local government. It is by no means universally loved—those with power seldom are—but to the outside eye it seems clear that the city of San Antonio has much to be grateful to its Conservation Society for; and perhaps for nothing more than its rescue of that unregarded stretch of river which so nearly disappeared for ever.

LOWER SWANSEA VALLEY—*Wales*

The problems of the Lower Swansea Valley, in South Wales, are altogether different in scale and complexity. They were perhaps the most daunting of their kind so far tackled by any municipality anywhere.

The mining valleys of South Wales run down from the Black Mountains towards the coastal strip which forms the hinterland of a string of ports, now less busy than they used to be. One of the more westerly takes a line from Ystradgynlais, through Pontardawe, to Swansea, a city of 184,000 population.

Coal has been mined in the area since the fourteenth century. After Abraham Darby's technical breakthrough at Coalbrookdale, it was only a question of time before the quality and accessibility of Swansea coal brought the smelting industries there. Copper came to Landore, in the Lower Swansea Valley, in 1717; by 1800 there were nine copper smelters in the area; in 1810 the big Hafod works opened up, eventually to employ 300 men; at its peak, around 1860, the industry there was smelting two-thirds of all the copper ore imported into Britain. With industry came new transport networks. Parallel with the River Tawe, which bisects the Lower Valley (and east and west Swansea), was constructed a canal—both running into the dock system. Brunel bridged the Tawe in 1847 and thereafter rail links spread northwards. Villages were built by the industrialists to house their workers. Over all the chimneys—at one time more than 300 in number—belched their smoke and fumes. 'On a clear day', wrote Charles Frederick Cliffe in 1848, 'the smoke of Swansea Valley may be seen

Above: the Maritime Museum in the Maritime Quarter, which marks the southern end of the Lower Swansea Valley project. Below: to the north, the Forest Park now clothes the unbelievable dereliction of thirty years ago . . .

. . . then a landscape of rotting desolation and gross pollution. Right: Dockside buildings refurbished for the Maritime and Industrial Museum; the grandstand of the big regional sports complex; the new multi-purpose leisure centre.

at a distance of forty to fifty miles,' and went on to note that the copper smoke 'has on several occasions afforded employment to the gentlemen of the long robe . . .'

It was not only the workers who died. Trees died, cattle and wildlife died, the land itself died. No tree in the valley today is much more than twenty years old. As copper smelting declined, zinc and steel and tinplate expanded—but only for a time. From the turn of the century numerous small companies amalgamated or were taken over. After World War I works were abandoned. The last pit closed in 1931. Steel was concentrated on large coastal sites at Newport and Port Talbot, tinplate at Velindre in Carmarthenshire. The last two works of any size in the Valley stuck it out until 1980, when they too shut down thus ending two and a half centuries of metal processing in the area. They left behind a sinister panorama of devastation and desolation to beggar description: a silent and seemingly endless desert, poisoned, sterile, incapable of supporting life; of grotesquely sculptured mountains of slag and waste, stained black and yellow and orange; of crumbling buildings and the stumps of once-tall chimney stacks; a polluted river and areas of polluted surface water. The word 'heritage' is used glibly today; Lower Swansea Valley represented a most bitter heritage of a particular kind from the first Industrial Revolution.

Reports and recommendations were made from time to time over several decades. Little was done. Apathy settled over the area and many came to believe that the sheer scale and complexity of the task of reclamation was such that it could never be undertaken. Some small schemes were implemented. The greater part of the area continued to fester. One man, however, was able to set the wheels in motion: in the late 1950s Robin Huws Jones, of the University College of Swansea, proposed that the Government and Swansea Borough Council should sponsor an interdisciplinary, fact-finding study, to be based on the University College, which would enable an overall, co-ordinated view to be taken of all the factors involved.

A working party was established in 1960; a four-year study was put in hand; in 1961 Kenneth J. Hilton was appointed Executive Director of the Project. The terms of reference included physical, social and economic factors; recommendations for future uses were to be made. The Project's studies, in which six Departments of the University College were involved, covered the establishment of vegetation, with large-scale trial plots; the state of the River Tawe, its culverting and flood protection; roads and transportation—it recommended filling in the canal and establishing a new road system; the environment and housing—in particular the development of parkland and amenity uses was proposed; suitable sites for new industry; visual enhancements; the use

of derelict land; and economic aspects of all these factors. These studies were completed in 1966—the year of the Aberfan disaster when an old coal tip (in another valley) engulfed a school and more than a hundred people, mainly children, died. The Report was published the following year and Swansea Borough Council was able to act on the recommendations with the substantial government aid towards land reclamation which came in the wake of Aberfan. Concurrently with this work the Project had teams of volunteer labour on specific tasks; the Territorial Army was called in to demolish and clear buildings; a complete photographic record was undertaken. In 1968 in the light of the Report, the City Council prepared a new plan for the Valley, itself put in hand a number of reclamation schemes, and, most important of all, began to acquire land. In 1964 the City owned less than four acres; by 1978 it had acquired over 720 acres (300 ha); by 1981 it had acquired or was negotiating for all the remaining land required.

Much remains to be done but already today the Valley bears little resemblance to the nightmare panorama of a generation ago. Most of the seven million tons of waste have been removed—in one operation alone, 330,000 tons of slag were removed from the Kilvey Hill tip to a site two miles to the north, which was being prepared for development. There have been problems of soil treatment, leading to the die-back of first seasons' growth, but large areas have been grassed and the Forestry Commission has planted 250,000 trees on the 180-acres of Kilvey Hill Forest Park. (Experiments were conducted with some thirty species, but only birch, alder, Japanese larch and lodgepole pine have been found to flourish.) Schools have been regularly brought into the work throughout, and the Conservator has special responsibilities for involving them to the full.

Five distinct parks are envisaged within the valley. At the lower end lies the South Dock and maritime quarter. Part of the then derelict South Dock was filled in during the early 1970s for an inner relief road which was to run between the city and the sea; the motorway was abandoned, the dock dug out again, and a package of new waterside developments is well on the way to completion—not on the scale of Baltimore's Inner Harbour, but fulfilling for Swansea a not dissimilar role. A new marina is a runaway success. Three hundred vessels were quickly moored there on its opening in 1983, and facilities are being extended for two hundred more. 'Maritime Village', of 700 new houses, was well advanced by mid 1986. The area boasts an excellent Leisure Centre (built on the site of an old railway terminus), a theatre, an arts workshop, and the city's maritime and industrial museum, housed in an adapted quayside building with a scarlet and white lightship moored alongside. A planned 146-bed hotel hit snags but looks like being in

New housing backs the marina in the Maritime Quarter.

the pipeline again. By the mid 'Eighties nearly £8 million from the Council had leveraged about £54 million of private capital.

Immediately to the north lies the 'city park' of twenty acres on the site of the filled-in North Dock. This green area, apart from some retail and leisure shopping, will provide pedestrian routes to the city centre, and link with the walking, picnicking and fishing of the Riverside Park, which, running northwards, holds the whole system together—and which is designed to soften the social divisions between the east and the west of the city. Sea trout and salmon are once again being caught in the river; a tidal barrage is proposed to maintain water levels.

Northwards again lies a big leisure park of 240 acres (100 ha) now wooded, with a sizeable lake, Pluck Lake. Eventually the park will house a £10 million regional sports complex to Commonwealth Games standard, with 3,000-seat grandstand (the all-weather running track is already complete). Stretching between this and the M4 motorway is the 'Enterprise Park' of 775 acres—the first (1981) Enterprise Zone to be designated in Britain. Here the initial work had to be put into the installation of all the infra-structure services; thereafter above-ground results began to multiply. By 1981 over thirty property deals had been concluded by the City Council, which would provide around 480,000 sq ft (48,000 sq metres) of new floor space to the value of nearly £8.5 million. Five years later, over 230 firms, employing some 3,000 were in fact trading there—half to two-thirds of them new undertakings. A new 120-bed hotel sits by the lake. Not far away is the 'Lakeside Technology Park'—the first of its kind in West Wales. Of the £40 million by then spent on the Zone, about £9 million had come from the Council (largely on infrastructure), with an additional £7 million in grant aid from the Welsh Office and from the European Community. In all, total investment in the Valley at the time of writing stands at over £200 million.

The development method employed by the Council in the Enterprise and Maritime Parks area has aroused widespread interest elsewhere. The Council buys the land, prepares a detailed planning brief, and then invites developers to tender. Schemes are then granted 'deemed planning consent', with details being approved as work progresses. On or near completion, the Council grants the developer a lease. By this means a financial ratio of public/private spending of 1 to 5 or 6 has been achieved, in conjunction with a reasonable degree of control.

What lies ahead? Swansea has twice been short-listed, but pipped to the post, in the National Garden Festival series. (For the Lower Swansea Valley even to have been considered would have seemed unbelievable a quarter of a century ago.) However, other proposals, perhaps of even greater long-term significance, are on the drawing board, most notably for the construction of a barrage to dam the Rive Tawe near its mouth. The tidal rise and fall in Swansea Bay is exceptional—at thirty feet, or ten metres, only the Bay of Fundy in Newfoundland has a greater range. At low tide extensive areas of mud are left. If the funding can be found to build the barrage, it will transform the river into a pleasant cruise-way and at a stroke create quite new amenity and leisure uses. No less will it represent the culmination of thirty years of intensive effort in the Lower Swansea Valley—effort that seems likely to gain momentum for many years to come.

GASWORKS PARK—*Seattle*

To the west Seattle faces Puget Sound and the scatter of islands which eventually coalesce into the Olympic peninsula; eastwards the city faces Lake Washington. Between these, the built-up area is threaded through by waterways and lakes, and on the north shore of one of these, Lake Union, is Gasworks Park.

It is a site of just over twenty acres (eight ha) projecting southwards into the lake so that it is surrounded on three sides by water, and has nearly 2,000 feet of shoreline. From 1906, it was occupied for half a century by the Washington Gas Company, whose works are said to have polluted the area to the point of shortening the life expectancy of the inhabitants' canaries. With the coming of natural gas the plant became redundant, and was virtually abandoned in 1956. The site has been described as 'a nightmare of industrial blight'—a rubble-strewn, oily waste, dominated by the rusting hulks of the abandoned plant. Nonetheless, facing downtown Seattle across the water, it had once been a favourite wooded picnic spot and the City had eyed the site for many years as suitable for an additional public park. The Council now moved to acquire it, for nearly $1.34 million spread over ten years; the Gas Company undertook to demolish the plant and level the site (a commitment from which it later withdrew, owing to the falling price of scrap metal). It was an allocation of $1.75 million from the 'Forward Thrust' initiative of 1968 (see page 228), with some funding from other sources, which enabled the City Council to clear the final payments on the site and to finance its redevelopment as a park.

In September 1970 the Department of Parks and Recreation commissioned the landscape architects Richard Haag and Associates to prepare a plan for the area; a site office—to which, as at Byker, the public were encouraged to come—was opened the following January. Haag was quickly faced with a problem. There was no natural soil on the site, and no plant life; the area was compacted, rendered sour and sterile by oil and hydrocarbon contaminates, and laced through with intricate underground pipework. It would be prohibitively expensive, if indeed possible at all, to create there the traditional sylvan city park.

On the other hand Haag became more and more fascinated by the giant structures remaining from the gas plant: the generator towers 50 feet high, the purposeful yet mysterious pipework with its rich variety of forms. They had at once the timelessness of all ruins and, as had already been pointed out by Richard Wagner, an architect member of a nearby houseboat community, something of the quality of modern 'junk' sculpture on an enormous scale—though actually to commission sculptures of this kind and size would have been unthinkably costly. Haag proposed that substantial elements of the works be retained, as the core of a new kind of park, unlike any other, which would complement rather than compete with others in the city.

It was a courageous throw. Not many local authorities would have been prepared to consider so bizarre a concept. However, Seattle has never been averse to impossible ideas, from World's Fairs to Freeway Parks. In 1971 Haag's proposals were approved in principle by the Parks Department; his final plans the following year. The public, on their side, remained unconvinced. Both main newspapers were relentlessly critical; anguished letters were delivered to the City Hall; there were objections from the family of Myrtle Edwards, an earlier chairman of the Parks Board, after whom it had been proposed to name the park. Controversy continued throughout a year of public meetings and presentations; nonetheless final approval was given by the whole City Council in 1972. The park was opened to the public in 1975.

Gasworks Park, as it has emerged from Haag's

hands, retains six generator towers, the pre-cooler towers, the boiler house and exhauster building. The boiler house, re-roofed with acrylic, has been converted to a picnic shelter; the exhauster building, similarly re-roofed, has become a children's 'play barn', its brightly painted equipment forming ready-made climbing frames over which children clamber delightedly. The area has a certain rough simplicity. There are no trees, but the soil has been improved sufficiently to allow for grassing (over eight miles of piping were excavated) and there has been a good deal of recontouring. To the south a 'great mound' has been formed (largely of unremoved waste) which is

surmounted by a monumental 24 ft sundial sculptured with shells, shards, carvings, castings, mosaic and *objets trouvés* by Charles Greening and Kim Lazare, and for which the viewer forms the stylus. The summit of the mound offers a commanding view across the sailing boats on Lake Union to the central city.

The Lake is very much a working lake, with repair yards, houseboats, foreign warships, yachts, seaplanes and hydrofoils. The park not only provides a marvellous spot from which to watch all this, but will itself have a ship museum (four old ships are scheduled to be moored there)—perhaps to be joined eventually by small shops and a floating restaurant. Haag would like to see a camera obscura in the largest of the towers. The city is acquiring a railway track right-of-way to form a hiking and cycle trail linking three major new parks.

So much of industry's detritus is regarded unthinkingly, or has been until very recently, as ugly and depressing. In Gasworks Park pop groups play, couples wander hand in hand with wondering smiles on their faces, children tumble over their bright mountains of gears and valves, kites fly from the great mound. Gasworks Park is very much a fun place—it shows on the faces of those who use it and the level of use has outstripped all expectations. The park is easy now to take for granted, but how many towns, one wonders, would have had the courage and imagination to do likewise? 'I'm amazed' says Haag, 'every time I go down there, that I actually pulled it off.'

Downtown Seattle (below), seen from the north shore of Lake Union—site of one of the most remarkable urban parks anywhere. Here (facing page), a gasworks stood for half a century, until abandoned in 1956. When the city purchased the site for a park, many of the generator towers and structures were left as giant 'sculptures'.

The West (A4, M4)
Guildford (A3)
Oxford (A40)
Acton

6
MANAGING THE URBAN ESTATE

'GOD made the country and man made the town.' Cowper's simple truth, wholly true anyway as to its second half, needs constant reiteration, for we are too frequently gripped by a kind of fatalism where the shaping of our towns and cities is concerned. If the places where we live are sliding into visual disorder, it is not because malevolent cosmic forces are at work; it is the result of our own collective apathy. That we are still *capable* of investing our surroundings with dignity and elegance is evident from the preceding pages. How is it, then, that we so rarely do so?

The stereotype villains are familiar: the wicked developer, out to make a quick killing; the arrogant architect, dreaming up monuments to his own vanity; the bureaucrat planner, weaving abstractions which are irrelevant to the real needs and wishes of the community; the ignorant (and doubtless corrupt) local politician who is

In the city of today, there is no place for 'them' and 'us'; we are all responsible. This market at Portobello Green, in London, was developed under an urban motorway by an independent community group, with assistance from official and unofficial sources.

blinkered by short-term expedients. Mix in the elitist, middle-class conservationist, obstructing progress at every turn; the lay-about building worker on strike for more money; the media-man who distorts the real issues by his cheap, black-and-white sensationalism . . . Like all caricatures, these contain a grain of truth, but, as a collective whipping boy, the picture simply will not do. It constitutes society's way of excusing its own massive indifference and distancing itself from the decision-making process.

How then do we move forward? The broad conclusions of the previous pages lie one within another like a nest of Chinese boxes. Integrated environments can be achieved only by integrated teamwork. However, our normal administrative machinery is ill-fitted to achieve this, and we therefore have to explore improved frameworks for urban collaboration and management. Yet these can only become effective if there is broad agreement on goals and objectives, which in turn postulates a common environmental language, a common ethic, which is understood by all sectors of society.

First, the mechanics. Change in the city straddles traditional boundaries and responsibilities. Too seldom are the efforts of the many agencies concerned, public and private, aligned and co-ordinated. Too often is there a gross mismatch between the timetables of political tenure and annual accounting on the one hand, and the long lead times involved in sustained environmental change on the other.

We have seen how local authorities came into existence to provide certain services to the community. They remain geared to the provision of such services, and the responsible departments give their principal loyalty to the maintenance of the machinery for this. (Oddly enough, there is no comprehensive statutory power in Britain's extensive planning legislation enabling local authorities to carry out environmental improvement schemes as such.) As a result authorities have difficulty in tackling complex issues involving more than one service, one department at a time. Even at a simple level. In 1982 a London council, having sited a new bus station next to a primary school, was faced with the necessity of moving the school, at a cost of at least £600,000, because of the noise and the fumes. The Council states: 'It was basically a mix-up. There was not enough liaison going on between council departments.'

Take a typical inner city site . . . On one side of the road a terrace of Victorian housing is being rehabilitated by the local authority housing department, with some government grant aid. Across the road is a school, the responsibility of another, higher-tier authority; its play-space, well maintained but clearly inadequate, abuts some considerable waste ground in the possession of the first authority. On the far side of this is a dead-end spur road, the relic of some unrealized plan a generation ago; waist-high weeds push through the cracked tarmac, an abandoned bed and a builders' skip are among the rubbish; on to this look the windows of a block of council flats. Litter is abundant everywhere. There is no off-street parking.

This is an area which clearly needs help. Why cannot the two local authorities get together to rationalize the open space between their properties? Why has the Highways Department not bothered to close the dead-end road so that it can be brought into some sort of use—perhaps pooled with the rest to make a mini-park, or a landscaped parking space, or offered to a local group as a site for an adventure playground, or as allotments for the rehabilitated terrace? Why has the local authority done so little about the litter? Why has the school not got its pupils on to some tree planting? It is at this level, not just for big 'important' projects, that *teams* have to be assembled, so that all concerned, even the street cleaner, feel part of a co-ordinated effort in which each can take a personal pride.

If situations such as this can become commonplace where a mere couple of public authorities are concerned, imagine the complexities when private landowners, residents, utilities and a fistful of commercial interests are part of the mix. There is need for new forms of estate management on the city scale, which will link the clout of the official agencies, the thrust of business and industry, the enabling spark of the unofficial organizations, the commitment of individuals. The time has come to turn the administrative problem upside down: to stop wondering what this or that agency might be doing in addition to its traditional functions, and to ask instead what it is that needs to be done—and then create the agencies or consortia necessary to handle it.

There is no blueprint, nor should there be. The means will vary according to local needs, circumstances, finances, personalities. However, there now exists a great range of precedents. Many have been apparent in the preceding pages; there are a great many more in a great many countries.

In Britain, a benchmark was notched up when, a quarter of a century ago, the Civic Trust initiated a series of co-operative clean-ups for shopping streets. For the first time teams of architects and designers were studying the potential of *existing* streets: their buildings, spaces, lighting, signs, street furniture, overhead wires, landscaping. For the first time traders were looking at their own premises in the context of the street as a whole. For the first time citizens were sitting down with their Council, the bus company, the police, representatives of government departments. The results were so startling that within a year or two some 400 towns were embarked on similar projects. The fundamental concept in which they were grounded is still, however, but fitfully grasped.

It has latterly been developed in the American 'Main Street' programme (see page 221) while the city of Norwich, where the Trust's first pilot exercise was mounted, fruitfully elaborated the precedent in its 'Heritage over the Wensum' project (see page 227). The Civic Trust itself moved into more complex situations. In the mid 1960s it brought into harness eighteen local authorities in the Lee Valley, to the north of London, to create out of 8,000 acres (3,250 ha) of idle or 'dormant' land a 25-mile regional park. We have seen something of its achievement in Wirksworth, in Derbyshire. In the mid 1980s, the Trust was instrumental, in a consultancy capacity, in working with Calderdale District Council, in West Yorkshire, to initiate a ten-year programme of environmental improvement for the whole 200,000 population area, embracing six main towns, including Halifax, and some splendid countryside. The Council has set up a special team, outside the normal departmental framework, to carry the programme forward; additional staff have been seconded to the team from the private sector; working groups been established in each of the towns, and project leaders appointed for local sub-programmes.

Three other examples at random . . . In France, the PACT-ARIM movement has worked since 1942 to improve living conditions, revitalize areas, conserve, and make day-to-day environments more pleasant. (PACT stands for *Protéger, Améliorer, Conserver, Transformer*: ARIM for *Associations de Restauration immobilière.*) Working through some 170 local associations (with 5,000 voluntary administrators) the movement rehabilitated half a million dwellings in the nineteen seventies (accounting in 1980 alone for one fifth of all such work in France), and environmental improvements programmed in 1,000 communes. In America, the Trust for Public Land, founded in 1973, in its first six years acquired wasteland to the value of over $35 million (at an actual cost of half that sum) for leasing to Neighbourhood Land Trusts for reclamation and maintenance. In London, the North Kensington Amenity Trust has, since the middle 'Seventies, brought into community use 23 acres (9.3 ha) of dead land around and under an elevated motorway; it has created industrial units, workshops, offices for local community organizations, a nursery centre, a market, sports pitches, a community centre and various other forms of leisure provision.

At the administrative level, pointers abound that authorities, the private sector, the professions, voluntary bodies are, here and there, beginning to feel their way towards new forms of co-operation. Local authorities *do* sometimes exchange information. In West Germany Bamberg, Rothenburg and Lübeck do so on their conservation programmes. The Municipality of Amsterdam offers free architectural advice to property owners. Edinburgh New Town Conservation Committee has instituted an insurance scheme for householders, which, by annual inspection of their property, provides them with an early warning system and essential repair work. The Netherlands has a computerized central data bank of information, daily updated, on the availability of premises on the market. Luxembourg has a national register of craft skills suitable for work on historic buildings. France's *Jeunesse et Patrimoine* mounts international training courses in restoration for young people.

And so on. A handful of agencies and initiatives which have broken new ground are sketched in, in a little more detail, in Appendix 1. The sad fact remains that, for any given city, most of these things would still be exceptional; they have yet to become part of everyday practice. There is need of new communications channels to allow communities everywhere more easily to learn from the experience of others. (A start has been made here by 'The Planning Exchange' in Glasgow, Scotland, which issues regular and informative fact sheets about official and unofficial initiatives nationwide.)

At the same time purposeful community effort predicates a wide measure of agreement on goals and objectives, long-term no less than short-term. Today the radical reshaping of towns is seldom possible, perhaps even desirable. Yet an *idea*, a vision, has to be created of the city towards which we wish to move. If a strong armature for change is to be established, setting firm reference points by which the future can increasingly claw back order and pleasure into our muddled settlements; if significant momentum for improvement is to be created and *maintained*, then the small-scale changes which are open to us must form part of a long-term strategy which is not subject to the stops and starts of political and economic expediency.

As James R. Ellis recognized in his clarion call to Seattle (see page 228), this is not easy. Society, as we do in our daily lives, has to make complex trade-offs between the options open to it. On the whole our towns and cities rate low among the priorities. We have for long been living beyond our environmental means and have not yet begun to grasp the order of investment needed to *maintain* our cities, let alone improve them. Governments, councils, tax payers, rate payers are all convinced that we cannot afford to do more. But, as every householder knows, the postponement of essential work leads to a much greater outlay in the long run. If urban decay is allowed to drift unchecked, the time could come—perhaps not so far distant—when the investment required to check it will seem so crippling as to be politically unacceptable.

By what right do we pile up problems of this magnitude for succeeding generations? There is no such thing as an absolute shortage of money. Western civilization is today infinitely richer than it was when it created the great cathedrals and Baroque cities of Europe—for that matter their Georgian and Victorian equivalents. Today we choose to spend our money differently; on additional television channels, on flying half-empty aeroplanes around the world, on football pools, or on overheating our buildings to the point where we have to half-strip for comfort—Houston's annual bill for air-conditioning amounts to $700 million, so imagine world expenditure on heating; on piling up food surpluses to plough back into the earth, on paying armies of unemployed to do nothing; on stockpiling more armaments than could ever be required in the most total of total wars. Such expenditure betokens changed values. In discussing the design and care of our cities we are discussing the nature and values of society itself.

How then, in a pluralistic world, are more sensible priorities to be established? Can we overcome our factionalism, our special pleadings, our adversarial and confrontational habits, and learn to find common ground, to share a common ambition, a common objective? Our towns and cities belong to all of us. 'Us' and 'Them' is a recipe for muddle, inertia and, finally, collapse. Somehow the house owner, the shopkeeper, the company director, the commuter, the immigrant, the man throwing his take-away fast-food junk in the gutter, the kink with the aerosol—somehow the individual citizen has to be brought into closer contact with the decision-making process by which his surroundings are shaped. Widespread participation, if it is to be more than perfunctory, is an untidy and time-consuming business—but it may well save time, and needless confrontation, later. It is certainly the only way by which improvement, rooted in the community, can develop organically.

Participation demands that fundamental options and implications are spelled out more clearly and more honestly than at the moment, both nationally and locally. An annual joust of politicians and administrators behind closed doors, in which each departmental interest seeks to maximize its share of next year's cake—or at least to minimize any threat to reduce its slice compared with last year's—is unlikely to explore the real options: the *real* net gain to the community and nation of spending more on this and less on that. Participation requires open government.

No less does participation presuppose some understanding of the issues involved on the part of the citizen. To hand a previously uninterested adult a detailed breakdown of all the factors in a planning issue which have to be brought to some sort of resolution is not very different from handing him for the first time a textbook grammar of a foreign language he has never learned. The enlargement of environmental understanding is a lifelong process, but it must surely begin with the child.

Everyone responds to urban quality when it is about them; to *envisage* it is made much more difficult for most by the very nature of our educational systems, based as they are upon the verbalization of thought. People are not trained to apprehend shapes, forms, spaces, colour, texture and the inter-relationship of these things. As a result, most of them never truly use their eyes at all. They do not *see* the brutalities of overhead wirescapes, the sheer ugliness of the parking lot, the banal vulgarity of outdoor advertising. 'You can get used to anything' wrote Bernard Shaw, 'so do be careful what you get used to.' How are such as these to *imagine* the potential of a run-down area, or the effect of a modern addition to a building of classical symmetry, or the way the spaces running into one another on the plan will really look when complete? How are they to participate in the corporate planning of their town?

There are straws in the wind. Concern is on the increase, sometimes dramatically so. It is fed by greater coverage in press and television, by 'interpretation' programmes, urban study centres, town 'trails', awards schemes, citizens' groups. Most important of all, perhaps, recent years have seen fresh efforts to bring environmental education into the schools. To open young eyes to the nature of their surroundings does not necessarily require the environment to be presented as a 'subject' in its own right. The town is a teaching resource of infinite riches, which can be drawn upon throughout the curriculum.

Why is it so important? Urgent problems confront the nations today—famine; the unemployment which goes with economic collapse; terrorism; the threat of nuclear war. Is it not frivolous to fuss about the nature of our towns? In truth, environmental quality is no longer, if ever it was, an optional extra. It has become fundamental to the very future of whole communities, whole peoples. It bears directly upon the ability of outworn industrial areas to find new ways of earning their living; upon the ability of collapsed inner cities to attract new investment; upon the ability of historic towns to bolster their economies through tourism. Planning is more than remedial; it can offer alternative futures. But there is more to the question even than that. It is a matter of what we ourselves want to be. If standards are allowed to slip in one direction, they soon begin to slip in others too. With pride of place goes confidence. With loss of pride of place goes a little of our self-respect, a little of our national, and local, and personal identity.

We end, then, as we began: with recognition that the city is ourselves, mirroring with precision our needs and our activities, our values and our aspirations, our confusions and our contradictions.

Three hundred years ago, life for the great was fairly primitive, for the great majority harsh in the extreme. Standards of living have since then changed out of all recognition. But with every material advance, perceived needs are pitched that much higher. Western society is now gripped by a materialism so intense that personal possessions, personal comfort, personal mobility, override all else. Can we summon sufficient collective faith in the future to nail the 'what-has-posterity-done-for-us?' ethic?

We get the surroundings we deserve. Ulysses, home from Troy, exclaimed that, having seen the habitations of men, he knew their minds. Common agreement on goals will not be reached overnight; new strategies will have to be fought for. Is it worth the hassle, the slog, the disappointments, the reverses? The stakes are very high. One does not have to be one hundred per cent determinist to believe that, if *we* shape our cities, so do *they* in some measure shape us. In working to give them grace and dignity, to make them a pleasure to live in, we are not only enriching day-to-day life for ourselves. We are helping to design the future of civilized society.

That is the measure of the challenge we face.

APPENDICES & INDEX

Appendix I:
MECHANISMS AND AGENCIES

Reference has already been made to a number of the innovative frameworks through which very different sectors of society are feeling their way towards an active participation in urban improvement. Here are seven more examples, which I believe to be unique of their kind, and which seem to offer lessons for elsewhere. The first three are examples of 'enabling machinery', assisting local groups to achieve what they might not otherwise be able to do. The next pair contrast interventions by trade unions and by a large industrial company. The last two illustrate the corporate endeavour of two particular cities.

America's High Streets

Bridge-building between public and private enterprise has often lacked a methodology. In the United States a formalized yet flexible approach, has been evolved by the Main Street Center. The Main Street programme was initiated by the National Trust for Historic Preservation's Midwest office in 1977 in three towns: Galesburg, Illinois; Madison, Indiana; and Hot Springs, South Dakota. So successful were the results that, in 1980, the direction of the programme was moved to Washington, under Mary C. Means its initiator, and expanded to embrace six more States competitively selected from 38 applicants, each of which had chosen five towns to form its own test-bed network.

To service these six States and their thirty towns in a three-year programme, the Trust set up a 'Main Street Center' in conjunction with the International Downtown Executives Association (IDEA), and with financial support from Federal sources and corporate and foundation grants.

The essential purpose of the programme is to revitalize the commercial thrust and competitiveness of Main Street—hard hit by the outward drift of population and the proliferation of out-of-town shopping centres—by building on its traditional qualities: architectural character and personal service, reinforced by local ownership and a general sense of community.

The restoration and cleaning up of buildings and shop fronts, many of them 'improved' over a quarter of a century by the addition of totally inappropriate cladding and clip-on features, is seen as an integral part of wider environmental improvements—better parking provision, landscaping and so on—together with a degree of economic restructuring and the stimulation of even greater entrepreneurial imagination by the business community.

The emphasis is upon *local* initiative. Each town has a project manager, who is given a basic training course of a week at the outset. Subjects covered include organization, promotion, design, financial strategies and recruiting new business. Two years later he or she is given another week to study the real estate development process—forms of partnership, tax implications, the management of rehabilitation, marketing commercial space, etc. These and other training programmes (within the first two years some 500 people had completed courses) are set up by the Main Street Center, which also offers technical assistance, produces publications and films (its first 29-minute film has been seen by over 10 million people), monitors progress and provides a central reference and information point. (In 1981, in co-operation with Urban Investment and Development Company, the Annual Downtown Data System [ADDS], used by 35 large cities, was adapted for use in Main Street Towns. The ADDS survey monitors job creation, new business starts and failures, square feet of space in active use, buildings rehabilitated, housing units created, rents per square foot, etc.) Wherever possible, existing national, State and local resources are brought into play. Over one hundred consultants of standing have been persuaded to give their time to four-day visits to each town by 'resource teams' which meet community leaders, observe problems, assess the towns' opportunities, and help to formulate approaches to realistic goals. The teams thus act as catalysts.

Towns do not decay overnight; their revitalization cannot be achieved overnight. The Main Street programme has all along emphasized the cumulative, incremental nature of the process. Almost by definition early progress can only be pinpointed by random indicators which vary from place to place. Thus, in the five Texas towns, all banks and building societies (savings and loan associations) chipped in to create 8–9 per cent loan pools for downtown façade work. In North Carolina the National Bank assigned a 'business development officer' to each of the State's five towns there; a State preservation trust did the same in Georgia. Buildings scheduled for demolition have been saved and adapted for new uses; a Massachusetts seminar attracted 275 bankers from all parts of the State; special festivals and fairs have drawn large crowds. Overall, progress was sufficiently evident by 1982 for Texas and North Carolina to have added five more towns to their original five, and for Georgia to have added four; five other States had initiated their own independent programmes along similar lines; a comparable nationwide programme was being mounted in Canada, under Heritage Canada, and now flourishes.

In fact, by late 1984, more than 100 towns were participating. Between 1980 and 1984 650 façades had been renovated; over 600 buildings had been rehabilitated at a cost of $64 million; over 1,000 business starts had been monitored, against 500 failures. In September 1984 the threads were drawn together in a national 'video-conference'—a 5½ hour affair, opened by President Reagan, which brought together at 442 broadcasting centres some 15,000 traders, planners and civic leaders from 2,000 towns.

Overall, it is estimated that every dollar of public funding has generated $11 of private investment. This is impressive, but perhaps even more important in the long run is the way the programme has bridged the strategy gap which so often exists between local-government thinking and the needs of private enterprise. The Center's hope has been that eventually all States will integrate work of this kind with their other economic development programmes. Such is the impetus which has already been generated—by the mid 'Eighties, nearly 300 cities were participating—realization of this hope seems more than likely.

The Architectural Heritage Fund

We have seen something of the work of revolving funds in saving older buildings. By definition, the revolving fund technique means that eventually, one way or another, expenditure on the restoration of a property will be recovered. However, most local trusts—if they are at all active—are chronically short of money. Few can meet the costs of acquisition and building work solely from their own resources. Some, to all intents and purposes, have no liquid assets at all.

They are forced, every one, to juggle with such grants and loans as may be available. But even official grant aid—if available—is normally payable only when the work has been completed, and to the satisfaction of the agency concerned. Nonetheless, the builder on the job is likely to be demanding progress payments every few months. In other words there is a cash flow problem in the middle of the operation, which normally can only be met by loans from a bank or similar source. Apart from the fact that it is not always easy to obtain loans on property which may be considered less than commercially desirable, interest charges, depending on the state of the money market, can be cripplingly prohibitive. There have been times in recent years when, in a number of countries, the going rate of interest has risen to 18 to 20 per cent—but even at half that level, interest can form so sizeable an item in the budget as to put paid to the project's viability.

It was to resolve these problems that The Architectural Heritage Fund was created in Britain. The Fund's broad purpose is to provide short-term, low-interest loans to assist local trusts and other appropriate charitable bodies to acquire and rehabilitate any buildings which merit conservation. Its origin lay in a 1971 Civic Trust report to the government on 'Financing the Preservation of Old Buildings', which pointed the need for a fund of this kind. When the Council of Europe designated 1975 as 'European Architectural Heritage Year', and the UK Government asked the Civic Trust to administer the three-year campaign in Britain, the creation of such a fund was established as one of Britain's specific aims. The Government offered to match, pound for pound, finance up to £½ million raised from the private sector. This was achieved and the Fund came formally into existence in the summer of 1976.

The Fund is controlled by a Council of Management of ten members—five nominated by the Department of the Environment and five by the Civic Trust. An Applications Committee deals with the details of requests as they arise. Day to day administration has been in the hands of the Civic Trust. Loans—normally within 50 per cent of the gross cost of acquisition and restoration—are for up to two years. Where the building is sold after rehabilitation, interest is calculated at 5 per cent per annum; in addition the Fund reserves the right to gear repayment of the loan to the selling price of the restored building—so that, for example, if the Fund advances 40 per cent of the cost of acquisition and restoration, the loan repayment would be calculated as 40 per cent of the selling price. In such a case the Fund allows the *gross* cost of the project to be offset against sale proceeds, thus enabling the borrowing trust to retain the full benefit of any other available grant aid. A loan of, say, £100,000 for two years at 5 per cent is thus the equivalent for the recipient trust, at market rates of 10 per cent, of a grant of £10,000—except that the money remains intact to be used again and again indefinitely. The Fund protects its capital by taking a first charge on the property concerned, if the building is to be resold after restoration. Where there is no intention to resell, a guarantee of repayment from a bank, local authority or comparable corporate body is required.

During its first ten years the Fund made loans totalling more than £4 million towards more than 100 projects (with no single bad debt). It is estimated that the total cost of building work made possible by these loans was of the order of £20 million or more at 1986 prices. The size of individual loans ranged from £2,000 for work on a 1911 cinema, to £250,000 for the £1¼ million rehabilitation of 57 terraced cottages in Derby dating from the mid-nineteenth century. During the ten years 1975–85 the number of local building and preservation trusts rose from about 20 to more than 80—with more constantly being formed. At the same time the scale of their undertakings tended to increase. At any given moment the Fund's forward commitments are now well over £1 million. By 1982 it was clear that demands upon the Fund were about to outstrip its capacity to respond. Since then two appeals broadly on the same basis of matching public/private contributions, have raised its capital to over £2.6 million. It seems likely, however, that yet more will be required if momentum is to be maintained.

COMTECHSA

In the environmental field, voluntary effort is not enough. Money is needed, and, above all, technical expertise. There are over 70 Community Design Centres in the US which offer free architectural and planning advice to local voluntary groups, the prototype for which was the Philadelphia Architects' Workshop. In Britain, 40 comparable organizations formed themselves, in 1983, into ACTAC—the Association of Community Technical Aid Centres. To some extent the role model here has been Liverpool's COMTECHSA—Community Technical Services Agency Ltd. The Agency provides the services of architects, landscape architects, planners and other consultants to voluntary and community organizations initiating projects on land (for example bringing areas of waste land into effective use) or in buildings (for example converting and finding new uses for redundant structures). COMTECHSA was set up in 1979 through the 'Vacant Land and Buildings Steering Committee', an *ad hoc* group drawn from the voluntary, statutory and commercial sectors active in the city. It is funded through Liverpool City Council's Inner City Partnership Programme, one of a series of joint programmes set up in designated areas by local and central government.

What is special about COMTECHSA is that it is a non-profit-making co-operative, registered under the Industrial and Provident Societies Act (traditionally, in Britain, 'Friendly Societies' were a form of mutual insurance against sickness and old age). Voluntary and community groups in the City are eligible for membership on payment of a £1 share; membership entitles an organization to use the services of the staff, and to nominate and elect the Council of Management which directs the agency's affairs and to which its staff are accountable. To a degree COMTECHSA may perhaps be compared with the experimental Community Law Centres in Britain, through which solicitors are allowed to provide free services.

COMTECHSA's services are free to organizations without adequate funds; if, later, grants or other sources of money become available for the project concerned, fees for the services received are payable. The degree of assistance can vary widely. Work on site may be supervised either by consultants or COMTECHSA; the Agency itself has powers to buy, sell or exchange property; to build; and to resist other parties in the Courts. The maintenance of urban sites—in particular of landscaping while it is becoming established—is notoriously tricky. To meet this the Society has set up a related agency, Community Maintenance Ltd, which, within two months of its formation, was dealing with 21 sites—a number which continued to increase weekly.

During its first three years 145 organizations became members of COMTECHSA. The staff of eight (six paid for out of Inner City Partnership money, two from free income) responded to at least the same number of enquiries and over £1 million worth of development was carried out. Income (in 1982) stood at about £90,000, of which some £70,000 was received in grants, with £20,000 or so from fees. Professional fees earned by those members of the staff funded through the Inner City Partnership Programme have to be returned to the programme—which, in its early days, gave the agency some financial credibility with the local authority.

Leslie Forsyth, COMTECHSA's Secretary (and himself an architect-planner), has cited three problems in particular of the many an agency of this type faces: inadequate professional training ('we have not only to provide technical aid but also raise money, involve groups and consider employment prospects, while most schools continue to produce "designers"'); the problems posed by strict financial-year budgeting; and maintaining the interest of members in the co-operative when their individual project is complete. Nonetheless COMTECHSA has produced results, and at a very modest cost.

These paragraphs are written in the present tense but, since 1984–85, COMTECHSA's future has been problematical. Liverpool's left-wing Council then decided to bring the organization under its own control, thus, ironically for self-proclaimed democrats, at a stroke destroying COMTECHSA's most special characteristic—the employment of the staff by the client-users themselves, through an elected committee.

Our next two examples are of interest as showing unusual initiatives, negative and positive, by the two sides of industry—labour and management.

Green Bans in Australia

Trade Unions have sometimes taken action over the environmental conditions in which their members have been forced to work. Unique to Australia—so far—has been a response from this quarter to unwanted development; in a series of actions dating from 1969, a number of construction unions decided to withhold their labour from sites where they disapproved of what was proposed.

A first foray in this direction had been made in the late 'Sixties when certain unions saved the Great

Barrier Reef from mining and drilling, but the movement began in earnest at Kelly's Bush, two miles up the Parramatta River from Sydney Harbour Bridge. Here thirteen housewives had come together to try to save twelve acres of open land near their homes from 'luxury' townhouse development. Reminded of the Great Barrier Reef precedent—though not without misgivings—they sought support from the two unions primarily concerned. These proved sympathetic and referred the matter to the New South Wales Trades and Labour Council, which in turn formally expressed its 'total opposition to the development on the site.' Concurrently another union, the NSW branch of the Building Construction Employers and Builders' Labourers' Federation (the BLF), had itself approached the housewives' group. The BLF had developed a radical leadership of three communists, Jack Mundy, Joe Owens and Bob Pringle, and as a result was on uneasy terms with the Sydney Trades and Labour Council—from which in fact it was in process of being expelled. Nonetheless the BLF and, two months later, the Trades and Labour Council (which meant also the bulldozer drivers' union FEDFA, the Federated Engine Drivers and Firemen's Association) had all voted to refuse to work on the site.

In one sense, as was to be expected, their action was inconclusive. The State government felt bound to avoid the precedent that would be created by the acceptance of such an imposed solution after all the official planning procedures had been gone through. The dispute dragged on and nine years later was still unresolved. On the other hand, nine years later, Kelly's Bush was still undeveloped.

Through the 'Seventies well over one hundred 'Green Bans' were applied in Australia. It was Mundy, Secretary of the NSW branch of the BLF, who coined the term, in contradistinction to the 'black bans' previously used to describe certain union boycotts. By 1978, according to Richard J. Roddewig in his useful account of the movement, Sydney claimed to have instituted 43; Melbourne between 25 and 30; the Victorian BLF over 50. Possibly a quarter or so involved the preservation of historic buildings; the remainder were concerned with open spaces—including an underground car park for the Sydney Opera house which would have killed three big fig trees in the Royal Botanic Gardens above. The combined value of the projects affected by the Sydney bans was estimated in the late 'Seventies as amounting to 3 billion Australian dollars.

It is not easy to gauge the long-term significance of the Green Bans movement. In the wake of Kelly's Bush, the BLF established two principles for their involvement in such cases: first, an appeal for help had to come from a local group—that is to say, the union would not itself initiate such action; secondly, the appeal had to be approved at a public meeting in the neighbourhood—that is to say, the cause and the unions' involvement had to have a degree of public backing. As the decade unrolled, the economic pressure resulting from the unions' actions mounted, so that developers began to seek the unions' views on projects at an early stage. On the other hand, in 1975, a number of members of the NSW BLF were expelled, including its three leaders, and with their departure the ideological tenor changed. Although the new leaders continued to proclaim their intention of protecting the heritage for future generations, thenceforward the job implications of such actions were to weigh more heavily and the Union in fact lifted *some* of the Green Bans it had earlier imposed.

Perhaps, in years to come, the Green Bans of the 1970s will appear as part of the process whereby planning and participation felt their way towards maturity in Australia. Although Australia's framework of planning control has been adapted from the British tradition, public participation is much less in evidence and much power resides with the State Ministers of Planning, at whose discretion development proposals are largely approved or rejected (and who may, as a result, be the subject of intensive lobbying). Since the Australian States remain the main agencies for developing housing, transport, schools and hospitals, often water and sewerage, and other public utilities, they may be said to have a built-in historical-bias towards development and a disinterest in conservation. It was only in 1974, for example, that the first historic buildings legislation was introduced by the Victorian government, and subsequent legislation has done little to strengthen that Act. However, Australia has been no more immune than the rest of the developed world from the shifts of public opinion which became evident throughout the 'Sixties and 'Seventies; the Green Bans movement will perhaps prove to have been one of the means by which that changed opinion made itself evident to government.

Private Industry, Public Quality

Leaders of great industrial corporations are prone to speak of the 'social imperatives' which nowadays impel business and industry to support the most diverse programmes and initiatives. Sponsorship and charitable donations have been directed towards medical research, art exhibitions, sporting events, education, the social sciences and many, many other fields. Architecture, however, has rarely figured in their lists. Certain companies—IBM, Olivetti, Braun among them—have made their mark largely by their overall design policies; others have created architectural bench-marks with particular buildings—for example, Lever House and the Seagram building in New York, Pirelli in Milan—or have donated parks and leisure facilities to a community. Unique, however, is a form of patronage exercised by the Cummins Engine Company in Columbus, Indiana.

Columbus is not a big place—its population is less than 40,000—but it happens to be the home of the largest producer of diesel engines in the United States. Cummins, which began life at the end of World War II, now employs over 11,000 locally and dominates the employment scene; through its head, J. Irwin Miller, it has come also to dominate the whole nature and appearance of the town.

In the mid 'Fifties, Columbus had need of new schools—eleven were in fact built—and the Cummins Company, through its charitable trust, the Cummins Engine Foundation, made an extraordinary and enlightened offer. The Foundation would pay the architects' fees for these schools provided that architects of sufficient distinction were used. The Schools Board could choose the designer for each project from a list of at least six names, each list itself having been drawn up by two distinguished nominees of the American Institute of Architects (there were some obvious prohibitions, such as that the same architect must not be chosen twice). Twelve months had to be allowed for the design process; architects had to be given responsibility for the whole building, its landscaping, and any later additions. The offer was not only taken up but was subsequently extended to embrace *any* new public building in Columbus. There are today maybe a couple of score of modern structures in and around the town, of which the greater number have been funded in this way. However, the story does not stop there. The stimulus has spread to the private sector, and a number of buildings of great interest have resulted quite independently of the Foundation's programme—though clearly stimulated by it.

The roll-call of practices represented here would be impressive in a much bigger city. Names include the Architects Collaborative, Gruen Associates, Elliot Noyes, I. M. Pei, Kevin Roche and John Dinkaloo, Saarinen (the story really began when the elder Saarinen's First Christian Church, completed in 1942, was underwritten by Irwin Millers' uncle, W. G. Irwin; the designs for Eero Saarinen's North Christian Church of 1964 were completed only days before his death), Skidmore Owings and Merrill, Venturi and Rauch, and Harry Weese. When a downtown block of Victorian shops was given a Civic Trust type face-lift in 1964, it was planned by Alexander Girard. In front of Pei's library stands Henry Moore's 'Large Arch' sculpture.

The Chamber of Commerce has tagged Columbus the 'Athens of the Prairie'. It is not quite that. The town's attitude to planning is relaxed, focusing for the most part on land use and growth patterns rather than aesthetics and urban design. Densities are low, and the spaces between buildings slack. A renewal plan, backed by Federal funds, to clear and redevelop one quarter of the central area of the town, resulted in the brown glass Columbus/Courthouse Centre, which, admirably done though it is in its own terms, is surely out of scale with its Victorian setting. And although

Zaharako's 1900 marble Soda Fountain, with its fabulous pipe organ, remains in good commercial health and is the subject of local picture postcards, the conservation ethic does not, it would seem, go very deep; a 1975 historical survey had to be initiated by Bartholomew County Historical Society, and proposals to tear down the 1895 City Hall for a parking garage were initially backed by the City Council. It is in keeping with the Cummins/Miller role that the building still stands only because Cummins promised to purchase it if no other suitable buyer should emerge; as also that the liveliest part of the Columbus/Courthouse Centre, an enclosed civic space embracing an exhibition hall, a stage, two movie theatres, a children's playground, a restaurant, snack bar and conference rooms, enlivened by Tinguely's kinetic sculpture 'Chaos I' which groans and clanks and at intervals hurls cannon balls down zigzag chutes, was a gift to the city by the Miller family. (As indeed it is in keeping that Cummins vans may be noticed in the town monitoring the atmosphere.)

Columbus, then, is more remarkable for its individual buildings than for its urban design—though it would be churlish not to mention the exceptional landscaping of some of its open-air parking spaces. The point has already been made that a number of these buildings fell quite outside the Cummins scheme: for example SOM's low glass container for the town's newspaper, *The Republic* (after dark the yellow offset presses can be seen turning in the machine room, surrounded by the attendant bustle of editorial and printing staff): and the glazed addition to an earlier building by Kevin Roche, John Dinkaloo & Associates for the Irwin Union Bank and Trust Company (notable for its use of a laminate of two layers of glass, one sprayed in reflecting stripes to reduce heat absorption, and for the discretion with which the extension emerges on to the street—see page 103).

Nonetheless, there are many towns of 40,000 which have no single modern building of any distinction. That Columbus can boast so many is attributable solely to the patronage exercised by its largest employer—a patronage sharply focussed on the specific objective of architectural quality, but exercised through normal civic machinery. In money terms it has cost the Cummins Foundation some millions of dollars, but, unlike so much industrial sponsorship of more ephemeral activities, its results will enrich the community for generations. Cummins has carried the ethic of the philanthropic nineteenth-century industrialists like Salt and the Cadburys and Leverhulme into the second half of the twentieth century. Are there no others to emulate their example?

Finally, two examples of what becomes possible when a community's citizens and agencies really decide to work together . . .

Heritage over the Wensum

The English cathedral city of Norwich has generally guarded its architectural heritage well, has tackled the problem of modern infill more skilfully than most and was the first British town to create a traffic-free shopping street (which is still one of the best detailed). The city can boast a strong sense of community and it is not surprising that it was in Norwich that the Civic Trust, in 1959, initiated its first co-operative street improvement project—to become known in North America as 'The Norwich Plan'.

The heart of the city is bisected by the River Wensum. The real centre of gravity—marked by the cathedral, castle, city hall and market square—lies to the south of the river; north lies a sector of the mediaeval city, the Coslany district, or 'Norwich over the water', where weavers came in the sixteenth century, dissenters congregated in the seventeenth and eighteenth centuries, but which, in the nineteenth, declined into an area of small workshops and traders. Around 1860 the population of Coslany was 7,000; a hundred years later it was a mere 300. It was on the edge of this district, in Magdalen Street, that the Civic Trust's 1959 project was mounted.

The following year the Norwich Society began to campaign for the river to be opened up to the city by development and a riverside walk. Ten years later the Council acquired two riverside sites for construction; at the same time, some historic buildings in the area were being restored. Under the stimulation of European Architectural Heritage year 1975—the run-up for which began in Britain at the end of 1972—a consortium of interests was brought together, jointly to work on a comprehensive scheme of combined renewal and conservation, to be known as 'Heritage over the Wensum'.

The prime mover was the City Council; the other organizations involved were the Norwich Society, the Norwich Preservation Trust (itself a joint agency of the Society and the Council), the Norfolk Association of Architects, the Magdalen Street and Anglia Square District Assocition (the local traders' organization), the Church, the 'Norwich over the Wensum Group' of local residents started by the Vicar of St George Colegate in 1970.

In addition two special building companies were created by the Council in partnership with one of the main construction firms in the area, R. G. Carter. The first of these, Colegate Developments, was a one-off, single venture company having as its purpose the execution of a £500,000 housing scheme on the site of an old timber yard. The nearly 3-acre site was conveyed to the company at 1972 values; 70 per cent of the profits were to accrue to the Council. The other company, Colegate Investments, was set up to undertake the restoration of the properties belonging to the Council. In this case the company was given hundred-year leases at a peppercorn rent; half the annual profits were to go to the Council. The advantage of these arrangements lay in the introduction of private capital into the programme, in conjunction with the Council's freedom from tax.

A Steering Committee was set up to co-ordinate the work, to monitor the progress and to initiate additional activities. This was linked to the advisory Conservation Panel of the Council's Planning Department; a Working Party was formed around the existing Conservation Group of Council officers.

Each organization took certain items of the programme under its wing. For example, the Trust undertook a restoration and infill scheme on an important corner site at Queen Ann Yard. A Norwich Society team undertook a 'townscape survey' and came up with twenty sets of proposals for general environmental improvements, nearly all of which were in fact implemented. The traders put up the money needed to restore the finial to the charming Octagon Chapel. Young people from schools, Scouts and the YMCA, among other projects, cleared the river bed, repaired a jetty, cleaned the walls of a church, and helped turn a derelict river site into an informal public garden.

In all, over 40 projects were undertaken. To meet the aim of increasing the resident population from 300 to 700, 122 Council dwellings were created at Hoppers Yard; 40 town houses were built at Friars Quay; with 12 infill units elsewhere. The most handsome and interesting old buildings were restored. Some 4,350 sq metres of office space was created in 1975, with 3,000 sq metres more planned. Access to the river was created at a number of points. The whole programme was costed at £2 million (1975 figures), though more has been done in the area since then.

'Norwich over the water' today bears little resemblance to the decayed district of the 1960s. Over and above the new life which has been brought to Coslany, however, profound interest attaches to the way it was done. 'Heritage over the Wensum' proved the Civic Trust's Magdalen Street lesson over again, but on a larger and more substantial scale. The lesson is simple enough. It is that by working together to agreed objectives, the different sectors of a community will achieve infinitely more than would otherwise be possible.

Seattle's 'Forward Thrust Committee'

'Metropolitan communities must work together and think ahead or face worsening survival options. A sustaining standard of life will *not* automatically be provided for our children.' Thus began a report to the citizens of Seattle and King County in the State of Washington, over the signature of James R. Ellis, Chairman of the 'Forward Thrust Committee'. 'We have the means and talent to create the city we want within our time. Young men and women looking for a cause beyond self, can find it here.' 'Successful civic action represents thoughtful communication between officials and citizens. It is not officials telling citizens what is good for them, nor is it citizens demanding more than they are willing to pay for. It is a continuing dialogue. It is listening, learning and hard work on both sides.'

King County embraces the city of Seattle, for the most part a comfortable, prosperous 'company town' —Boeing provide by far the greatest number of jobs —of around half a million population, clambering over seven hills and well-nigh surrounded by water, so that it commands wonderful views in many directions. The city's cheeky World's Fair of 1962 (cheeky in the sense that it thumbed its nose at the juggernaut machinery established to settle the order in which the great international Expos shall take place) was probably the only one of its kind since the Great Exhibition of 1851 to make a profit. The Fair gave impetus and confidence to the decade. Downtown buildings pushed upwards; the city administration was sharpened up by strengthening the powers of the mayor; citizens' groups became active, lobbying successfully *against* a proposed Bay Freeway, and *for* such things as the clean-up of the Pioneer Square district and the retention of the Pike Place Market. In the forefront of the environmental lobby was a very remarkable man, James R. Ellis, an attorney. In the middle 1950s he began to press for improved local government and planning machinery, and scored a resounding victory with the creation of a $135 million sewerage system for the whole metropolitan area, resulting in greatly reduced water pollution and a cleaner coastline.

In a 1965 speech to Rotary, Ellis returned to his longer-term theme and proposed a 'massive investment' in a whole package of improvements. So persuasive was he that City and County put together a committee of 21, which in turn brought together some 200 community and civic leaders, drawn from King County, Metropolitan Seattle, the City itself and the State of Washington, to appraise the needs, strategies and investment required adequately to shape Seattle's future. The operation, formalized under a Board of Trustees and given the name of 'Forward Thrust', spanned the years 1965–70, and turned into the largest programme of public improvements undertaken by an American city.

Three main committees dealt with economic analysis, legislation and priorities. Eleven specialist committees studied particular areas of concern: traffic and highways; health, safety and welfare; utilities (including pollution, energy, flooding, the undergrounding of overhead wires, etc); parks and recreation; culture and entertainment; schools; urban redevelopment; airport and seaport facilities; multiple use of facilities; quality in environmental design; and a final committee was created to monitor government and local government progress. It must be borne in mind that all this was largely voluntary effort. At the end of Forward Thrust's five-year lifespan, it was estimated that there had been 966 committee meetings; and that 67,000 man-hours had been given freely by citizens, plus 8,700 hours of professional office time—more than doubled by their out-of-office time.

This, however, was no talking shop exercise. After a year's work, the various committees came up with a total requirement for some $5 billion, related to hundreds of recommended projects. Clearly, not all of these could be put in hand simultaneously. The slimmed down legislative package finally put to the local authorites concerned called for $2 billion expenditure, of which $819 million was to be found through local bond issues. Eighteen enabling Acts had to be passed; the detailed proposals then had to be put to the voters and approved by 60 per cent of the votes cast.

Not all won through. An ambitious mass transit proposal was one casualty. Nonetheless the electors did pledge $333 million in 7 major bond issues (by Seattle and King County), plus two State bond issues of $65 million. Of this, no less than $158 million, plus nearly $9,350,000 in matching funds from the State and Federal Government, were voted for parks and open spaces. Two schemes thereby made possible —Freeway Park and Gasworks Park—have been referred to in earlier pages. In all, this particular vote made possible the acquisition, development or improvement of 5 regional parks, 19 major urban parks, 30 community and County parks, 14 local parks,

50 vestpocket parks, 100 neighbourhood parks, 25 waterfront parks and beaches, 10 playgrounds, 8 playing fields, 13 swimming pools, 3 youth camps, 3 golf courses, boating facilities, trails and scenic drives, a woodland zoo and an aquarium. $2 million was made available for tree planting and landscaping; £6,600,000 for undergrounding overhead wires.

A second package of proposals costed at $615 million, including proposals which had been rejected in 1968, was put to the electorate in 1970. But Boeing was now in difficulties, and was having to cut its work force by around 65 per cent. Seattle suddenly found itself with unemployment running at double the national average. Forward Thrust's proposals were rejected, and before the end of the year the organization was wound up. The effects upon Seattle of its labours and its thinking, however, were profound and long lasting. Of the 370 separate projects commissioned in 1968, 200 had been completed a decade later. The Design Commission set up to advise on Forward Thrust projects proved so successful that City and County extended its authority to cover all public capital improvement projects. A citizens' commission, 'Seattle 2000', was brought into being in 1972. The Pioneer Square area, once written off, in the 'Seventies was finally brought back to life. Pike Place Market was saved from demolition and today hums with activity. A free downtown bus service, 'Magic Carpet', was introduced in 1974.

It would not be unrealistic to claim that all the improvements effected in Seattle between 1968 and 1978 were rooted, directly or indirectly, in the climate of opinion generated by Forward Thrust. The campaign provides a dramatic indication of how the vision of one private individual, if it be compelling enough, can bring a whole community to action; and of how, by intensive and disciplined effort, an essentially independent group can energize the official machinery and work with it to more ambitious ends than would otherwise have been possible.

The costs, in relation to the size of the programmes indicated, were tiny. Forward Thrust's operating and campaign expenses amounted to about $530,000, contributed by more than a thousand business firms and individuals.

Appendix II:
REFERENCES

The full academic machinery of references seems unnecessary in a broad-brush sketch of this kind—most of the historical references will be familiar anyway. However, I am anxious to pay tribute to those present-day sources on which I have leaned particularly heavily—in addition to the titles figuring in Appendix III—and to indicate the origin of some of the possibly more surprisng figures and statements used. The short list is as follows:

1 Jane Jacobs, *The Economy of Cities*. USA, 1969; Jonathan Cape, London, 1970.
2 *World Conservation Strategy*. International Union for the Conservation of Nature and Natural Resources, in collaborations with UNESCO and FAO.
3 Figures from *Forum* 1/82, Council of Europe.
4 Reported in *Building Design*, 5 September, 1986.
5 *The Architects Journal*, 29 October, 1986.
6 Robert Venturi, Denise Scott-Brown, Stephen

Izenour, *Learning from Las Vegas*. MIT Press, 1972; revised edition 1977.

7 *Basic Road Statistics* 1986. British Road Federation, London.

8 1977 Report of the UK King Inquiry into *Serious Gas Explosions*.

9 I am indebted for these figures to Oliver Marriott's *The Property Boom*. Hamish Hamilton, London, 1967.

10 All figures from the 1986 mid-year survey by Messrs. Richard Ellis, London.

11 Robert Kaufman, in a talk to a Royal Institute of Chartered Surveyors' Conference, May 1980.

12 Stichting International Water Tribunal, Amsterdam, 1982.

13 Report in *The Times*, London, of a five-year study by Dr Timothy Hunt, of St John's College, Cambridge, published in 1977.

14 *Canadian Heritage*, Feb.–March 1985.

15 Mexican Health Ministry, reported in *The Times*, 28 August 1985.

16 Reported in *Time* magazine, 24 August 1981.

17 *Digest of Environmental and Water Statistics*, No. 8, HMSO, London.

18 Peter Hall, *Great Planning Disasters*. Weidenfeld & Nicolson, London, 1980; Penguin Books, 1981.

19 Preservation options were explored in greater detail in P. A. Faulkner's three Bossom Lectures at the Royal Society of Arts: A *Philosophy for the Preservation of our Historic Heritage*, printed in the Society's Journal, Vol. 126, 1978.

20 Quoted by David Warren in his article 'Living Above The Shop' in *Heritage Outlook*, Vol. 1, No. 6, 1981.—Civic Trust, London.

21 Colin Buchanan, *Traffic in Towns*, HMSO, London, 1963.

22 *Bypasses and the Juggernaut. Fact and Fiction*. Civic Trust, London, 1983.

23 Edmund N. Bacon, *Design of Cities*. (See Appendix III).

24 William H. Whyte, 'The Humble Street: Can it Survive?' in *Historic Preservation*, Jan./Feb. 1980, Preservation Press, Washington, DC.

There is considerable documentation and literature on many of the 'case histories' cited, though not all of it is generally available. Over and above what I have gleaned from such papers, and the assistance given me by those named in the Foreword, I have to acknowledge my debt to the following:

Emile Fallaux and Jaap Woudt, *Guide to the Zaanse Schans*. Inside Books, Amsterdam, 1982.

Charles B. Hosmer's *Preservation Comes of Age. From Williamsburg to the National Trust* 1926-49 (see Appendix III) for his account of the development of Colonial Williamsburg.

The *Lowell Preservation Plan* of 1981 is central to an understanding of current programmes in Lowell.

Amongst much documentation on the subject, Roger Kain's contribution to *Planning for Conservation* (see Appendix III) entitled 'Conservation Planning in France: policy and practice in the Marais' is exceptionally detailed and useful.

Brambilla and Longo's *Learning from Baltimore* (see Appendix III), and in particular for Mayor Shaefer's remarks quoted in these pages.

The basic account of Wirksworth's revitalization was published in 1984 by the Project, in association with the Civic Trust, as *The Wirksworth Story. New Life for an Old Town*. This has been updated by successive annual reports by the Project.

It is impossible to write about the Lower Swansea Valley without reference to Lavender's *New Land for Old—the environmental renaissance of the Lower Swansea Valley* (See Appendix III), and to publications by the City Planning Department.

I am wholly indebted for my information on trade union action in Australia to Richard J. Roddewig's most interesting study *Green Bans. The Birth of Australian Environmental Politics*. Hale & Iremonger, Sydney; Allenheld, Osmun/Universe, New York; with the Conservation Foundation, Washington, DC, 1978.

Appendix III:
SOME FURTHER READING

Many shelves of books, studies, papers, legislation, reports, plans and other documentation exist on each and every aspect of the town touched on in these pages. A complete bibliography would itself run to hundreds of pages. The professional reader will know how to pick his or her way through all this material. What follows is a very short (and arbitrary) list of titles which may be of interest to the general reader who is minded to follow up some of the issues raised in the foregoing pages.

GENERAL

Cities and People, by Mark Girouard (New Haven and London, Yale University Press, 1985). A panoramic view of the development of the Western city.

The Culture of Cities, by Lewis Mumford (London, Secker and Warburg, 1938). Now a period piece, but remains an essential overview of the subject, and a powerful indictment of the modern 'megalopolis'.

Towns and Buildings, by Steen Eiler Rasmussen (Liverpool University Press, 1951) is an altogether slighter but nonetheless charming introduction to the growth and character of towns.

Townscape, by Gordon Cullen (London, Architectural Press, 1961), is the book which taught a whole generation how to look at, and experience, the elements which make up a town's character.

The Image of the City and *What Time is This Place?* both by Kevin Lynch (Cambridge, Mass. MIT Press, 1960 and 1972 respectively) offer equivalent insights from an American viewpoint.

ARCHITECTURE

Architecture: Nineteenth and Twentieth Centuries, by Henry-Russell Hitchcock. (First published 1958, fourth [second integrated] edition, London, Penguin Books, 1977). An authoritative and fascinating standard text.

Form Follows Fiasco, by Peter Blake (Boston/Toronto. Atlantic Monthly Press/Little, Brown and Company, 1977), demolishes some of the pretensions of the Modern Movement with wry gusto.

Morality and Architecture, by David Watkin (Oxford, Clarendon Press, 1977), does another hatchet job on the same subject.

PLANNING

City Fathers. The Early History of Town Planning In Britain, by Colin and Rose Bell (London, Barrie & Rockcliffe, The Cresset Press, 1969; Pelican Books, 1972). Readable and illuminating.

The Death and Life of Great American Cities. The Failure of Town Planning, by Jane Jacobs (New York, Random House 1961; London, Jonathan Cape, 1962). A powerful and influential plea for urban diversity, and against the accepted planning wisdom of the earlier post-war years.

The Evolution of British Town Planning, by Gordon E. Cherry (London, Leonard Hill Books, 1974). A professional history.

Great Planning Disasters, by Peter Hall (London, Weidenfeld & Nicolson, 1980; Penguin Books, 1981). Awful warnings department.

TRANSPORT

Creating Livable Cities, edited by Norman Pressman ('Contact', University of Waterloo, Canada, 1981). A symposium of contributions from many quarters, primarily on the problems of traffic exclusion and pedestrianization.

Traffic in Towns. C. D. Buchanan, et al. (London, Her Majesty's Stationery Office, 1963.)

CONSERVATION

The Character of Towns: an approach to conservation, by Roy Worskett (London, Architectural Press, 1969). An experienced architect-planner offers a sensitive view of conservation realities.

The Conservation of European Cities, edited by Donald Appleyard (Cambridge, Mass., MIT Press, 1979), a thoughtful gathering together of European experience.

The Future of the Past. Attitudes to Conservation 1147–1974, edited by Jane Fawcett (London, Thames & Hudson, 1976)—good on nineteenth-century conflicts and philosophies.

Planning for Conservation, edited by Roger Kain (London, Mansell, 1981), is volume III of a trilogy 'Planning and the Environment in the Modern World'. It contains valuable contributions on programmes and approaches of different periods in different countries.

The Presence of the Past. A History of the Preservation Movement in the United States before Williamsburg, by Charles B. Hosner, Jnr. (New York, G. P. Putnam's Sons, 1965).

Preservation Comes of Age. From Williamsburg to the National Trust, 1926–1949, by Charles B. Hosner Jnr. Two volumes. (University Press of Virginia, 1981). The above three volumes constitute the definitive history of preservationist thinking and action in the United States.

The Protection and Cultural Animation of Monuments, Sites and Historic Towns in Europe, edited by Dr Hans Dieter Dyroff; Co-ordinator Gerd Albers (Bonn, German Commission for UNESCO, 1980). An uneven but, in the better sections, valuable compilation on conservation legislation and practice in European countries and Canada.

Saving Old Buildings, by Sherban Cantacuzino and Susan Brandt (London, Architectural Press, 1980). Useful case histories of the adaptation of old buildings for new uses, culled from a number of countries.

URBAN DESIGN and RENEWAL

Architecture in Context, by Brent C. Brolin (New York, Van Nostrand Reinhold Company, 1980), is one of the very few books specifically addressing itself to the problem of designing new buildings into existing settings.

Design of Cities, by Edmund N. Bacon (London, Thames & Hudson, 1969). Insights into the creative principles of urban design by the planner of post-war Philadelphia.

The Grassroots Developers; a handbook for Town Development Trusts, by David Rock (London, Royal Institute of British Architects, 1980), provides a useful overview of innovative approaches by self-help and voluntary groups in the UK context.

The Social Life of Small Urban Spaces, by William H. Whyte, (Washington, DC. The Conservation Foundation, 1980), is essential reading for anyone concerned with the design of urban spaces and mini-parks.

Streets Ahead (London, Design Council, 1979). A well illustrated collection of articles on the design of urban spaces and street furniture.

Streets for People: a primer for Americans, by

Bernard Rudofsky (New York, Doubleday and Company, 1969), offers a rich mine of pictures and comment—by no means only for Americans as the title implies—on what makes streets live.

PARTICULAR PLACES

Learning from Baltimore, and *Learning from Seattle*, by Roberto Brambilla and Gianni Longo (both New York, Institute for Environmental Action/Partners for Livable Places, 1979 and 1978 respectively). Excellent and well presented studies of how two cities have managed their environmental affairs.

New Land for Old—the environmental renaissance of the Lower Swansea Valley, by Stephen J. Lavender (Bristol, Adam Hilger, 1981), gives a full account—up to the date of publication—of the history, decline and reclamation of the Lower Swansea Valley.

The Wirksworth Story. New Life for An Old Town (London, The Wirksworth Project/Civic Trust, 1984).

Index

Numbers in italics refer to illustrations